a letter from Chris Cleave's editor

Gold is Chris Cleave's first novel since the publication of *The Other Hand*.

That book was shortlisted for the Costa Novel Award, sold half a million copies in paperback in the UK and was a global bestseller. In the USA it stayed in the *New York Times* Top Ten for over a year. Across the world, millions of you read it, loved it and told your friends and family about it.

And now we have *Gold*.

Like *The Other Hand*, it is a story of ordinary people doing extraordinary things. Chris has a rare gift for not just showing you his characters' lives, but also making you feel what they feel. I believe *Gold* is even better than *The Other Hand*, and he says that if it is, it's because of the feedback he has received from you, his readers. In his own words:

'The way you talked about my last book gave me the licence to push myself even harder with the next one. You showed me that there are intelligent, warm-blooded, curious readers out there who I can write up to'.

If you are one of those readers, we hope this is another book you want to tell your friends about. If you would like to discuss it with Chris and with others, you can join the conversation on his website or Twitter.

We look forward to hearing what you have to say.

Suzie Dooré
Editorial Director

www.chriscleave.com
facebook.com/ChrisCleaveBooks
twitter.com/chriscleave
#goldnovel

Chris Cleave's debut novel *Incendiary* won the Somerset Maugham Award, among others. His second, the Costa-shortlisted *The Other Hand*, was a global bestseller and sat in the *New York Times* Top Ten for over a year (under the US title, *Little Bee*). Both books were shortlisted for the Commonwealth Writers' Prizes. He lives in Kingston-upon-Thames with his wife and three children, and welcomes readers at www.chriscleave.com and twitter.com/chriscleave.

just a taste of the praise for Chris Cleave:

What they said about *The Other Hand:*

'Searingly eloquent.' *Daily Mail*

'A powerful piece of art . . . shocking, exciting and deeply affecting . . . [a] superb novel . . . Besides sharp, witty dialogue, an emotionally charged plot and the vivid characters' ethical struggles, *The Other Hand* delivers a timely challenge to reinvigorate our notions of civilized decency.' *Independent*

'This is a slow release of dirty secrets, surprises and wonderment. Hooked from the start by Little Bee's voice, you stay in thrall to the bittersweet end.' *Scotland on Sunday*

'Impresses as a feat of literary engineering . . . the plot exerts a fearsome grip.' *Daily Telegraph*

'In a novel that tackles serious and uncomfortable subject matter, Cleave's writing makes one laugh and despair in equal measure. * * * * ' *Time Out*

'I felt the same excitement discovering this as I did Marina Lewycka's *A Short History of Tractors in Ukrainian* and Paul Torday's *Salmon Fishing in the Yemen*. There is an urgency here, an inability to put it down and a deep sense of loss once finished. It is a very special book indeed. Profound, deeply moving and yet light in touch, it explores the nature of loss, hope, love and identity with atrocity its backdrop. Read it and think deeply.' Sarah Broadhurst, *Bookseller*

'By turns funny, sad and shocking.' *Sainsbury's Magazine*

'Book clubs in search of the next *Kite Runner* need look no further than this astonishing, flawless novel.' *Library Journal* (starred review)

'So far it's the best book of 2009, no question.' *Metro* (US)

'A better book than Chris Cleave's *The Other Hand* may be published this year, but I wouldn't bet on it. This exquisitely written story of a Nigerian refugee and a British glossy magazine editor is the most powerful novel I've read in a long time . . . it's also a very funny book about brave, funny people who the reader quickly grows to love . . . But the heart of the book is Little Bee; naïve yet insightful and sophisticated, damaged yet capable of great courage and humour, she is an unforgettable character. I finished *The Other Hand* in tears, and I still can't get it out of my head. Just read it.'
The Gloss (Ireland)

'Warm, witty and beautifully written.' *Sunday Tribune*

'Big themes, high emotion and cliff-hangers aplenty. . . an enormously affecting investigation of love, guilt and global responsibility, told with a bittersweet urgency.' Justine Jordan, *Guardian*

'An exhilarating, disturbing read.'
James Urquhart, *Independent* (Books of the Year)

' . . . [an] immensely readable and moving second novel . . . Cleave uses his emotionally charged narrative to challenge his readers' conceptions of civility, of ethical choice . . . The character and voice of Little Bee reveal Cleave at his finest . . . An affecting story of human triumph.'
New York Times

'Will blow you away. . . the best kind of political novel: you're almost entirely unaware of its politics because the book doesn't deal in abstractions but in human beings . . . thoroughly satisfying if also heart-rending.'
Washington Post

'An ambitious and fearless gallop from the jungles of Africa via a shocking encounter on a Nigerian beach to the media offices of London and domesticity in leafy suburbia . . . Cleave immerses the reader in the worlds of his characters with an unshakable confidence.'
Lawrence Norfolk, *Guardian*

'One of the most vividly memorable and provocative characters in recent contemporary fiction . . . heart-warming and heartbreaking . . . viscerally stunning . . . Cleave paces the story beautifully, lacing it with wit, compassion, and, even at the darkest moments, a searing ray of hope.'
Boston Globe

'Cleave has a Zola-esque ability to write big, and deeply . . . Cleave makes the reader think about political issues and care about his characters.'
USA Today

'Every now and then, you come across a character in a book whose personality is so salient and whose story carries such devastating emotional force it's as if she becomes a fixed part of your consciousness. So it is in Chris Cleave's brilliant and unforgettable [*The Other Hand*] . . . What elevates this novel even further is Cleave's forceful call for all of us, the floating masses of a globalized, socially isolating modern world, to look after one other.' *Seattle Times*

'The charge, then: buy this book. Resist opening it until you are ready to start reading, for once you begin you'll find yourself unable to stop . . . Prepare yourself for Cleave's poignancy, his control, and the pathos he so effortlessly evinces. Expect astonishment, for this is a work inspiring in depth and style; a work that alters perceptions.' *Bookslut.com*

' . . . will amaze and delight you, and break your heart. It's one of the finest books I've read in years.' *ShelfAwareness.com*

What they said about *Incendiary:*

'Stunning.' *Newsweek*

'Stunning.' *New York Times*

'Stunning.' *Bookmarks Magazine*

'Stunning.' *International Herald Tribune*

'Masterful.' *The Age*

'Mesmerizing.' *Washington Post*

'Terrifying.' *The Baltimore Sun*

'Unforgettable.' *The Miami Herald*

'Hilariously sympathetic and convincing.' *San Francisco Chronicle*

'Dark, tense and undeniably provocative.' *Metro*

'Searing . . . poignant and compelling . . . Utterly believable
and mesmerizing.' *Newsday*

'Richly sardonic and often disarmingly poignant . . . How can one fail
to be impressed and moved?' *Guardian*

gold

chris cleave

SCEPTRE

First published in Great Britain in 2012 by Sceptre
An imprint of Hodder & Stoughton
An Hachette UK company

1

A CIP catalogue record for this title is available from the British Library.

Hardback ISBN 978 0 340 96343 2
Special Edition Hardback ISBN 978 1 444 75641 8
Trade paperback ISBN 978 0 340 96344 9
Ebook ISBN 978 1 848 94575 3

Printed and bound in the UK by Clays Ltd, St Ives plc

Hodder & Stoughton policy is to use papers that are natural, renewable
and recyclable products and made from wood grown in sustainable forests.
The logging and manufacturing processes are expected to conform to the
environmental regulations of the country of origin.

Hodder & Stoughton Ltd
338 Euston Road
London NW1 3BH

www.hodder.co.uk

For Cecily

Tuesday 24 August 2004

Changing room, Olympic Velodrome, Athens.
Women's sprint cycling Olympic gold medal race

Just on the other side of an unpainted metal door, five thousand men, women and children were chanting her name. Zoe Castle didn't like it as much as she'd thought she would. She was twenty-four years old and she sat where her coach told her to sit, beside him, on a thin white bench with the blue protective film still on it.

'Don't touch the door,' he said. 'It's alarmed.'

It was just the two of them in the tiny subterranean changing room. The walls were freshly plastered, and little hardened curds of the stuff lay on the cement floor where they'd fallen from the trowel. Zoe kicked at one. It came detached, skittered away and dinged against the metal door.

'What?' said her coach.

Zoe shrugged. 'Nothing.'

When she'd visualised success – when she'd dared to imagine making it this far – the floors and the walls of every building in Athens had been Platonic surfaces, hewn from an Olympian material that glowed with inner light. The air had not smelled of drying cement. There hadn't been this white plastic document wallet on the floor, containing the manufacturer's installation guide for the air-conditioning unit that stood, partially connected, in the corner of the room.

Her coach saw her expression and grinned. '*You're* ready. That's the main thing.'

She tried to smile back. The smile came out like a newborn foal – its legs buckled immediately.

Overhead, the public stamped its feet in time. The start was overdue. Air horns blared. The room shook – it was so loud that her back teeth buzzed in her jaw. The noise of the crowd was liquidising her guts. She thought about leaving the velodrome by the back door, taking a taxi to the airport and flying home on the first available jet. She wondered if she would be the first Olympian ever to do that simple, understandable thing: to quietly slope off from Olympus. There must be something she could do with herself, in civilian life. Magazines loved her. She looked good in clothes. She was beautiful, with her glossy black hair cropped short and her wide green eyes set in the pale, haunted face of an early European saint. There was the slightest touch of cruelty in the line of her lips; a hint of steel in the set of her face that caused the eye to linger. Maybe she should do something with that. She could give interviews, laughing backstage after the show when the journalist asked did she know she looked quite a lot like that British girl who ran off from the Olympics – what was her name again? *Ha!* she would say. *I get that question all the time! And by the way, whatever did become of that girl?*

Her coach's breathing was slow and even.

'Well *you* seem okay,' said Zoe.

'Why wouldn't I be?'

'Just another day at the office, right?'

'Correct,' said Tom. 'We're just clocking in to do our job. I mean, what do you want – a medal?'

When he saw how she looked at him, he raised his hands in supplication. 'Sorry. Old coaching joke.'

Zoe scowled. She was pissed off with Tom. It wasn't helping her at all, his insouciance – his pretence that this wasn't a huge deal. He was usually a much better coach than this, but the nerves were getting to him just when she most needed him to be strong. Maybe she should change coaches, as soon as she got back to England. She thought about telling him now, just to wipe that faux-wise smile off his face.

The worst part was that she was shivering uncontrollably, despite the unconditioned heat. It was humiliating, and she couldn't make it stop. She was already suited and warmed up. She'd given a urine sample and eight cc's of blood that must have been mostly adrenaline. She'd recorded a short, nervy piece to camera for her sponsors, signed the official race entry forms, and pinned her race number to the back of her skinsuit. Then she'd removed it and pinned it back on again, the right way up. There was nothing left to occupy these terrible minutes of waiting.

The crowd went up another frenzied gear.

She slammed the flats of her hands down on the bench. 'I want to go up there! Why are they keeping the door locked?'

Tom yawned and waved the question away. 'It's for our own safety. They'll let us up once security have checked the corridors.'

Zoe held her head in her hands and rocked back and forth on the bench. It was torture, being locked in this tiny room, waiting for the race officials to release them. She couldn't stop her body shaking and she couldn't take her eyes off the metal door. It trembled on its hinges from the crowd noise. It was a strong door, designed to resist autograph seekers indefinitely or fire for thirty minutes, but fear came straight through it.

'God . . .' she whispered.

'Scared?'

'Shitting myself. Honestly, Tom, aren't you?' She looked up at him.

He shook his head and leaned back. 'At my age the big event isn't what scares you.'

'So what is?'

He shrugged. 'Oh, you know. The lingering sensation that in pursuit of my own exacting goals and objectives I might not have been as generous in spirit as I could have been with regard to the needs and dreams of the people I cared most about, or for whom I was emotionally responsible.'

He popped the gum he was chewing, and inspected his nails. Zoe seethed.

From the stands above them, a fresh cheer shook the building. The announcer was whipping up the crowd. They roared Zoe's name. They stamped harder. In the changing room the temporary strip light went off and flickered back to life by stuttering increments. A sudden rill of dust fell from an unfinished break in the plasterboard ceiling.

Tom said: 'You think this building will hold?'

Zoe exploded. 'Shut up, will you? Shut up, shut up, shut up!'

Tom grinned. 'Oh come on, this is just another bike race. It's gravy.'

'Five thousand people aren't screaming for you.'

He leaned close and took her arm. 'You know what you should be scared of? The day they aren't shouting your name. Then you'll be like me. You'll be the dust collecting in the cracks between the boards of the track. You'll be the spit drying on the chewing gum stuck underneath the seats. You'll be the sound of the brooms

4

sweeping up after the crowd has pissed off. You'd rather be all of that? Would you?'

She shook her head, sulkily.

He cupped a hand around one ear. 'What? I can't hear you over the noise of all this love! Would you rather be the girl no one remembers?'

'No, for fuck's sake!'

He smiled. 'All right then. So now get your arse out there and win!'

The two of them looked at the closed metal door, then down at the floor, then back at each other. A moment passed.

Tom sighed. 'Nice pep talk, though, wasn't it? I maybe peaked too soon.'

Zoe glared at him. She was ready to spit.

Overhead, the crowd's stamping was incessant. Plaster dust fell continually now.

She fixed her eyes on the door. 'Why don't they come? We've been down here for*ever*.'

'Maybe this is our personal hell. Maybe they never come, and the crowd just gets louder and louder, and we're left alone for eternity with our thoughts.'

'Don't even joke, okay? I feel guilty enough.'

Tom looked at her carefully. 'Because of Kate?'

Zoe was surprised at the relief she felt when Tom said Kate's name. Underneath all the last-minute details of her preparation – the tightening of shoe cleats, the polishing of visors – she hadn't realised how much it had been eating her.

'She should be here,' she said. 'It should be me and her in this final.'

Her coach squeezed her knee. 'Good girl. But you didn't force Kate to stay at home. She made her own choices.'

'Still . . .'

'I want you to say it, Zoe. I want to hear you say *Kate made her own choices.*'

Zoe stared at the floor for a long time. The roar of the crowd accelerated every torpid molecule of air in the little unfinished room. The vibration of their stamping feet rose through the steel frame of the bench and shimmied the white plastic seat beneath her.

Slowly, she raised her eyes to her coach's.

'Kate made her choices,' she said softly. 'And so did I.'

Tom held her gaze.

'Good,' he said finally. 'And now put it out of your mind. Okay? That there is life; this here is sport. You only need to think about the next ten minutes.'

She swallowed. 'All right.'

He laughed. 'Well then, don't look so terrified.'

'Listen to that noise. I *am* terrified.'

'Look, Zoe. You've done all the hard work. You've made it to the final. Your worst-case scenario here is to be the second fastest rider on the entire planet. The very worst thing that could happen in the next ten minutes is that you win an Olympic silver medal.'

'Exactly.'

'You're scared of getting silver?'

She thought about it, then nodded. 'I'd rather fucking die.'

'Honestly?'

'Honestly.'

She took a long, deep breath, and the trembling in her body subsided. When she looked back at Tom, he was smiling.

6

'What?' said Zoe.

'Young lady, I believe you're finally ready for your first Olympic final. Now do us both a favour, and go up there and win it.'

'But the door . . .'

Tom grinned. 'Was only ever in your mind.'

She stood up and pushed on the metal door with two fingers, tentatively. It swung open easily, on oiled hinges, and the roar of the crowd swelled louder. The door banged against its stop and rang with the deep note of a bell.

She stared at him, wide-eyed.

'What?' said Tom, shooing her away. 'Go on. You're really bloody late, as it happens.'

Zoe looked back at the open door and then at him.

'You're actually pretty good,' she said.

'Get to my age, you'd better be.'

The tall, whitewashed stairwell leading up to the track was silvered with sunshine falling from the high skylights in the velodrome roof. On the wide white riser of the very last step, in blue stencilled letters that were nearly straight, the Olympic motto read: *Citius, Altius, Fortius.*

Zoe breathed a deep, slow lungful of the hot, roaring air. The hairs rose on the back of her neck. Everything that had passed was excused, gone, and forgotten. The crowd was screaming her name. She smiled, and breathed, and took the first step up into the light.

203 Barrington Street, Clayton, East Manchester

On a tiny TV in the cluttered living room of a two-bedroom terraced house, Kate Meadows watched her best friend emerge from the tunnel into the central arena of the velodrome. The crowd noise doubled, maxing out the TV's speakers. Her heart surged. The baby's bottle was balanced on the TV, and the howl of the crowd raised concentric waves in the milk. When Zoe lifted her arms to acknowledge the crowd's support, the answering roar sent the bottle travelling across the top of the TV. It teetered on the edge, fell to the floor and lay on its side, surrendering white formula from its translucent teat to the thirsty brown hessian of the carpet. Kate ignored it. She was transfixed by the image of Zoe.

Kate was twenty-four years old and since the age of six, her dream had been to win gold in an Olympics. Her eighteen years of preparation had been perfect. She had reached the highest level in the sport. She had shared a coach with Zoe, and trained with her, and beaten her in the Nationals and the Worlds. And then, in the final year of preparation for Athens, baby Sophie had arrived.

This was an old TV and the picture quality was terrible, but it was quite clear to Kate that Zoe was now sitting on a twelve thousand dollar American prototype race bike with a matte black monocoque frame made from high-modulus uni-directional carbon fibre, while she herself was sitting on a Klippan sofa from Ikea, with pigmented epoxy/polyester powder-coated steel legs and a removable, machine-washable cover in Almås red. Kate was well aware that there were victories to which such a seat could be ridden, but they were small and domesticated triumphs, measured in infants weaned and potty-training campaigns prosecuted to dryness. She ground her knuckles into her temples, making herself remember how in love she was with Sophie and with Jack, who was in Athens preparing for his own race the next day. She tried to exorcise all jealous thoughts from her head, kneading her temples till they hurt, but God forgive her, her heart still ached to win gold.

Under the coffee table Sophie picked over the fallen mess of breakfast and lunch, cooing happily as she brought cornflakes and non-specific mush to her mouth. The doctor had said she was too poorly to travel to Athens, but now the child seemed effervescent with health. You had to remind yourself that babies didn't do these things deliberately. They didn't use the kitchen calendar to trace out the precise schedule of your dreams with their chubby little fingers, and then plan their asthma and their allergies to clash with it.

It was sweltering in the living room. The open window admitted no cooling breeze, only the oppressive August heat reflecting off the pale concrete of their back yard. Kate felt sweat running down the small of her back. From next door, through the shared wall, she heard the neighbour vacuuming. The hoover groaned and thumped its bald plastic head against the skirting board, again and again, a lifer despairing of parole. Crackling bands of electrical interference scrolled down the TV picture, masking Zoe's face as she lined up to start the race.

The two riders were under starter's orders now. A neutral voice counted down from ten. Up at the start line, behind the barrier, Kate caught a glimpse of Tom Voss in the group of IOC officials and VIPs. At the sight of her coach, her pulse quickened to prepare her system for the intense activity that his arrival always signalled. Adrenaline flooded her. When the countdown in the velodrome reached five, she watched Zoe's hands tense on the handlebars. Her own hands tensed too, involuntarily, grabbing phantom bars in the stifling air of the living room. Her leg muscles twitched and her awareness sharpened, dilating every second. Kate hated the way her body still readied itself

9

to race like this, hopelessly, the way a widow's exhausted heart must still leap at a photo of her dead lover.

There was a commotion by her feet, and an excited squeal. She reached down to lift a small electric fan from the floor to the coffee table, out of the way of Sophie's exploring fingers. Its breeze was a relief. On the TV, the starter's countdown reached three. Kate watched Zoe lick her lips nervously. *Two*, said the starter. *One*. Sweat was beading on Kate's forehead. She reached out and turned up the speed on the fan.

The picture contracted to a bright white dot in the centre of the TV screen, then sparked out entirely. From next door the whine of the neighbour's hoover descended in pitch and faded through a long, diminishing sigh into silence. Through the wall she heard the neighbour say: *Shit*. Kate watched the blades of the fan relinquish their invisibility as they slowed to a stop. She looked at the fan dumbly, feeling the breeze on her face fade into stillness, wondering why a breeze would do such a thing at the exact same second the TV went on the blink. After a moment she understood that something had blown in the fuse box. As usual, it had taken half the street's electricity down with it.

She felt a rare pulse of self-pity. Only these little things set her off. Missing the Olympics was too big and blunt to wound in anything but a dull and heavy sense. It was like being etherised and then smothered. But Jack's plane tickets when they arrived had been sharp enough to cut. The packing of his send-ahead bag had left an ache, and a specific emptiness in the wardrobe that they shared. Now the electricity burning out had left her burned out too.

A second later she laughed at herself. After all, everything could be fixed. She looked in the kitchen drawer until she found fuse wire, then took a torch into the understairs toilet where the fuse box was. Sophie screamed when she left the room, so she picked her up and held her under one arm while she juggled the torch and the fuse wire in her other hand, standing on the toilet seat to reach the fuse box. Sophie wriggled and squawked and kept trying to grab the wires. After a minute of trying, Kate decided she cared about not electrocuting her daughter more than she cared about watching Zoe race.

She put Sophie back down on the living room floor. Immediately the baby brightened up and resumed her endless quest for dangerous objects to put in her mouth. Fifteen hundred miles away the first of the best-of-three sprint rounds was over by now, and Zoe had either won or lost. It felt weird not to know. Kate clicked the TV on and off, as if some restorative element in the wiring of the house – some electronic white blood cell – might have healed the damage. No picture came. Instead she watched herself, ten pounds heavier than her racing weight, still in her nightie at three in the afternoon, leaning out of the reflection in the blank black TV screen.

She sighed. She could fix the problems with her reflection. Some hard miles of training would put the leanness back into her face, and her blonde hair wouldn't always be scraped back into a tight bunch to keep it clear of Sophie's sticky grip, and her blue eyes were only hidden behind her ugly glasses because she just hadn't found the strength to get dressed and go to the shops for the cleaning fluid for her contacts. All of this could be sorted.

Even so, as she watched herself on TV, she panicked that Jack couldn't possibly still find her attractive. It didn't do to dwell on thoughts like that, so she slumped back down on the sofa and phoned him. Behind his voice when he picked up was the roar of five thousand people.

'Did you see that?' he shouted. 'She killed it! She won like she wasn't even trying!'

'Zoe did?'

'Yeah! This place is unbelievable. Don't tell me you weren't watching?'

'I couldn't.'

She heard him hesitate. 'Come on, Kate, don't be bitter. It'll be you racing next time, in Beijing.'

'No, I mean I actually couldn't watch. The power's gone out.'

'Did you check the fuses?'

'Gosh, Ken, my Barbie brain did not entertain that option.'

'Sorry.'

Kate sighed. 'No, it's okay. I tried to fix the fuse but Sophie wouldn't let me.' Straight away, she realised how sulky that sounded.

'Our daughter is pretty strong for her age,' said Jack, 'but I still reckon you should be able to kick her arse in a straight fight.'

She laughed. 'Look, I'm sorry. I'm just having a shitty time here.'

'I know. Thank you for looking after her. I miss you.'

Tears formed in her eyes. 'Do you?'

'Oh my God,' he said, 'are you kidding? If I had to choose between flying home to you and racing for gold here tomorrow, you know I'd be right back on that plane, don't you?'

She sniffed, and wiped her eyes. 'I'm not asking you to choose, idiot. I'm asking you to win.'

She heard his smile down the phone. 'If I win, it's only because I'm scared of what you'll do to me if I don't.'

'Come back home to me when you win gold, okay? Promise me you won't stay out there with her.'

'Oh Christ,' he said. 'You know you don't even have to ask me that.'

'I know,' she said quietly. 'I'm sorry.'

Through the phone connection, the noise of the crowd peaked again.

'The second race is starting,' Jack shouted over the roar. 'I'll call you back, okay?'

'You think she'll win it?'

'Yeah, absolutely. She made round one look like a Sunday ride.'

'Jack?'

'Yeah?'

'I love you,' she said. 'More than ice cream after training.'

'I love you too,' he said. 'More than winning.'

She smiled. It was a perfect moment, and then she heard herself ruin it by saying: 'Call me when the race is over, okay?'

She cringed at herself for being so needy; for putting this extra demand on him. Love wasn't supposed to require the constant reassurance. But then again, love wasn't supposed to sit watching its own reflection in a dead TV while temptation rode a blazing path to glory.

Whatever Jack said back to her, the crowd drowned it out by chanting Zoe's name.

She clicked the call off and let the phone fall softly to the washable, hard-wearing cushion covers. It wasn't just that she'd stopped believing she would ever get to the Olympics. Now, if she was really honest with herself, she wasn't even sure if she could win the kind of races you rode on kitchen chairs and sofas.

She stared with glazed eyes through the window. In the shimmering heat of their little back yard, a squirrel had found something in the bottom of a crisp packet.

She thought: *Is this my life now?*

She held her hands to her temples, more gently now, and timed the pulse in them against the second hand of the living room clock. It had been months since she'd trained hard but even now – even with this stress – her heart rate was sub-sixty. The second hand was back where it started, and she'd only counted fifty-two. Sometimes this was the only small victory in her days: this knowledge that she was fitter than time.

She looked up and saw that Sophie was mimicking her, trying to press her own tiny hands against the sides of her head. Kate laughed, and for the very first time Sophie laughed back.

Kate brimmed with euphoria.

'Oh my God, darling, you *laughed*!'

She dropped to her knees, picked Sophie up and hugged her. Sophie grinned – a gummy, prototype grin that faltered and twitched lopsidedly and then shone again. She gurgled noisily, delighted with herself.

'Oh, you clever little thing!'

Wait till I tell Jack, she thought, and the thought was so light and so simple that she suddenly knew everything would be okay. What did it matter if Zoe won gold today, or if Jack won gold tomorrow? Kneeling here in the untidy living room, holding her baby close and breathing the warm curdled scent of her, it was impossible to believe that anything mattered more than this. Who even cared that she had, until recently, been able to bring a bicycle up to forty miles per hour in the velodrome? It seemed absurd, now that real life had begun for her – with its real progression through these lovely milestones of motherhood – that anyone even bothered to ride bicycles around endless oval tracks, or that anyone had had the odd idea of giving out gold to the one who could do it quickest. What good did it ever do anyone to ride themselves back to their point of origin?

God, she thought. *I mean, where does that even get you?*

After a minute, during which her heart beat forty-nine times, she smiled wearily.

'Oh, who am I kidding?' she said out loud, and Sophie looked up at the sound of her voice and produced an experimental expression, unique to her, and perfectly equidistant between a laugh and a lament.

Eight years later, Monday 2 April 2012

Detention deck 9 of the Imperial Battle Station colloquially known as the Death Star

The Rebel – the kid – resisted, so they locked her in a dark metal holding cell that smelled of machine oil. It was too much for her and she grinned and wriggled with excitement. She clung to her father. He held the kid's skinny neck in the crook of one arm and squeezed with just enough pressure to restrain her, or to convey silent affection, the way fathers will apply forces. The child squirmed to escape, giving the hug an aspect of violence: parenting didn't seem to change much, wherever you went in the universe.

Two Imperial Stormtroopers stood guard over the pair. They exchanged a look, decided that the detainees were secure for now, and nodded. Leaving the detention block of the Death Star, they slipped discreetly out of a side door and emerged into the bright April light of the car park. They took off their helmets, shook out their hair, and bought two takeaway teas from a catering van. They were both thirty-two. They were athletes in real life. They had sponsorship deals, and privacy issues with the press, and body fat below four per cent. In the world rankings for sprint cycling on the track, they were numbers one and two.

'The things I do for you,' Zoe said. 'It's far too hot in these.' Strands of black hair were stuck to her forehead with sweat.

'I could do with a wee,' said Kate. 'How are you meant to go in these costumes?'

'They weren't designed by a woman.'

'The Death Star wasn't designed by a woman. There'd be curtains. There'd be a crèche.'

Zoe shook her fists at imaginary higher-ups. 'Yeah! Can't you brass hats figure out some way of balancing motherhood with suppressing this damned Rebel Alliance?'

Kate shook her head sadly. 'With insubordination like that, you'll always be a Stormtrooper.'

'You're wrong,' Zoe said. 'They'll recognise my zeal and my passion. They'll promote me to the command of their battle station.'

'Don't flatter yourself. They'll take one look at your personality profile and make you a droid. Highly specialised, but basically single.'

'Oh, get fucked,' said Zoe, smiling. 'I wouldn't swap for your life.'

A cold squall rippled the yellow-brown puddles of the film studio car park. On the far side, in a blue people carrier splashed with mud, the next group of ticket-holders for the *Star Wars* Experience was already looking for a parking space. Kate checked her watch. The Death Star was theirs for another twenty minutes.

'We'd better get back in to Sophie,' she said.

The two women rushed their teas. Zoe looked at Kate over the rim of her cup.

'Be honest with me,' she said. 'Is Sophie dying?'

'No,' Kate said, without hesitation. 'The chemo's going to work. I'm one hundred per cent sure she's going to get better.'

'Honestly?'

'We've proved it before. When she first got sick, the chemo worked and she went into remission. This is just a little relapse, and now the chemo will work again.'

There must have been doubt in Zoe's face because Kate began pursing her lips and nodding her head determinedly. Zoe watched the certainty building; going up the dial and into the red. One hundred and five per cent. One hundred and ten.

'Okay,' she said. 'Okay. But do you really think these day trips help? They don't just exhaust her?'

Kate smiled. 'Let me worry about that.'

'Let me ask, at least. As your friend.'

Kate's smile stiffened. 'Would I put her through all this if it wasn't helping?'

Zoe touched her arm. 'Of course not. But are you sure you don't organise these trips slightly for your own peace of mind? Just so you can be doing everything in your power as a mother, I mean.'

'What, and you're an expert on motherhood now?'

Zoe recoiled as though she'd been slapped. Slowly, she collected herself and looked down, twisting her hands together.

Kate faltered, then stepped forward and took her hand. 'Shit, Zo, I'm sorry.'

Zoe turned her head aside. 'No, no, you're right. I was out of order. I know what you go through.'

Kate moved to put herself back in Zoe's eyeline, then held her gaze. 'I know what you go through, too. This must make you think about Adam.'

'It's fine,' said Zoe. 'And you know what else? Your hair's all fucked up.'

Kate laughed. 'Oh, have I got helmet hair?'

18

'You think that's bad? I've got Stormtrooper's tits. I swear to God, these costumes are so tight . . .'

Under the relief, Zoe's heart was still snagged on the wire of the fence her friend had put up between them. She wished she hadn't brought up the subject. She needed to learn when to keep her mouth shut, which was nearly always.

She looked down into her Styrofoam cup, where an inch of tea – the same yellow-brown as the puddles – was reaching the temperature at which the warmth no longer disguised the bitterness. You could get tired of being unattached, of having no partner to undertake patiently the task of winnowing your days from your demons and showing you which was which. You could get to hoping for a companion of your own – and yes, even a child – despite the overwhelming evidence that children too were bottomless, echoing wells of need into which exhausted women like this one, her best friend Kate, endlessly dropped brave little pebbles of certainty and anxiously listened for a splash that never came.

'We really should get back to the Death Star,' Kate said, pulling Zoe back from miles away.

'Hmm?'

Kate pulled her Stormtrooper helmet back on, and her voice was changed to a metallic rasp by the modulator built into the face guard. 'The Death Star? Big round naughty spaceship? Promising acting debut, got a bit typecast, never appeared in another film after the *Star Wars* series?'

Zoe rolled her eyes.

'Oooh,' said Kate. 'Touchy.'

Zoe flicked her hair back, suddenly irritated.

19

'Listen,' Kate said, 'it's that time of the month and I've got a blaster, so don't start.'

Zoe looked carefully at her, gauging the extent to which things might now be back to normal between them. It was hard to tell. Kate might be smiling, or she might not. This was the thing with Stormtroopers: they only showed the multi-purpose expression moulded into the face plates of their helmets – a hard-wearing, wipe-clean, semi-mournful expression equally appropriate for learning that one's soufflé, or one's empire, had fallen.

Command module of the Death Star

The battle station hung in the cold black vacuum of space. Sophie Argall could feel the vast metal mass of it under her feet. It was huge. It had its own gravity, though it didn't seem as strong as Earth gravity. Sophie realised there was extra bounce in her legs. Standing on the bridge of the Death Star was like standing at home would be, if Dr Hewitt had just told you that your leukaemia had gone into remission.

Sophie reviewed the data. She was eight. The Death Star was younger. Sophie didn't know by how much. The Death Star was defended by 10,000 turbo-laser batteries and 768 tractor-beam projectors. A crew of 265,675 kept it running, kept it clean, and did the cooking and laundry for 52,276 gunners, 607,360 troops, 25,984 Stormtroopers, 42,782 ship support staff, and 167,216 pilots and technicians. Despite these precautions, both the Death Stars built before this one had been destroyed. Statistically, the chances of a Death Star surviving combat were zero. The chances of Sophie surviving acute lymphoblastic leukaemia were better than ninety per cent. When you considered the odds, it was presumptuous of the battle station to be exerting a gravitational pull on her.

Sophie knew the stats by heart. She had drawn pictures of the Death Star a thousand times, in felt tip and in crayon, but nothing had prepared her for standing here, on the bridge, looking out through the portholes at the stars. She listened to the low electronic hum of control circuits and the soft cool hiss of the air conditioning.

They had taken the Argall family car – a silver-grey Renault Scénic – to the space port at the film studios: Sophie, her parents, and Zoe. The car ride had taken three hours and thirty-six minutes, which Sophie had timed using the stopwatch feature on her iPod. She'd listened to the original *Star Wars* soundtrack by John Williams and the London Symphony Orchestra. She'd made crosshairs with her fingers and aimed them out of the windows on the motorway. The Nissans and the Fords were friendly Rebel craft. The Mercedes and the BMWs were hostile TIE fighters.

They'd used a transporter to get from the film studio car park to the Death Star. It had taken forty-nine seconds. The transporter had looked like an ordinary lift, but it hadn't been. Dad had been captured with her, as soon as they stepped out of the transporter. As far as Sophie knew, Mum and Zoe remained at liberty somewhere within the Death Star.

Sophie was still amazed to be here. She had to keep looking down at herself, to check that all the atoms in her arms and legs had made it okay through the transporter beam.

Two Stormtroopers patrolled the bridge in their pristine white armour. They checked the settings of every switch on every control panel. They spoke to each other in terse, metallic voices. Their helmets had full visors so you couldn't see their faces, but you could tell they were nervous. There was a rumour that Darth Vader was arriving in his personal shuttle. Sophie's mouth was dry and her heart pounded. She held her dad's hand and squeezed tightly.

She knew none of this was actually real, but that didn't mean it wasn't happening. On the rare days she was well enough to go into school now, school never felt real either. The other girls had moved on. They were into YouTube, and they thought she was weird for still being into kids' stuff. She tried to get into the things they were into, but the truth was that she didn't want to learn the dance moves from pop videos – she wanted to be a Jedi knight.

Leukaemia didn't feel real either. They put tubes into you and pumped you full of chemicals that made your ears ring and your skin go so transparent that you could see right inside yourself. You could touch the tubes with your fingers, and look at your tendons with your own eyes. It was possible that you weren't dreaming – it just didn't seem very likely.

After a while you stopped worrying about what was real. The rare school days lasted six and a half hours, and then they were gone. Life lasted till you were very old – with odds of ninety per cent – or for another few months, with odds of ten per cent. Being here on the Death Star would last as long as it lasted. That was how you had to look at it.

Her dad knelt and put an arm around her. 'You're not scared are you, big girl?'

Sophie shook her head. 'No.'

She made her voice sound as though the question had been stupid, but Vader was coming and the truth was that she was more scared than she had ever been in her life – more scared than she'd been in January when Dr Hewitt had told her the leukaemia was back. It was important not to worry Dad, though. It was harder for him.

'You prisoners, stop talking!' said one of the Stormtroopers. Then, in a softer voice: 'Are you guys all right for drinks and so on? Can I get you a juice or a biscuit?'

Sophie asked: 'Is there Ribena?'

'Magic word?' said the Stormtrooper.

'Is there Ribena, please?'

'Of course,' said the Stormtrooper, and produced a carton from a blue isotherm bag.

'We've got one of those bags at home,' said Sophie.

'Wow,' said the second Stormtrooper. 'Small universe.'

The first Stormtrooper spun around to look at the second, then quickly turned back to Sophie.

'Prisoner!' said the Stormtrooper. 'Our master is expected at any moment. When he arrives, you must stand at attention. If you are invited to speak to him, you must address him as "Lord Vader". What must you address him as?'

'Lord Vader,' said Sophie in a small voice.

'What's that? I can't hear you,' said the Stormtrooper, cupping a gloved hand to the place on the helmet where an ear would be.

'Lord Vader!' said Sophie, as loud as she could. She was tired from the long car journey. Her voice had a slow puncture and it was letting out air.

'That'll do,' said the Stormtrooper, and went off to whisper to the other.

A hush fell on the bridge. The Stormtroopers stiffened to attention. Sophie's legs trembled. The music of "The Imperial March" sounded from hidden speakers. An involuntary whimper came from

Sophie's throat. A blast door opened. Clouds of dry ice billowed. Darth Vader emerged from his vapours, stood mightily in silhouette, and stepped onto the bridge. His respirator hissed and clicked.

He stared at Sophie and Dad, and nodded slowly.

'So,' he said. 'The captured Rebel fighters.'

Sophie felt urine running down her legs, shockingly hot. It splashed on the brushed steel floor. The noise was undeniable.

She looked at the pooled urine on the floor, and felt tears coming. This was going to really freak Dad out.

She looked up at him. 'I'm fine,' she said. 'I'm fine.'

There was a moment of surprised silence on the bridge. Vader's respirator wheezed.

'Uh . . . are you all right?' he said.

'I think she's let a bit of wee go,' Dad whispered.

'What?' said Vader.

'Oh, where are my manners? I mean, I think she's let a bit of wee go, *Lord Vader*.'

Vader held up his hands, black-gloved palms outwards.

'Hey,' he said. 'Don't make me the bad guy here.'

The nice Stormtrooper came over, knelt beside Sophie and put an arm around her.

'It's okay,' the Stormtrooper whispered. 'It happens.'

Sophie looked up at Dad's face, which was lined with concern. She couldn't bear that she'd done this to him. She began to cry.

Darth Vader bent down and patted Sophie on the shoulder.

'What's that tube going into you?' he asked.

'It's . . . it's a . . . Hi . . . Hi . . . Hickman line,' Sophie sobbed.

Dad folded her into his arms. 'It's to get the chemo into her.'

'Ha!' Vader said. 'You call that a line? You should see me when I take this helmet off. I have so many wiggly lines going into me, I look like a plate of spaghetti.'

Sophie giggled between her sobs. A perfect green bubble of snot swelled from her nose, stretched to molecular thinness and shrank back again, like the membrane of a calling frog.

'You're a very brave young lady,' said Vader.

After her tears, Sophie had a hammering headache and a rending in her guts and a pain in her side that made her want to curl up.

'I'm fine,' she said, looking up at Dad. 'I actually feel great.'

He smiled. She smiled back. This was good.

Afterwards, when they'd got Sophie cleaned up, Darth Vader lifted her to sit on his shoulders. They watched the huge monitor screens on the bridge, which showed the galaxy lying before them and shimmering.

'Would you like to choose a world to destroy?' Vader said.

'Why?' said Sophie.

Vader shrugged. 'It's just something I offer my guests.'

'Does it have to be a world? Could you blow up my bad blood cells?'

Air sighed from the grille of Vader's face plate. He waved a gloved hand at the star field.

'I can do you anything on that map,' he said.

Sophie pointed at a bright star in Orion. 'Let's say those stars are my white blood cells and that one's a bad one.'

'Fine,' said Vader. 'Commence death ray initiation sequence.'

Sophie held up her hand. 'Sorry, but it's not actually a death ray if it's saving my life.'

Vader pointed at the big red button labelled DEATH RAY. He said: 'It's the only ray we've got.'

'Oh. Okay.'

Vader crouched down to let Sophie press the button. A low drone built slowly to a crescendo. The lights flickered. They all watched the monitor screens as the eight green beams of the death ray converged into one, shot out across space and heated the core of Sophie's bad blood cell until it exploded in a shower of bright sparks across the blackness of space.

They watched the sparks crackle and fade back into perpetual darkness.

Car park, Pinewood Studios, Iver Heath, Buckinghamshire

Jack carried Sophie out to the car while Kate and Zoe were still changing out of the Stormtrooper costumes. She was shattered. She clung on around his neck and buried her face in his chest.

Jack shifted her weight onto one arm. Her head lolled. He extracted the car key from the back pocket of his jeans, popped open the car door and eased Sophie into her child safety seat. He handled her like a patient cop with a drunken perp, laying one hand on the crown of her head to stop her banging it on the door frame. One of the last remaining clumps of her hair came detached. Lifted on the wind it rose briefly into the ragged sky, then floated down into the mud. Jack followed its progress with his eyes, then turned back to his daughter. He didn't say anything.

Sophie sat with her eyes half closed, uncooperative, while Jack worked to install her. She was sluggish, like a reptile waiting for the sun to warm her. On the other side of the car park, mammalian children in red Wellington boots and striped bobble-hats giggled and splashed each other with the tawny water from the puddles.

Sophie's Hickman line was in exactly the wrong place for the seat-belt where it rode across her collarbone, so they always needed to tuck a folded tea towel under the belt. He checked that it protected the Hickman line, and that the seatbelt still ran smoothly.

He squeezed Sophie's knee. 'How about that Vader?' he said.

Her eyes came open. 'He was *so* cool,' she said. 'You remember how he's actually Luke Skywalker's father?'

Jack grinned. 'He is?'

Sophie nodded. 'He actually *tells* him? In *Empire Strikes Back*? Right at the end?'

Jack made a face as if he was weighing up the information. 'You don't want to believe everything a guy in black leather knee-boots tells you.'

The animation left Sophie's face and a worried, provisional expression took its place. 'What?'

Jack's stomach fell. He was an idiot for breaking the bubble. 'Sorry, big girl. Forget it.'

He went to stroke her cheek, but she turned her head away and folded her arms. Now Jack felt terrible for teasing her. This was what she dreamed about – what she believed in – while the other girls on their street rode their bikes and had Hannah Montana sleepovers.

The guy who played Darth Vader had handled the Sophie situation pretty well. Better than Jack would have done, probably. People were actually okay. The man probably made – what? – ten quid an hour; eighty a day? In that stifling black costume, patiently helping under-tens select worlds to destroy.

Jack wondered if he should have tipped Vader.

He got into the driver's seat and made sure that the Hickman line emergency kit was still in the glove box of the car beside the sterilising gel, in case Sophie began haemorrhaging through the line and it needed to be clamped.

'Can you stop kicking the back of my seat, please?'

'Sorry, Dad.'

He plugged his phone into the cigarette lighter to charge, in case something happened en route and they needed to call in an emergency. He pulled the road atlas from beneath the passenger seat and memorised the route home to Manchester. Then he checked which hospitals were close to the route, and tried to recall which ones had accident and emergency departments. This was in case Sophie began fitting, or lost consciousness, or was stung by a wasp or bee and needed a precautionary injection of adrenaline to stop her small body going into shock.

'Can you *stop* kicking my seat?'

'Sorry.'

He winked at her in the rearview mirror. He didn't mind, really. If anything he liked it – found it reassuring that she wound him up in the ways a normal kid might.

A movement in the mirror caught his eye, and Jack turned in his seat to see Kate and Zoe starting out across the car park. Zoe's head was down. Kate was walking slowly, making it easy for Zoe to come alongside her if she wanted to, but Zoe walked a few paces behind. He wondered if she regretted having come along.

He leaned across to make sure that the small cylinder of emergency oxygen for Sophie was accessible in the side pocket of the passenger door. He checked its airline for kinks or obstructions. He gave the spigot on the head of the cylinder a quarter turn and put the oxygen mask to his ear to check it was delivering. Then he closed the oxygen tap and replaced the cylinder in the door pocket.

He looked up again and adjusted the rearview mirror to watch Zoe and Kate approach the car. They paused while something was said, then they briefly hugged. He knew he wasn't the most sensitive observer but the signs were hard to miss today: these rushes the two women made to the brink of disintegration, followed by the check, and the careful backing down. They'd been like this all the way down here in the car. It was always an intricate friendship to navigate, this bittersweet affection of rivals, and yet it seemed more urgent today.

Kate got in the back seat next to Sophie, took her cheeks in her hands, and went to kiss her on the forehead. Sophie squirmed and took evasive action, the way any healthy eight-year-old tomboy would. Jack smiled. You collected these signs of normality. You took them to the bank, knowing that if you saved up enough of them then the compound interest would eventually grow your deposit into a child in remission.

Zoe got into the passenger seat next to Jack.

He glanced across at her. 'Everything okay?'

She tilted her head. 'Why wouldn't it be?'

Jack said nothing.

'What?' she said.

'Let's go, for God's sake,' said Kate from the back.

He shrugged, released the handbrake and reversed five yards. Sophie announced that she needed a wee. Jack smiled. It was all the Ribena – the Stormtroopers had been very free with it. He eased the car five yards forward again, re-applied the handbrake and sat looking straight ahead.

Kate undid Sophie's seatbelt and helped her to go at the edge of the car park, tucked away behind a van. Jack and Zoe watched the pair of them.

'You're more dad than human now,' she said.

He ignored the jibe. 'You're frazzled today.'

Zoe snorted. 'You know how to make a girl feel special.'

'Overtraining?'

'Overthinking, maybe.'

'It was good of you to come. It means a lot to Kate.'

He let himself look across at her.

She said: 'Sometimes it all gets a bit heavy, you know?'

Jack gripped the wheel a little tighter. 'Are you okay with it?'

Zoe thumped her chest lightly above her heart. 'It just gets me more than it used to. I mean, Sophie's so ill . . .'

'But you're fine?'

Zoe hesitated. 'Fine . . .' she said, seeming to test the feel of the word in her mouth as if it hadn't been used for some time, like *house-wife*, or *Rhodesia*. 'Fine,' she said. 'Yeah. I mean . . . fuck, how could I not be?'

Jack turned to look back through the windscreen, and they sat in silence as Kate pulled Sophie's jeans back up and brought her back to the car.

'What are you two talking about?' Kate said as she swung open the car door.

'The Tour de France,' said Zoe.

'Oh, I've heard of that,' said Kate.

She re-seated Sophie and re-attached her seatbelt. Jack watched in the mirror and knew what his wife was thinking: how skinny their child was becoming. In three months of relapse she'd lost half the weight she'd put on in three years of remission. He reached out a

30

hand behind the headrest of his seat and Kate took it, and they squeezed. The pressure created a fixed point in time, to which so many accelerating events could be anchored.

With Sophie safely strapped in, Jack drove away.

'Sophie?'

'Yeah?'

'Next time you kick the back of my seat, I'm taking you back to the Death Star to be brought up by the Sith.'

'Sorry, Dad.'

He slowed almost to nothing on the speed bumps of the film studio's exit road, and he checked in the rearview mirror to make sure that Sophie wasn't jolted too much. When he pulled out onto the main road, he drove defensively. He'd been on a course to learn how, since it was unlikely that any kind of road traffic accident would improve Sophie's prognosis. Jack planned in which direction it would be safe to swerve in case the green Mercedes waiting at the upcoming junction pulled out early. When it didn't, his eyes moved on to the next car ahead, and then to the mini-roundabout after that.

'Sophie . . .'

'Yeah?'

'Kicking.'

'Sorry, Dad.'

Jack was thirty-two years old, he was an Olympic gold medallist, and he was one of the top five quickest male cyclists in the world.

He said: 'Sophie? If I'm going too fast you just tell me, okay?'

On the motorway they drove in the slow lane, wedged between lorries. Sophie knew it was to keep her safe. This was the effect she had on people: they drove twenty per cent slower, they gripped the handles of boiling saucepans twenty per cent harder, they chose their words one fifth more carefully. No one was going to blow a tyre and crash her, or spill a pan and scald her, or say the words *worry* or *die*.

She wanted to tell them that it all just made you twenty per cent more scared, but she couldn't do that. They did it to cope with how they felt. She felt bad for making them feel that way.

Out of the side window, she saw normal families cruising past. They were mostly families who weren't on the good side like the Argalls or on the dark side like the Vaders. They were families who weren't anything except on their way to the zoo or the shops. Quite often you could see them squabbling as they drove past. Their mouths moved crossly behind the glass. It was like a museum of human families, where the display cases moved past you without labels. Sophie wrote the labels in her head: *Mum Bought the Wrong Crisps* or *Dad Won't Let Me and Chloe Listen to the Chart Show*.

When Sophie got bored of watching the other families, she watched *Star Wars* in her head. She'd seen the films so many times now, she didn't need the DVDs. She watched the AT-AT Walkers attacking the Rebel base on the ice planet Hoth, to take her mind off how sick she was feeling. She felt so bad today, it was scaring her. Everything hurt. Her head pounded, her vision was blurry and her bones ached the way they did when it was freezing and you were out on a long walk and the rain just kept getting harder. Waves of nausea rolled over her and gave her the icy chills.

It was incredible how Skywalker flew his fighter ship. It was because he was a Jedi. There were special cells in your blood, called midi-chlorians, that made you a Jedi. Sophie knew the changes in her blood that Dr Hewitt thought were leukaemia were actually just the start of midi-chlorians forming. You couldn't expect Earth doctors to diagnose it right – they would be lucky to see a single case in a lifetime of medical practice.

Even so, when she felt as sick as she did today, there were times when she thought she would never become a Jedi. Even at sixty miles per hour, she was uncomfortable. The rumble of the road surface was shaking her up and making her insides hurt. How would she ever be able to fly a ship at hundreds of miles per hour between the feet of an attacking Imperial Walker?

She swallowed. 'It's okay if you want to go faster,' she said.

Dad shook his head. 'We're good like this.'

Sophie looked at Dad's wiry forearms on the steering wheel, and then she looked at her own. She squeezed her fists to make her muscles bulge.

'You okay?' said Mum. 'What are you doing?'

'Nothing.'

The veins in her arms were dark blue and thin and led nowhere, as if someone had taken a biro and drawn the wiring diagram of a useless droid on her body before stretching human skin over it. Her dad's veins bulged like cables under the skin and made purposeful lines, powering the blood back to his heart. Dad was the strongest man in the world, probably. She didn't understand how Dad could look at her – at the fragile, sickly sight of her – and not be scared. She had to try to seem strong and brave.

'It's okay if you swerve a bit,' she said. 'I don't mind.'

Dad looked at her in the rearview mirror. 'And why would I do that?'

'There's actually a TIE fighter chasing us.'

In the front passenger seat, Zoe looked serious. 'Right. Divert maximum power to the aft deflector shields please, Sophie.'

Sophie grinned and pressed the button on the side of the child seat that executed Zoe's order.

'Fire the turbo-lasers!' said Zoe, and Sophie did.

'Make sure you lock on to their coordinates!'

Sophie was amazed that Zoe was so good at this. When the TIE fighter was destroyed and they were all safe again, she relaxed in her seat. 'Thanks, Han!'

Zoe turned and there were tears in her eyes, which was something that Sophie didn't get. She hadn't complained and she'd tried really hard not to look ill, and it made her a bit angry and sad if people felt sorry for her.

She made sure to keep smiling.

'It's okay,' she told Zoe. 'I actually feel great!'

Beetham Tower, 301 Deansgate, Manchester

Zoe got out of the car. As it drove off, she waved the Argalls away and watched Sophie's new-moon face watching her back, through the rear window. The child's eyes fastened unselfconsciously on her own, the way her brother Adam's used to, and the fact that there was no reproach in them only made her feel worse.

She realised she was actually trembling. She'd hardly slept, and then the Death Star had upset her, and the car journey back had been worse. Sophie really looked as if she was on her way out, and Kate was in denial, and Jack . . . well, she couldn't decide what Jack thought.

A single day with that family had felt like the whole of her life. She didn't know how they could bear it. There was an insane amount of emotion, but nothing sufficiently concentrated to cry about at any particular second. It was impossible.

She decided she would go up to her apartment and drink coffee. That seemed a reasonable thing to do. She could easily imagine a woman with more manageable emotions than she had at this moment saying to herself, *You know what? I think I'll grab an espresso.* This was the best she could hope for today: to do the things that ordinary people did, and to hope that by some kind of sympathetic magic their ordinary sense of wellbeing would accrue to her.

The early April rain was falling. The pavement in front of the Beetham Tower's lobby was cordoned off with tall orange cones and red and white safety barriers. A yellow crane was hoisting olive trees up into the sky, one by one. Zoe stopped to watch. There were a dozen trees waiting to go up. They were eight feet high, with their trunks swathed in bubble wrap and their roots balled into orange sacks. In the vortices of wind that spun around the foot of the high tower, the undersides of the olive leaves flashed as they turned, all at once, as if at an unseen signal, like shoals of silver fish.

Zoe wrinkled her eyes against the rain and watched a tree spinning on its halter, mirrored in the windows of the tower as it rose up into the slate-grey sky. The lift had been going on for two days now. The trees were going up to the penthouse, one floor above her own apartment. Management was making a 'green space', with birds and plants and a water feature. It would be nice up there – a souvenir of Earth.

Zoe wanted to watch the trees going up but she couldn't stay too long out on the street before people would begin to recognise her. Over the road from the tower there was a ninety-six-sheet backlit billboard. It showed an image of her own face, twenty feet high, her big green eyes framed with green hair and green lipstick. Her hand, the nails painted green, was holding a bottle of Perrier dripping with condensate. *Best served cold*, said the text on the advertisement. Across the right-hand third of the billboard, as tall as her face, were the Olympic rings glazed with a frosting of ice.

She looked up, to where the looming orange shape of a wrapped tree was disappearing into the cloud base. The smudge of colour hung for a moment at the limit of vision, then surrendered to grey. Zoe felt a panic that she couldn't pin down.

She slipped away before any passers-by spotted her, and entered the lobby of the tower head-down. She hurried across the marble and took the lift to her apartment on the forty-sixth floor.

Inside, with the roar of the city five hundred feet below, she dropped her single Yale key into a wide pewter dish that served only that purpose. The chime the key made in striking the dish was the only sound. Beside the dish, a very old dented aluminium water bottle was the only other item on the black high-gloss hall stand. She removed her trainers, balled newspaper into the toes, racked them, and put on the grey felt slippers that were exactly where she had left them.

She tried to remember the name of the man she'd left sleeping in her bed. He'd been sweet. Tall, Italian-looking, a few years younger than her. Carlo, she was pretty sure, or Marco. A something-o with a grin that said this was in no way serious. Still, sometimes you hoped.

She called: 'Hello?'

No answer.

There was no note on the fridge, no message on the kitchen counter. She checked the living area – nothing.

In her bedroom the bed was trashed – she remembered them doing that – and his boxer shorts were in the corner where she'd thrown them. The rest of his clothes were gone. Her four gold medals weren't on the shelf where she'd put them, and for a second her heart stopped. Then she saw them glinting under the edge of a pillow, and picked them up. She held the cold metal to her chest, and sighed. He was an arsehole for not leaving his number, but he wasn't a thief. She supposed she'd been lucky again – if you could call it luck.

There was a stillness in the apartment, and maybe the ghost of the smell of him.

She made an espresso with the built-in coffee machine and went to sit on an armless, low-backed charcoal-grey sofa in the living area. Clouds obscured the view from the floor-to-ceiling windows.

She'd only been living here a week. On the two days of clear weather she'd been able to see the National Cycling Centre, where she trained and competed, three miles away to the east. It had looked like the domed grey back of a beetle; as if it might crawl away from her through the understory of industrial estates and logistics hubs that fringed the city. Looking to the horizon through the binoculars the estate agent had left, she'd also seen the mountains of Snowdonia, the Anglican cathedral in Liverpool, and Blackpool Tower and beach. Her third night she'd watched lightning storms, and seen the wind boiling over the Cheshire plains.

Now there was nothing to see, only grey. It was hard not to feel like a ghost. Zoe held up her hand in front of her face and was amazed she couldn't see through it. She stood, moved to the kitchen area and ate a dry slice of multi-grain bread. The texture of it was reassuring. She drank a glass of water and went back to sit in the living area.

She wondered if this was supposed to be her life now, moving alone between these designated spaces, inhabiting them according to patterns of usage envisioned by the architect.

Paolo – that had been his name. She flipped open her laptop and found him on Facebook. He was even better-looking than she'd remembered. It had been a nice night. The sex had been good, but it was more than that. There had been a tenderness – something that had moved her. She was slightly surprised he hadn't left a note.

She closed her eyes and let herself believe that he was on his way up in the lift, right now, with flowers. She smiled. It was silly, but you had to believe these things were possible. Just beyond your sight, life might be moving in ways that were moments away from being revealed to you. It was a mistake to take disappointments at face value. You were only ever a tap at the door and a dozen fresh-cut blooms away from happy.

She opened her eyes and clicked on the man's profile. Her smile disappeared. She read what he had written about her, and saw the photos he had posted from her apartment, half naked, with her Olympic golds around his neck. Then she read again what he'd written. She was *insane in the sack*. She was *aggressive*. She *had to be on top*.

She phoned her agent. 'I think I might have a slight issue,' she said carefully.

Afterwards she put the phone down beside her on the sofa, leaned back, and looked around her at this place she'd bought with a thirty per cent deposit that the Perrier sponsorship had afforded her, plus a million-pound mortgage that she had no prospect of continuing to pay unless she won gold in London in four months' time and landed another sponsorship deal.

The extra pressure helped her push through the pain threshold in training. You had to keep yourself desperate – as wild as you'd been when you'd had nothing. You had to double up your stake each time, or watch as someone more frightened than you were rode you off their wheel.

It amused her that this place she'd bought to scare herself was trying so hard to be soothing. The walls were painted in Farrow & Ball. They had the quality of neither reflecting nor absorbing. The shade was called *Archive*. The tall plate-glass windows responded to the external light level, sparing one's pupils the stress of it all.

On a low ironwood coffee table beside the sofa there was the new copy of *Marie Claire* with Zoe's face on the cover, smiling. She flipped through it. She was *fiercely determined*. She was *ruthless and unstoppable*. She was *driven by her demons*. This is what they wrote.

None of it felt like her. She closed her eyes and tried with her breathing to calm the panic that was spreading from her stomach. There was no traffic noise; no sound of the neighbours' TV; nothing. This high above the world's surface, the thing the estate agent had marketed as privacy felt quite a lot like solitude. This high above the city she'd climbed out of, the silence seemed irrevocable.

She didn't know what she'd been thinking. Maybe that she could leave her problems forty-six floors below, on Earth.

She tried to focus on her breathing. She wished Tom were here. He would know what to say to help her work through how she was feeling. Since she'd met him, at nineteen, she'd trusted him to get her through the difficult days. The trouble was that the difficult days weren't the race days any more. Competing in an Olympics didn't scare her now. The thought of stepping up into the full roar of the crowd, in London, seemed simple and natural and good. It was ordinary days now that frightened her – the endless Tuesday mornings and Wednesday afternoons of real life, the days you had to steer through without the benefit of handlebars. Off the bike she was like a smoker without cigarettes, never sure what to do with her hands. As soon as she got off the bike her heart was expected to perform all these baffling secondary functions – like loving someone and feeling something and belonging somewhere – when all she'd ever trained it to do was pump blood.

She shuddered, and picked up her phone to call Tom. She pulled up his number and paused. She knew he would ask her to formulate the problem for him, and she tried to think what to say this time. Probably she should lead with a question about her diet, or her Pilates regimen, and then let Tom work out what was really wrong. This was often what she did now, when she called him. She was a champion, after all, and it was humiliating just to say out loud: *Please, I'm not coping.*

She hesitated, gazing out into the grey mist that cloaked the city. An Italian olive tree ascended silently past the window, spinning slowly as it rose.

Barrington Street, Clayton, East Manchester

Jack turned into the Argalls' home street and slowed down to walking pace as he edged the car over the potholes. He looked in the rearview mirror to check he wasn't shaking Sophie around too badly. The rain had eased, and half a dozen children wrangled their bikes lazily down the long, straight ribbon of road between the banks of identical redbrick Victorian terraced houses, each with its single step and low wall separating a painted front door from the pavement. The children stopped their bikes to blow bubble gum and watch the Argalls pull up outside their house.

Jack opened his door, stepped up and out into the last of the rain, and frowned.

'Don't you kids ever go inside?'

The tallest child was a girl of eight in pink leggings, white trainers and a green parka with the hood up. She inched her bike forward from the others, gripped the brake levers, and tilted her head to one side. She wrinkled her nose and looked at Jack as if he was slightly retarded.

'There's nowt on telly, is there?' she said. 'Just shite.'

He frowned.

'What?' said the girl. 'I only said *shite*. Is that not a word in fuckin' Lapland or wherever you come from, Mr Argall?'

She leaned over and spat on the road. A long strand of drool failed to detach, and she sucked it back like spaghetti between the gap in her front teeth, looking amiably at Jack all the while.

'I come from Scotland,' said Jack. 'You'd know it if it came on TV. Bagpipes? Kilts? Heroin?'

'Whatevs,' said the girl. 'Is your Sophie all right?'

'Ask her yourself, Ruby. She does talk.'

Kate had got out of the car and was leaning back in to undo Sophie's straps. The girl footed her bike up to her.

'Mam left a cake for you, Mrs A. On your step.'

Kate looked up and there they were, one Tupperware box and one metal biscuit tin on the front step of their house.

'Two cakes,' she said. 'That's so kind.'

'Nah, the tin is from Kelly's mam. It's biscuits, but I wouldn't eat them if I was you because Kelly's mam's dirty.'

'Ruby, honey, that's not nice,' Kate said.

Jack gave her a look over Ruby's head that said, 'Yeah, but . . .' and she tried to keep a straight face.

41

'Let's have you out of there, Sophie,' she said, cradling her daughter's head as she lifted her out of the car.

Sophie looked over Kate's shoulder at the other girl. She blinked against the drizzle.

'All right, Soph?' said Ruby.

'*Amazing*,' said Sophie. 'We actually went to the Death Star and we actually met Darth Vader and it was really him because otherwise *why would I have these memories?*'

Ruby rolled her eyes. 'When are you coming back to school?'

'I don't know, do I?'

'Soon, Ruby,' Kate said. 'When she's better.'

'You've missed two months now,' Ruby said. 'Miss any more and you'll have to go in thicky maths with Barney and he'll show you his willy.'

Sophie shrugged nonchalantly. 'Already seen it.'

Ruby smiled, then she reached up quickly and took Sophie's hand. She looked into her eyes for a second and tilted her head forward, as if she was trying to direct forces from inside herself, through her arm, into Sophie's body. Then she let go of her hand, popped her bubble gum and pedalled away to join the other children riding circles in the street.

Sophie let Mum carry her inside. The house smelled of toast and bike oil. Her parents' road bikes hung on hooks in the hallway. Mum set her down on her feet and she kicked her way through the chaos of shoes, unpaired gloves and discarded coats on the hallway floor to get to the toilet under the stairs.

Sophie bolted herself into the toilet and collapsed on the floor in the dark. She leaned her back against the wall and closed her eyes. That half a minute of talking with Ruby had wiped her out. It was good, though. Mum had seen it, Dad had seen it. That counted for an hour when they wouldn't worry. After that she knew she would start to see the lines creeping back into their faces, and hear the sharp edge coming back into their voices, and notice the little sideways glances they shot at her while they pretended they weren't looking. They would start to have arguments with each other, about stupid things like training hours and long-grain rice, and they wouldn't even know why they were doing it. She would know, though. It meant that they were scared for her all over again, and she would have to do one of the things that made them forget it for another hour.

If you were in the car, you could kick the back of the seat. That made them annoyed, which was the opposite of scared. If you were in the house, you had more choices. You could answer back or be lippy, which made you seem less ill. You could do a drawing. You could hurry up the stairs, and make a lot of noise so they noticed you doing it, even if you had to lie down on your bed afterwards for ten minutes. You could make it look like you'd eaten all your toast, even if you had to post it down your T-shirt and flush it in the toilet later. You could play boys' games like Star Wars that had fighting and spaceships and made you look tough, even if you weren't tough enough to ride a bike.

Night was more difficult. At night when you had nightmares, and when Mum or Dad came running, you could tell them it was about a wolf or a robber – the stuff that healthy kids had nightmares about – and not Death, that made you so scared you could never even make your voice come out to call for Mum and Dad. When you got Death, you just had to keep quiet. Other nights, you could pretend to be asleep when Mum came in to check on you at 10 p.m., 1 a.m. and 4 a.m. If you set your iPod alarm for five minutes before hers, you could make it seem as though you slept soundly, even if you were really reading *Star Wars* comics half the night.

There were a hundred things you could do to make Mum and Dad not worry. You could polish your own shoes, and clean your teeth, and get dressed nicely, even though you were so tired all you wanted to do was lie down and close your eyes. You could talk about the future – they liked it when you talked about the future, so long as it was close. If you said, 'Tomorrow, can I go to the shops with you?' it made them happy, because it meant you were being optimistic. Dr Hewitt called it *positive engagement* and it was a sign that you weren't suffering from the thing everyone was most scared of, which was *failure to thrive*. So if you said, 'Can I go to the shops tomorrow?' they would say 'Great!' But if you said, 'Next year can we go to France for our holidays?' then they would get a hollow look in their eyes, and give each other those sideways glances, and say something like, 'Let's just take it a day at a time, shall we?'

If you wanted them to not worry, there were also a hundred things you could not do. You could not cough, you could not be sick, and you could never say you were tired or sad. If you actually were sick there were ways to hide it, and if you actually were sad there were ways too.

There were so many ways to make Mum and Dad not worry, it was easy to think of a thing for every single hour. The only hard bit was that all of it made you very tired, which was one of the main things you had to never be. That was why you had to rest like this sometimes, in the toilet, in the dark.

Now that she'd rested, Sophie reached up and pulled the light cord. The wooden handle had come off the end and got lost, and Mum

44

had tied on one of her Commonwealth gold medals in its place. It swung in the light of the bare bulb, flashing as it spun.

Music started up from the kitchen. Sophie smiled. Dad was in a good mood. The Jesus & Mary Chain were doing 'Never Understand'.

Dad's music was shit.

Through the toilet door she could hear Dad singing along. It sounded like anyone's dad singing words. Sophie loved the moments when Mum and Dad were happy. If you concentrated and arranged them in your memory then you could collect them, like old copper coins, or crystals.

Sophie pulled herself upright on the hand basin, sat on the toilet seat and peed. This time her urine was a bright lime green. She was glad Mum and Dad couldn't see it, because it would freak them out. She flushed the toilet and washed her hands carefully in the little basin with the cake of soap that had been formed by pressing together the tailings of the last two. She dried her hands on her jeans. Through the door she heard her parents laughing in the hallway. Mum was telling Dad to shut up with his singing.

Sophie stood on the toilet seat to look into the mirror above the hand basin. She had to check how she was doing, every day. She did it in here, so no one could see. She took off her *Star Wars* baseball cap and examined her scalp. She had one lock of hair left now, hanging down over her forehead on the left side. In the mirror there were dark circles under her eyes. That was just the effect of the harsh overhead bulb. Her face seemed thinner, though. She put her hands to her cheeks, ran her fingers over the cheekbones, and felt the sharp edges of them. She was scared for a moment, but then she realised it wasn't the leukaemia. This was just what it did to you, the microgravity of the Death Star. It made you waste away. This was probably what all the Stormtroopers looked like, under their helmets.

She put her baseball cap back on and checked herself in the mirror. She rubbed her cheeks to put colour in them. She planned what she would do now: go into the kitchen, look healthy for about a minute, tell Dad his music was rubbish, then go upstairs to her room and lie down. No, she would say 'Your music's *shite*,' the way Ruby would say it. And Dad would grin, and drop to his knees and play-fight with her, and Mum would laugh when she saw them, and that would be one more hour when Mum and Dad wouldn't worry.

'*Shite*,' said Sophie quietly, practising the word.

Bathroom, Flat 12, The Waterfront, Sport City, Manchester

Tom Voss still remembered how it had felt for him, back in Mexico in '68, to miss out on Olympic bronze by one tenth of one second. He could feel the anguish of it even now, in his chest, raw and unavenged. Forty-four years later he still noticed the sharp passage of every tenth part of every second. The inflections of time were the teeth of a saw, bisecting him. This was not how other people experienced time. They noticed its teeth indistinctly in a blur of motion and were amazed to wake up one day and find themselves cut in half by it, like the assistants of a negligent magician. But Tom knew how the cut was made.

He took a call from Zoe's agent while he was soaking in the bath, persuading his knees to unlock.

'She's been sleeping around again,' the agent said. 'It's all over Facebook.'

'Facebook?' said Tom.

'It's a social networking site, Thomas. People use it to exchange information with friends. A *friend* is someone who—'

'Ha ha,' Tom said. 'I know what Facebook is. Zoe's got a lot of likes on it, right?'

'Ninety thousand, last time I looked.'

He held the phone between his ear and his shoulder while he massaged his knees. His inflamed ligaments weren't responding to the application of ibuprofen rub. In truth, he knew they would only respond to him applying several decades of top-level coaching insight to his own life. It was maybe time to admit that a sixty-six-year-old man shouldn't be doing clean and jerk with a heavy barbell. But hey. There were accountants who bollocksed up their own taxes. There were doctors who smoked Marlboro Reds. Why should he be the first old man to listen to himself? He was a sports coach; he wasn't some kind of bloody pioneer.

'So anyway,' the agent was saying. 'She sleeps with this guy, and apparently he wakes up and realises who she is, and he goes and plasters it all over the internet. Where, right at this moment, the salacious details are being read by every single person on Earth with the exception of the Chinese, because Facebook is blocked there, and you, because you are a reactionary old man with no interest in fun stuff. You want me to read you the filth he's posted?'

'Not really.'

'I'm going to read it to you,' she said, as if he'd never spoken.

Tom heard her out, but he didn't know what he was supposed to do with the information.

'I'm Zoe's coach on the track,' he said finally. 'Who she takes to bed is her own bloody business.'

47

'Agreed,' said the agent, 'but this is just to keep you in the loop, and to suggest that—'

Tom growled. What did a loop have to do with it? Why couldn't people just say: *I wanted to give you the information?*

'Is everything all right?' said the agent.

'Christ, that's a huge philosophical question.'

'You made a sort of . . . noise.'

'Yeah, actually I growled at you. It's an Aussie thing. And I guess it worked, because you stopped talking.'

'Look, I'm just trying to help, okay?'

'What you're trying to do, darling, is protect your fifteen per cent.'

'She's the face of *Perrier*, Tom. It's worth protecting.'

'Look. If fizzy water wants a face, that's fizzy water's problem. My job is to help Zoe win gold in the sprint in the London Olympics in 127 days' time.'

'Yes, and what *I'm* saying is that we're on the same side here. Surely it can't help her focus, to be all over Facebook like this?'

'I won't disagree, but what do you want me to do? Shut down Facebook? I'll check with my broker, but I'm pretty sure I don't own it.'

'Could you just have a talk with Zoe? She respects you.'

Tom smiled, and his voice softened. 'Flattery will get you everywhere, honey, but don't kid yourself. I've been trying to calm Zoe down since she was nineteen. If I had my way I'd keep her asleep whenever she wasn't training or racing. I'd pop one of those little tranquiliser darts into her with a blowpipe, like they do with tigers in the wild. But what can I do? I'm a coach. All they give us is a whistle and a stopwatch.'

The agent murmured sympathetically. 'Well I hope you can do

48

something, because this will be all over the papers tomorrow and these things have a habit of spiralling. You should at least encourage her not to give them any more ammunition.'

Tom sighed. 'I'll pull her in and see what I can do. That's all I can say.'

'Thanks, Tom. I owe you one.'

'Yeah, well, maybe you can make me the face of something.'

The agent laughed. Through the phone, it sounded like a goose honking with its head jammed in a half-empty Lyle's Golden Syrup can. 'And what would you be the face of?'

'I don't know. Nurofen? I use a lot of that.'

'I think they'd be looking to cast someone young and pain-free.'

'That's ironic.'

'Ah, but that's showbusiness.'

Tom clicked off the call. He thought it over for a minute, then texted Zoe to be at his flat in an hour. If he was going to assert some authority over her, it had better be on his patch. Rule number one of tiger training: make sure the beast knows it's coming into your territory.

Zoe texted back straight away: *OK boss.*

Good girl – she knew what it was about. She'd show up, he'd tell her off, then he'd make them both a cup of Earl Grey and send her on her way.

He felt a lurch of worry for Zoe. He had tried so hard to get it right with her. He'd been a terrible dad himself, but Zoe and Kate sometimes felt like his second chance. He cared more than he probably should, on his salary, for these two women he'd trained since they were nineteen.

He let himself daydream about what he'd do to the guy who'd

smeared Zoe all over the internet. They were pretty good, these vengeance fantasies. With functioning knees, you could kick all kinds of shit out of a fellow. This was one of the many advantages that wishful thinking held over reality.

Still, he did care about Zoe. She was hard to read, and maybe that's why he liked her so much. For all he knew, she really believed in the good-looking losers she fell for. He often tried to talk about it with her but she always made a joke of it, as if arriving for her early morning training session with her heart in tiny pieces was an everyday evil to be endured, like losing an earring, or not finding a seat on the bus. She was defensive, and sometimes that came out as sarcasm. And she was right – what would he know about a young woman searching for love? But if Tom had to pin it down, he'd say she was more vulnerable than reckless.

He added more hot water to his bath. The trouble was, he saw stuff in men that Zoe could never see. He knew what the awful bastards were like.

'Present company excepted,' he said aloud.

Steam rose. He couldn't blame Zoe for being desperate. The odds against her finding love rose every day. She was only getting more notorious, and men were only getting worse. The planet was filling up with good-looking young worldlings built entirely of opposites, cancelling themselves out and – speaking as a bloke – leaving nothing you'd honestly want to go for a drink with. This new species of guy paired city shoes with backwoods beards. They played in bands but they worked in offices. They hated the rich but they bought lottery tickets, they laughed at comedies about the shittiness of lives that were based quite pointedly on their own, and worst of all they were so endlessly bloody gossipy. Every single thing they did, from unboxing a phone through to sleeping with his athlete, they had this compulsion to stick it online and see what everyone else thought. Their lives were a howling vacuum that sucked in attention. He didn't see how Zoe could ever find love with this new breed of men with cyclonic souls that sucked like Dysons and never needed their bag changing in order to keep on and on sucking.

Tom swore at himself and put the thought away. The agent was right: he was an old man. Also, he was probably thinking about Zoe too much.

He wasn't supposed to have a favourite, and the truth was that he didn't. Kate was the more naturally gifted rider, Zoe levelled the score with pure determination, and Tom liked them equally.

He checked his watch – forty minutes to go till Zoe arrived. His watch was a Casio, it was splash-proof, and it did exactly one thing, which was to tell the bloody time. This was another point of difference between him and guys these days. They all wore James Bond watches with separate chronometer dials, resistant to a depth of one thousand metres. What the hell did they think was going to happen to them? That they would be thrown clear from the high street stores where they worked and sink to the bottom of the Mariana Trench, from which they would swim clear only due to their ability to time events to the split second? Those guys wouldn't know a fraction of a second if it jumped up and denied them an Olympic medal. They had no concept of what could be won and lost in one. Time was wasted on this new breed of man who could spend a whole night with a woman and then upload it in less than a minute.

He sighed. He knew he wasn't being fair. Whatever was wrong with Zoe, it was about more than this latest man. Away from the track, her judgement was shitty. Take this new apartment of hers.

One lucky break with that endorsement gig – those Perrier ads, because of her looks – and she'd gone and got herself mortgaged up higher than a career in track cycling could ever pay down. As her coach, he should literally talk her back down to Earth. Get her out of that apartment and back to ground level, back to where athletes hunted gold for the glory of it. It made him sick, to be honest, the way the agent had turned Zoe's head. But he knew how it went: you lost all human perspective, living alone. You didn't have anyone to say: mate, you're being a dick about this.

He worked on getting his knees to bend, as a prelude to standing in the bath and towelling dry. He massaged his knee joints again to ease the ligaments, swearing rhythmically under his breath. Finally, in pure frustration, he banged his fists on the backs of the knee hinges. The pain flared and his knees flatly refused to comply. They mocked him, dumb and inarticulate.

The bath water had cooled. He raised one stiff, straight leg and reached for the hot tap again with his big toe. The toe scraped up the chain of the bath plug, each tiny chrome-plated link marking off one thirtieth of a second against his waterlogged skin. He managed to spin the hot tap but there was no more hot water. He realised he was getting cold. His knees were adopting their coffin configuration. He told them: 'Don't get used to it, you work-shy little bastards. I'm having you cremated.'

The longer he was stuck here, the worse the situation got. About a heartbeat ago, at the age of twenty-two, he had been the Australian national champion in pursuit cycling and the Australian number two in the sprint. And then, so recently that he could still hear 'God Save the Queen' ringing in his ears, he'd won two Commonwealth silvers. He really had experienced every tiniest increment of time in the four decades since then, and yet here he was, surprised to be suddenly old and crippled. Turned out the rope didn't care if you noticed every daisy on the path to the gallows.

He tried to push himself out of the bath by placing his palms flat on the rim and heaving his wiry body up to a point at which he might be able to manoeuvre a buttock onto the edge, raise his legs over and fall in a reasonably controlled fashion onto the blue bathmat, catch his breath, and drag himself across the floor to pull himself upright on the rungs of the heated electric towel rail. Sweet bollocks, he thought. This is actually my best-case scenario right now, to fall out of this bath and land on the floor of this modernist bathroom in this two-bedroom flat with its double-glazed units and its Juliet balcony giving onto the partially obscured canal view in this regeneration project of a residential block, twelve thousand miles from where I was born.

The cold gripped him now, and he didn't have the strength in his arms to lift himself out of the tub. He thought for a long time about what to do, but a plan wouldn't come. The problem now wasn't that he was one tenth of a second short of the podium. It was that he couldn't get out of the bath. He fought back tears of frustration. He hadn't wept since 1968, and he wasn't about to give the twenty-first century the satisfaction.

Lars Homestead, Great Chott Salt Flat, planet Tatooine, Outer Rim Territories, Arkanis Sector, 43,000 light years from the Galactic Core. Upstairs

When Sophie was a Jedi knight was the only time she didn't feel exhausted. She lay on her stomach on her bed on her home planet,

53

wearing Skywalker's black robes. She had his lightsaber at the ready, and she was reviewing footage of herself on her iPad. On the screen she was explaining the lie of the land to C-3PO, a protocol droid.

'Well,' she was saying, 'if there's a bright centre to the universe, you're on the planet that it's furthest from.'

Sophie's lips moved as she watched herself speak the words on the screen. Through the wall of her bedroom, she could hear Dad singing in the bath. Through the window she heard children laughing and calling to each other as they rode their bikes in the street. By scrunching the earphones into her ears, she muffled the noise. It was a distracting phenomenon, that Earth sounds could be heard way out here on Tatooine. It had to be some kind of spatio-temporal effect caused by the gravitation of the planet's twin suns. As a Jedi, she tried to tune it out. Time and space were training wheels on a bike – you were pretty limited until you could ride without them.

The walls of her room were lined with *Star Wars* posters. The lampshade hanging from the ceiling was the Death Star under construction. On the floor beside her bed was her most precious thing, a perfect model of Han Solo's ship, the *Millennium Falcon*. It was two feet long, and open to reveal the interior. There were the twin Girodyne SRB42 sublight engines, the Isu-Sim SSP05 hyperdrive generator, and the Novaldex stasis-type shield generator. Something she worried about was that the ship didn't have a toilet. There were Corellian Engineering Corporation AG-2G quad lasers, both dorsally and ventrally mounted, there was a complex network of underfloor smuggling compartments, but there was nowhere to go for a wee. Even when time and space meant nothing to you, a trip across the universe was a long time to hold it in.

From the street outside, the noise of the kids shouting was getting louder. Singing in the shower next door, in another galaxy, Dad was misremembering "Over the Rainbow".

Sophie decided to review all the footage again, to see what could be learned. She watched the whole of *A New Hope* and *The Empire Strikes Back* on super-fast-forward, slowing down whenever she got to a scene with the *Millennium Falcon* in it. Still nothing about any loo.

She'd been feeling pretty sick already, and the super-fast-forward made it worse. Her stomach cramped and her saliva ducts produced a sweet, metallic water. She ignored it and switched to *Return of the Jedi*. There wasn't much of the *Falcon* in this footage, and pretty soon she was back to the scene in the Death Star where Skywalker finally confronts Vader.

She slowed it down, watching herself getting zapped by the powers that radiated from the Emperor's fingers.

'Feel the power of the dark side.' This is what the Emperor was saying.

All she really felt was sick.

'Luke,' said Vader. 'I am your father.'

In the bathroom, Dad was singing, 'Lemon drops, in some kind of lullaby with chimney pots . . .'

Her concentration wavered. It was getting hard to block out her life on Earth. Outside her window, the children were screaming and giggling. She kept the earphones in and stood on her bed to see what was happening. Through the window she saw Zoe arriving on a bike. The kids in the street had fallen in line. They were riding behind her down the street. Zoe was laughing and playing up to it, weaving along the road, leading them all in looping patterns.

Next door, Dad sang: 'If jolly little rainbows fly above the blue-birds, why, precisely, can't I do that kind of stuff too?'

'Search your feelings,' said Vader. 'You know it to be true.'

She watched Zoe stop outside the house. Now that Sophie was standing up, the nausea was worse. She felt the sick trying to come up, and she took sharp breaths to force it down again.

'Noooooo!' screamed Luke in her earphones.

Downstairs, the doorbell rang and she heard the front door opening.

The vomit tried to come up again. Her concentration was gone. She took out her earphones and she was Sophie again, suddenly spent, in her upstairs bedroom on Earth. She hurried to the door, then stopped, sweating and jiggling from one foot to another. Dad was in the bathroom – she couldn't be sick in there. And Mum and Zoe were downstairs, so she couldn't run down and use the toilet under the stairs. She held her hands over her mouth as the nausea came in waves that rose higher and higher. She looked around the room, in panic, for something to be sick in. The wastepaper basket was wicker. Her pencil case was too small. She climbed on her bed and tried to unscrew the Death Star lampshade, but she was too small to reach it properly, and the sick was coming now, and there was nothing she could do to stop it.

She stepped off the bed, knelt on the floor, and threw up into the *Millennium Falcon*. Hot sick flooded the underfloor smuggling compartments. It shorted out the Koensayr TLB power converter, and rose to the waists of the action figurines of Skywalker, Kenobi, Solo and Chewbacca. They said nothing; just stared at her in disgust. When it was finished, Sophie was so tired that she could hardly wipe away the long strand of mucus that trailed from her mouth.

Her head throbbed. She didn't know what to do. Downstairs, Zoe and Mum were talking. She heard their voices getting louder.

Mum said: 'I'll just go up and see if she's okay to leave.'

Sophie's heart hammered. She grabbed the top section of the *Millennium Falcon*, snapped it on to the base, and shoved the model under her bed. The sick sloshed inside it, but it was contained. She jumped back into bed, pulled the covers over her and plugged her earphones back in.

'I will not fight you, Father,' said Luke.

Mum appeared in the doorway. She smiled at Sophie. 'How are you feeling, darling?'

Sophie looked up from the screen. She shrugged. 'Fine.'

'Need a hug?'

Sophie shook her head. She couldn't let Mum come into the room and smell the sick. Sophie saw the hurt in Mum's face. It was okay. Hurt was better than worried.

She pointed at the screen. 'This is an important bit.'

Mum nodded. 'Okay. I just came to see if you're good for a while. Zoe wants me to go round to Tom's with her.'

Sophie shrugged and looked at the screen.

'Look,' Mum said, 'I can say no to her, if you need me.'

Sophie shook her head. 'I'm fine. I'll just watch this.'

Mum sighed. 'Well, if you're sure. Dad's just in the bathroom if you need him.'

Sophie felt the sick rising again. Under the duvet, she clenched her fists to keep it down.

She said: 'Just *go*, will you? You're making me miss the best part.'

Mum looked at her for a moment, then turned and closed the door behind her. Sophie rolled out of bed, took the top off the *Millennium Falcon*, and threw up again. The sick rose to the middle of Skywalker's chest. Sophie knelt on the floor, panting.

Remembering the look on her mum's face made her want to cry, so she put the earphones back in.

'If you will not be turned, you will be destroyed!' said the Galactic Emperor.

She turned the DVD off.

The front door slammed, and from outside in the street she heard the snapping sounds of Mum and Zoe clipping into their pedals.

'Is she okay?' Zoe said.

'She's just off in her own world these days,' Mum said. 'It's like she doesn't want to connect with me at all.'

Their voices faded as they rode off down the street.

Sophie knelt with her arms crossed over her stomach. She watched Chewbacca, now up to his armpits in sick, looking at her accusingly.

If she hadn't felt so bad, she'd have laughed. She could actually hear the Wookiee's mournful cry.

Bathroom, Flat 12, The Waterfront, Sport City, Manchester

Tom tried again but he still couldn't get out of the bath. He needed warmth to get the necessary strength, and he needed strength to get out and get warm. It was like a shitty version of *Catch-22* where you were stuck in a bath instead of a bomber squadron. It was too bloody realistic, was what it was, plus Zoe was going to show up in five minutes. Say what you liked about the girl, she was never late. As someone who made her living by arriving milliseconds ahead of the quickest people on earth, Zoe seemed to find punctuality less challenging than civilians did.

He heaved up again on the edge of the tub, using all his upper body strength. A cold muscle tore in his shoulder and he splashed back down into the bath.

'Oh you treacherous little bastards,' he said to his left deltoid group.

He shivered, massaged the shoulder and thought about the situation. When you analysed it, his best-case now would be to die of hypothermia, nice and quick, before Zoe got here.

The doorbell went. He sighed, picked up his phone, and dialled Zoe. She answered after a couple of rings.

'Listen to me,' he said. 'I might as well be up-front about this. I'm stuck in the bath. My knees are locked.'

'Shit. I mean, okay. Has someone got the key?'

'Christ, Zo. Who would I give a key to?'

'I don't know.'

'No, you don't, and that's because you have a basic lack of curiosity about other people's lives. Now Kate, on the other hand—'

'She's with me.'

'What?'

'I thought if I brought her, you wouldn't tell me off so much. Do you want us to break the door down?'

'Shit, I don't know. Can you?'

'Hang on . . .'

He heard a splintering, then the sound of his front door slamming back against the doorstop.

'. . . yeah,' said Zoe. 'That'll be all the gym work you make us do.'

'Wait there,' said Tom. 'Okay? Don't come in yet.'

The only thing he could reach was the bubble bath, and he emptied out a third of the bottle and whipped up a froth so they wouldn't see his bony body with his skin hanging loose from the depleted muscles, and his cock hiding from the cold.

He forced himself to relax. This was just a bad situation, that's all. He could get them to pass him a towel, or something. A way could somehow be found to preserve everyone's dignity as the girls helped him out of the bath. This was just one of those unfortunate moments in life, like going to dinner parties. You didn't need to enjoy it to survive it.

They'd get it over with, him and the girls, and then they'd laugh about it afterwards over coffee. It wasn't as if he was asking to have his arse wiped or anything. In fact that was exactly the line he would use to make the situation okay.

'You'd better come in,' he shouted.

He heard their footsteps in the hall and he looked towards the bathroom door, preparing the wry grin he was going to use when they entered. Then, on the far side of the bathroom, he saw his partial denture standing in three inches of Listerine in its glass on the side of the basin; the six front upper teeth, moulded in acrylic and stained progressively over the years to match his real teeth. His stomach lurched. He pushed his tongue to the front of his palate and found the concavity there, with its twin surgical steel pegs that docked with the denture. He didn't know what he'd been hoping for – that his teeth might be in two places at once, simultaneously there in the glass and here in his mouth. Somewhere in his mind his front teeth were scattered white seeds on the boards of a velodrome track. But Christ, he didn't want that memory.

Seeing his falsies in the glass gave him a desperate strength, and he hauled up again on the sides of the bath. This time he was able to heave himself over the rim. He collapsed on the floor like wet meat and dragged himself to the basin, racing the girls' footfalls as they came up the hallway. The gap in his teeth was a nakedness worse than nudity. He went faster, dragging his useless legs across the lines in the linoleum, and he felt every tenth of every second cutting into him.

He heard the bathroom door opening just as his hand reached up and found his denture. He grabbed it, brought it to his mouth and fumbled it with his freezing hands. It bounced off the rim of the sink and spun through the air. It sank, with the discreet splash of a near-perfect dive, into the toilet bowl.

He said: 'Oh . . . fuck *you*, life.'

Kate and Zoe found him collapsed on the floor, a slug trail of water stretching from the bath to his feet, his skin wrinkled from prolonged immersion and goose-bumped with cold, twisting his neck to look up at them, and wearing nothing but a toothless grin.

'You should see the state of the other guy,' he joked. It was the best he could do in the circumstances.

Zoe put her hand to her mouth, between laughter and shock. Kate blinked at him over Zoe's shoulder.

Tom sighed. 'Well don't just bloody stand there, admiring my birthday suit.'

Zoe took down his dressing gown from the peg on the back of the door and wrapped him in it. She knelt beside him and took his hand. Her eyes flicked around the room, looking for an explanation.

'Knees completely locked,' he said. 'Trouble exiting the watery grave.'

'Should I call an ambulance?'

He grimaced. 'Call the vet. Have me put down.'

The girls were shaken, he could see. He was a fixed point in their lives, and God knew they needed fixed points. He'd better get back to being one, but he was shivering so hard his legs were banging on the lino. He was flapping like a landed fish.

61

'Let's all just relax,' he said. His mouth was John Wayne and his body was Flipper the dolphin.

Kate said: 'Can I get you some blankets or something?'

He waved the idea away. You got to a certain age and kindnesses became these invisible flies to be swatted.

'What can we do?' Zoe said.

'You, sweetheart, can sell your luxury apartment. It's not good for you. Come and live in my spare room, I'll cook you three meals a day and keep you out of mischief.'

She raised an eyebrow. 'That's what you brought me here to say?'

'Yeah,' he said. 'You can go now.'

'Can we lift you?' Kate said.

'Catherine, honey, I'm sixty-five kilos. You could bench-press me.'

She laughed. 'Would you put some clothes on first?'

'Maybe. If you train hard.'

She made as if to punch him. 'You're an arsehole, you know that? I thought you'd had a heart attack or something. I was worried.'

'You kids worry at the drop of a hat. When I was your age it hadn't been invented.'

Zoe squeezed his hand. 'You're *frozen*.' She looked at him, and he was amazed to realise that she actually cared about him. He felt the sting of tears and fought them back.

He coughed and looked away. 'Let's get me on my bloody feet, shall we?'

They got him upright, and he took most of the weight on his legs as they helped him into the living room and sat him in a chair by the simulated fire. Zoe brought the duvet from his bed, laid it over him, and turned the simulation on.

'Oh, the fucking glamour,' he said.

62

He started shivering harder then. The cold had hit him worse than he'd thought. Kate brought him a tea and he closed his hands around it, trying not to jitter the whole lot out of the mug.

He had to get on top of the situation.

'Okay, you two,' he said. 'Different speech from the one I was planning. We have eighteen weeks and a day till the first heats in London. Every minute counts, and look at me. I'm the oldest coach in the business, and this is the last Olympics for both of you. I have to advise you, as your coach, that you might want to think about working with a guy who has knees.'

He watched their faces to see how they reacted. But they turned away from him. They looked at each other. Something passed between Zoe and Kate and they looked back to him, their minds clearly made up.

'No,' Kate said. 'You're our coach. Who else would put up with us?'

Zoe nodded. Her face was calm. 'Don't bring it up again, please.'

Tom swallowed. 'You're both bloody idiots,' he said.

He walked painfully to the kitchen and did something he hadn't done since Mexico '68. He allowed exactly two tears to roll down his cheeks. Then he coughed, wiped his face dry and went back to the living room.

'I'll get both of you to the Olympics, though,' he said. 'And that's a simple promise.'

'Yeah, yeah,' said Zoe. 'But what happened to your *teeth*?'

'Ask me again and you'll be picking up your own.'

Kate laughed. 'But seriously?'

'Seriously,' he said. 'A nice girl like you doesn't want to know how I lost my teeth.'

* * *

Back outside, Kate said: 'I reckon he crashed.'

Zoe shook her head. 'I reckon he had them removed so he could give better blow jobs.'

Kate winced. 'You need help.'

Zoe showed her the middle finger. '*You* need an extra foot of pace in the finishing straight.'

'I'm quicker than you.'

'No you're not.'

'I'm way quicker,' said Kate. 'When I let you win sometimes in training, I'm just messing with your head.'

Zoe threw her a dark look. 'When I let you mess with my head sometimes in training, I'm just winning.'

Their road bikes were chained to a railing outside Tom's flat. It was dark, and the drizzle was colder now. They unlocked their machines, wiped rain off the saddles, and set the front and rear lights flashing. Kate strapped on a helmet and zipped up a yellow reflective vest; Zoe didn't bother with that stuff.

Zoe grinned when Kate looked up.

'What?' Kate said.

'Race you to my new place.'

'What, your sky palace? Your high-rise Xanadu?'

'Go on, take the piss. If you had these cheekbones you'd be living up there yourself.'

'I'm not like you. I don't need the affirmation.'

'God!' said Zoe. 'If you weren't a bike racer you'd be one of those chubby yet strangely judgemental columnists.'

'If you weren't a bike racer you'd be working through your esteem issues in porn films, getting banged by men with calf tattoos.'

Zoe threw back her head and laughed the bright, carefree laugh she only used when a joke frightened her, but when she looked back at Kate her face was composed.

She said: 'Yeah, but we're racers, so let's race.'

Kate didn't see how she could say no. She'd overstepped, and now she had to give something.

'Okay,' she agreed. 'If you really need to.'

'Ooooh!' said Zoe, twisting her toes with excitement and flapping her hands at her sides like a chick attempting flight.

Kate felt the tension released and she could only laugh – Zoe really did love to race. The stuff they couldn't talk about was more unbearable by the day. At least they could duel it out on the bikes. It was more dangerous than fighting but safer than conversation.

'Let's go,' Kate said.

'You know the way, right?'

'Yeah, yeah. Just give me your apartment key, will you?'

'Why?'

'Well I'm going to get there before you, aren't I? I can go up and put the kettle on, have a nice cup of tea waiting for you.'

'Save it for the bike.'

The two women clipped into their pedals and rode out into the cold black drizzle, streaks of red trailing from their rear lights. By tacit agreement they took it easy for the first couple of minutes, keeping each other close as they wove through the slow traffic rolling into the city centre. Then, as they rode past City of Manchester Stadium, they looked across at each other, nodded, and picked up the pace. Theirs was the easy, loping style of riders who made no distinction between their skeletal systems and the bones of their bikes. They dug in and accelerated to race speed.

They had a clear run for a mile now, west along Ashton New Road into the city centre, and although it was only one lane in each direction there was a wide band of chevrons between the lanes. They raced along that median strip, side by side, one rider now dropping back to slip-stream the other before accelerating into the lead. Twice they had to swerve into the margin of their lane to dodge oncoming motorbikes, filtering in the other direction along the central strip. Zoe clipped a wing mirror, a horn blared out, and she screamed with excitement.

Zoe was happiest when she was street racing. It was dirty and it was fast and everything you could see wanted to kill you. The car drivers were either dozy and inattentive, or alert and seething, and either affliction might make them suddenly swerve out and hit you. The white chevrons you rolled on were slick in the rain, and slippery with spilled diesel, and strewn with broken windscreen glass that could shred your tyre and spill you into the path of traffic. If you fell you could only roll like a gymnast and hope you hit the kerb before you hit a car. The rain got in your eyes and made the approaching headlights a blur of speed and glare, and in the midst of this chaos you were racing another human being at the top of her game, so your heart rate was on the rivet and the adrenaline blitzed your senses.

They went quicker. Zoe grinned into the wind. This was pure racing because there was no prize and no glory and no one knew who you were. There was no recognition and no fame. You could ride to a place beyond yourself. This was what she loved. When she raced like this, she couldn't think about her life. You were intent on not making the tiniest error. You could ride so fast that the speed fed on itself and your wheels began to roar in the dark and your heart was going so hard that you thought one more beat per minute might kill you, and then suddenly you heard a motorbike and you looked round and you saw the white headlight behind you, and somehow you went even faster. Lights flashed past like laser bolts. You leaned and you wove and you accelerated. Street racing was the only part of her life where Zoe felt in control. It was the only time she could ride past a twenty-foot-high floodlit billboard of her own face and notice only the helpful illumination it gave to the road surface.

Kate and Zoe jockeyed for position on the narrowing central strip, first one pulling ahead, then the other. They were perfectly matched. After nearly a full mile, with lungs bursting, neither could open up a gap on the other. The central strip was getting too skinny for them to come alongside each other in safety, and twice they bumped shoulders and had to hold their line hard not to careen off into the cars.

Two hundred metres ahead, a set of traffic lights marked the T-junction where their route went left onto Great Ancoats Street. The lights were green.

Kate looked up the roadway and judged the point at which the lights could show amber and she would still carry on rather than braking. Without signposting it in her body language, she suddenly kicked hard and opened up five bike lengths on Zoe. This was a power play in a street race: you dug extra deep for a few seconds, way beyond your aerobic limit, knowing that if you gapped your rival then there was a chance the traffic lights would catch them after letting you through. The risk was that the lights might not change, in which case your rival could cruise past you as you drowned in your own oxygen debt.

Kate risked it, grimacing as the pain in her body began to spike. She badly wanted to win. To beat Zoe now, even in a play race like this, would be to lodge a negative association in Zoe's mind the next time they lined up together on a serious start line. She kicked harder. At this intensity a single second seemed unendurable, and twenty unimaginable. By an effort of will, she called the image of Sophie into her mind. This was how she coped with suffering. She thought: if I win this race, Sophie will get better. There was no logic to it, but her mind above one hundred and sixty beats per minute of heart rate had no use for logic. As she powered on through the dark, she visualised Sophie ahead of her, and the image pulled her forward.

Zoe knew the traffic light trap by heart and she'd been expecting Kate to jump ahead. She steeled herself and powered up her pedal stroke, refusing to let her rival open up more of a gap. She looked at the roadway, and now she was judging the point beyond which an amber light would not stop her. Her muscles were in agony, but she didn't acknowledge pain. Her tyres slipped and skidded from the lateral force as she cranked the bike forward so hard that the frame gave out cracking noises.

Kate was operating at her limit. Just as the pain in her muscles and her lungs reached an unendurable pitch, the lights went amber. She was still fifteen metres short of the point on the roadway that she had marked as the absolute point of no return. She had a flash of relief: she could brake now. She risked a quick look behind her to check that Zoe was thinking the same. But Zoe was going for it. Eyes glazed, rocking from side to side in a trance of effort, Kate didn't think she'd even noticed her looking back.

Kate hesitated. Was she being too cautious? She was only five metres short of her judgement point now, and the light was still amber, and there was a pretty good chance she could carve through the left turn while the light had only just turned red. She flicked a glance right, across the face of the junction to where the traffic waited in the last second of its own red light. It was a dual carriageway.

There was a black Volvo and a blue BMW at the front. There was a courier motorbike filtering up the outside. Kate watched the cars tinted orange in the overhead lights of the junction. They looked okay. Neither of them stood out as obvious psycho wheels. Odds were that they wouldn't go like dragsters off the amber light.

Kate stamped down hard for two pedal strokes, then hesitated again. She thought about Sophie. Suddenly the zone into which she was travelling seemed as starkly demarcated as the painted stop line on the carriageway suggested. She was the mother of a young child. Was she seriously assessing the risks involved in riding out at full speed onto a T-junction that was about to be overrun with traffic? She pictured Sophie's face, and her daughter's eyes connected so forcefully with her tendons and forearm musculature that without even thinking about it, she was braking so hard that her wheels almost locked.

When the lights went amber, Zoe noticed Kate's hesitation and upped her pace instinctively. She was thirty metres short of her own decision point, but she wasn't thinking about that. She was thinking about Adam. Here, at her physical limit, she felt her dead brother watching her with the same curious, unabashed gaze that Sophie had shown her earlier that day. Here was this ripple in time again, widening from their shared point of origin, keeping pace with her however fast she tried to outride it.

As Kate slowed, Zoe swerved and whipped past her. She flashed across the hard white stop line and ran the red light at twenty-five miles per hour, leaning hard into the perpendicular left turn with her wheels squeaking on the wet tarmac, at the very limit of adhesion.

30-metre cordoned-off section of the nearside carriageway, Great Ancoats Street, at the junction with Ashton New Road, Manchester

The driver of the blue BMW told the investigating officer that he hadn't had anywhere to go. He was three quarters of the way across the intersection and accelerating through maybe fifteen miles per hour when Zoe appeared in his lane, a wheel-length ahead of his bumper. He'd had less than one second to react. To his left there'd been the black Volvo; to his right, the motorbike courier. He'd managed to get a touch on the brakes but he'd still clipped Zoe's back wheel. He'd felt something go under his tyres and he was pretty shaken up because he thought it had to be her.

'I don't know what to say,' he told the investigating officer.

The officer had an incident form on his clipboard, and a ballpoint pen on a string. 'You could say she turned into your braking distance,' he said. 'That way it'll be clear for your insurance.'

Measuring up the scene, and judging from the marks on the road surface and the detritus of shattered registration plates and indicator light housings, the investigating officer was inclined to endorse the male motorist's account. The female pedal cyclist had come off her machine and rolled across the carriageway, probably passing fractionally ahead of or fractionally behind the motorcycle before coming to rest against an illuminated bollard on the central traffic separation island. She'd been fortunate to walk away with cuts and bruises.

Her pedal cycle – this is how he described it on the road traffic incident form – her pedal cycle had come off worse. He lifted the wreck of it into the back of his patrol car, its frame snapped and the rims twisted. It had gone under the wheels of at least three vehicles. The cyclist was sitting upright now, wrapped in a silver thermal blanket and shivering in the back of the on-scene ambulance while her friend comforted her.

When he set out the facts of the incident on the form on his clipboard, and came to the final box headed SUMMARY, he didn't reckon it was any more complicated than this: that the injured party had continued into the path of oncoming vehicles, while the friend had applied the brakes. This was just how the world was. There were two kinds of people when a light turned red. One kind accelerated, the other kind braked. It was Eve and Adam, Abel and Cain. There wasn't any use doing your head in about it. Not on his pay grade, anyway.

His pen hovered for a few seconds above the box headed OTHER COMMENTS, but no words came. The officer clicked the button that retracted the pen point, shrugged, and winced as cold rain dripped from his uniform cap between his neck and his hi-vis jacket. He wondered what the hell it was in this woman's life that meant she couldn't just brake like everyone else.

Interior of Iveco Daily 40C15 first-responder ambulance, unit number 72, North West Ambulance Service

Rain streamed down the rear window as the paramedic made Zoe comfortable sitting upright on a stretcher. The stretcher had an information panel indicating that it was rated for patients weighing up to 400 kg or 880 lb.

'It's the weight of an adult female buffalo,' the paramedic said, inviting the conversation away from the fact that the casualty had wilfully ridden into the path of moving traffic.

Kate smiled and looked to Zoe to respond, but Zoe turned away and frowned at the rain.

Kate filled the silence. 'Do you get many buffalo?'

'We get ladies who just really like doughnuts. We actually have a crane to get them on the stretcher. We call it the Krispy Kreme Express.'

Kate laughed, but Zoe was still zoned out. Kate held on to both of her hands as the paramedic used tweezers to pick grit out of a deep graze on her forearm. Kate wasn't expecting Zoe to flinch, and she didn't. If you were very attentive, you could feel the slightest twitch of Zoe's fingers each time the tweezers connected.

'Would you look at me?' Kate said softly.

Zoe looked out of the rear window.

'Look at me!'

Zoe turned to her, exasperated. The paramedic paused in his work until she was still. When he resumed, the morsels of grit he removed from her arm made little clicking sounds as they fell into a surgical steel dish. The ambulance moved at the speed of the traffic, its sirens off. Twin overhead tubes secreted a bright sickly light.

Kate said: 'Why did you do it?'

'I wanted to win.'

'You could have been killed.'

'I wasn't thinking.'

'No. Well. Clearly.'

Zoe screwed up her face in irritation. 'Oh, what are you? My mother?'

'I've known you longer than she did.'

Zoe was looking out of the window again. 'Yeah, but if I'd gone under that car, it would've made things simpler for you.'

Kate reached up and turned Zoe's face back to hers.

'Look at me. If you'd gone under that car, I'd have died too.'

The paramedic paused again and the small percussions of falling grit stopped.

Zoe said: 'I don't see why. You have things to live for. You have everything.'

'Not everything.'

Zoe exhaled irritably. 'Christ, Kate. It's a lump of yellow metal on a shiny red string.'

'Easy to say when you've won it.'

'You think?'

'You know what,' said Kate, 'I don't even care. So long as we both get to that final in London, and we're both on that podium, I don't care which of us wins it.'

'No, nor do I,' Zoe said. 'So long as it's me.'

Kate smiled and shook her head. 'Honestly, Zo, what are we going to do with you?'

'I'm fine.'

'Really, though? I'm worried. You seem a little bit out of control.'

'The road was wet, Kate. Crashes happen and we bleed. The girls who couldn't handle the damage dropped out of this game years ago.'

Kate sighed. 'I'm not talking about crashes. I'm talking about real damage.'

Zoe looked away, and Kate squeezed her hands. 'We don't always have to be psyching each other out, do we? We can call a truce. We can talk about what's bothering you.'

'Nothing's *bothering me*.' Zoe took her hands out of Kate's to put air quotes around the phrase.

Kate hesitated, then took Zoe's hands again. 'It's Adam, isn't it?'

Zoe looked at her sharply. 'No.'

'It is though, isn't it? I know you. When you get like this, it's because you're thinking about him.'

Zoe looked at her steadily. 'I'm thinking about boys and shopping.'

The paramedic resumed his work in silence and the ambulance rolled on through the slow, rain-soaked traffic.

Kate didn't know how to handle her friend when she was like this. If you closed your eyes you could believe you were talking to a drunk at a bus stop – one of those puffy-eyed women who were alternately morose and acerbic, squinting through their own cigarette smoke while their fingers spun a thread of imagined oppressions from the air and knitted them into a shroud. But when Zoe went on a downer like this, she did it from behind those clear green eyes in that perfect face with its unblemished skin and its Olympian glow of health. The incongruity shocked you, like being punched in the face by a Care Bear.

'Want to come home with me after the hospital?' Kate said. 'Have a bite to eat with us?'

'I'm not hungry,' Zoe said, as if that was an answer to a question Kate had asked.

Kate had to remind herself that Zoe wasn't always like this, and that she was always sorry afterwards. She cared enough to try to explain, at least, and that was how Kate had first learned about Adam. Years ago, well before Athens, Zoe had got into one of her moods and done something so viciously personal that Kate had actually lost a race at the National Championships because of it. In the weeks that followed Zoe had been incandescent with remorse. That was how it had seemed to Kate – that her friend

74

had actually flickered with a pale and anxious light that sought to expel the shadows cast by her behaviour. She'd invited Kate to lunch – begged her to come – and they'd met up at one of the best restaurants in town, The Lincoln. Kate couldn't have afforded the place, and she doubted if Zoe really could either.

In the busy dining room clad in Carrara marble, a low-slung hipster with a three-day beard and a linen suit was playing Debussy in shoes but no socks. Zoe inhabited the room naturally, un-made-up in jeans and a loose grey tank top but still attracting covert glances. Kate ducked down behind the menu and failed to find one single item on it that didn't seem expressly conceived to worsen her power-to-weight ratio on a bicycle.

She was furious with herself for accepting this invitation to a reconciliation that was looking more and more like a bid to humiliate her.

She looked up in misery and saw Zoe watching her back with a panicked look.

'Shit,' said Zoe, 'this isn't helping at all, is it?'

'Oh no, this is great,' said Kate. 'It's really nice.'

Zoe held up her hand. 'Wait,' she said. 'I can fix this.'

She stood, crossed to the pianist and sat down lightly beside him at the piano stool. The *Préludes* faltered for a moment as she whispered something in his ear, then they picked up again with a hint of *allegrezza*. Kate saw the pianist's grin as Zoe came back to the table.

'There,' she said.

'What did you say to him?'

Zoe flicked a hand dismissively and blew a strand of hair off her face. 'I said I'd give him my number if he made you laugh.'

Kate felt a surge of anger. 'It's not funny.'

'I know. I'm sorry. I treated you like shit, Kate, and I don't know how to make it right.'

As Kate looked into Zoe's eyes, trying to work out if she was being sincere, the pianist segued seamlessly into Britney Spears' 'Oops! . . . I Did It Again', with sober classical phrasing and a completely straight face.

Kate couldn't help smiling.

'I don't know where my head goes,' Zoe said. 'I want to win so badly, I forget that you're *you*. That we're friends.'

Kate felt her anger dissolve in the bubbles of the mineral water and the impressionistic flourishes with which the pianist was retrofitting Britney's *chef d'oeuvre*.

'Well,' she said. 'Just don't forget again. Write it on your fucking hand or something.'

Zoe bit her lip. 'I know I have a problem with relationships. I told you . . . I tell everyone that I'm an only child, but actually I had a brother and I lost him when I was ten, so . . . you know. Boring old story. People get too close, I push them away. I'm sorry.'

'God, no, *I'm* sorry. Oh Zoe, you should have said something.'

Zoe looked up. Her eyes were brimming, but the pianist lurched into Kenny Loggins' 'Danger Zone', *grandioso*, and she laughed instead.

'It's not something you say, is it? You're the first person I've told.'

'In Manchester?'

'Or any other planet.'

'Doesn't Tom know?'

Zoe frowned. 'It's not a performance issue.'

'Still, I think it's the sort of thing you should tell him.'

'I think . . . it's the sort of thing you should tell your best friend.'

Zoe waited for Kate's reaction. Before Kate could think what to say, a waiter arrived and placed plates before them, covered with silver cloches. He whisked away the cloches, gave a half bow and glided away. On each of their plates were 150g of plain steamed wild rice, 60g of chopped raisins, 100g of canned tuna in brine and a 30g carob-coated ProteinPlus PowerBar in its blue and yellow wrapper.

Kate blinked, incredulous.

Zoe grinned. 'I asked Tom what was on your eat sheet for today. I knew the menu would freak the piss out of you.'

Kate stared at Zoe, while the pianist threw in a quick *intermezzo* of baroque variations on the theme from *Knight Rider*.

'What?' said Zoe.

Kate studied her for a moment longer, then smiled and shook her head. 'Nothing,' she said. '*Bon appétit*,' which was easier than trying to find the words to explain that just sometimes – in the rare moments when she wasn't causing quite serious mental discomfort – being friends with Zoe was like being knocked dizzy by grace.

This was what Kate was thinking about as the two of them rode the ambulance to the accident and emergency unit.

'Are you okay, though, Zo?' she said. 'Really, I mean?'

Zoe looked at the ragged mess of her forearm, then back at Kate. 'Yeah,' she said softly. 'I'll mend.'

Flat 12, The Waterfront, Sport City, Manchester

When the girls left the flat, Tom was tired. He retrieved his denture from the toilet, scrubbed it down with bleach, rinsed it and re-inserted it. He stuck the front door shut with duct tape and put the chain on it. He sat down in front of the simulated log fire and took two Nurofen and an inch of red wine for his joints.

77

He came awake to the sound of his own sobbing. He was disorientated. He made it to the kitchen on his stiff knees and boiled the kettle for tea.

He breathed. It was okay. It was okay. Here were the blue and white ceramic kitchen tiles. Here was the old work surface with all its rings and scratches that you could run your fingertips across. It was okay. You had to stop thinking of these dreams as proof of damnation. They were just your bloody neurons crackling and fizzing, like jaded ladies fabricating gossip.

On balance he was not guilty. He'd made a fair job of his life, that's how you had to look at it. After his own Olympics he could have stayed in Oz and had people buy him drinks for a few years, but he hadn't done that. He'd made a good decision; flown out here to try a new life as a coach. He'd started a family, too, and it hadn't worked out, but he'd had this idea that if he could help other kids, it would make up for the mess he'd made with his own.

He couldn't even remember much about his boy now. Maybe it was a good sign. At some point all the okay stuff you did had to start cancelling out the bad things, even the memories.

He'd got into coaching with the juniors, and when BMX came along in the 80s he'd had a lot of success. BMX was *Wacky Races* – all those kids with their full-face helmets and their legs hammering like tiny steam pistons. He let the races take care of themselves and he worked with the kids between competitions to find out where they were coming from, so he could help them be mentally stronger. A kid's psyche was a hundred times more powerful than an adult's. If you could work out which kid was racing away from their past and which one was racing towards their future, then you unlocked a lot of power.

When it came to race day, his kids were always on their game and they won every bloody trophy in sight. He loved those furious little shrimps who only came up to his waist. He especially adored the angry kids. You helped them to win enough times, and bit by bit their grin on the podium was a little bit less *fuck you*, and a little bit more *hey, I'm secretly enjoying this*. Maybe he was still waiting for that moment to arrive with Zoe, but he was patient and he knew he'd live to see the day she smiled an uncomplicated smile.

He'd done an okay job with his life. If you put it all on the scales – your own attempt at parenthood on the one side, and all the kids you'd helped on the other – then who could say where the bastard thing would balance? You just did your best with every hour – that's all you could do.

He poured the boiling water and stirred up a tea. Squinting at the clock on the cooker, he made out that it was just before 9 p.m. He was no fool. He was going to give his dream half an hour to vacate the building before he risked sleep again. He sipped the tea and leaned against the kitchen counter. His knees hurt, but he didn't dare sit down in case he couldn't get up. He didn't need the girls to have to rescue him again.

Still, wasn't it a hell of a thing that they'd looked after him?

He'd always believed that the most important thing was the results. He'd imagined that the thing that would make him happiest would be seeing his athletes improve. After years of getting kids to the top of BMX, he'd been promoted to run the Elite Prospects Programme for British Cycling. The idea was to take the seventeen-, eighteen-, and nineteen-year-olds with the best record on the track at national level, and see which of them had the stuff to go international. It was death or glory for those kids, and they ran the programme out of the best venue they had, which was the National Cycling Centre at Manchester Velodrome. It was the big time for Tom. He got to pick the athletes he wanted to work with. Most often he picked girls. They tended to think harder about what they were doing than the guys ever did, and that suited Tom's coaching style, which was more confidant than drill sergeant.

He'd picked his girls, and then he'd picked the best of the girls, and finally he'd dropped everyone else for Zoe and Kate, because he couldn't think of anything more sensible to do with his life than to get those two to the top. He'd given his best years to them, and all he'd ever wanted was to see them achieve. But the truth was, Zoe's four Olympic golds and all of Kate's near misses didn't mean half as much to him, now, as the fact that his two girls still believed in him even when all the evidence pointed to their coach being a decrepit old wreck.

Tom chucked the last of his tea in the sink and went back to lie down on his bed.

He felt good for once, he really did. Maybe the deal was that life had to break your body down before you could see it. Maybe there wasn't any other racket in town except this one that brought you to your nadir and challenged you to build yourself back up from it, then showed you that what you'd done at least meant something to someone.

Tom laughed with his head on the pillow. He felt drowsy again, and he closed his eyes. He could almost see the rest of his life, and it looked pretty simple now. He'd get both his girls to the Olympics, he'd watch the best one win, and then he'd retire and take his knees back to Oz; maybe even buy the old house if it still stood. He'd drink red wine on the veranda and be at peace with all that had happened.

You weren't a finished man till you could look at your memories and be . . . not unmoved, but unafraid of them.

Cubicle 12, Accident & Emergency department, North Manchester General Hospital

Kate squeezed Zoe's knee. 'I should get home,' she said. 'Jack and Sophie will be wondering where I am.'

Zoe smiled. 'Cool. Thanks for staying with me.'

'Will you be okay?'

Zoe looked at the slim, good-looking doctor who was carefully taping a sterile dressing over the graze on her arm.

'I think I've got everything I need.'

Headquarters of the International Olympic Committee, Lausanne, Switzerland

In a sports administration unit on a high floor of a modernist office building, six middle-ranking officials were gathered around a mid-century burr walnut boardroom table. They were finalising a small change to the rules governing the running of Olympic track cycling. It was nearly midnight, and they wanted to get it done and go home to their families. Tomorrow they would be reviewing modern pentathlon. There were half-empty cups of cold black coffee and half-empty cans of warm Diet Coke on the table. Subordinates were dispatched to vending machines. Clauses were redrafted. In the long corridor outside, the cleaners were vacuuming the carpets.

The officials were changing the rules for entry into the Olympics, to satisfy stakeholders in TV scheduling operations in the US, Europe and Asia. The schedulers demanded that fewer riders should participate, because they wanted fewer heats and more finals in Olympic primetime. They needed this to satisfy secondary stakeholders – the advertising buyers in twelve hundred regional markets – who needed to deliver better value to their clients. The clients were squeezed because the bankers had sucked the marrow out of the money, so the customers had less to spend.

The officials agreed, therefore, that the competition in the velodrome would need to be accelerated. This was what had become of the world that children used to ride their slow bicycles through in careless arcs. Time had been restructured like bad debt. The long languid hour had been atomised. Manifestos were shrunk to memes and speeches were pressed into soundbites and heats were truncated into finals and it wasn't the officials' fault if the consequence of all this devaluation was that an old man would now have to choose between two riders who'd grown up with him, and a girl suspended between life and death would now feel that fragile cord unravelling.

The officials locked the revisions into their documents and stood up from the boardroom table. As they walked through the empty building, trading small talk about their families, lights on automatic detectors sensed their presence and flickered on with low, metallic popping sounds. On timing devices, they stayed illuminated after the stakeholders had passed, then clicked off in the order in which they had first been lit. It was as if another group of officials, silent and desirous of darkness, had stalked the first group through the building. The corridors became silent and still.

The officials took the lifts directly down into the underground parking facility. They climbed into the mannered black or silver-grey vehicles – Volkswagens, Audis, Volvos – that were available to middle-ranking administrators in the organisation. Some of them played music, others preferred to drive in silence. If they thought about it at all on their short journeys home to their families, it would seem to them that they had only made a small change to the competition. It wouldn't even make the papers.

Cloud City, Outer Rim Territories, Anoat Sector, in high planetary orbit 60,000 km above the surface of the gaseous planet Bespin, 49,100 light years from the Galactic Core, grid coordinates K-18

Sophie was fighting Vader, with lightsabers, on the observation deck of Cloud City, the sun a livid purple as it set beyond the boiling gaseous clouds of the planet far below, when the alarm on her iPod went off. She woke slowly and killed the alarm. She ignored the weakness that weighed down her limbs. She knew what she had to do. This was a Jedi mission, and Jedis didn't worry about being ill.

She switched on her battery-powered lightsaber. It glowed green. It was light enough to see by. She climbed out of bed and tiptoed into Mum and Dad's room. She stood at the foot of their bed, with the lightsaber raised so she could see them. It was fine. They lay close together in sleep, with her head resting against his chest, as was the custom on Earth.

She tiptoed back to her bedroom and leaned the lightsaber against the wall. Kneeling, she pulled the *Millennium Falcon* out from under the bed. She carried it perfectly level, so that the vomit would not slosh and leak.

'Easy, kid,' whispered Han Solo. 'One false move and this old crate will tip out of control.'

'Hey, this is nothing,' whispered Sophie. 'This is just like manoeuvring my land speeder back home.'

She piloted the *Millennium Falcon* down the stairs, evading hostile TIE fighter patrols and stepping on the edges of the treads so that space-time wouldn't creak. In the kitchen she docked the *Falcon* on the draining board, removed the top section, and tipped out the vomit carefully into the sink. The smell was awful, but she was very used to it. She turned on the cold tap and sluiced water through the model until all the vomit was gone and the action figurines were clean again.

'Are you *done* yet, kid?' whispered Han Solo. 'This water is *cold*.'

Chewbacca just made his mournful noise.

'Relax, won't you, you big ball of fur?' whispered Sophie. 'Do you want the Empire to be able to track us by our smell?'

When the *Falcon* was clean, she ran water into the sink and swirled it round and pressed the last few chunks through the apertures of the plughole. Then she towelled off the *Falcon* and the figurines, clipped the top section of the model on again and navigated back up through the asteroid belt to Cloud City. Halfway up the stairs, where the gravity was exceptionally heavy, she got space-sick and had to rest for a few minutes. She sat down in the dark, feeling the burning in her chest and the nausea rising from her stomach. After a while it subsided, and she stood up and carried on.

When she reached the landing, she made a mistake. She moved too quickly in the dark, and she stumbled. The *Millennium Falcon* lurched and scraped against the wall.

'Watch it!' said Han Solo. 'She may look like a heap of junk, but she's the fastest smuggling ship in the galaxy.'

Sophie froze. From her parents' bedroom, she heard someone stirring.

84

Dad's voice came, heavy with sleep. 'Is that you, big girl? Are you okay?'

Sophie tiptoed the last few steps into her bedroom, tucked the *Falcon* under the bed, and slipped under the duvet.

'Sophie?' called Dad. 'Is everything all right?'

'I'm fine,' she called back. 'Everything's fine.'

'That's my girl,' said Dad.

She closed her eyes, made the jump to hyperspace, and headed back to Cloud City.

Tuesday 3 April 2012

Flat 12, The Waterfront, Sport City, Manchester

Tom woke with the April light seeping through his curtains and the DJ on his clock radio announcing heavy traffic coming into town.

He stood, opened the curtains and let the thin, bright sunlight wash over him. Yawning, he eased himself into his desk chair, taking the weight on his arms so as not to overstress his knees. He sparked up the software he would need to make Zoe and Kate's training schedules for the week, and while it was loading he checked his email.

The first email was from the locksmith, about his broken front door. The second was from his boss at British Cycling.

Tom, it read, *bad news. Late last night we received a memo from the IOC, who will shortly announce a change to the entry criteria for the London 2012 qualifiers. Only one athlete per Olympic nation will now be allowed to contest each sprint event in London. You will need to have a word with Zoe and Kate ahead of the IOC announcement, as obviously only one of them can now qualify.*

The email continued with offers of support and an assurance of a forceful appeal against the IOC's rule change – complete with a warning against investing too much hope in that appeal.

'Oh God,' he said quietly, and read the email again.

He sighed, letting his head sink slowly down to the desk.

He'd met the girls on the same day, in 1999, when he was running the Elite Prospects Programme. He'd been running two Prospects classes a year back then, at Manchester Velodrome, and at each event he'd had exactly three days to screen a dozen kids for talent. It wasn't much time. He'd developed a trick over the years: on the first day he sat behind the front desk of the velodrome and pretended to be the receptionist. That way he could talk to the new kids as they arrived, and check out their attitude when they weren't on their best behaviour. You got a better insight when you saw them that way.

Zoe arrived first on day one, nineteen years old, tall and fierce in a black puffa jacket, with black eyeliner and a shaved head. She didn't smile, but hey. Tom respected a kid who showed up early. If you arrived first, you claimed the space. On the track, the others would be waiting for your move in the sprint. They'd be looking for that little twitch in your leg muscles that showed you were starting to put down the power. And by the time they were able to react, you'd already be that tiniest fraction ahead. By arriving one hour early at the velodrome, a kid could gain one tenth of a second on the track. These were the ratios that victory was made of.

Zoe walked right up to the reception desk and dumped her kitbag on it.

'Morning, miss,' Tom said. 'What can we do you for?'

Zoe looked past him and through the turnstiles that divided the entrance hall from the velodrome proper. She said: 'Elite Prospects Programme.'

Tom grinned. 'We're a prospect, are we?'

She wasn't in the mood to play. 'Zoe Castle. I'm on the list. The coach is Thomas Voss.'

'Voss? Not that old guy?'

She rolled her eyes. 'Look. Could you please just check on the list?'

Tom looked around on the desktop, affecting perplexity.

'They probably haven't put it out yet,' she said. 'I'm early.'

'Early for what?'

She obviously couldn't handle it any more. 'Look, I told you. I'm here for the—'

'Well, let's just hope your riding's as quick as your temper, Miss Zoe Castle.'

She gave him a dark look, and Tom buzzed her through. She managed to get the handles of her kitbag stuck in the turnstile and fought with it for a minute before she got them free. Her fuse was completely blown. Tom watched her with the shocked but thrilled expression of a child who'd banged on the glass of the reptile house and woken up something furious.

He gave her a minute, then followed her through into the velo-drome. He liked to watch how an athlete reacted to this space. Twelve thousand seats rose all the way to the domed roof, so high that the light from the glass panes didn't penetrate down as far as track level. Wide square bars of sunlight fell through the huge void and faded to a fossil grey that only just put a shine on the varnish of the track. It was a bright winter morning, but down at track level it was twilight. Tom watched Zoe reach trackside and drop her kitbag near the start line. The echo rolled through the empty space.

She took off her shoes and socks and stepped out onto the track, testing the angle beneath her bare feet. She walked a lap, anticlockwise. On the straights the angle was shallow, but on the turns the banking was so aggressive that her feet only just kept traction. She broke into a jog and then into a run, and Tom felt the hairs go up on his neck as she stretched out her arms and screamed into the echoing space.

Thirty minutes later, with Tom back at the reception desk, Kate showed up. She was wrapped against the cold in two fleeces and a bobble-hat, her blonde hair sticking out from under it.

She smiled at Tom. 'Sorry. I'm too early, aren't I? I didn't know how long it would take to walk from the hotel. I mean, I can come back later if it's . . . you know.'

She stopped, halfway between the revolving entrance door and the reception desk. Tom tilted his head and watched her.

'I'm here for the Elite Prospects Programme?' she said. 'It is today, right? I got the letter from this place. But maybe there are lots of different sessions? I'm sorry to mess you around.'

Tom put his elbows on the table, cupped his chin in his hands and smiled at Kate. 'Deep breath.'

She took one, and laughed. 'Sorry.'

'Let's start at the beginning. Were you issued at birth with a name, honey?'

'Oh. Yes. Sorry. Yes. Catherine Meadows. Kate.'

Tom blinked at his clipboard.

'Catherine Anne Meadows, North of England Champion on road and track at Under-12, Under-14, Under-16 and Under-18. Our file is showing a tidy set of results for you, but nothing for the last six months. Did we forget to keep winning?'

She blushed. 'No.'

'So?'

'I haven't raced.'

'Injured?'

She looked at the ground. 'My dad died. Sorry.'

'And you thought screwing up your racing career might bring him back?'

She looked up at him again, shocked.

'We tell it like it is here, Kate. When you're as good as you are, so long as your legs are still attached, you bloody well keep riding. Okay?'

She blushed even deeper. 'Sorry.'

Tom smiled. 'I'm sorry for your loss. Do you have all your kit with you?'

She came up to the reception desk and showed him her kitbag. 'I think so. I mean, I've just brought what I used to race in. I don't know if I've got the right stuff.'

Tom looked at her. 'You really don't, do you?'

'Don't what?'

'Know if you've got the right stuff.'

She stood there and let her arms drop to her sides. She was perfectly flustered now.

Tom leaned back in his chair. 'You're all right, Kate Meadows. We'll get you back on track. Go through, and the coach will be with you at nine.'

He checked in the other kids as they arrived. At nine o'clock, when all of them except Jack Argall had showed up, he closed the reception desk and went through into the velodrome to observe how his new prospects interacted with each other in the half light.

They were eleven altogether, six girls and five boys. The boys sat together high in the stands, slouching in the flip chairs and talking about Keats and fine bone china, or whatever it was that boys talked about when they were about to spend eight hours racing each other. They looked like standard athletic models with few moving parts. Zoe stood with her feet shoulder-width apart and watched them from the brightest place trackside, where everyone could see her. She laid out her kit across the best seats and moved as if she owned the place. Tom watched her watching the other girls warm up.

Four of them were friends from the English junior circuit: Clara, Penny, Jess and Sam. Tom had been to watch all of them compete. They sat together on the floor in the technical area, laughing and helping each other with their stretches.

Tom watched Zoe analysing their form. Clara was bulky, a weightlifter on a bike. She would be unbeatably powerful right up until the moment when her muscles filed a polite request for oxygen. Tom could see Zoe dismissing her with her eyes. Penny was harder to call. She was helping Clara to stretch, one hand on the small of her back while Clara touched her toes. Penny's arm on Clara's back was skinny, scrawny even. She'd clearly been training for long distance; her body fat looked close to zero and her muscle mass was right down. She looked more like a triathlete than a track star. Her face was sharp, and when she laughed at something Clara said, her gums looked shrunken. It was a fine balance – one tiny fraction too much training could do it – between being acutely fit and chronically ill. Penny didn't look as if she was getting it right. Zoe seemed to relax.

Jess and Sam were sitting face to face with the soles of their feet touching, gripping each other's wrists for leverage and working together to stretch their backs alternately. Jess was pretty, her hair dyed with crimson streaks. She'd had a tattoo done on her lower back, a stylised sun with a face and a mane of sunbeams. Each time she stretched, the sun rose over the waistband of her track pants. She had a good back and she stretched like a gymnast, springy and resilient. But maybe she was too slight to impose her will, physically, on a contested situation. When a narrow window opened up just ahead of you on the track, you needed to have the power to go instantly to another level and leap through that gap before it closed. Jess looked as if she had good power, but maybe she didn't have that jump. Studying her, Tom gave her fifty-fifty, and when he looked back at Zoe he could see she was curious too.

He saw her attention shift onto Sam, but it was obvious that Sam didn't have it. She had a stiffness in her back when she stretched and a brittleness in the way she held her shoulders that made Tom wonder if she was carrying an injury. She wasn't smiling, and Tom could tell she was feeling the superior force flowing through Jess's body as they stretched together. Perhaps she was suddenly wondering what she was doing there.

That only left Kate. Tom watched Zoe homing in on her. While the other girls were wearing their club warm-up kits or their champion's colours, Kate wore a plain yellow tracksuit, a hooded civilian number from Adidas. It had oversized draw-cords around the waist and the hood. She looked around the velodrome, as excited as Zoe had been but without the sense to hide it. Everything about her body language was giving away a psychological advantage to anyone who could be bothered to watch.

Tom saw Zoe stand as Kate approached her.

Kate smiled, stopped, and left a space for Zoe to come the rest of the way if she wanted to. Some people left those careful empty spaces for others, just the right shape to accommodate them. These people, Tom knew, were rarely champions.

He watched as Zoe smiled back, coldly, then cut Kate down with her eyes and turned away.

Tom wished she wasn't right, but he couldn't argue with her conclusion. Kate's results were the best of any of the girls on the programme, but the fact was that she was the kind of girl who would stop training when her dad died. Zoe was different. She struck Tom as the kind of girl who, if her family ever got in between her and training, would kill them herself.

It didn't matter if Kate beat her this week. Bit by bit, race by race, year by year, a girl like Zoe would stay afloat in the sport while Kate slowly sank under the weight of real life. Tom had seen it a hundred times.

It was ten past nine, and Tom was about to go trackside and introduce himself to the prospects when a boy jumped the turnstiles and headed for the track. He was six foot. He was all muscle. He wore a T-shirt that said 'The Exploited'. He had blue jeans, wild black curly hair and headphones hanging round his neck.

Also, the kid looked quick. He looked wind tunnel tested. He ran down the steps from the entrance like a rock star running into a stadium. He shouted 'Hello! Hello!' He dropped his kitbag. He stood on the track in the middle of the start line, clapped his hands and all the kids went quiet.

Tom hung back, fascinated.

'All right, everyone! Gather round! My name's Jack Argall and

I'm the assistant coach. Thomas Voss is indisposed, and he's asked me to take charge. I will be taking you through various warm-up exercises and assessing your suitability for each of the track disciplines. Right, so if I could have the lads in a line here . . . that's right . . . and the lasses in a line here . . . thanks, that's lovely . . . and if I could have you all jogging on the spot for two minutes, just to get the circulation going.'

Tom watched open-mouthed as the kid marshalled the riders into lines, chivvying them in a thick Scotch accent.

The riders all jogged on the spot. Even Zoe stalked out onto the track and warmed up. Jack applauded.

'That's very nice, very nice indeed! Okay, so now if I could have the lads jogging around the track in an anticlockwise fashion . . . thanks . . . that's very nice . . . and if I could have the lasses do some upper body stretches for me, hands clasped behind your backs and extend your chests forwards . . . thanks, that's very good. A really good stretch now, ladies, the ones of you who are most flexible will be given the quickest bikes.'

The girls laughed but they pushed their arms back and their chests out. Kate strained till her veins bulged. The boys jogged back round to the start line.

'Right, lads!' Jack said. 'You can give me another lap, but this time jogging backwards. And lasses, I want you to stand with your feet a shoulder-width apart and touch your toes. Ah yes, that's very nice. Show me how low you can go.'

Watching from high in the stands, Tom couldn't help laughing. The boys were struggling to run backwards on the track, with the angle of it. They stumbled. There was swearing. The girls had their bums in the air and their hands on the ground.

'Right, gentlemen,' Jack shouted. 'I want you to carry on jogging backwards, only now I want you to slap your thigh with the palm of the opposite hand on every second step, and on every eighth step I want you to slap the back of your neck with both hands. The one who's best at it, I will be reporting to the coach that he has the best coordination.'

The boys were terrible. There were slaps and falls and swearing echoing through the velodrome. The girls started laughing and stood up from their stretching to watch the boys. On the far side of the track the boys were losing it. It was falling into chaos.

Jack grinned at the girls. 'Now, ladies, if I could have your kind attention, I have a terrible admission. My name really is Jack Argall, but Thomas Voss didn't ask me to do this. I'm just one of you. I have no idea where Thomas Voss is, to tell the truth. So I would just like to take this opportunity to inform you girls that I am the reigning Scottish National Champion on a push bike, that these are my real biceps, that I am currently single, that all of you are extremely beautiful and stretchy, and that at this exact moment I'm the only male athlete in the building who isn't looking like an arse and doing the backwards Bavarian slap dance. I thank you.'

He bowed. From the waist. With a flourish.

There was silence from everyone. Kate started laughing, and Jack winked at her. It turned into a coughing fit, and Jack touched her on the elbow. 'I'm sorry, are you okay?' he said. Kate nodded at him, tears streaming.

The boys came back to the start line. They were seeing the funny side. They swore at Jack, and he put up high fives. Everyone was laughing now, or nearly everyone. Zoe stepped up to Jack. She was as tall as him. She looked him in the eyes. Her face was an inch from his, and she was shaking. The laughter stopped.

Zoe said: 'Who. The fuck. Are you?'

Jack spread his hands wide. 'Aw, come on! I was just playing!'

'Get a good look at us, did you? How was it?'

'Well, to tell you the truth, very pretty . . .'

Zoe punched him in the gut. She put her full weight behind it. It caught him unawares, and he staggered and bent double.

'Now,' she said. 'Look at me differently.'

Jack got his balance back. He smiled, held up a placatory hand. 'Please . . .'

Zoe slapped him across the face, and the sound echoed around the velodrome. Tom felt it. He physically felt the sting and felt the breath catch in his chest.

Jack was rubbing his face.

'Remember that feeling,' Zoe said quietly.

All the kids stared at her in the half darkness. Her eyes were wild. Her face was white. The echoes took too long to die away.

'The fuck are you all looking at?' Zoe shouted. 'Is this not serious for you? This isn't Girl Guides. This isn't something I do on Saturdays so my mother can have the house free to tidy.'

As they stood in shocked silence, Tom took his phone and made a quick call to the velodrome's control room. The floodlights powered up from orange to white. The shadows shrank, the velodrome filled with light and the prospects stood caught in it and blinking.

Tom walked calmly down to the track, taking some weight off his knees on the handrail. He looked them all in the eye.

'Okay, guys,' he said. 'My fault entirely, I reckon. Jack, you're a dick. Are you injured?'

Jack rubbed his face. 'No.'

Tom said: 'Zoe, you're a menace. Are you sorry?'

She looked straight at Jack and shook her head.

'Well, can I rephrase? Zoe, if we all agree that Jack's behaviour was out of order and we were wrong to laugh, will you agree to take out your aggression on the track?'

She shrugged. She made a face that could be read both ways. Tom was old enough to take that, while it was on the table.

'Well okay then.' He held up his hands. 'Look, I'm Tom Voss. I'm not proud of what happened just now. I play the receptionist trick every year. I'm a decent coach but I only get three days to sort out which of you might cut it internationally, so I go undercover and learn the psychology. I think I've learned all I need. Now, let's ride, shall we?'

The prospects smiled. They couldn't help it. Their bodies changed. From standing stiff, they loosened. Their knees bent slightly, their fingers flexed. Balance shifted from heels to balls of feet. Calves tightened and breath quickened.

Tom grinned back at them. 'Christ, you lot are like bloody wolves! Never let it be said you bastards aren't keen.'

He issued bikes. They were pretty basic. The frames were heavy steel with dents. He let them fine-tune the bikes to size and had each of them write their name on their machine, in marker pen on masking tape stuck to the top tube. He watched them peel off the last rider's name.

He told them to strip down to their race kits and warm up for half an hour. He had them do slow laps, each of them watching the others, circling like ships in a whirlpool.

Tom observed as they orbited him. He analysed their form and after a dozen laps he already knew which three of them would make it to the highest level. Under these shadowless arc lights he saw that

Zoe, Kate and Jack would graduate to the big events. They would be the ones to race one on one around the banked wooden curves of the world's velodromes – these gladiators' arenas, encircled by the roaring crowd, where human speed and human loneliness were contained so that they might be witnessed. They would become the most powerful athletes on earth, propelling their silent machines to speeds where the air started to scream.

In the velodrome their sprints would last for less than two minutes, but the making of those minutes had begun before his eyes. They would come up in the sport together, have these angry confrontations together, love and loathe and make up together, and peak together in their late twenties and early thirties. They would match each other breath for burning breath, pedal stroke for pedal stroke at the speed of a swooping bird, and win or lose by millimetres. The tiniest error – the lightest touch of wheel on wheel – and bones and bikes would shatter. They would wear no protective armour, only aerodynamic suits that showed off every lean and sculpted muscle. They would wear mirrored visors, hiding their eyes. They would become unknowable. Their minds as they raced would transcend. They would be aware of the swirling vortices of their rival's slipstream; of the precise burn in every particular fibrous strand of each muscle group; of the constantly fluctuating parameters of heat, humidity and surface texture that determined the limits of tyre adhesion on each square centimetre of the track. They would be aware of the hope they were chasing and of the failure that stalked them, they would be aware of their future and their past, and they would be aware of every pixel of the moment, from the knots in the boards of the track all the way up to the plaits of the little girl in a blue checked dress in row thirty-eight, catching her breath as she realised she wanted to be just like them. The jurisdiction of the psyche in their races would remain unmapped by literature or science. More would be known about the minds of hunting sharks.

The best Tom could do for these kids was to coach them to Olympian level, where they rode to destroy each other, once every four years and for less than two minutes each time, on the greatest of the world's stages. They would ride for the thousands roaring in the stands and the three billion watching at home. The winner would receive their own childhood dreams of glory, smelted into a disc and presented back to them on a ribbon. The medal itself would be sixty millimetres across, three millimetres thick, made of silver and gilded with six grams of pure gold. Tom remembered when the gold medal used to be solid – but these days, what was?

Tom watched as the warm-up period ended. He saw Kate's latent strength, and Zoe's perfect flow, and Jack's incandescent energy. They were looking over at him now, excitedly, waiting for his signal that would end the warm-up and start the action.

He held the starting whistle between his lips. When he gave the signal, these people's lives would change in ways they couldn't yet know. It would be harder for them than they realised, because outside those exalted two minutes of each race, they were condemned to be ordinary people burdened with minds and bodies and human sentimental attachments that were never designed to accelerate to such velocities. They would go through agonies of decompression, like divers returning too quickly from the deep. They would have this one certain, strange and mercurial quality, these unknowable people with their eyes hidden behind visors: at exactly the moment they crossed the finish line, they would become human beings just like anyone else.

Tom hesitated. He held the whistle ready, but he didn't have the heart to blow it.

And then Kate swooped down from the high side of the track and brought her bike to a stop beside him. She took off her helmet and beamed at him, and Tom felt his heart melt. He frowned back at her sparkling blue eyes and her cheeks pink from the warm-up.

'What?' he said. 'Shouldn't you be in school?'

She gave him the middle finger. 'Can we bloody race yet, or what?'

He laughed. All her hesitation and her awkwardness were gone. She was a different girl on the bike. This was what you did on the track, for better or worse – you raced yourself. And for a while at least, you could win.

'Race?' said Tom. 'Ah, so that's what you're here for.'

He blew the whistle and called the riders in to him.

Now Tom picked his head up off the table and looked at the email again.

You will need to have a word with Zoe and Kate ahead of the IOC announcement.

There was no sense whingeing about it. It was on him, and he wasn't going to shirk it. If you were honest, you called these heartbreaks in to you the moment you blew that whistle.

Beetham Tower, 301 Deansgate, Manchester

Zoe woke on the dark sheets of her own bed in the first wash of the pale April light. It was always like this. The slightest hint of dawn snapped her eyes open and sent adrenaline surging through her limbs. Immobility was impossible. You couldn't train your body up to this pitch and also require it to lie still, however nice that would be.

Beside her was the junior doctor who'd checked her over in A&E the night before. Seeing that no bones were broken, and since his shift finished at eight, he'd offered her a lift home and she'd offered him a euphemism. Coffee was probably the one she'd used – she didn't recall.

In sleep he'd taken up a position along the far edge of her bed, lying on his side, incurved like a closing parenthesis. She stroked his cheek and he didn't respond – he was in deep sleep. Zoe ran light fingers over the soft skin of his shoulder. His stillness moved her.

There was a language of sleeping together and most men shouted it. Even good lovers became strident in sleep; fidgeting, sprawling, holding on to you. As if you needed to be held. As if it was against all odds that you had managed, for thirty-two years, not to fatally injure yourself by tumbling out of your own bed due to the absence of a relative stranger to anchor you.

Zoe stroked his cheek again. His eyes opened. They were pale green, and something stirred in her. He looked at her blankly for a moment, then closed his eyes again without waking. They worked the juniors a hundred hours a week, she'd heard.

Asleep, he looked really young. Zoe liked the tidy, self-contained way he slept. She hadn't wanted the sex as much as she wanted to share this space with another human being, forty-six floors up in the clouds. Sex was cheap money that you could print on demand and use to buy a reprieve from loneliness till morning.

Afterwards the man had collapsed, exhausted. He'd said this nice thing that had made her smile: 'In my professional opinion there is quite literally nothing wrong with you, Zoe.'

'I might want a second opinion.'

'I might want some sleep.'

She'd laughed, and they'd lain together quietly in the dark. She'd felt his heart beating, and he'd felt hers. The rate of it had made him anxious to the extent that he'd taken hold of her wrist to measure her pulse.

'I don't mean to worry you, but . . .'

She'd ruffled his hair. 'My pulse is thirty-nine. I know. It's okay, I'm not dying. I'm superhuman.'

He'd smiled sleepily. 'What are your special powers?'

'Oh, you know, I just like to keep myself fit.'

He didn't know who she was, and she hadn't told him. It was easier to be herself that way. She'd kissed him, and he'd fallen asleep with the lightest touch on her wrist. She'd lain there, listening to his breathing. She hadn't moved her wrist from beneath his hand. Her whole life was filled with people who knew who she was, and who gave her training schedules, and who took her pulse day in and day out. They measured her maximum heart rate, her lactate threshold heart rate, her heart rate at optimal power output. It had felt good to lie quietly in her own private darkness beside this man who seemed to care, however slightly, what her heart was doing when it was resting.

In the feeble dawn light Zoe pulled the duvet up around the doctor's shoulders and left him alone to sleep.

In the living area she put the news channel on mute while she did two hundred abdominal crunches, eighty side planks and sixty seated oblique twists with a medicine ball. She stretched, then showered with her grazed arm held high to protect the surgical dressing. She towelled her hair and made espresso. Standing at the floor-to-ceiling windows she sipped it as the sun rose over the wide human sprawl of Manchester. The bright light connected with the post-exercise glow in her chest and she felt weightless and uncomplicated. For the first time since moving into this high tower, she felt okay about it.

She smiled to herself, and bounced on the balls of her feet.

These were the moments of happiness; you had to take them. You had to notice the minutes of stillness where memory was clement and the surface of your life was the mirror of an unruffled sea. You could almost believe you had raced so hard that you had outrun the past. The sensation was indistinguishable from that of being forgiven.

Spires reached, glass burned, painted gasometers gleamed in the new light.

Zoe stretched up on her toes, steadying herself with one hand against the glass. Slowly, she sank back down to her heels as her face became still again. The act of realising she was happy had been enough to set the moment's foundations crumbling. Sooner or later, the junior doctor would have to take the lift down to the street and emerge, in yesterday's clothes, to be confronted with a twenty-foot-high billboard image of her face. Once he knew who she was, the process of disintegration would begin the way it always did.

She made another espresso, her hands shaking slightly, and went to look in on him sleeping. He'd shrugged off the duvet again and his slender back glowed in the rising sunlight. She remembered the curve of it in darkness; the sense of complicity she had felt with him.

She sat on the bed with her back against the headboard and her knees drawn in to her chest, waiting for him to wake up. She fidgeted, weighing whether to stay or to go for a run. If she did, she wondered if he'd still be here when she returned. She pressed a button and a screen rose silently out of the foot of the bed. She put it on to the morning show, with the sound off and the closed captioning on. Pirates had taken a freighter off the Somalian coast. Arsenal had lost quite badly. A planet had been discovered in a nearby solar system, at approximately the right distance from its sun to theoretically support life. The newscaster imparted these things without presuming to order them hierarchically.

The text message alert on her phone went off, startling her and bringing the man awake. He sat up in bed and blinked at her. When his eyes adjusted, he smiled.

'Hi,' he said.

'Hi. I'm sorry I woke you up.'

'I'm not.'

He reached up and touched her hip. She hesitated. The morning hadn't stolen his looks.

She looked down at her phone. The text was from Tom, asking her to put aside an hour at the end of afternoon training.

'Everything okay?' said the man.

'Fine. Just the office.'

'What time do you go in?'

'Oh . . . you know. I'm working from home today.'

'Want me to leave you in peace?'

Zoe smiled. 'No.'

They lay on the duvet and their bodies were lit by the mute TV as the captions flashed. *There has been more protest in Pakistan's troubled North Waziristan tribal region, say officials* as he kissed her body and *sixteen civilians were reported buried alive in the rubble of a building destroyed by an unmanned drone* and she rolled him onto his back and knelt over him and *dignitaries began arriving for the official opening of the London Olympic Velodrome* and she closed her eyes and bit down on a moan and opened her eyes and there she was, suddenly face to face with herself.

Through eight years of time she stared out of the TV screen from the top step of the podium in Athens, in the infamous clip where she looked miserable. The TV showed her stepping down from the podium and journalists shoving microphones in her face, asking her how she felt.

Zoe blinked. She remembered exactly how she'd felt. With all the adrenaline crashing out of her blood, unconsoled by the gold medal that hung around her neck, she'd lost her nerve like a terrified child who had suddenly found herself in a grown-up's body and wished the nightmare would end.

Oh, I feel very happy, said the closed captioning, in yellow, to indicate that the words had come from her.

You don't look happy, said disembodied green text on the screen.

Honestly, said the yellow text beneath her speaking face, *no one is as happy as me.*

The TV showed the soft line of her mouth in the moment when she had understood that victory changed nothing. That had been after the sprint final. The next day she'd won gold again, in the individual pursuit, and that had felt no different. Gold came out of the ground, and she had felt the weight of it dragging her back down there.

Zoe realised that she had frozen in the middle of sex. She became aware of him pushing up into her, nudging her back into motion. She couldn't respond.

'Is everything okay?' he said.

'Yes, everything's fine.'

'Is it?'

'Yes.'

'God, nothing terrible's happened, has it?'

His eyes followed hers to the screen. Blue text: the sports presenter's voice superimposed on the archive footage of her podium moment: *There she is, Little Miss Sunshine.* The shot cut to the two presenters laughing on the newsroom sofa. The confirmation in white text: [LAUGHTER].

The picture cut back to the archive footage of her, pale, mumbling the national anthem.

Blue text: *And now of course she's in the news for all the wrong reasons.*

Red text: *Some pretty racy details doing the rounds on Facebook, and now these further revelations in this morning's paper.*

Blue text: *Apparently she's been described as 'sexually aggressive'.*

Red text: *Now there's a surprise!*

[LAUGHTER]

Now they were showing the front page of Britain's biggest daily. Her face stared out of the page, beneath the Olympic rings.

XXX-RATED, was the headline. It was the thirtieth Olympiad.

Beneath her she felt the man's body shift.

'Oh my God,' he said softly. 'It's you.'

'Yeah,' Zoe said quietly.

She moved off him and sat with her chin on her knees, watching the pictures.

'I didn't recognise you,' he said.

She shrugged. 'I'm smaller in real life.'

Red text: *Thirty-two years old. Scandal aside – and we should stress that this latest story is only allegations – is thirty-two too old for a realistic Olympic prospect?*

Blue text: *Well, thirty-two is old for any professional athlete, Doug, and even if Zoe is still selected for London after this, there's no doubt it will be her last Olympics.*

Beside her on the duvet, the man touched her hand. 'You should have said something. You should have . . .'

'What? What should I have done?'

'You should have told me who you were.'

She flashed irritation at him. 'You didn't tell me who you were.'

He spread his hands in despair. 'I was wearing a name badge.'

'Oh, please,' said Zoe. 'I was wearing my fucking face. Excuse me for not *actually* having green lips and hair.'

He looked at her and his face softened. 'You're beautiful. You're not at all like they make you out to be.'

She gave a quick, bitter laugh. 'What – the ice queen? The frozen-hearted destroyer of rivals?'

'I'm sorry,' he said. 'I just need a moment to get my head around this.'

On the TV the red text said: *Have you been able to speak to her?*

Blue text: *No, her agent tells us she isn't available for interview today.*

He stared at her. 'You told me you worked in an office.'

'I'm sorry,' she said. 'It's just that when people find out who I am, *this* happens.' She waved her hand at the TV.

The doctor flushed. 'What, you think I'm going to run to the papers now?'

She looked at him for a moment, then shrugged. 'If you do, then at least tell them I'm an all right person, okay? Tell them . . . I don't know. Tell them I offered you breakfast.'

The TV cut to an image of the high street of a provincial town in the rain. Bunched under bright umbrellas, charity collectors outnumbered shoppers.

Is consumer confidence returning to the high street? said white text.

Zoe stood. 'I don't have much in the cupboard that normal humans eat. I mean . . . I can offer you rice, or dried fruit? Or rice *and* dried fruit, if you're going for a PB today.'

'PB?'

'Personal Best. Like when you're training and you really smash it up and you clock your quickest lap. You want to be fuelled up for it.'

'We don't really have PBs in A&E.'

She raised an eyebrow. 'So how do you motivate?'

'Mostly we just resuscitate.'

She pulled on her bathrobe and went to the kitchen area to make two more coffees while he looked for his clothes. The hissing of the espresso machine was the only sound in the apartment, as it pumped steam into the silence but failed to entirely fill it.

When he was dressed he came up to the counter in the kitchen area and she leaned across and took his hand.

'I'm sorry,' she said. 'It would really be okay if you stayed for breakfast.'

He was helpless in his confusion. Zoe squeezed his hand. 'It'll blow over by tomorrow. And anyway, I'm B-list. It's not like they'll start stalking you. Actually, I'd really like to see you again.'

'Yeah, but this is . . . I mean, God. I don't know if I'm up for all this.'

As he said it, he looked away from her to the window and swept the Manchester cityscape with his hands. The gesture seemed to link their situation with a billion tons of masonry, and Zoe felt the sudden concrete drag of it.

'But I *like* you,' she said. 'Can't you ignore what they're saying about me? It's jealousy, that's all it is – they hate me because I'm successful and they're just little people who've never done anything with their lives. And they sit on their arses and criticise the way I'm living, and it's like they're stealing my life from me. The more they criticise, the less I can have a normal relationship, and the less I can have a normal relationship, the more they criticise. I can't win, and now if you're standing here and telling me you care about what the papers will say, then that does my head in because I'm a winner, okay? I'm a winner and I can't fucking win.'

She realised she was failing to keep the desperation out of her voice; to hold back the rising anger as she squeezed his hand tighter.

She let go of it, cast her eyes down to the kitchen counter and took a long, shaky breath to calm herself.

'Sorry,' she said.

He looked at her for a long time with his pale green eyes, then touched her shoulder.

'Look,' he said softly. 'Can I write down a number for you?'

He took a pen from his pocket and she passed him the copy of *Marie Claire*, flipping it onto its back so he wouldn't see her face on the front.

'Here,' she said. 'You can write on this.'

He clicked the point of the pen out and began to write a name and phone number across the face of the face of a rival brand of bottled mineral water. Zoe couldn't help laughing.

'What?' he said.

'Nothing. You've got really crappy handwriting.'

He grinned. 'Typical doctor, huh?'

'Mmm.'

Relief flooded her. It had been an awkward morning, but at least he was leaving his number. Mostly, the guys she liked didn't do that. She watched the strong, soft movements of his hand where it held the pen, and let herself begin to believe in the possibility of seeing him again.

He clicked the button that retracted the tip, replaced the pen in his pocket and spun the magazine around so that the phone number was the right way up for her.

She smiled. He smiled.

'This is the number of a very good friend of mine from med school,' he said gently. 'She's actually a clinical psychologist but I don't want you to get the wrong idea. She's just a very good person to talk with about anything that's on your mind. I can't imagine what you're going through with all this media intrusion, but it can't be very easy to deal with.'

Zoe felt an icy clutch in her chest, and forced herself to keep smiling. She smiled as if this was not utterly terrible, and not unbearably embarrassing, but instead exactly what she had been expecting and hoping for him to do at this exact moment in the long and troubled history of her romantic life: to write her a referral.

'Thanks,' she said. 'I'll call her.'

She smiled as he put on his jacket, grinned as he kissed her neatly on the cheek, and beamed as he prodded questioningly at the minimalist opening mechanism of the apartment's high-gloss olive-lacquered sliding front door.

'It's open,' Zoe said.

The man turned and smiled back at her for a moment.

'I'll be rooting for you, okay?'

'Yeah,' she said brightly. 'Great.'

The door slid open and then back between them on air-damped runners with a hydraulic closing system that made only the tiniest sound, hardly louder than her soft exhalation of breath as the smile could finally be abandoned to make room for the neutral expression her features fell into.

In frustration she slammed her free hand down on the kitchen counter, wincing as the movement tore at the wound under the sterile dressing.

She walked over to the windows, leaned forward and looked down over the city for a long time.

At nine in the morning, with the sun glittering on the wet streets far below, her agent phoned.

'You all right?' her agent said.

'Yeah. No worries. You're calling about the story?'

'Yes. You saw the TV? We need to wrap our arms around this situation. If we let them rebrand you like this, your sponsors will walk.'

'It'll blow over.'

'Do you want to take that risk? I think you have to give the newspapers something bright and shiny to distract them. And I mean before they go to press. Otherwise this could run another day, don't you think?'

'What do you want me to give them?'

'Any positive photo op would work. You need to be smiling. And showing a bit of skin.'

'Oh, please.'

'I don't make the rules, okay? I make fifteen per cent by imploring you to follow them.'

Zoe pulled her dressing gown tighter. On the TV, the closed

captions were trailing a daytime staple. *Jules Hudson and the team are in Worcestershire to meet Meg Cox and her teenage daughter Melissa. Melissa may be blind but that is not stopping her from achieving her dreams. With a great talent for music, she hopes the team can uncover enough items of value in their beautiful home to purchase a 12-string guitar.*

Zoe shivered. 'Okay. I'll do what I have to.'

Her agent's relief came through the line. 'I'm sorry. We both know you're better than this but it's the news cycle, you know? I mean—'

'Stop talking now. This photo op – what do I need to do?'

'We need to create a positive event. Something to generate sympathy.'

'Like what?'

'Could you visit some charity or something?'

'What sort of charity?'

'I don't know . . . something with kids?'

'You know how I feel about kids.'

'Okay. Sport, maybe?'

Zoe closed her eyes. 'I do enough sport.'

Her agent took this in for a beat. 'Well, can you rustle up a particular friend? Is there like a BFF angle we could work, a feature piece, something to make you look more human?'

'Well, there's Kate.'

'I'm not talking about a photo on the bike. We need you doing something interesting.'

'And bike racing isn't?'

'Darling,' her agent said. 'What humans are interested in is human interest.'

'Fine, so Kate and I will do something human.'

'You'd better. Or tomorrow's papers will eat you. And remember to smile in the photos, okay? You have a really lovely smile.'

Zoe was silent, thinking about Kate. Every now and then a moment came – like the aftermath of the previous day's crash – when she realised how close they'd become. It had meant everything to Zoe to have one person in her life, amidst the black rain and the blue flashing lights, who was picking her up off the road surface not because it was her job but because she wanted to. Later, in the back of the ambulance, they'd talked the way she imagined sisters might. It had scared her. Her reluctance to open up, her sharpness – it was a bid to put back some distance. She needed Kate but she didn't trust herself. She'd been more naturally equipped to deal with the relationship when all Kate had been was her rival – some-one to destroy on the track and demoralise off it.

'What's wrong?' said her agent.

'Nothing,' Zoe said. 'I was just remembering when none of this was about news cycles.'

'What, you still think it's about bicycles? You can't get all sentim—'

Zoe clicked off the call and closed her eyes.

The first day she met Kate, on the first morning of the Elite Prospects Programme, she'd only beaten her by psyching her out. She and Kate were the two quickest girls on the programme by far, and Tom had set them up for a head to head sprint over three laps.

They'd sized each other up. Zoe's heart had been fluttering. She couldn't think straight from the adrenaline. She sat on her bike next to Kate, on the start line. Tom held Kate's bike up and Jack held Zoe's. Zoe's skin glistened. She'd ridden three races in a row.

Kate said: 'Are you okay to ride? Don't you want to rest first?'

Zoe shook her head. 'I'm fine. I'm warmed up. It's you should be careful. How long have you been out of competition?'

'Six months.'

'Don't break anything.'

Zoe had meant it to be psychologically unsettling, but Kate seemed to take it at face value.

'Thanks,' she said.

Zoe began working up a hypothesis that Kate was maybe not all that bright.

Tom counted down: 'Five . . . four . . . three . . . two . . .'

Zoe looked down at Kate's pedals. She made her eyes go wide.

Kate said: 'What is it?'

Zoe said nothing.

Tom said: 'One . . .'

Kate looked down. She was confused.

Tom blew his whistle for the start.

By the time Kate looked up, Zoe was already ten yards down the track. It was an impossible lead to reel in over three laps, but Kate almost did it. On the line, Zoe only beat her by a wheel.

Kate said: 'Fuck!'

They rode two warm-down laps. They were gasping. They got off the bikes and collapsed. Kate drew up her knees and Zoe knelt beside her.

'Are you okay?'

Kate stared at Zoe. Her eyes were bloodshot. She said. 'I'll beat you next time.'

Zoe shook her head in some kind of admiration. 'You're fucking bionic,' she said.

Kate smiled. Jack came over, and when Zoe saw his hand on Kate's shoulder, and the way she looked up at him, a knife turned in her chest and she stalked away.

By the last day of the programme she was sitting apart from everyone whenever she wasn't racing. She ate lunch high in the dark stands above the banking at the south end of the velodrome. She watched Kate and Jack putting each other's numbers into their phones far below on the bright floodlit track. They'd been starry-eyed for three days.

She had a tray of fruit salad and she speared green grapes with a plastic fork as though each one of them had spited her. Tom climbed the stands to reach her. He held on to the handrail and pulled himself up with painful steps.

He said: 'You don't think she's his type, do you?'

'I don't think. I ride.'

Tom laughed. 'Still pissed off at me for the receptionist trick?'

She looked up at him, crunched an apple slice and said nothing.

'You okay?' he said.

She turned back to monitoring Kate and Jack. 'If I keep winning, yeah.'

'And if you don't?'

She shrugged. 'Not an option.' She screwed up her eyes to see them better.

'I like you, Zoe. I'm pleased you came on this programme. I can help you work through your issues, if you like.'

'I don't have "issues".'

'It's just that you don't seem very happy.'

'Like you are?'

'This isn't about me.'

'Because?'

'Because I'm the bloody coach.'

She drummed her fingers on the seatback in front of her.

After a while he said: 'You don't have to talk if you don't want to.'

'I know.'

Tom waited, but she didn't say anything else.

'Okay,' he said finally. 'Just so you know I'm here to support.' He stood to go.

As he was turning, she said: 'What happened?'

'To what?'

'To your knees. To you.'

Tom smiled. 'I'd just as soon not talk about it.'

Zoe smirked. She mimicked his tone. 'Just so you know, I'm here to support.'

'Shit, Zoe, I'm only doing my job.'

She looked away and smiled.

Tom said: 'Ah, I get it. You have to win *everything*. Even conversations.'

Zoe massaged the back of her neck. 'Yeah, okay. Sorry.'

Tom sat down again and put his hand on her shoulder. 'I'm a pretty fair coach. I've helped a lot of riders.'

She shrugged, but she didn't shrug his hand away. He squeezed her shoulder quickly and took his hand back himself.

Zoe stared down at the track. Kate and Jack were laughing, the arc lights full on them. Jack threw back his head and guffawed, and Kate stretched to punch him jokily on the shoulder, and light flashed on her hair and light sparkled in his eyes and both of them glowed with fucking light as if they were hollow and illuminated from the inside by searchlights of one billion candlepower, blazing through air-blown clouds of gold and silver glitter that filled their body cavities in the places where ordinary people had livers and lungs and intestines.

Zoe scowled. 'How come they like each other, just like that?' she said, snapping her fingers.

'Ah, it's chemistry, isn't it? You see it all the time as a coach. There's nothing on this earth more ready to fall in love with itself than youth at high velocity.'

Zoe opened her mouth to say something, then reconsidered.

'No, go on,' Tom said.

'Okay,' said Zoe. 'You ever fall in love?'

He laughed. 'Only twenty or thirty times a day. Doesn't count at my age. Apply the voltage and the frog still kicks, but it's dead as a disco on a Tuesday morning.'

'No,' she said irritably. 'I mean properly.'

Tom sighed. 'Love?' he said. 'Yeah. Shit. I mean, long time ago.'

'What does it feel like?'

'You're asking the wrong bloke. Like I say, it was in another life.'

Zoe was still watching Kate and Jack. She said: 'I just feel kind of flat inside, mostly. Kind of dead. And other times I get super angry.'

'Does it scare you?'

She thought about it. 'Yeah.'

Tom nodded acquiescence, like a doctor inclined to agree with his own diagnosis.

'What?' she said.

'Nothing. But I mean, surely that counts as an issue.'

'I'm just being honest about how I feel.'

'You're just being nineteen, Zoe. It gets easier.'

She made the hand signal of a mouth flapping away.

Tom smiled. 'No. Seriously. As your coach it's my solemn duty to inform you that you haven't seen everything yet.'

'Whereas, what? You have?'

'Time moves on, is all I'm saying. You'll find someone you care about.'

She gave him a hard look. 'I'm not scared of being alone. Are you?'

'Oh my God, are you crazy? I'm shit scared of being alone.'

They sat there for a couple of minutes, watching Kate and Jack. They didn't talk. Finally, Zoe passed Tom her fruit salad tray and he took a grape.

He said: 'Thanks.'

She said: 'Don't get used to it.'

Tom laughed; Zoe didn't.

'I want to race Jack,' she said.

'Are you kidding?'

'No. He pisses me off. Let me try to beat him.'

He looked at her sceptically and she looked back, forcing her face to be blank. She held his eyes and a certain sadness took shape between them. It made Zoe ache and she didn't know what the feeling was. Her own fragility, maybe. Her sudden doubt that she was stronger than days; that she could be the fixed object that time would curl around like smoke in a wind tunnel.

Tom said: 'I'm more of a bike coach than a matchmaker. I mean, if you fancy Jack you'd probably be better off just going down there and talking with him.'

Unexpectedly, Zoe blushed. 'I don't *fancy* him.'

'Then let it go.'

She tossed her head dismissively. 'Fuck letting go.'

Tom regarded her carefully.

'*What?*' she said.

He weighed two invisible masses in his cupped palms. 'You're going to end up on a podium or in a body bag. I'm trying to work out which.'

Zoe snorted. 'Like you care.'

'I'm paid to care, okay? This is my job. I strongly believe that with the right coach, you could be an incredible champion.'

'I don't need a coach. I just need to race.'

'Then I'll make you a deal, okay? If I let you race Jack, you let me coach you for a month. If you still think you don't need me at the end of that month, then I'll release you back into the wild. Maybe put some kind of tracking device on you, make it easier for the police to find your corpse.'

She grinned. 'Okay.'

Tom patted her on the shoulder. 'Good girl. Now look, how do you want to race Jack? You've got no chance if we make it a sprint race, have you?'

She looked down to where Jack was still laughing with Kate at the side of the track. He was big for a rider, six feet of muscle, and he had no body fat at all, just long bones with quads and glutes and abdominals deployed on the framework like an anatomical diagram. Zoe looked him up and down, and there was no lack of power.

'Distance?' she said.

'I can't disagree. Make him work a few laps and he might fade. Ever raced pursuit?'

Zoe nodded. Individual pursuit was the simplest kind of racing. The two riders started at opposite sides of the track and rode anti-clockwise, chasing each other down. You went hard from the start, and whoever caught the other rider was the winner. If no one made the catch, the winner would be whoever finished the distance first.

'Okay then,' said Tom. 'Fourteen laps?'

'Fine.'

They walked down the steps to the track, and Tom called the riders in and shouted out the rules of engagement. Zoe kept her eyes locked on Jack, and he watched her back with amusement. His eyes did something to her. She fumbled her helmet straps before finally getting the buckle to snap closed. She hid behind her mirrored visor and whispered *Come on, come on.* She controlled her breathing.

She closed her eyes tight and let all the buried fury come to the surface. Here was the deep rage she felt at herself. It started to rise in her, quicker and quicker, until she knew that if she didn't get on a bike immediately and turn it into forward motion, a scream was going to come out of her that would get her taken away from the group.

'Let's go,' she said with her eyes closed. 'Come on, come on, let's go . . .'

She let herself be ushered to the start line. Someone wheeled out her bike. Her body was shaking itself apart with adrenaline. She was alone on her start line. All the other riders on the programme wanted Jack to win. They were clustered round his start, on the opposite side of the track. Zoe was fine with that. But there was no one to hold her bike up for the start. Tom called for volunteers, but no one would. In the end Tom came over and held her bike up himself.

He took her arm, but she shook him off.

'Come on, Zoe,' he said quietly. 'Let's set a realistic expectation for you here. Just try not to let him catch you inside ten laps. If you hold him off till the last four laps, you and I will call that a win, okay?'

She managed to say: *O-k-k-k-ay.*

Tom shouted out to get ready for the countdown, and the girls were excited at the other side of the track, shouting *Go on, Jack! Kick her arse, Jack!* All thighs and glowing faces. Zoe looked across the centre of the velodrome and Jack was looking back at her, smirking.

She snapped her gaze away. Tom yelled out the countdown.

Ten seconds to go. Zoe stared at the line on the track ahead of her front wheel. The thin black strip that brought you back to yourself. She breathed hard, getting the oxygen into her blood. Focusing. She looked along the curved black line that bent gravity around the locus of her fury and called in all her demons and bound them together into one infinitely hot point of energy in the centre of her. She shook with the force of it. She held it on the very edge of control as the countdown reached its end. The absolute anger of her energy would kill her if she had to hold it for more than a few more seconds. She fought to keep it contained. The speed struggled hysterically to be born. For the three last impossible seconds she restrained it, focused between the race and the real world, under starter's orders. Her lips moved: she was praying for the whistle to go.

She felt the shriek of it down her spinal column. The sound connected directly with the life that she'd focused into one vengeful incandescent point. The whistle released that life into motion. She was stamping down on the pedals before her brain had heard the gun. She only became conscious twenty yards down the track. The first and last properly formed thought arrived: *Oh, look at this, I'm racing.*

The technique returned to her. All the training she'd coded into her body began to take control. Round the first steep curve, she eased down onto the saddle. She took her hands off the wide part of the bars, braced her elbows and settled into her aero position. Her brain churned out random chatter. It said *Fuck fuck fuck I am going to lose.* It said *Shoes, I need a new pair of shoes.* It said *Her name is Rio and she dances on the sand.* By this time her heart was doing 140 beats per minute and her digestion had shut down to save energy. Anger was transfigured into muscle burn. Muscle burn became speed. Her brain said *Indium, tin, antimony, tellurium.* Her brain said *I have seen things you people wouldn't believe.* When she got to the second steep curve she was on her line and getting into her rhythm, and her heart was already at 150, and her mind had gone numb and the edges of her vision were starting to blur. This was her body shutting down the blood flow to non-essential systems. Her brain gave one last chatter and faded into silence. *Great Burnham Wood. Eject! Eject!* Her heart rate hit 170. Involuntary whines escaped from her body. By six laps in, her heart rate was 190. She couldn't think or even recall her name, and she was almost blind. Then something surprising happened.

A very slow peace came over her. Every bitter joule of rage had been converted into speed. She was empty. There was no pain. The air whistled past her ears. She listened intently. That silent music was all there was. It was the sound of the universe showing her mercy. Finally, she was no one.

These were the moments.

But then it started to go wrong. Slowly, as a whisper at first and then an undeniable roar, she heard Jack's wheels behind her, and the ragged sound of his breathing. With eight laps to go, he was catching her. She was working at her maximum and so was he. Jack was just quicker. There wasn't anything to be done about it.

Being chased down by another human being is a very intimate thing. She'd never been caught before. She heard each gasp of Jack's lungs. She heard the catch in his breathing each time he reached the top of his pedal stroke. She heard the hiss of the airflow around him change its pitch as he dropped even tighter in to the frame of his bike. Her vision was down to a single bright green tunnel in a haze of black, as if she was riding with a tinted headlight. Behind the racing edge of the darkness there was only her breathing and Jack's, getting closer. Somewhere out there, other human beings were chanting Jack's name. The darkness filled with hallucinations. She saw the tall trunks of beech trees flashing past her. She saw green dappled shade and a tarmac road curving leftwards ahead. She heard a child's giggling over the noise of the airstream, and she stamped down harder, hoping that her heart would burst and she wouldn't have to hear it any more.

And then Jack said something to her. He didn't have to shout, because he was so close now. He said: *Sorry, Zoe.*

He was sorry. She knew it was the only kind of apology that meant something. With both of them at 200 heartbeats per minute, with the peace of exhaustion coming over her, she understood the effort it took him to say that. She realised what it must have cost him.

She could have simply accepted it. She could have eased up on the pedals, spun her legs out for a few slow laps, and let go. She wanted to. But some dumb anger, encoded by years and automated in her limbs, kept her pushing to the point of blacking out. She gave it everything. She was losing consciousness. Her steering bucked and twitched.

There was a bang.

At first she didn't know if she'd crashed or if it was Jack.

Her vision started to brighten. Colours returned. She was still upright and riding.

Later, when Tom explained to her what had happened, he said he'd never seen anyone hit the inside rails so hard. Apparently Jack had clipped her back wheel. The duty medics took one look and put him unconscious with an injection, right there on the track. They strapped him into a body brace to move him.

Afterwards there was an inquiry and they asked Zoe why she hadn't stopped riding. She told them she must have been in shock. Really, she didn't want anyone to see her face. She wanted to keep her helmet on, because its visor hid her eyes, and she needed to ride herself back together. If she could have kept on riding flat out, forever, then she would have. Instead she put in twenty slow laps and tried not to look at Jack lying unconscious. When they finally moved him, she dropped down to the centre of the velodrome to warm down on the stationary trainers they had there.

She was aiming to get her heart rate down from 160 to 80 in 10-beats-per-minute increments, spending two minutes on each step. She was down to 140 and a few of the other girls were coming by and giving her looks. She shrugged back. Because it wasn't as if she'd done anything except ride hard. And then Kate came over, tearful and shaking.

'Sorry, Zoe, but you could have killed him.'

She was down to 130 beats per minute.

'I held my line, that's all I did.'

'No, you cut right up across him. He swerved not to hit you. He didn't have a chance.'

'I wasn't trying to hit him. I was just trying not to lose.'

Kate stared at her. Then she sobbed – a single, sharp sob.

'Shit! It's just a fucking bike race, Zoe.'

Zoe couldn't hold her eyes. The sharp edge of misery forced itself back into her. It prised apart the calm that the race had given her. She fought against it, but the confusion was back. She looked down and shook her head slowly. 'I know. I'm sorry, Kate. I don't know what's wrong with me.'

Kate looked at her for a long time, then came close and touched her on the arm.

'Maybe you should talk to someone. You know? To a doctor.'

'Yeah.'

'Is there someone who can take you?'

'Yeah. I mean of course. Sure.'

Kate squeezed her arm. 'Who?'

She looked down at her heart rate monitor.

'Loads of people.'

'There's no one, is there?'

Don't admit it. That was the first thing Zoe thought. Don't show her any more weakness. You're going to be racing this girl for years. Don't give her an inch. Make up a family. Make up a partner. Make up a Pekinese, but don't tell her you're alone.

She said: 'Look, you're a nicer person than me. Let's leave it at that.'

'Please,' Kate said. 'I'm just saying we could go together to see someone, if you like. I mean, we're always going to be racing each other, aren't we? So I'd like it if we were friends.'

Thirteen years later, in her apartment on the forty-sixth floor, Zoe tried to hold her hands steady as she made her third double espresso.

You should talk to someone. That's what everyone said if they cared about you.

Happy people believed in someone. That was the difference between her and Kate, right there. Expecting company, people like Kate walked with a careful space beside them. Even in their worst moments they could imagine the possibility of someone. A magic someone who could glue them back together with words. That someone would need to be a good listener, and they would need to understand you very well, and you would need not to have killed them when you were ten.

Zoe drank the coffee and rinsed the cup and went to the bathroom for her second shower of the morning. She let the water wash the junior doctor away, and her agent away, and the memory of the crash with Jack away. When all of it was gone and she was alone again, she cried. There was no fuss. It felt mechanical: tears welling from a simple build-up of pressure. It was almost silent, just tears mingling with the shower water. Everything came out. She practised her London gold medal speech to drown out the ache in her body. *You know, I'm just pleased I gave it my best on the day and didn't let down the other members of the team and I have to say the support I've had from everyone and all the fans has been amazing and wow to see all those British flags thanks guys.*

203 Barrington Street, Clayton, East Manchester

Jack lifted Sophie to carry her downstairs, holding her carefully so as not to put any strain on the Hickman line. On the threshold of her bedroom, he paused.

'Are you sure I can't tempt you to get dressed, wee lassie?'

Sophie giggled and kicked. 'Nah!'

'Are you going to stay in these pyjamas your whole life, then?'

Jack felt but couldn't see Sophie's nod against his shoulder.

'Pyjamas? Really? Even when you go back to school? Even on your wedding day?'

Sophie nodded again.

'Even when you step onto the Olympic podium to hear them play "God Save the Queen"?'

'I'm not going to be an athlete, remember. I'm going to be a Jedi.'

'Ah, I forgot. Sorry.'

'You will be.'

'Is that a threat?'

'It's a promise.'

Jack laughed, then winced as Sophie punched him in the side of the head.

'Hey!' he said. 'I thought you were supposed to be a poorly tomboy.'

He squeezed the child just enough to make her giggle and squirm, but not so much as to provoke her white blood cells into any more unhelpful behaviour. You got a feeling for how hard to press.

He carried Sophie down and sat her at the kitchen table. Kate was already there, making tea in the big brown glazed teapot. She stirred it, brought it to the table and carefully covered it with the Union Jack tea cosy. Steam rose from the spout and wove soft coils through the weft of the April light. Kate wore knickers and a white T-shirt that rode up over her bum when she leaned over to fix the tea. Jack grinned.

'What?' she said.

'You're the sexiest woman alive who still favours the use of a tea cosy.'

She batted his hand away. 'You Scots. You're so insatiable.'

'Only because you're so invadable.'

She hissed *Stoppit!* and squirmed in his grip.

He kissed her neck, let her go and winked at Sophie. Kate went into the next room to fold clothes and Jack plugged his phone into the stereo and stuck on The Proclaimers singing '500 Miles', because it was Sophie's favourite and because what other way was there to start a day like this, with the hours of hard training still ahead and the clean rising sun the colour of children's promises?

Sophie joined in with the words. Jack loved how she liked The Proclaimers, the fierce wee men from Leith with their cheap jeans and their best Sunday shirts tucked into them, and their ugly glasses and hair. If they were still gigging maybe he'd take Sophie to see them one day, once she was better, so she could watch how they stood on the stage. The one with the acoustic guitar and the other one just with his balls, belting out this song like they were firing iron bullets into the guts of the devil himself. The chorus came on and Jack picked Sophie up and spun around the kitchen with her.

An AH would walk five HUN dred miles! An AH would walk five HUN dred more! Just tae BE the man who'd walked a THOUSAND MILES tae fall down at your door! Sophie shouted the words and Jack felt a furious love for her. It was a shout of defiance, was what the song was. It was the reason he and Kate and Sophie all knew she would get better. In his heart Jack was sure they could all win against this leukaemia just by being sufficiently Scottish.

After the music there were Sophie's chemo pills to be taken from their various brown bottles and arranged for the day. Sophie clung to his legs, wobbly after dancing.

'C'mon, Sophie. Sit down, big girl, hmm? I'm sorting out your pills.'

Shit, and now he'd lost count. Six of the tiny yellow capsules. Four of the blue and whites. Six of the red and greens. Into the old silver cup with the yellow ribbons on the handles that said CHAMPION. Sophie knew the order to take the pills in. They also had a printout of it on the fridge, in Comic Sans, with sunny clip art. It was fortunate that chemotherapy was so cheerful, really, otherwise Jack might have found it quite frightening.

The little hand was pulling on his leg again. 'Dad?'

'*What?*' Jack said. And then, more softly: 'What?'

'Need a wee.'

'So? You know where the toilet is.'

'Yeah, but I'm *tired*.'

'What, you can't be bothered to walk to the toilet?'

She smiled. 'Yeah.'

He grinned back, trying to keep things normal. Was she really too weary to move, or was she just winding him up? It was so hard to tell, sometimes.

Jack waggled an admonishing finger at Sophie. 'Don't go all English on me now.'

Kate skipped in from the next room, put her phone down on the table and lifted Sophie to her hip.

'It's okay,' she said. 'I'll take her.'

Sophie smiled, wrapped her arms around her and buried her face in her neck. Kate leaned over and kissed Jack, open-mouthed and unhurriedly, her free hand finding the small of his back under his T-shirt.

'You . . .' she whispered, and just like that his fear passed.

Jack sat at the kitchen table, watching her perfect arse as it receded, wondering what calculus life might possibly have used to ascertain that he deserved her. Maybe fate had simply become distracted, and counted the wrong pills out of the jars.

Understairs toilet, 203 Barrington Street, Clayton, East Manchester

Kate carried Sophie through to the loo and pulled the light cord for her. She took off her daughter's *Star Wars* baseball cap because the peak fell over her eyes when she sat down on the toilet seat. She waited for Sophie to pee. Sometimes wee sprayed forth from the child almost before her pants were down, or sometimes you could stand for more than a minute like this, waiting for her to go. Sometimes it was a false alarm, and you waited in solemn silence until it seemed safe for you both to stand down. This was the thing with chemo. There was nothing it didn't affect.

She thought about the text message she'd just received.

'Me and Zoe have to see Tom after training this afternoon,' she called through to Jack. 'Some kind of situation. Can you look after Soph a bit longer today?'

'No bother,' she heard Jack shouting back. 'I might bring her to watch you train anyway.'

Kate stood and watched her daughter's thighs tensing and relaxing as she tried to go.

'Do you want to come and watch Mummy and Zoe train? It might be quite cold in the velodrome.'

She half wanted Sophie to say no, but her daughter said: *Okay.* Wee had still not made an appearance.

While she waited, Kate revised the logistics for afternoon

training. If Jack was bringing Sophie to watch, they would have to leave for the velodrome with her kitbag bulging. They would need the oxygen cylinder and the Hickman kit and the list of on-call doctors. They would need Sophie's emergency injections, her inhaler, and the complete set of her *Star Wars* action figurines. And they would need the dozen small things that had somehow ended up in the bottom of the emergency bag. You forgot what they did, but you knew you'd remember the day after you chucked them out. Which would be more than shitty in their case. They couldn't let Sophie die because Mummy and Daddy binned the little adapter for her oxygen line, mistaking it for some detached part of an obsolete bike pump.

Zoe, on the other hand, would leave her apartment with just her cycling kit in a bag and one slim Yale key in the back pocket of her jeans. To get to the velodrome Kate and Jack would have to strap Sophie into her car seat, run through the safety checklist, then drive defensively past a dozen billboards with Zoe's face on them. Her green eyes, her green hair, her green lipstick on the rim of that green frosted glass. *Perrier: best served cold.* By the time the Argalls had run the gauntlet and made it to the velodrome, Zoe would have been warming up for an hour already. How could Kate compete with that? Zoe lived alone at the top of the highest tower in Manchester. Kate lived down here on Earth, with her family.

'Give up?' she said gently.

Sophie sighed. 'Yeah.'

She helped Sophie to pull her pyjamas up, and hugged her. She knew she'd be thinking about Sophie in the head to head training session that afternoon. Suddenly Tom's whistle would go and she would come back from distraction to reality; to Zoe being one tenth of a second ahead already. Freedom made Zoe quicker and sadder than her, and if Kate had the choice she wouldn't trade. Still, she had to work hard sometimes not to feel resentful. Even knowing what drove Zoe, even understanding what had happened with her brother, it was hard to forget the times she had put the fight before the friendship. Then again, maybe this was how everyone felt. Perhaps everyone struggled with the possessive flaw in human memory that hoarded the episodes you most wanted to let go. Maybe by the time you reached thirty-two, it was a miracle if you could completely forgive your friends.

Kate shivered, and forced the thought away.

She smiled down at Sophie and smoothed a thin strand of hair back from her daughter's forehead. The strand stuck to her finger and came away from Sophie's scalp at the roots. It was the very last of her hair. Sophie didn't notice.

Kate popped the baseball cap back on.

'Off you go and play with Daddy,' she said brightly.

When Sophie was gone, Kate folded down the toilet lid and sat heavily on it, collapsing as if winded by a blow. She stared at the clump of Sophie's hair on her finger. The tiny yellow roots trembled on the ends of the black strands like bulbs disinterred. She held the hair up to her lips and kissed it, feeling the softness of it on her lips and inhaling the slight scent of chemo and dust. Then she stood, lifted the toilet lid, let the hair fall into the bowl and pulled the flush. There was no point making a fuss about it. Jack could notice what had happened if he needed to; otherwise it was kinder if she didn't mark the moment. Deception was too strong a word for it. She thought about what she did as something a stage magician might accomplish: performing a sleight of hand, palming these ominous moments and directing the family's eye to other, healthier signs. This was the trick. A family was as sick as you let it be.

Kate watched the water cascading from the cistern into the toilet bowl.

The first time Sophie had had enough hair to cut, at the age of two, Kate had cut it herself. She'd put the first lock she snipped off into an album. She'd sellotaped the dark curl to the page, and written Sophie's name and the date in her best writing. She'd actually gone out to the corner shop to buy a pen that wasn't a biro.

And now here was the last lock of her daughter's hair, irrepressibly buoyant, floating in the toilet bowl. She pulled the handle again, but the hair wouldn't flush. In truth, life never would.

After Jack's crash at the Elite Prospects Programme, Kate hadn't known what to do. Tom had announced to the other riders that Jack had been taken to the Intensive Care Unit in North Manchester General Hospital, with broken bones at least. And that was the end of the programme, two hours earlier than scheduled. In dull shock, with her thoughts muffled like voices in fog, Kate had showered and begun walking from the velodrome to the train station. Her kitbag weighed heavily on her shoulder and her hair was still damp.

As she walked in the cold air she remembered Jack's hand on her arm, the long talks they'd had between races, the way he had playfully touched her face. She saw his fingers now, snapped and swollen, a sharp edge of bone protruding. Or was it his arm, or his legs, or his spine? Her mind flashed up these images. What was she doing, walking away? 'Longing' or 'attraction' were not the style of words she'd use for it. She just realised that she minded – that she needed to know – exactly which of his bones were broken.

And yet she squirmed at the idea of going to the hospital. To do what? To sit by his bedside and examine his hand, and, if it wasn't too badly broken, to hold it? It didn't feel as if she had any right. She'd only known Jack three days. But it felt wrong to do nothing; to board her train back home as if nothing important had passed between them. Was this merely a natural reluctance to leave the scene, simply because conversations with boys were not supposed to end like this – with the boy being immobilised by a sedative injection and removed from the scene of the conversation in a full brace by medical technicians in gloves and green overalls? For all she knew, every one of the other girls on the programme was having exactly the same thoughts. Hadn't Jack smiled at them, too? Had she been the only one whose heart had accelerated? Maybe what she was feeling was nothing out of the ordinary but – on the contrary – simply the sensation of being a commonplace and rather inexperienced northern girl, mistaking rain for rainbows.

Pedestrians faltered, corrected their trajectories and flowed by on either side as Kate stopped dead in the street.

She held her head and tried to think. There wasn't any established etiquette, in peacetime, to smooth out this sudden step from a nice flirtation to a serious hospital visit. There was no emotional jurisprudence; just this doubt about whether the feelings she might be beginning to have for Jack actually qualified her to feel that what she now wanted to do was to sit by his hospital bed and hold his hand in hers, and maybe to cry a bit. Yes, that was it – she wanted to cry. With, for, or about him, she didn't know.

If she had seen someone else in this wretched state, holding her head in the street, she would have politely averted her eyes. Was this normal? Did other women feel half mad like this? Or was this predicament unique to the intensity of the life she'd chosen? Perhaps she was not overreacting after all. Perhaps these were her real feelings, so sharp as to be suddenly unbearable, suppressed by thirteen years of hard training and now cutting the gum like adult teeth.

She groaned. This was why people didn't race bikes. This was why people didn't train for seven hours a day. This was why people allowed themselves to drink alcohol, and carry body fat, and chill out with friends in the evenings, so that they wouldn't have to cope like newborns with these unbearable feelings. Her heart was racing and her head was scrambled. She curled her hands into fists and squeezed her eyes tight with frustration.

The day's bright sunshine had surrendered to afternoon cloud, and now the first spots of rain darkened the pavement and sent the other pedestrians hurrying. Here was that startling new-rain smell of youth and fresh water, cutting through the traffic fumes of the city. She watched the crowds scatter and wondered which was more frightening: that she was just like other people, or that she wasn't. If they all felt how she felt, then how did anyone survive? How did you endure all the ripping and tearing, the disintegration as whole layers of yourself attached themselves to the surfaces of others, and came away completely from your core? If she let herself fall in love, there would very quickly be nothing left. A memory of her in the exhalations of these scattering crowds on the pavement.

She should go home. She had a training schedule that resumed at five the next morning. She had a job as a personal trainer at LA Fitness, and a college course that would make her a physio in two years. She had friends. She had people who needed her.

Kate started walking again, towards the train station. She was conscious of piloting herself, unhappily aware of the portentousness of each footfall that took her away from Jack and back to her life. She felt too small to have to think this big. She watched her trainers slowing again on the wet flagstones. She was very aware of the textures and the singularities beneath her feet. These were huge conversations for composite soles to be having with damp cigarette butts and the old hardened circles of chewing gum.

If she turned back and went to him now, she would be losing focus. She had planned to leave the velodrome at the end of the Elite Prospects Programme, take the train straight back home, and then wait to see if the call-up came from British Cycling. It had been a good plan, and now this. Her mind was sunset and sunrise all at once – a brilliant, half-lit mess. It was simultaneously the most exciting moment of her life and extremely painful and distressing.

She was nineteen. She stopped dead in the street halfway to the train station, changed direction, and ran to the hospital to see Jack.

She arrived breathless in a wide corridor outside the Intensive Care Unit. Both walls were lined with stackable brown plastic chairs. The nurses couldn't give her any information and they told her to wait. She sat for an hour, reading leaflets about death and its causes, and still there was no news. She was tired from the day of racing, so she lay across three of the chairs and covered herself with her coat.

She dreamed about Jack and when she woke she was wet between her legs and her chest was fluttering and it was dark outside. The hospital corridor was lit by overhead strip lights with dead flies trapped on the inside of their frosted acrylic housings. This was the first thing she saw, and the second was a middle-aged man's face looking down at her. She sat up, blinking. The man's face was Jack's, but half dead. She put her hand to her mouth and choked back a scream.

A woman was standing beside the man, holding his arm.

The woman whispered: 'You've *scared* her.'

Kate's mind yawed between her dream and this incomprehensible reality.

The man looked curious, or hostile, or both. 'Are ye here for Jack?'

Kate sat up and hugged her coat. 'Um. Yes.'

'Are ye a rider?'

'Yeah. I'm Kate.'

The man stared at her. His face was all mixed up with Jack's. It was freaking her out. She blinked hard, chasing sleep out. She pressed her knees together, suddenly ashamed and panicky. Images from her dream fell away. She wondered if she'd made any sounds in her sleep.

'Are ye the girl who made our lad crash?'

Oh God – these were Jack's parents.

She shook her head.

'So why are ye here, then?'

Kate realised she was blushing.

'Ah, let the poor lass alone,' said the woman.

'Robert Argall,' said the man. 'An' this is my wife, Sheila.'

Sheila was wearing blue jeans. Blue T-shirt. Beige suede boots with the suede worn shiny on the insides of the ankles. She was maybe forty. She was skinny and pale. She had dry hair and blue eyes with dark black rings around them. Not like someone who'd been beaten, but like someone who'd been eating poison. In small amounts, quietly, and for years. You looked at her skin, and it was slightly yellow. You could actually visualise her slipping away to the cupboard under the stairs, taking the lid off the shoe polish, and having a quick sniff and a lick. Then hurrying back to the kitchen to make Robert his tea. Robert looked . . . Kate didn't know. Like the kind of man who might drive you to try shoe polish.

Sheila smiled up at her quickly, then looked down at her hands and fiddled with a folded denim jacket.

Robert was smaller than his son. He was thinner, bald and ill-looking. Facially he did look a bit like Jack. But he'd smoked the life out of himself. His skin was yellow and leathered. Kate couldn't get her head around how beautiful Jack was versus how completely poisoned his parents looked. Jack was a bird of paradise hatched from a pickled egg.

Robert and Sheila sat down on the opposite side of the corridor, facing Kate. They left an empty chair between them. Robert dropped car keys on it and a folded-up newspaper, the kind with tits on page one with little stars superimposed on the nipples so that nobody could be offended. Next to the keys he put down a mini-lighter and a packet of ten Benson & Hedges. He wore a brown leather jacket with shoulder tabs. The air around him was filled with the bitter smell of cigarette smoke and cow. He didn't look at Kate. He stared at the wall above her head.

'Our son is here tae excel in the sport, no' tae go chasing after the lasses. So dinnae go gettin' any ideas.' He let his eyes drop down the wall until he was looking at Kate. 'Right?'

Even the whites of his eyes were yellow, the irises milky blue.

Sheila blushed. She crushed her hands around her jacket. She didn't look at Kate, but she said: 'We're sorry, Kate. Honest we are. But you don't know what it's like, where we're from. This is his chance to escape all that.'

She shook her head several times, quickly, to make it true.

Robert picked up his cigarette lighter. He flicked the spark wheel several times, also quickly, but without pressing down on the gas.

He said: 'We drove straight down when the hospital called. We didnae know if he was alive or *dead*.'

Sheila said: 'Alive or *dead*.'

'We came on the M6. And petrol a pound a litre. But he's our son.'

Sheila said: 'Our son.'

Kate heard herself saying: 'I'm sorry.'

She didn't know why she'd said it, and she was confused, and the sudden reality of waking out of her dream of Jack and into the presence of his parents was too much. She quickly said goodbye and picked up her kitbag and hurried away down the corridor.

Now she saw it. Her misreading of the situation had been excruciating. She wondered how she could have been so naïve as to confuse Jack's flirtation with anything deeper. Of course he said sweet things to the girls. And she'd had no immunity to it. All the years when the other girls had been inoculating themselves against boys through progressive exposure, she had been riding bikes faster and faster in circles and now here she was, sabotaged, outridden by these forces inside her.

She cringed with shame as she walked in her damp knickers with her heavy kitbag through the dark and the rain to Manchester Piccadilly, where she just made the last train up to Grange-over-Sands. Then, after the cab ride home and the sleepless small hours looking through her window at the black waves licking the beach, she rode her training bike back to the station and bought another ticket to Manchester. She was too exhausted even to be surprised at herself. She boarded the first train south and sat meekly in a corner of the quickly filling carriage. She wasn't even being brave. Her hands folded in her lap and her face angled to watch the rain as the high-speed airstream drew it in horizontal rills across the windows, she waited in simple acceptance for the humiliation she was sure was waiting for her.

She was a condemned prisoner on the walk from Manchester Piccadilly back to the hospital. She climbed the stairs to the ICU with heavy legs, and when she arrived in that corridor the nurses told her that Jack had been moved to a ward. With her head ringing from hunger and sleeplessness she navigated the bright primary-coloured signage of the corridors until she found where they'd taken him. She stood with one hand flat against the steel push-plate of the heavy swing doors. She didn't know how Jack would react when he saw her. With incredulity, maybe, and then embarrassment, and then pity. Her pulse hammered in her head and she felt her vision thinning, as if she might faint.

She pushed open the doors. On the other side, halfway along the half-empty ward, Jack was asleep on a bed. He lay on top of green sheets with his neck in a brace and one shattered leg in traction. Beside the bed in a brown stackable chair, with her shaved head and black puffa, looking as if she hadn't slept since the accident either, was Zoe. She was holding Jack's hand, tenderly, in both of hers.

When Kate entered the ward, Zoe looked up. Their eyes locked. The look Zoe gave Kate then – the fear and the challenge and the misery in it – was something that Kate could never forget, even now, all these years later, when she only thought of Zoe as a friend.

Kate tore off two sheets of toilet paper, folded them into one along the perforation, and laid the sheet carefully flat on the surface of the water in the toilet pan so that it covered the last lock of Sophie's hair. The cistern was full again now – time had renewed itself – and Kate pulled the handle and flushed the hair and the toilet paper away.

140

When she was sure it was gone she closed the lid and sat back down on it, under the light of the bare bulb. As she sat, she brushed against the light cord. She watched her old Commonwealth gold medal swing back and forth on the end of the grey, frayed string.

Kitchen, 203 Barrington Street, Clayton, East Manchester

Jack heard the toilet flushing for the third time.

He shouted: 'You okay in there?'

'Fine,' Kate shouted back. 'Just cleaning this bloody loo.'

Jack smiled. This was how Kate was – how they both were – tolerating the chaos and the grime of parenthood, but occasionally losing patience and making an example of a toilet bowl, or a sink, or a cooker, as if by administering a punitive cleaning, the other inanimate parts of their life might be shocked into falling in line. Maybe he should hire a cleaner. That would be good for both of them. And it might not do Sophie's health any harm to have the surfaces cleaned by someone whose heart was in it, rather than in the top one thousandth of one percentile of the population for ventricular capacity at anaerobic threshold.

Jack whistled a happy tune.

Here was Sophie now, shuffling back into the kitchen and sitting down abruptly on the blue and white tiled floor. She sagged like a roofline weary of the rain.

'Did you wash your hands, big girl?'

Sophie shrugged and stared at the floor. It wasn't like her.

Jack eased himself down next to her. 'You okay?'

'Great.'

'Sure?'

141

Sophie placed her hands palms down on the tiles, playing with her fingers, interweaving them.

Jack said: 'Do you feel poorly?'

Sophie hesitated, then shook her head.

'Good girl. You're getting better. If you feel tired, that's the effect of the chemo starting to have its way. We're four sessions into this round, aren't we? That's the feeling of your body getting better.'

Sophie rolled her eyes.

Jack smiled. When his daughter looked at him as if he was the afflicted one, she seemed like a normal healthy girl for a second.

'Sophie?'

'What?'

'Even if you think I'm full of shit, I'm still your dad, okay?' He squeezed her shoulders. 'We're going to beat this illness. We're going to stay defiant.'

'I'm going to stay strong.'

'You have to be defiant too.'

'What's the difference?'

'Defiant, Sophie Argall, is if you ever find yourself in front of a firing squad, you say no to the offer of a blindfold.'

'Why?'

'So you can keep looking for a way to escape, right till the last second. The captain of the firing squad asks if you have a last wish, and you say, "Yeah, gimme a cigarette," and you smoke it as slow as you can, and you look for an escape route and you find one. That's defiance.'

'That's smoking.'

'Yeah, but you know what I mean.'

'It gives you cancer. Dr Hewitt says.'

Jack grinned. 'Look, baby, you can tell Dr Hewitt from me that if I ever catch you smoking when you are not literally standing in front of a firing squad, I'll shoot you myself.'

His daughter looked up at him patiently. Jack felt some of the tiredness enter his own body.

'Oh, sweetheart. I say these things because I love you, not because I particularly want to see you get killed by bullets. It's just part of my job as a dad, okay? Same reason I'm strict about bedtime and brushing your teeth. Defiance at all times. Is that clear?'

There was no answer. Jack watched as Sophie tilted her head. Her expression was inscrutable.

'What is it?' Jack said.

'Are you sometimes not sure, Dad?'

'Me? No, I'm always sure.'

'You always sound sure.'

'Aye. Because I am.'

'Dad?'

'Yeah?'

Sophie closed her eyes. 'Nothing.' She swallowed again. The colour was gone from her face.

'Are you feeling sick?'

'No.'

Jack felt her forehead. 'You are a wee bit hot.'

'I'm fine.'

He held her hand and sat with her, there on the kitchen floor. Sophie leaned her head on his shoulder and kept her eyes closed.

Jack didn't feel sad; this was what sometimes surprised him. He loved hanging out with Sophie, even with all this going on. When she'd first been diagnosed, he'd never imagined that happiness would be possible again. The correct response to having a critically ill child seemed to be a kind of stoical calm, or an endless, heavy solemnity that could bring flying birds to ground and suck the brightness out of sunlight. Jack had felt that for the first year or so, but eventually you grew out of it.

You could only be sad if you let yourself join the dots; if you allowed the scatter of moments in their totality to have some kind of a downward trend that you might be dumb enough to extrapolate. If you just sat on the kitchen floor like this, enjoying the feeling of your bare feet on these chequered tiles warmed by this bright April sun, and you breathed in the ashy, medicated smell of your kid, then it was okay.

Being a rider helped. The only way you could bear the training, and certainly the only way you could endure the pain of the sprint, was to take life one fraction of a second at a time. You carried that attitude with you across the finishing line, and through the dressing room, and out into ordinary life with your kit still wet in your kitbag. One moment of pain was never unbearable unless you allowed it to have some kind of a relationship with the moments on either side of it. Atoms of time could be trained to operate quite effectively in strictly partitioned cubicles on the open-plan floor of the day.

Jack let Sophie fall asleep leaning against him. He smiled. You could practically hear the lightsabers humming in the girl's dreams.

Kate came in from the next room and looked down at the pair of them fondly. Jack thought she looked more tired than usual. He knew she found it harder than he did, to let the day wash over her. She was tired and sick of their daughter being sick and tired, was what it was. Jack tended to trust the chemo, but he knew Kate was always asking herself whether there might be some version of cutting her own heart out and offering it to the gods on a sharpened stick that she had somehow missed in her determination to do everything she could for Sophie. She stayed up late every night reading up on plasma or leuko-cytes, she got up early to bake a special kind of bread with wild grains and low gluten, and she missed training to organise days out for morale, like yesterday's trip to the Death Star.

'You two . . .' Kate said.

The sound brought Sophie upright. Confused, she looked up at Jack with eyes that struck him as eerily blank, like those of a fish after the life had been knocked from it.

Jack's breath caught in his chest. Fear, which he'd been holding at bay, had only needed one look to show him how negotiable his defences were.

When he looked again, Sophie was back inside her eyes.

He shivered. 'Would it help if I put on the special cheering-up music?'

Sophie widened her eyes in horror. 'Nooooo . . .'

Jack jumped up, connected his iPod to the stereo in the kitchen and selected the massed pipe bands of the Scottish Highlands playing a marching tune originally composed to be lethal to the English at a range of up to five miles, even in conditions of wind, rain and mist. Kate hurried out of the room. Jack cranked up the volume.

Tins moved on the shelves. The windows rattled and buzzed. Jack imagined the neighbours cringing. The houses shared a party wall, which Jack liked to think of as Hadrian's.

He lifted Sophie to her feet and shouted over the noise of the stereo: 'Christ, Soph! Get a load of those pipes and tell me you don't feel better already!'

She stuck her fingers in her ears. 'It's not helping!'

'What's that you say, big girl? I can't hear you above the sound of four hundred kilted Scotsmen telling leukaemia where to stick it!'

She tried her hardest to scowl but it came out as a grin instead.

'That's my girl!'

The two of them listened to the pipe bands for a minute, and Sophie even managed half a reel around the kitchen floor with him. Jack was happy, and given that there was a fixed quantity of happiness in the universe then he could only assume that in an equal and opposite kitchen somewhere on Earth, the father of another sick girl was listening to Mozart's *Requiem* and not dancing.

When Sophie needed to get her breath back, Jack took a Mars bar from the fridge, broke it in two, and offered half to her.

'Get that down you. All the vital food groups: toffee, chocolate, and the mysterious beige matrix that we must assume to be vitamins.'

He lifted her onto a kitchen chair and watched her chewing. The pipe bands finished up on the stereo.

'Dad, can I ask you something?'

'Sure thing, big girl. What is it?'

She sighed, her expression implying that Jack might not be the brightest light in the room.

'Is Mum okay?'

'Yeah. Of course. Why?'

Sophie dropped her eyes and flushed. She laid one hand on top of the other on the tabletop, then removed the bottom hand and put it on top. She repeated this, faster and faster, zoning in.

'What is it?' he said.

She stopped abruptly. 'Is she training hard enough?'

146

'Absolutely.'

'Did she miss training yesterday for me?'

'No. She had a rest day in her schedule. Me and Zoe too.'

'Honestly?'

Jack crossed his heart. 'Honestly.'

'I want Mum to win gold in London.'

'So do I.'

'It's her turn, Dad.'

He shrugged. 'There aren't turns in sport. They do it by whoever's quickest.'

She looked steadily at him. 'What if she isn't quickest, and it's because of me?'

He stroked her cheek. 'Oh, Sophie. I'm sure if you asked Mum, she'd say there were some things more important than winning.'

She held his eyes for a second longer. She blinked.

Straight away, he knew he'd said the wrong thing. She turned away. Jack turned her back to face him and she sat there passively, shoulders hunched.

Jack hesitated. Of course you could turn a child so that she physically faced you. This was something you could do when you were six foot tall and superhuman. The trick was in knowing what to say.

'Maybe you should talk to Mum about it,' he said gently.

Sophie shrugged simply. 'I can't talk to her like I can talk to you.'

'Why not?'

She sighed. 'I just can't.'

Jack felt a constriction in his chest – an ache – whether for himself or his daughter or his wife he didn't know. He'd never asked himself such a question. If he'd thought about it at all, he'd always felt that Kate was closer to Sophie. Ever since Sophie was born, the bond between them had been intense because of the amount of time he and Kate could spend at home, compared to people with real jobs. He probably knew his kid better than most dads did. Nevertheless, he'd sometimes felt guilty for his unshakable state of happiness, while Sophie was going through so much. He'd often worried that it had to be a certain detachment that permitted him to feel good, from moment to moment. Kate suffered more. She was the one who agonised about nutrition and nursing, she was the one who dropped everything when Sophie took turns for the worse, and she was the one who set her alarm three times a night to go and check in on their daughter. And yet here he was, apparently closer to her.

He dropped his eyes and stared miserably at the backs of his hands.

'I was the first person who held you, did you know that?' he said quietly. 'When you were nine hours old. I didn't know how to do it. They showed me how to scrub my hands and put on the latex gloves, and they showed me how to put my hands through the holes in the incubator. Then they stopped giving me the instructions. So there I was, with my hands sticking through the glove holes and your little body lying on the blue plastic pad and all the wee tubes and whatnot coming out of you, and I said "What do I do now?" And they said "Just hold her." And I was so scared I was going to drop you. I didn't know how to do something as simple as hold you, Sophie. Sometimes I still don't.'

'It's okay,' said Sophie. 'I don't mind.'

They hugged for a while, and then Jack carried her up to her room for a rest.

Kate came into the kitchen when he was back down there, making more tea.

She laughed. 'Real tea, in a pot? Okay, what have you done?'

He jumped at the sound of her voice and spun round. 'What?'

'You're the teabag in a mug guy. You only make me proper posh tea when you're sorry for something.'

'Really?'

'Yeah. Once when you forgot our anniversary and once when your dad got pissed and tried to kiss me.'

He frowned. 'I never realised.'

She kissed him. 'See? I can read you like a book.'

'Which book?'

'One of those early readers with a list of new-words-we-learned at the back.'

'And which new words did we learn?'

'Gorgeous, handsome, bloody, idiot.' She counted them off on her fingers.

He put his arms around her. 'Sorry,' he said.

'What for?'

'For being so bloody gorgeously idiotically handsome.'

'This is what my pot of tea is for?'

'Yeah. Don't drink it all at once.'

She twisted in his arms to look up at him. 'Really, though. Is something wrong?'

'If I make you a pot of tea it has to mean there's something on my mind? This is your contention?'

'Indeed.'

He raised one eyebrow. 'Well, I'm sorry for that. But honestly, nothing's wrong.'

'Truly?'

He hugged her tighter. 'Truly.'

After a while Kate switched on the radio, and they looked out through the kitchen window and drank their tea while The The played 'Uncertain Smile'.

'Remember this?' said Jack.

'Oh God, I do.'

'After my crash? Driving up the motorway? When you still thought I was an egotist?'

'I still think you're an egotist *now*.'

He looked at her to see if she was being serious, but she was looking out of the window and he couldn't tell. He followed her gaze. Propped against the little shed in the small, sunny back yard, Sophie's bicycle was rusting.

Bathroom, 203 Barrington Street, Clayton, East Manchester

When Kate went upstairs, she found Sophie vomiting into the upstairs toilet. She was puking undramatically, with the resignation of a girl doing something less pleasant than cleaning her teeth but less arduous than homework.

Kate rushed to her. 'You poor thing,' she said, stroking Sophie's cheek and feeling the hot dryness of her skin. 'Why didn't you call?'

'I'm fine,' said Sophie, wiping her mouth.

'Have you been feeling poorly?'

Sophie shook her head.

'It was just really sudden?'

'Yeah.'

Kate ran a flannel under the bathroom tap and cleaned her up.

'Feel better now?'

Sophie smiled up at her. 'Much better.'

Kate held her tight, and sighed. She must have fed her something wrong, which was bad of her because Sophie could eat so many things. This is what the dietician told her. Sophie had allergies and intolerances, of course, which was normal with leukaemia and diminished immune function. The dietician told Kate that she just had to be imaginative. *Don't obsess on what's prohibited*, he insisted. *Think of the millions of things in nature. See it this way: your daughter can eat almost anything.*

And he was right, thought Kate, so long as it wasn't food. She rinsed the flannel and wrung it out. Sophie was wheat intolerant and she couldn't do shellfish. She could eat fresh fruit and sparingly cooked vegetables and she liked those things about as much as other kids did. Also, she had no resistance to germs. Everything got boiled or peeled. Theoretically she could eat fish. The dietician had told Kate: *Fish is nature's superfood, Mum. It's nutrition with fins. It's lunch with a face on the front. Your daughter will live till she's ninety on fish.*

Sophie hated fish, though. She made outraged faces and spat it out. Because as well as having leukaemia, she was eight. There were multiple protocols to treat leukaemia, but the only known cure for being eight was being nine. In the meantime, no fish. Or yeast. Or soy. Or ground nuts. Or nuts from trees. Or citrus fruit. Sometimes Kate opened the fridge and just stared. Why, she didn't know. In case they'd invented a more edible kind of food, perhaps, and she'd cleverly bought it without remembering. She could sometimes stand there for a whole minute, gazing into the bright white light as if a cure might be hidden between the baby sweetcorn and the carefully scrubbed new potatoes.

She was sure she hadn't fed Sophie anything on the banned list, and yet here was this vomit. She sat on the edge of the bath and phoned the dietician, while Sophie sat with her back against the warm radiator and played with her *Millennium Falcon*.

Kate had to go through the hospital switchboard and ask to speak to the food doctor. There was an assumption on the paediatric unit that the technical vocabulary would bamboozle you. If you asked for the dietician they would say, 'Do you mean the food doctor?' and you would have to say, 'Yes please,' and that would be another ten seconds of your life that you'd never get back. The nutritionist was the food doctor, the haematologist was the blood doctor. The first time they had met Sophie's paediatrician, he'd bounded up to them and said, 'Hi! I'm the baby doctor!' After a while, you learned to play up to your role in the pantomime. The script was that you were not very clued up, but the doctors were patient and kind with you, and all of the children were brave.

After some paging, the food doctor came on the phone. 'And how are we today, Mum?'

'Sophie's been sick. We haven't even done breakfast yet, and I wondered if you had any ideas to settle her stomach.'

'Well, Mum,' the dietician said, 'what you have to understand about leukaemia is that it is a condition affecting the blood, and because blood is such an important part of the little one's body it will affect all her systems, so you have to be prepared for food tolerances to change . . .'

Kate zoned out and let her eyes defocus on the bathroom tiles. She didn't know what she'd been expecting the dietician to say. *Try Marmite*, perhaps, or *Custard always goes down well*. Instead she was getting this lecture, apparently aimed at parents with head injuries, and yet there was still a certain comfort in it. Sometimes, even with Jack in the house, she felt alone. It could feel as if you were only orbiting the planet that normal families lived on. Hospital voices on the phone reassured you, like the babble of mission control. They made you feel that at least you were orbiting something substantial, and not simply drifting in space.

She heard Jack's steps coming up the stairs. He stood in the bathroom doorway, watching her for an explanation. She mimed sticking two fingers down her throat, pointed at Sophie and the toilet.

Jack clapped his hand to his forehead.

Kate mouthed: *What?*

'I fed her a Mars bar. Just a half. I thought it'd be okay.'

Kate was too relieved to be angry. She put the dietician on speakerphone. Jack listened for a moment, then grinned and mimed words coming out of his arse, swirling in eddies and dispersing in the air of the room with an odour that was disagreeable to him. Sophie and Kate giggled, which stopped the dietician mid-flow.

'Is everything all right, Mum?'

'Yes, I'm sorry, everything's fine. Look, something's come up – I'm sorry, I'll have to call you back.'

She clicked the phone off and stared at Jack. 'You twat,' she said simply.

Jack aped the dietician's voice. 'Oh, for goodness' sake, Mum, you're thinking in a much too narrow way. Consider all the very many foodstuffs that exist on this big wide planet of ours. Have you tried tractor grease and tiger milk? Have you tried cuttlefish roes and wolfsbane? No? Then kindly do so at once, before phoning up to bother me with news that your daughter has puked up a Mars bar.'

That made Kate laugh, and Sophie too. Jack knelt and gathered them into him, and they hugged on the bathroom floor in the little house, and it seemed true to all of them that a moment like this was worth the unceasing work of ignoring the little things that might spoil it.

National Cycling Centre, Stuart Street, Manchester

Before training that day, at the velodrome, Jack's coach gave him the news about the Olympic rule change. Jack listened without changing his expression. Then he nodded and said: 'Fine.' He strapped on his aerodynamic helmet, clipped in to his pedals, and trained so hard he almost blacked out on the track.

He warmed down from the bike session, then hit the basement gym. There was an energy in him, a fury. He got rid of some of it with abdominal work, then he began clean lifting an eighty-kilo barbell, just snatching it up and slamming it straight above his head. Some of the guys from British Cycling were warming down in the gym. They were all national-level athletes themselves, and they stared at Jack as if he was a freak.

The mood he was in, he could have lifted more. He tried to wear himself out but he couldn't. He felt muscle fibres ripping and forced himself to stop before he ruined something. There was still so much furious energy. He showered and stood with a towel cinched around his waist, looking at himself in the mirror above the basin in the locker room. He caught his own eye, held it for a second, then somehow walked away before he punched the mirror.

It was two in the afternoon. He jogged home to pick up Kate and Sophie and drive them back to the velodrome for Kate's training session. All the way home he rehearsed how to give Kate the news about the rule change. He slowed to a walk as he got closer to home. The walk got slower, became a dawdle. When he finally turned his

154

key in the door, Kate was standing in the hallway, impatient. Her annoyance turned to concern when she saw his face.

'What is it?' she said.

Jack's courage left him. He forced his face to become calm. He said: 'Nothing. I'm sorry I'm late.'

Kate had packed a bag with all Sophie's bits in it as well as her own, so all Jack had to do was drive. His legs ached from the track work, his shoulders hurt from the weights, and his fingers would hardly grip the wheel. Ideally he'd be horizontal at this moment, in recovery, with his legs slightly elevated and an ice pack on his deltoids. At the elite level it wasn't the training that set you apart – all the guys trained themselves to the edge of destruction. Victory lay in how well you managed the recovery phase.

'Don't kick the back of my seat, please.'

The kicking stopped. He glanced in the rearview mirror. Sophie was hunched in her car seat with her arms crossed tight. She looked out at the traffic, her eyes huge under her baseball cap.

'So why were you late?' Kate said.

Jack shrugged. 'I'm sorry, okay? Dave wouldn't let me go.'

'He's your coach, Jack, not your boss.'

'Don't nag me, please.'

'Then don't be late, please. This is shit for me.'

'Twenty minutes late. It's not the end of the world.'

'Twenty-five minutes.'

'Don't be petty. You're not a petty person.'

She shot him a look that said: No, but you're an arsehole.

He drove through traffic that was sluggish and getting slower. He thought about recovery. You were meant to have time to your-self, to settle your thoughts while your body replenished the energy and fluids you'd lost in training, and set about new protein synthesis. You weren't supposed to be on the go, twenty-four hours a day, juggling sport and this illness.

The truth was, with their final Olympics only four months away, he and Kate were getting tireder each day. And now here was this rule change, and suddenly the pressure on them was doubled. It was another heavy blow to take. Last year the IOC had announced that the individual pursuit had been axed from the Olympics. It had been hard for all of them, to have one less chance to medal, but it had been hardest of all for Kate, since the pursuit was her best event. She'd taken the news uncomplainingly, rebuilt her body into a new configuration to focus everything on the sprint – and now this. He tried to find the words to give the news to her, but he could hardly think about it coherently himself.

In the passenger seat beside him, Kate snapped her fingers impatiently. Zoe would have been warming up for half an hour already. Kate probably imagined that this was her biggest problem at this moment in time. She exhaled loudly.

'Can I help you?' he said.

She pointed at a gap in the traffic that had just closed ahead of them. 'You could have got through there.'

'Maybe.'

'Definitely.'

Jack hit the steering wheel with the palm of his hand and looked away. She was putting this crawling traffic on him, as if it was somehow his fault that everyone in Manchester had picked this exact moment to jump in their vehicles and go to buy geraniums, or deliver photocopier toner, or whatever people did with their time when they didn't have an Olympics to prepare for.

Sophie started drumming her feet against the back of his seat again; Kate clicked her fingers. Jack thought: *Of course, this is my main job, ferrying these women around.* He realised the thought lacked dignity, but it was hard not to feel resentment. His competition wasn't as close as Kate's, but still. There was only one male sprint place for London in play, and only so many joules of energy in his body. His rivals would be chilling out right now, recovering. They'd been clever enough to choose wives without sports careers and kids without cancer.

Jack cursed himself for thinking it. He nosed through the slow-moving traffic and tried to grip the wheel. He carefully changed lanes to put a high-sided van between their car and one of the billboards of Zoe.

Kate said: 'This lane's even slower.'

'So I made a mistake.'

She looked at him sharply. 'Are you okay? You're being shitty.'

'*I'm* being shitty?'

'Yeah.'

He kept his eyes straight ahead. 'I'm being fine.'

'Training go all right?'

'Yeah, I ripped it up.'

'You're not smiling.'

'I'm knackered, Catherine. Okay?'

'*Catherine?*'

He raised his arms. 'Sorry.'

She sighed. 'Yeah, me too.'

'I'm knackered, Kate, truth be told.'

'What, even your little face muscles?'

She made a mischievous face and jabbed his cheeks insistently until she raised a smile.

'That's better,' she said, and straight away it was.

Jack's mood evaporated. He clicked on the hazard warning lights, brought the slow-moving car to a stop in the right-hand lane and leaned across to kiss her. They kissed while the outraged traffic blared and diverted around them. Motorists made the sign of mental incapacity, stabbing their fingers at their temples to indicate the locus of the deficiency. It made Sophie anxious.

'*Come on!*' she whispered. '*Move!*'

Jack felt for her, but he wasn't in a hurry. Now that his irritation was gone there was the post-training high, a cosy analgesic cocoon within which it was hard to prioritise the needs of the impatient world over his own. Reluctantly he pulled back from the kiss. In moments like this an old anxiety struck him with fresh shock: he couldn't understand why she had chosen him, and why she had stuck with him through everything that had happened, and why she continued to stick with him. Sometimes he felt like a clawed animal who'd been given a rose to hold. He knew just enough to know it was beautiful, but not enough to know how to look after it.

Kate was welling up, and Jack wiped away her tears with his thumbs. Behind them, Sophie was freaking out. Outside, the car horns had massed into an imbroglio of indignation. Their fellow motorists were beginning to make the other sign, of the extended middle finger, with its implication that there was some rectum or some vagina into which something – possibly the finger being displayed, or possibly some other item for which the displayed finger was a proxy, signifier or understudy – might usefully be inserted in such a way that it would expedite the plaintiff's journey to whichever furniture superstore or cross-platform marketing meeting constituted their immediate destination. This soon after lifting heavy barbells, Jack found that it was hard to take people or their hand signals particularly seriously.

'You'd better drive,' Kate said. So he did.

'*Finally!*' said Sophie, in such a prissy voice that it made all three of them laugh.

The traffic seemed to ease up a little.

Trying to keep his voice casual, Jack said: 'That text from Tom, this morning – did it say what he wants to talk to you about?'

Kate shook her head. 'Just to put aside some time after training. I'm sure it's nothing.'

Jack kept his eyes straight ahead.

When Dave had given him the news that morning, his first thought had been how he was going to secure his own place in London. He'd thought about how he could train harder. He didn't care if he had to train the world to spin the other way on its axis. That place in London was going to be his.

Turning, now, into the car park of the velodrome, Jack realised how typical it was of him not to have thought about what the news meant for Kate until afterwards, in the locker room. When his head was in the game, the existence of others – even the ones he loved – could easily not occur to him for hours on end. People just flickered in and out of his awareness, like figures in a dark room where some unbidden hand turned the light switch on and off at times not of his choosing. As soon as he remembered them, he wanted to do the right thing. That was all you could say in his defence, he supposed.

He parked and went to help Sophie out of her seat. He lifted her to his hip and nudged the rear door shut. His eyes met Kate's across the roof of the car. She was hopping from foot to foot with the anticipation of imminent training. The kitbag swung on her shoulder and her hair blew in the wind that whipped around the grey dome of the velodrome. Now would be the moment, if he was going to do it. He should tell her about the rule change, and give her at least the tiny psychological edge of knowing before Zoe did.

But here she was, happy, and here was Sophie in his arms, excited to be out of the house for once, thrilled to be allowed to watch Kate training. Jack realised he wasn't going to say anything. The next hour, the next minute, even the next ten seconds of happiness was as far as his mind wanted to think. While there was laughter in bathrooms, and kisses snatched from traffic, and smiles in windy car parks, let it persist. Jack held on to the moment and held on to his wife's small warm hand as they walked the short distance from the car to the velodrome entrance.

Kate hurried off to change and Jack took Sophie to sit by the track. He sat her down carefully on a stacking chair beside the technical area and wrapped a black fleece blanket around her.

'Comfy?'

'Yeah.'

Sophie pulled the top edge of the blanket over her head to make a Jedi cowl. Her eyes were fixed on Zoe as she warmed up with smooth, fluid laps of the track. On the steep curves at each end Zoe swung high, all the way to the top of the banking at the apex, hung for a moment between energy and gravity, then swooped back down to the black line with a rising note from her wheels. She wore a white skinsuit and a white helmet with a black visor that flashed with the reflected lines of the track.

Sophie was transfixed. She raised her hands towards Zoe, fingers slightly bent.

'What are you doing?' Jack said.

Sophie frowned, annoyed that he'd broken her focus.

'I'm using the Force on her.'

'Why?'

Sophie dropped her hands and stared at him. 'To make her crash, of course.'

Jack opened his mouth, but he couldn't think what to say. Sophie turned away and raised her arms again. He left her to it, kissed the top of her head and walked over to Tom in the technical area.

'Zoe's looking good,' Jack said.

Tom reached up to shake his hand. 'Excuse me if I don't stand. Bloody knees are worse than ever.'

'Yeah, Kate said. You ever going to have them operated?'

'Mate, I'm going to have them amputated. More trouble than they're worth. Going to get my feet attached straight to my arse, cut out the middle man.'

'Works for penguins.'

'Yeah, it's a southern hemisphere thing.'

They watched Zoe working the track.

'You told her yet?' Jack said quietly.

Tom shook his head. 'When did you get told?'

'Before training this morning.'

'I was going to tell the girls after. Keep their heads in the game for this session at least.'

'Might do the same if I was you.'

Tom looked up at him. 'You say anything to Kate?'

'It's on you, feller. I'm only married to her.'

Tom kept his eyes on Jack's. 'You didn't know how to tell her, right?'

'Something like that.'

'Me neither,' Tom said, dropping his eyes. 'It's a bloody shame, is what it is.'

'You know how they're going to work it yet?'

Tom shrugged. 'There'll be a formal qualifier for the place. In three months' time, a few weeks out from the Games. We'll see which one of them is quicker on the day.'

'You got a hunch?'

'Don't ask me that.'

'But have you?'

Tom kept his face neutral. 'Three months is a long time, isn't it?'

Jack felt his stomach go. 'You think it's Zoe.'

Tom didn't answer. He turned away to watch Zoe riding. She was working half-sprints now, slowing the bike on the straights and then powering up to enter the bends at speed before easing it back down again. She was keeping it loose and fluid, still warming up, not maxing out. She looked completely in charge.

They watched her in silence for a few laps.

'You confident about winning your own place?' Tom said finally.

'Sure,' Jack said.

Tom nodded, his eyes still on Zoe. 'I was talking with Dave just now. He said you were "quietly confident".'

'I don't know about quiet. I told him I could turn up at the qualifiers with a BMX and a drogue parachute and still lap the other guys.'

'You always were a cocky bastard.'

'I used to be worse.'

Tom turned to him. 'I remember. What I've never figured out, though, is why you race. You don't fit the mould. Kate, she wants to know that she's done her best and she wants to make you and Sophie proud. Zoe, it's like she's pursued. I mean she's more scared of losing than she's glad about winning. But you, it's like you only race at this level because you can.'

Jack grinned. 'I only race at this level because I got kicked out of Scotland.'

Tom laughed.

'What, did I never tell you the story?'

Tom shook his head.

'I started riding when I was maybe ten,' said Jack. 'I was into the street racing up in Leith, and we used to crash every day. Pops got sick of taking me to A&E, so he talked me onto a Scottish Cycling programme. Decided I'd be safer racing indoors. And Pops was a chain-smoker – I mean, I can only imagine him sitting in the coach's office, reeking of cancer and telling him what a healthy wee family we were. Anyway, they gave me a proper bike and I beat every junior in Scotland. Pursuit, sprint, any individual event – it didn't matter. I was physically incapable of losing. I hit sixteen and the coaches were feeding me substances hitherto unknown – you know: vegetables and fruit. Feeding me properly was like cheating, that was what the main coach told Pops. Riders were giving up competing against me at that point, and races were getting cancelled all across the Highlands and Lowlands. That was when all the Scotch coaches got themselves together for a parley. They said to themselves: For the sake of our own careers, we have to get this young man out of Scotland.'

'And that's how your call-up came for British Cycling?'

'I didn't even want to go. I was mostly out on the town, chasing girls, and I got home off my head one night and this letter was waiting for me. I'd been entered for the Elite Prospects Programme at the

Manchester Velodrome, and could I please bring with me a towel, a wash kit, and appropriate riding clothes for a full day of racing. I guess you wrote the thing yourself, right? And at breakfast I had a hangover and Pops said: *What was that letter?* And I was like: *It is from the English, Father. They are begging me to be their lawful king.* And Pops said: *No, but seriously?* And I told him what the letter was, and how I wasn't going to go to Manchester. I mean, it had never occurred to me to leave Scotland, the same way it had never occurred to me to leave my senses.'

'So what persuaded you?'

Jack smiled. 'What Pops did was, he got on the phone. A fortnight later, the day before Prospects, a pal of his knocked on the front door, and this pal just happened to be the former Light Middleweight Champion of the whole of Scotland and the Outer Isles. You know the kind of guy – I mean, he had tattoos on his neck and his arms depicting imaginative acts of violence. Jim, was his name. I answered the door and Jim grinned at me with these two rows of gold teeth. And Pops said: *Jim's here to put you on the train to Manchester.* I tried to do a runner, but Jim grabbed hold of me. He was like: *You'll enjoy England*, and I was like, *No I fucking won't.* So Jim grabbed the back of my hair and stood me up off the floor and squashed my face against the wall. *You'll like England*, he said. *The climate is mild and the folks have delightful manners, which it shall be their gentle pleasure to teach you.* And I was gasping for air by this point so I just went: *Yes, Yes, I'm sure I shall love it terrifically.* And Pops said this thing that's always stayed with me. He said: *It's for your own good, Jack. I will not see you end up like me.* And I said: *But I like you, Pops.* And he said: *Well, you'll like me more when you win gold.*'

'And did you?'

Jack sighed, watching Zoe making her slow loops around the track.

'I never told him how much it meant to me, and of course he died the year after Athens. Gasping his lungs out through an oxygen mask. If it hadn't been for what he did, I'd be headed the same way.'

'Mate,' said Tom. 'Sounds like he wasn't all bad.'

Jack watched Zoe as she leaned into another fluid lap. 'You do what you can, don't you?' he said finally.

Kate emerged onto the trackside in a blue skinsuit, tying her hair back. She hurried up to Tom and kissed him on both cheeks.

'Sorry,' she said.

Tom tapped his watch. 'Nine minutes late, honey.'

'Sorry, there was traffic and—'

'It was my fault,' Jack said. 'I was late to take over with Sophie and—'

Tom silenced him with one raised finger and used his eyes to push him back outside the technical area. Now that the training session was on, the dynamic had shifted.

'We got your bike ready,' Tom told Kate. 'On the off-chance you were planning to show up.'

He pointed out a heavy black butcher's bicycle with a huge wicker delivery basket on the front, propped up on its kickstand beside the warm-down bikes in the centre of the velodrome.

Kate groaned. 'You're not actually going to make me, are you?'

'Count yourself lucky. If you're late one more time, I'll make you race on it.'

Kate sagged her shoulders theatrically and walked over to collect the bike. It was a long-established penalty – for every minute you were late, you did a warm-up lap on the butcher's bike. As Kate wheeled the bike up to the track, Zoe, still circling, took her hands off the bars and began a slow handclap that echoed around the empty velodrome. Kate winked across at Sophie.

'Want to come for a ride?' she said.

Sophie's eyes widened. 'Can I?'

Kate wheeled the bike over to where she was sitting, and held it up while Jack lifted Sophie carefully into the wicker basket on the front.

'You okay, big girl?'

Sophie nodded and clung to the rim of the basket, only half sure.

'You'll be fine.'

Jack steadied the bike as Kate climbed on and eased it out onto the track. She kept it steady and careful, hugging the black line at the bottom of the track, and a slow grin spread across Sophie's face. Zoe played along with it, swooping down towards them, overtaking and then allowing herself to be overtaken in return. She swerved and twisted in their slipstream while Sophie yelled with delight and called to Kate to ride faster.

Forest moon of Endor, Outer Rim Territories, Moddell Sector, 43,300 light years from the Galactic Core, grid coordinates H-16

Sophie opened the throttle on the repulsorlift engine and sent the speederbike flashing between the trees. The airstream felt good on her face as the acceleration kicked in. Behind her own machine, an Imperial scout was giving chase. Sophie gripped the handlebars tight and threw in some evasive manoeuvres. This Imperial scout was good. Whatever Sophie did, the following bike matched her turn for turn. Her pursuer seemed to know what Sophie was going to do, almost before she knew it herself. Sophie felt a sense of awe along

166

with the excitement. This wasn't just any Imperial soldier. Maybe this was Vader himself.

'Faster!' she shouted, and she felt the speederbike accelerate.

Down on the forest floor the droid C-3PO was looking concerned, anxious bag of bolts that he was. *Are you sure you know how to ride that thing safely?* That's what his silly mechanical face seemed to say.

'Relax,' came Han Solo's voice through the rushing air. 'A joyride isn't supposed to be safe.'

Trackside, National Cycling Centre, Stuart Street, Manchester

Jack's chest tightened as he watched the three of them riding, and he was relieved when Zoe glanced across at him. He implored her with his eyes. She stared at him for a moment, inscrutable behind her visor, and he shivered.

He was relieved when she called off her mock pursuit. She pulled alongside Kate and Sophie, matched their pace and started up a running commentary in the style of the TV pundits:

'And Sophie Argall is in the lead as they go into the straight. This has to be the most awesome performance by an eight-year-old that the Olympics have ever seen. She's destroying the opposition now, and watch that determination on her face as she powers around that final bend, and now here she is in the home straight – can she make it? They said it was impossible but oh my goodness she's done it, the girl wonder from Manchester, she's only gone and taken gold!'

As they crossed the finish line, Sophie raised her arms in a victory salute. Jack noted Zoe's smile beneath the line of her visor as she peeled off to carry on her warm-up. It was rare to see Zoe connect with Sophie like that. It was rare to see her connect with anyone.

He lifted Sophie carefully out of the basket and sat down with her by the track. The excitement had left her shattered. Jack pulled the fleece blanket back around her and held her on his lap.

He watched Kate and Zoe sparring. Kate got her real bike up to speed for a few laps and then Tom had the two of them do power intervals – ten seconds at full exertion followed by a minute to bring the heart rate back down. Jack kept his arms around Sophie as he watched. Every time the two riders flashed past, Sophie whispered, 'Come on, Mum, you're so much quicker!'

Watching the two women, Jack wasn't sure. It had never been easy to choose between them.

In the hospital, after the crash, Zoe had held his hand. He'd woken up from anaesthesia and seen her looking down at him with an expression more like sarcasm than sympathy.

'You took your sweet time,' she said.

'To . . . ?'

'To be conscious. I got so bored.'

Jack glanced around. It seemed from the many beds with their green sheets and modesty curtains that they were on a hospital ward, or in some kind of budget hotel concept that probably shouldn't catch on. The girl was saying she was sorry for some crash.

Jack said: 'What crash?'

Concussion had set him back a couple of days. He half recognised Zoe, though. Remembered her name, even, but not where he knew her from. He found himself smiling at her. It seemed safest. He remembered having had an argument with her once. Either recently or long ago. Maybe he'd been very drunk. Maybe he still was – maybe that was the problem. He wondered why she was holding his hand.

'Sorry, are we . . . going out or something?'

She smiled and shook her head.

'Would you like us to? You're very attractive.'

'God,' she said. 'You're ridiculous.'

She didn't stop smiling, though, and they began talking. She told him how they'd fought at the velodrome, and yes, he remembered it now. He remembered her hitting him, in a rage. He must have pushed all her buttons.

She seemed different now. All of the hardness he remembered, it melted away as she talked. She was beautiful. She struck him as kind of sad, or maybe angry, or maybe she was just talking about fetching tea and a biscuit – he was finding it hard to follow her words. Her voice was slipping in and out of phase like the rainbow of sounds at the end of 'Bold as Love'. And all the while here was a white thing in a green sling angling up and away from him. After the longest time he realised that the white thing was his own leg, in plaster, suspended from the ceiling on a chain. This was a weird place to put it. He could see his toes sticking out from the plaster cast, and by making the right movements in his brain he could make the toes wiggle. It was hard, though – it made him cross-eyed with concentration, like bringing a plane in to land. Just wiggling his own toes. He laughed, interrupting whatever she was saying.

'What?' she said, irritated.

'My *leg*!' he said, incredulous. 'The fuck is it doing up there?'

She began explaining the crash to him again, but he cut her off.

'Just feel under my blanket,' he said. 'See if this leg's still attached to me, at least.'

'Under your blanket?' She smirked. 'You'll be lucky.'

He grinned back. 'Can't blame a man for trying.'

'Are you always like this?'

The question confused him. The morphine was wearing off. He lost his train of thought, and noticed his broken leg all over again. This time, it hurt.

He looked up and saw Zoe more clearly now. Pale; intense; head shaved like a penitent.

'Tell me about you,' he said. It was something you were meant to say, and he said it to give himself some time.

Her green eyes stared off into space. 'Ah, you don't want to know.'

'I do.'

Her eyes snapped back down to his and he saw a flash of anger, but it quickly dissolved into uncertainty. 'Yeah?'

He felt sorry for bringing that expression to her face: she couldn't work out if he was playing with her.

He squeezed her hand. 'Really.'

Something in her eyes closed itself off, and she laughed. 'Forget it.'

When she laughed it unsettled him. Her eyes did something different from her face.

A nurse came and gave him more morphine.

'I love you, nurse,' he told her. 'You're the most beautiful creature I've ever seen.'

When the nurse had gone, Zoe shook her head. 'The fuck is wrong with you?'

The question confused him. Then he noticed his leg again. 'I think it's this,' he said. 'Oh my God, I think I might have broken it.'

Hours went by. His parents came and went in a blur of morphine and concussion.

When he woke it was daylight again and Zoe was still holding his hand and Kate was there in the ward, staring at them without words. As soon as Jack saw her face, he remembered her. She was the girl he'd talked with at the track, the one he couldn't keep away from. He'd loved the way she laughed, and shrugged off defeat; the way she turned every negative positive. She was gentle good energy, and it made you feel simpler and stronger being around her.

She looked devastated when she saw his hand in Zoe's.

He tried to sit up but his ribs were cracked, and he fell back to the pillow in pain.

'I'm sorry . . .' he said.

'No, no, I'm sorry,' Kate said. 'I didn't realise you two were . . . I . . .'

'Oh, it's not . . . I mean . . .' He stumbled on his words as Kate's lip began to tremble.

'I'm sorry,' she said, 'I'm just so tired. I think I'll just . . .'

'No, please, it's just that . . .'

Jack took his hand away from Zoe's, but Kate was already turning to go. They watched her back disappearing down the ward.

'Fuck,' Jack said, raising his head and slamming it back down on the pillow.

Kate's trainers squeaked on the floor as they covered the length of the ward. The heavy doors swung closed behind her at the end of the room.

Zoe said: 'Want me to fetch her back? Your choice.'

They watched the swing doors returning to stillness in diminishing oscillations. When they were motionless, Jack found it quite possible to believe that the scene had not just happened.

He sighed. 'Nah.'

He reached over to touch Zoe's hands again, but she took them back into her lap. Which was understandable but also a bit over-dramatic, he felt.

171

'Okay, I'm a bad person,' he said simply.

'No. It's fine. I mean, she's cute.'

'Is she? I mean . . .'

'Don't shit me, okay? You've been flirting with her for three days.'

'Well, you know, that's what I'm like. There's less to me than the bike I rode in on.'

'Is that meant to make me feel better?'

Jack was suddenly tired of apologising. There was a throbbing pain in his leg and ribs, now that the morphine was wearing off again.

'I don't care how it makes you feel,' he said.

She blinked. 'Thanks for the information.'

'My pleasure.'

They were silent for a minute, then Zoe sniffed and leaned back in her chair. 'I know she's more your type anyway.'

He smiled. 'Really? What's my type, then?'

She shrugged. 'Pretty happy. Pretty normal. Pretty pretty.'

'As opposed to . . . ?'

Zoe managed a half smile. 'I'm ugly on the inside. I'll mess your head up.'

'Aye, I've used that line myself. *I'm a bad boy, I'll break your heart.* It's a good one, really sexy.'

'You think I'm joking.'

'You won't do it to me,' Jack said. 'I mean, look at me. I'm indestructible.'

Zoe smiled and shook her head. 'No one's indestructible.'

'Try me,' he said.

He stretched out and took her hand and pulled her down towards him. She resisted at first, then she let him pull her close. She wasn't smiling now. With their lips almost touching, she said: 'No one's indestructible, Jack.'

The movement of her lips brushed them against his. This was their first kiss, this thing that started out as a warning, and as their lips touched he thought about Kate. He didn't like that. He couldn't understand why the flash of her face came, or why it bothered him. Nothing had happened between them in the three days of the programme, which wasn't his usual style. They'd flirted but she'd held herself back and if he'd thought about it at all, he'd imagined that would make her easy to forget. It nagged at him that he was thinking about her now, at exactly the moment when his body was insisting he shouldn't. Kissing Zoe was good, and it made him think of Kate, which was inexplicable, like getting ready to leave the house and putting on your jacket and shoes and opening the front door and instead of seeing the street, seeing your own hallway looking back at you.

Zoe stayed with him all day and then all of that week. There were kisses and whispered conversations, and all of it was good, and slowly the sense of unease subsided and he stopped thinking about Kate when Zoe touched him. He grew used to her lips, and he liked listening to her, and he followed the morphine down into a graceful state just above pain and just below happiness. The ward was starting to fill up. Now that it was getting busy, the nurses began to enforce visiting hours. Zoe had to leave between 6 p.m. and 9 a.m., but the first minute the nurses let her back in, there she would be, pushing the swing doors open. She sat by his bedside for hours. She would slide her hand under the sheets to place it against his heart. He would let his own hand wander from her arm, to her knee, to her thigh. On the second day she suddenly took it and slipped it quickly under her waistband. She cupped it there for a few seconds while the other patients ogled *Countdown*, blaring out from the TV. While the rest of the ward watched contestants trying to configure six numbers to produce a randomly chosen total, Jack felt the warmth of her sex. It was a juxtaposition he found easy to confuse with the sensation of falling suddenly and delightedly in love.

They dared each other on. He loved how Zoe didn't give a shit – didn't really care if they were caught. He loved how she slipped her hand further down under the sheets and cupped his balls and whispered in his ear: *When we get out of here you're not safe*. He was nineteen and drowning in morphine and he didn't see the harm in it. This was a game they played: while the ward bustled with patients and their visitors, she would cover her lap with a blanket as if she was cold, and he would slip his arm underneath and she would read him sports articles from the *Daily Mail* in the most matter-of-fact voice she could muster. *Whenever football lovers gather to reflect on the beauty of their game, they will talk of the night Manchester United gave Juventus a two-goal start before calmly proceeding to place a shroud over Turin. This will rank forever among the most magnificent comebacks in the annals of the European game.* A visitor on the ward would only have noticed the very slight cracking of her voice on 'calmly proceeding', and the sudden flush of blood in her cheeks. Afterwards she would lean back languorously in her chair and read the horoscopes in a dreamy voice.

'Taurus,' she said. 'You will meet a tall dark stranger. And somehow or other she swears to God she will find a way to give you a blow job without anyone on this ward noticing.'

'It doesn't really say that.'

'You're right, it's the *Daily Mail.*' She peered again at the newsprint. 'The actual phrase they use is *lewd sex act.*'

'I've never met anyone like you,' he said.

'That's why you're still happy,' she said casually.

The next day *Antiques Roadshow* came on the TV. It was popular in the ward, and all eyes were off them. She quietly drew the curtain most of the way round the bed and ducked down under his blankets, and Jack closed his eyes and felt certain that a bond was forming between them that would by some process – the mechanisms of which were yet to be established in his mind, but in which his faith grew even as an old lady got to the head of the queue clutching a painting by a local watercolour artist and Zoe brought him to the point of no return – would by some process lead to a shared happiness that would occur between them for some unspecified period – a lifetime, for example, and in locations still to be determined – a rented studio flat, perhaps, with bikes hanging in the hallway, and then a bigger flat, and then maybe a small house with a kids' room . . . Lazy with pleasure, afterwards, as the TV drifted into the news, this was how Zoe seemed to him: like a future unhurriedly condensing from the white-hot gases of youth, like a star not in a rush to be formed.

He began to feel that he loved her.

This is what he said to her on the fifth day, and he knew straight away that it was a mistake. He told her in the grey light of a tedious afternoon in that ward that was no longer an empty stage on which they shone alone, but which was increasingly crowded with the needy and the sick, who brought with them their own visitors with their corpulence and their flatulence and their rustle of carrier bags full of paperbacks and fudge.

'Sorry?' Zoe said distractedly.

For a moment he saw her eyes alight on him as they ranged across the ranks of patients.

'I mean there's an amazing connection, don't you think?'

The words sounded really stupid, even to him.

'Connection?' she said.

The nurses were distributing trays of tepid food prepared in huge stainless steel kitchens, not with carelessness or even incompetence, but with a kind of indifference to any quality of comfort or sustenance that might be contained within it. A tray of it landed on the wheeled table that bridged his bed, smelling of neutralised masala under its shiny dome with its lifting hole into which a finger could be inserted. Jack was suddenly aware of the dangerous ordinariness of it all – the speed with which their uniqueness had been diluted. The ward – the world – had absorbed them.

'I don't even know what you're talking about,' she was saying. 'It's like your mouth is going mwah mwah mwah.'

His desperation overflowed. 'I love you, Zoe.'

She stopped. 'Oh . . .'

'What?'

She ran her hands over her scalp and exhaled deeply. 'Wow . . .'

Jack's heart was hammering in his ears.

'Look,' she said. 'This is a bit quick for me. I mean, I only came here in the first place because Kate was into you, and now—'

Jack gripped her hand. '*What?*'

She stopped and looked at him. 'Oh. I thought you got that, no? Kate was obviously going to come here, so I thought I should be here when she did. What? Don't look at me like that. She came, and you made your choice.'

Jack dropped her hand and tried to sit up. 'Kate was into me, so you . . .'

'Look. She's going to be my biggest threat on the track, for sure, so I thought—'

He stared at her.

'What?' she said again. 'I'm just saying that's why I came in the first place. I stayed because I like you, so don't get all stressed. But *love* is . . . you know. No offence, but it's a bit sudden for me. I really like you, but love . . .'

Jack rubbed his eyes. 'You're here to psych Kate out?'

She shook her head. 'Is the morphine making you slow? I *came* to psych her out. I stayed because of you.'

He ran his hands through his hair. 'When were you going to tell me?'

She laughed nervously. 'Oh. I just thought you got it.'

'No, of course I didn't *get it*. That's not how my head works, Zoe. That's not how anyone's head works.'

She struggled to keep her smile. 'I'm sorry. I think about racing too much, probably. I mean, if that's—'

He struggled to keep his voice to a whisper that wouldn't carry to the neighbouring beds. 'That's fucked up, is what it is!'

She strained to keep her voice low. 'What's fucked up is saying you love someone when you don't even know them. I do what I want, okay?'

'Oh, very good. So how long do you want to stay with me? Just till you're sure Kate isn't coming back?'

She looked sadly at the floor. 'Don't be a dick, Jack.'

They watched each other in silence. Slowly, Jack let his weight sink back down to the pillows.

She took his hand and he let her hold it without reciprocating her pressure.

'I like you,' she said. 'More than I thought I would. I really want to believe I could be with you.'

He sighed. 'I like you too.'

'I liked meeting your parents. You know? Seeing where you come from.'

He looked sharply at her. 'You met them?'

'When they came to visit. You don't remember?'

He shook his head. 'Did Dad try to chat you up?'

'He was furious with me for making you crash. He grabbed my arms and shook me.'

Jack groaned.

She smiled. 'It was fine. I mean, once he felt my muscle tone, he was already looking for the first convenient moment to stop.'

'I'm sorry.'

'No, I liked him,' Zoe said. 'I liked both of them. They're a unit.'

'Mum repeats everything Dad says, you mean.'

She squeezed his hand. 'You'll end up marrying someone like that.'

'I won't.'

'You will. You'll marry some saintly woman who tidies up your mess.'

He shook his head. 'I don't want to end up like my parents.'

'Everyone says that.'

'Don't you?'

She stared at the ground. 'Mine are gone. Dad didn't stick around, and Mum killed herself when I was twelve. I was fostered.'

She looked up and saw him watching her. 'So? It happens. So what?'

He held his hands up. 'No, nothing.'

'No, go on, what?'

He said: 'That's pretty intense, is all.'

She stared at him. 'Intense . . . ?'

He spread his hands. 'Yeah, I mean—'

She laughed, and he saw the bitter flash in her eyes again. 'You just told me you loved me. Sorry for being *intense*.'

She scraped her chair back and stood. He reached for her wrist but she pulled her hand away.

'You're going?'

A tear escaped and she brushed it away. 'I can't stay.'

Jack watched her go, and each step she took down the ward left an ache he knew he would have to fill with morphine.

When visiting hours began the next day, Jack watched the doors at the end of the ward. Each day he waited, but she never came back to the hospital.

A fortnight later, when he was still high on painkillers, the doctors released him to a programme of intensive physiotherapy. Jack sat in an NHS wheelchair in the hospital's main lobby and took out his phone to call his parents to pick him up. He paused, watching a game show playing on the TV on its high bracket above the reception desk.

He changed his mind and dialled another number. She picked up, out of breath. 'Yeah?' She sounded as if she'd been running.

'It's me,' he said.

A long pause. 'I deleted your number.'

'I'd have done the same.'

'Yeah.'

'I hurt you.'

'It's fine. Look, I'm running, so—'

179

'Kate, please. I want to explain. I was concussed. I didn't remember you till after.'

'You remembered Zoe.'

'Not at first. And then she didn't let me forget.'

Another long pause. In the background, he heard the sound of traffic. She said: 'Are you okay?'

'I don't know. Just recently I was the quickest rider in the galaxy, and now I'm in a wheelchair with . . . I'm checking my pockets here . . . nine pounds forty and a four-millimetre Allen key and three paracetamol. My leg needs another operation. I've got vertebral fissures. The doctor reckons it's fifty-fifty whether I'll race again.'

'Shit. I'm sorry.'

'Don't be. I could beat odds like that with an egg whisk.'

She laughed. 'Did the doctors say they could do anything about your ego?'

'No, I'm afraid it's gone secondary. It's completely inoperable.'

'You're completely impossible.'

He smiled. 'Are you okay?'

She sighed. 'I spent a week hating myself, then a week hating Zoe, then a week hating you. I was just getting round to me again.'

'Sounds like I phoned just in time.'

'Stop it. Are you seeing her?'

'No.'

'Did anything happen between you?'

'Nothing good.'

'So now you're phoning me?'

'Well, you are the only English girl I know who hasn't tried to kill me.'

She laughed again. 'What makes you think I won't?'

'I made a mistake. I got taken in, and I'm sorry. That's all I rang to say. And good luck, and be a little bit careful of Zoe. She's all right, but she'll do stuff to win that isn't healthy.'

She paused. 'Thanks.'

'Great. Well. I'll see you around, okay? I guess I'll see you on the track.'

'Yeah. Get better, okay? And thanks. Thanks for calling.'

She hung up, and Jack sat in the wheelchair in the hospital reception lobby. He gripped the chromed hand rims of the wheels, applied some torque, and wondered how it would feel to race one of these things. Not too bad, probably. You'd want to get one of those fancy chairs, with the aero position and the caster wheels way forward like a Formula 1 car. Then you could really tear it up. He held the image too long, and the morphine high was crumbling. He stared at his phone, thinking of Kate's voice, and a hollow sadness crept into his chest. His broken leg throbbed, elevated on the front rigging of the chair.

For the first time in his life, he felt breakable. He sank down into the cracked vinyl upholstery of the wheelchair, and his eyes half focused on the TV. Two contestants, equipped with buzzers, were guessing the prices of retail items. He watched and tried to learn, in case his injuries were going to make him a civilian.

His phone rang.

'Look,' Kate said. 'Where are you?'

'I'm in the hospital. Just psyching myself up to call my folks to collect me.'

A slight pause. 'Don't move,' she said.

She walked into the lobby a little under two hours later, still in her running kit.

'I'm an idiot for coming,' she said, smiling shyly. 'I stopped twice on the M6. I nearly turned around.'

'You look amazing,' Jack said.

She shrugged. 'You look like shit.'

They didn't talk much. They listened to Radio 2 on the motorway north in the old VW Golf she'd borrowed from a work friend. As they passed Preston the sun came out, and The The came on the radio playing 'Uncertain Smile', and Jack reached across to put his hand on her knee. She picked it up without drama and carefully gave it back to him, keeping her eyes on the road. He liked the way she drove, too close to the wheel with her hands bunched up at the top of it, frowning through the windscreen as if she was navigating something more complicated than a flat, straight strip of tarmac with neat lane demarcations, populated by evenly spaced cars travelling at velocities that closely approximated their own.

It was only later that he found out she'd had a problem with her contacts, and didn't want him to see her in her glasses.

At the time he said: 'You drive like an old lady.'

Again, the slightest of pauses. 'An old lady wouldn't let you in her car.'

When they stopped for coffee at a service station she had to take the wheelchair out of the back for him and set it up. He wheeled himself to the disabled toilet and parallel parked next to the high porcelain bowl, reversing himself into position and then ankling his trousers and hoisting himself across. He pissed sitting down, gripping the big chrome safety rails for balance and trying not to think of all the bed-sore arses that had sat where his now rested. When he wheeled himself back out to the car park, the wheelchair picked up dog shit and smeared it on his right hand. Back at the car he sat there wiping it off on a tissue she gave him, while she explained how she wasn't promising anything. It was a long speech. He got the impression she'd been practising it in the middle lane of the motorway, all the way down south.

Her flat was one small room looking out over the brown water of the bay, with a bed that folded down. Since he was the one with spinal injuries, he slept on the bed while she lay on an air mattress on the floor. During the day she went out to her job at the gym while he did his physio exercises and read her cycling magazines. She didn't have a TV. In the evenings she trained on her road bike and came back late. He cooked pasta for her, reaching up from the wheelchair to use the sink and the cooker.

Twice a week she drove him to his physio appointment in Manchester, and every morning she supported his head and neck while he lay on the floor and did his abdominal exercises. When for the first time he was able to stand up from the wheelchair and balance unassisted, she was there to see him do it, and she was there to hold his hands and help him down into the chair when the pain in his back got too much.

That time was full of flashes of progress followed by setbacks. In the second month he walked from her flat to the corner shop and back, then lay in bed for two days and nights with back spasms. On the second night of that she came into the bed and although she still wouldn't kiss him, she slept with her arm around him and her face pressed into his neck. The next morning, though, nothing was said and they started the day as normal, each one careful to avert their eyes while the other dressed.

A happiness was growing between them. It felt normal when, on the first day he could walk that far, he walked to the gym where she worked. It felt natural that she kissed him in the car on the way home. They shared the bed, and the air mattress was propped up against the wall. On the first day it seemed too dramatic, or too definitive, to pull the stopper out of it. The next day Kate was out till late, and Jack idled in the house, eyeing it, but a unilateral deflation seemed presumptuous. On the third day, while Jack was out walking around the block, Kate got as far as putting her hand on the stopper. It was already too good to be true, this thing that was happening between her and Jack. She didn't want to jinx it. By the end of the week they had both stopped seeing the mattress. Besides, its top edge was useful for draping training kit on after it came out of the wash. It stood against the wall for a month, slowly leaking, sagging as their bond became firmer, until it lolled so badly that it no longer made a useful clotheshorse. Then Kate dealt with it matter-of-factly, its talismanic qualities forgotten. She laid it on the floor, pulled out the stopper and rolled it to expel the vestigial air. The room that she and Jack now shared so easily was suffused with the uncertain breath that she had blown into the mattress on the first night he arrived.

Zoe's first call to Jack came after four months, while Kate was away at the National Championships and he was out on one of the long, slow, painful rides that marked the start of his rehabilitation on the bike. He was taking it steadily, not pushing himself too hard. His phone went when he was halfway up a long incline in the Duddon Valley, and he was grateful for the excuse to stop and see who it was.

When he saw Zoe's number, he hesitated with his thumb on the green button. It was a brightening day with a fresh breeze, and distant clouds trailing rain in tendrils. The air held the scent of sheep and wet bracken. He was in a good place. He was happy to be on the bike, and enjoying the scenery. He could have easily ignored the call.

Still, the thing with Zoe seemed far away in time and distance. It would be harmless to talk.

'I can't believe you're not here at the Nationals,' she said when he answered.

'I'm still getting strong.'

'So Kate told me. I just beat her in the final. I'm the National fucking Champion! I'm still out of breath.'

'What did you do? Loosen her spokes?'

'I just rode straight past her. It was easy. She's been doing you instead of doing training.'

'That's low.'

'It's true. You're making each other soft. She's dragging you down to her level.'

'You're calling to gloat?'

'I'm calling because I miss you.'

She was getting her breath back, and her voice was soft and urgent now. In the background of the call, a velodrome crowd was shouting. Jack felt a cold rush of adrenaline.

He took the phone from his ear for a moment and looked down over the valley. In the breaks in the cloud shadow, nudged on by the breeze, golden patches of sunlight rode across the low hills and up the flanks of the high fells. Ravens called from the sheltered oaks and the bleating of sheep carried from the flocks grazing above the bracken line.

'Kate and I are doing just fine,' he said.

'You should be back in competition by now. She's not good for you.'

'What wasn't good for me, Zoe, was breaking my back.'

She laughed. 'That's such a tight-arse thing to say. Even your voice sounds tight. You're getting domesticated.'

He laughed too. 'You're tripping. I love Kate, okay?'

'Love, love, love. You drip that word around like chain lube.'

He couldn't pretend to be amused any more. 'I know what I feel.'

'Kate, though? I mean, I like Kate too, and she's pretty enough, but she has this terrible habit of coming second. Have you not actually noticed that?'

He ended the call, furious, and glared out at the ruined day. The hills were still beautiful, the light was still subtle and soft, but all of it felt far from the action now. He pocketed the phone, got back on the bike, and rode the rest of his route with an angry intensity. His lungs burned and his muscles ached but the suffering felt good again. He'd reconnected with the power inside him, and the realisation that it was Zoe who'd put his head back in the game only added to the venom with which he attacked the hills. When he got home to Kate's flat he was spent, but there was an energy in him that the ride hadn't managed to dissipate. He stood in the shower and thought about Zoe.

Thirteen years later, she could still get inside his head just by looking at him. Jack hugged Sophie close and tried to concentrate on his daughter while Tom finished the girls' warm-ups and lined them up for a head-to-head sprint. Tom put Kate on the inside line and Zoe on the outside. They edged their front wheels up to the start line. They looked across at each other.

Tom blew the whistle.

'Watch this,' Jack whispered to Sophie.

They started very slowly. They stood on their pedals, looking across at each other, their eyes unreadable behind the mirrored visors. They sized each other up and waited. Kate edged forward, and Zoe moved to cover her. With exquisite balance, tiny movements of the handlebars and little changes of pressure on the cranks, they manoeuvred for infinitesimal advantages of position. Kate, on the inside line, could be direct. The outside line was subtler, and longer, but Zoe could ride higher on the banking so that any attack would be launched with the assistance of gravity. The riders sped up by imperceptible degrees. Kate eased ahead, still travelling very slowly, craning her head back to watch for any response. Zoe lingered behind, poised to ambush her if Kate's attention wavered for an eye-blink.

Jack knew it wouldn't. He hardly blinked himself. You didn't see better racing than this. They'd been doing this since they were nineteen, and they knew each other's style. Each rider perfectly anticipated the other, and no advantage was conceded. Now Kate and Zoe slowed again, and converged, and leaned shoulders on each other. They slowed to an absolute halt and became motionless, each unwilling to risk giving away the tiniest advantage of body position by turning their head to watch the other. They watched instead for any alteration in the stark outline of their arc-lit shadows conjoined on the maple boards of the track. They balanced together, listening for any telltale acceleration in the other rider's breathing.

Using each other for balance in that moment they resembled neither rivals nor team mates but, in the intimacy of their mutual dependency, lovers.

Sophie said: 'They've stopped.'

Jack squeezed her arm. 'No. They're just starting.'

When it happened, it happened incredibly fast. Without surrendering any premonition at all, Kate twitched and made a break. Zoe responded, the power in her legs instantly up to maximum. Now each rider was making snap decisions, picking her course by instinct, by immediate and irrevocable reaction to what the other rider had done. You steered left or right and you couldn't ever take it back. Within seconds the air was shrieking as they parted it. On the second lap Zoe closed the gap and tucked in to Kate's slipstream. The two riders worked explosively, on the limit of human force. On the third and final lap Zoe pulled alongside Kate in the final straight and you saw the skull beneath the skin as her jaws gaped for air. The two riders crossed the finish line, flat out, lungs bursting, throwing their bikes forward, looking across at each other to see who had inched it. Always, this was how it ended, whether the audience was three or three billion. Kate and Zoe looked not to the line on the track or the flags of the umpires or the banners of the crowd, but at each other.

Slowing, their wheels rumbled in the echoing space.

'Who won?' said Sophie.

Jack looked at Tom with the question in his eyes.

Tom shook his head. 'Mate,' he said. 'Too close to call.'

Changing room, National Cycling Centre, Stuart Street, Manchester

After training Kate felt tired and good. Head-to-head training was always a battlefield, but she'd held her own. She'd put down at least as much power as Zoe, and she hadn't risen to any mind games. And that bit at the start, with Sophie in the basket of the butcher's bike – that had been fun. Zoe didn't feel like the threat she once was.

She hurried into the shower before her muscles could cool, took her time to dress, then sat in front of the mirror to sort her hair out.

Zoe was already changed. She took the comb out of Kate's hand and stood behind her to sort out her tangles. Kate let her, wincing at the brutal way Zoe dealt with knots.

'Your hair's fucked,' Zoe said.

Kate yawned. 'My hair can be combed out.'

Zoe caught her inflection. 'You're saying my life can't?'

'I'm just saying you should lie low for a bit.'

'Not an option.'

'Because . . . ?'

'Because the papers go to print at nine. I've only got three or four hours to do something, you know? My agent says I have to give them a photograph, today. Something family-friendly.'

'What are you going to do? Sleep with a Teletubby?'

Zoe laughed. They were keeping it almost weightless. To Kate, conversation with Zoe often felt like walking on ice while clinging to almost enough helium balloons to counteract your weight. You lowered yourself gingerly onto the surface. This was the kind of lightness they had now. It wasn't unusual, Kate supposed. This was just friendship: this faith to believe that you could grab more balloons as the baggage you carried multiplied. You got on with it; of course you did.

'So what are you going to do?' Kate said.

'I'm getting the Olympic rings tattooed. Here. Photo op.'

Zoe indicated the place by sweeping the comb along her uninjured forearm, then resumed work on Kate's hair.

'This afternoon?' Kate said.

'Why not? There's a place round the corner. Want to come and get yours done too?'

'Zoe. Be serious. I'm me.'

'So? Be you with a tattoo.'

'That should be their slogan.'

'They don't need a slogan. They've got needles and ink and baldy

189

men with ponytails and latex gloves and . . . ooh, it's so *sexy*, Catherine! Say you'll come with me!'

Zoe hugged her around the neck and dropped her face close to Kate's, making a pouting face in the mirror.

Kate shook her off. 'What about this meeting with Tom?'

Zoe stood straight again. 'No time. We'll sneak out the back door. I mean, what's the old man going to do? Run after us?'

Kate made a sceptical face. 'Seriously. With the newspapers . . . shouldn't you just stay off-radar for a bit, Zo? I mean, I would.'

Kate felt the comb stop moving for a moment, and looked up to see the unguarded expression Zoe wore in the mirror. The look said: *Yeah, but that's you, isn't it?*

The look said Kate didn't have the face, didn't have the imagination, didn't have the charisma to think any bigger. Kate watched Zoe trying to take the look back, trying to turn it into something less judgemental, but it was out there now.

She tried not to mind. It wasn't as if she was unaware that next to Zoe she was less mysterious and less attractive and less interesting. But you got used to these facts, and it was easy to tie each one of them to an equal and opposite lightness. For example, she was a great mother, she really was. She was helpful and patient with Jack and Sophie. She was quite intelligent. She had learned a huge amount about blood disorders and developmental nutrition. She noticed other people's feelings.

She tried to give Zoe back a look that was neither intimidated, nor tipping over the other way into aggression. It came out looking slightly bovine. God, it was sometimes so hard to know how to *be* around Zoe. Something about Zoe always made Kate feel like a good person and a coward, both at once. When she thought about Zoe's relationships it was sometimes with a serene sense that thank God *she* wasn't like that, but more often it was with a kind of tired fascination – not that her friend was insatiable, but that she herself was grateful for so little. For the longest time, she'd just been happy that Jack was happy with her. That had been the extent of her ambition.

When she'd found out that Zoe had been phoning him, right at the start of their relationship, it wasn't just that she'd felt threatened. She was sure that Jack didn't love Zoe, and the proof was that it hadn't gone further than phone calls. She was sure that Zoe didn't love Jack, either, and that she was only after him to destabilise Kate. What disheartened her was the realisation that Zoe considered it all to be part of the race. This was before they were friends – there was no good history between them yet to offset the hurt.

It was the start of the off-season. The National Championships were behind them, and Tom ordered them to take a month away from training to let their bodies recover from the summer of racing. Kate tried to rest but it was tedious, cooped up in the flat she and Jack were renting in East Manchester. Jack had been told to relax too, and he lay on the sofa with his legs up and his earphones in, glassy-eyed from the forced inactivity, nodding his head to jigs and reels and Scottish indie rock. She tried to forget Zoe's phone calls but every time Jack's phone rang – his mother checked in on him constantly, and his coach made sure he wasn't training – she imagined it was Zoe, which was probably, she thought, exactly what Zoe wanted. She read novels listlessly, or she got halfway through and chucked the books against the wall, disgusted that the protagonists could never seem to just sort themselves out. There was rarely much in the characters' lives that Tom wouldn't be able to fix by breaking down the problem into solvable components, or by calmly unpacking their psychology, or occasionally just by ordering them to brace up. She felt sorry for Anna Karenina and Clarissa Dalloway and Holly Golightly, that they couldn't simply phone their coach, and glad that she herself would never get so tangled up in life's knots.

Nothing happened, day after day. The sky was slate grey and the roads were black with rain. The radio, with a soundtrack of Christmassy bells, was already offering to consolidate all your credit card debts into one easy to manage monthly payment.

Kate sat at the window, brooding, watching the cars crawling through the November sleet. The off-season was a presentiment of death. There was no action on the track, and the sporting press lost interest in you completely. The disconnection was as sudden and absolute as if a switch had been thrown. All summer they fought over you for photos and gossip and interviews, and then they went quiet and you lived until spring in an obscurity so complete that only you knew you were still alive. You inhabited the town like a ghost, wandering without purpose. You'd been so busy training and competing and doing interviews all year that you'd made no civilian friends to hang out with, and yet you didn't want to see your friends from the sport. Sometimes there were off-season get-togethers but they were awkward affairs where the riders stood around making in-jokes about cycling. They were like office parties where all the nibbles were optimised for protein delivery and no one got drunk and photocopied their assets.

Kate climbed the walls in the flat. One afternoon, after a fortnight of resting, she gave up and put on waterproofs and took her training bike out into a full gale. She headed up into the hills of the Peak District, and with each turn of the pedals she felt better. Rain lashed her face and she opened her mouth, liking the untamed taste of it. She rode through Glossop and out along the Snake Pass, climbing the long, steep gradient into a gusting headwind and relishing the burn in her legs. The wet road rose through the scrubby moorland and the low pines – she knew each twist of it by heart. It was the only big climb on the standard loop that all the riders did once a week in training: east out of Manchester, a whirl around the Peak and then home. She settled into the rhythm of the hill, standing in the pedals when the road kicked up, easing down into the saddle where the gradient relented a little.

The summit of the pass came into sight two hundred yards ahead, with another rider cresting it from the opposite direction. It was windier up on the top, without the shelter of the hill, and the other rider was getting blown all over the road as she began to descend, too fast on the wet road, yellow waterproof whipping in the gusts, no crash helmet, eyes screwed up against the rain.

'Zoe!' Kate shouted as the rider flashed past her.

She stopped, panting, and watched Zoe skid to a halt fifty yards downslope. Zoe turned her bike in the road and pedalled back up the hill to her, smiling.

Kate half regretted calling out. Maybe she was stupid to try to be friendly. It wasn't as if she'd forgiven Zoe. Still, the adrenaline of the climb made her bold, and maybe the fortnight of isolation had left her glad to see anyone.

Kate returned Zoe's smile as she approached.

Zoe shouted over the noise of the wind: 'What are you doing up here?'

Kate was still out of breath. 'Two weeks. Sitting around. I was going mental. You?'

Zoe laughed. 'I've been out here every day. Don't tell Tom. I'm a nuclear submarine. Stop running the turbines, I melt down and take civilisation with me.'

Kate smiled again. 'Headed home?'

Zoe nodded. 'Unless you fancy some company?'

Kate sniffed and wiped rain off her face with the back of her glove. She looked down at the ride computer on her handlebars. 'I'm doing another forty-five, fifty,' she said.

Zoe scanned the sky to cross-reference this information against the strength of the wind and the heft of the rain clouds.

'Via a nice hot coffee?' she said.

Kate hesitated, then laughed. 'Go on, twist my arm.'

They rode to the top together and cruised the four downhill miles to the Snake Pass Inn. They left the bikes outside and sat down either side of the fire. They didn't talk at first. They arranged their shoes to dry, took off their waterproof tops and steamed as the coals glowed.

Zoe held her coffee in both of her hands to warm them, watching Kate over the rim of the cup.

'What?' said Kate finally.

'I'm sorry,' said Zoe. 'I'm sorry for the phone calls.'

Kate looked sharply at her. 'Going to make a habit of it?'

Zoe dropped her eyes. 'No. It's done. I'm over it.'

'Fine, then.'

Kate took off her gloves and draped them over the brass fender of the fireplace. They sizzled as the water boiled out of them.

'You sure?' said Zoe. 'I'm forgiven?'

Kate smiled, feeling the weight lift off her too. 'Yeah.'

Zoe raised her coffee cup. 'Drink to it?'

Kate smiled at Zoe's bedraggled hair and her hopeful expression. For the first time, she realised that Zoe might be okay.

'Not with coffee,' she said. 'Let's have a glass of wine.'

Zoe looked panicked. 'Wine?'

Kate nodded. 'French people make it from grapes. It comes in red or white.'

Zoe frowned, trying the feel of the word in her mouth. 'Wine . . .'

'Oh, come on,' said Kate. 'It's off-season. Live a little.'

She went to the bar before the adrenaline of the climb could desert her and ordered two glasses of Pinot Grigio. She hadn't drunk in a pub since her sixteenth birthday and she was surprised by the size of the glasses the barman gave her – there was almost half a pint of wine in each. She dug into the back pocket of her gilet for money, paid with a damp £20 note and was surprised by how little change she got back.

Back at the fire she passed a glass to Zoe and sat down.

'Cheers,' she said.

'Cheers.'

They clinked. Zoe sniffed the wine, eyed it sceptically, then drained the glass. She put her hands to her mouth, rocking. 'Ew. God. Yuk.'

She reached into the pocket of her waterproof for a caffeinated energy gel. She tore the top off the sachet, sucked out the gel, swallowed and made a face.

'God,' she said. 'They taste better on the bike, don't they?'

Kate laughed. 'Most people go for bar snacks.'

'Most people didn't just ride eighty miles in that wind,' said Zoe. 'I could eat the actual bar.'

She got up and went in search of food. Kate sat looking into the fire, feeling the warmth bringing her fingers and toes back to life, sipping her wine and liking the unaccustomed glow. They were the only people in the pub, and outside, the storm was building. Water streamed down the windows and the wind delivered buffeting gusts that drowned out the sound of Robbie Williams on the jukebox.

195

Zoe came back from the bar with a tray of sandwiches and two more glasses of wine. Kate's eyes widened.

'What?' said Zoe. 'I got him to make them with wholegrain.'

'You know what I mean.'

Zoe motioned to the window with her head. 'Yeah, but who wants to go back out there right now? There's freezing cold water actually coming out of the sky. I should never have moved up north.'

Kate snorted. 'This is the south, love. You should try it up in the Lakes. Our rain comes in from the Arctic.'

'I'm from Surrey,' said Zoe, sipping her wine with her little finger extended. 'Our rain comes in bottles labelled Evian.'

Kate laughed and finished her first glass of wine to catch up.

Zoe eyed her. 'It's not a race, you know.'

Something in Zoe's eyes struck Kate as a challenge, and she drank her second glass of wine straight down without thinking about it too hard. Zoe followed, and they put down their glasses at the same time.

'Photo finish,' said Zoe. 'Crowd goes wild.'

'I think you might just have edged it,' said Kate, thinking the opposite.

They sat together, looking into the fire.

After a while Zoe said: 'What was it like?'

'What was what like?'

'Growing up in the Lakes.'

'I don't know. Wet.'

'Any brothers or sisters?'

Kate shook her head.

'Me neither,' said Zoe. 'Only child. Were you happy?'

Kate thought about it. It wasn't a question with an easy answer, and it freaked her out a bit that Zoe had asked.

'Why?' she said finally.

Zoe held up a hand. 'Sorry. My mouth.'

'No, it's okay.'

The wine's first rush ebbed away from her. With the warmth of the fire creating a burgeoning gravitational field and the wind outside shrieking, she started to regret the second glass. She ought to think about riding home to Jack. She imagined him lying on the sofa. She imagined coming in from the rain, soaked to the skin, and letting him warm her up. He would take her in his arms and help her peel off her kit and . . . well. It was nice to have someone to go home to.

Zoe was eating a sandwich. She sighed, threw the crust down and nodded at their empty glasses.

'Best of three?' she said.

Kate smiled. 'We should head back. It'll be dark in a couple of hours.'

'We could dial a taxi. Put the bikes in the back.'

Kate hesitated, thinking of Jack. 'I really should get going.'

It came out sounding rather formal, and the tiniest flicker of desperation in Zoe's eyes made Kate wish that she'd been able to find a warmer way of saying it.

'Of course,' Zoe said quickly. 'I was only kidding.'

'Oh, right,' said Kate, dropping her eyes and giving a small self-deprecating laugh that she hoped was enough to make her out as the one who had embarrassed herself.

Zoe began collecting together her gloves and waterproofs. 'You heading home?' she said.

'Yeah,' Kate said. 'You?'

'Oh, I'm going to my boyfriend's.'

'Great,' said Kate, thinking about the ride home. 'In town?'

'No,' said Zoe, gesturing south. 'It's that way.'

Outside, after the glow of the fire, the wind and the rain were even stronger. Zoe turned left and Kate turned right and it wasn't until half an hour later, while she was rolling down from the hills and the first of Glossop's streetlights were turning the rain red with the glow of adolescent sodium, that Kate realised there was nothing at all in the direction Zoe had indicated – nothing for fifty miles except the bleak and rainswept Peak with its sodden hills black against the wet grey disc of the setting sun. She wondered if there really was a boyfriend, or whether Zoe was still out there in this weather, riding a lonely arc from the fading glow of the alcohol to the clutch of the gathering night.

The more you got to like Zoe, the harder it was to know how she made you feel. In the changing room, Kate let her eyes fall away from Zoe's in the mirror, while Zoe combed her hair. She watched herself. She hated these mirrors with their harsh halogen lights: they showed you nothing but the truth. Her face had aged in the last few months, this was undeniable. She'd kept the looks of her early twenties beyond their return date and now life had chosen this year, of all years, to call in the loan. The mirror didn't admit to the possibility of a time when she had been radiant, when there had actually been a difficult choice for Jack to make between Zoe and her. Now she really looked like a mum, and Zoe still looked like a model. She tried not to feel resentful. It had been her choice, after all, being a mother. No one had forced her to do it.

And here she was, thirty-two and looking it, and here was Zoe, asking if she would come with her and get a tattoo. Time clawed at the back of her neck in the sharp, insistent strokes of Zoe's comb.

Zoe watched her in the mirror, waiting for her response with that same almost perfectly concealed desperation she'd shown by the fireside on that rainy training ride, the first day they'd become friends. Silence settled and the inchoate moment persisted.

'Yeah, fuck it, Zo,' Kate said suddenly. 'I'll come to the tattoo place with you.'

Made in Manchester tattoo studio, Newton Street, Manchester

Zoe called her agent and her agent had a photographer despatched to the tattoo studio. He arrived after forty minutes, on a scooter. He was young and convinced of his charms. Zoe needed good shots, so she smiled as if she concurred. Kate smiled too, and the pap took the pictures while the tattoo artists worked.

Zoe was having her forearm inked with a triple X, beneath Olympic rings the size of fifty-pence pieces.

In the chair next to hers, Kate was getting the rings done small, the size of five-pence pieces, exactly where Zoe had known she would: high on her shoulder blade where a T-shirt would cover them.

When the shots were done, Zoe signed the pap's shirt for him with a magic marker. She handed it to Kate so she could sign too, but the pap was already turning to leave. Zoe watched the hurt flicker across her friend's face, then the quick recovery. She felt for Kate. Something caught under her ribs, and she allowed the feeling to swell for a moment. It reassured her that she felt something. It wasn't as if she was heartless.

A moment later, Kate seemed to be over it. She got on the phone to Jack, giggling as she admitted to him what they were doing.

'We're just down the road! We're having *tattoos*.'

She whispered the word, elongating the 'oo' into a delighted exhalation of wonder at her own daring.

Sometimes Zoe wondered if Kate was ever going to grow up. She listened to her friend on the phone. There was a hesitancy in her voice – a timidity, almost – in the way she broke the news of a little ink to the man she'd been married to for eight years. *Jack*, for goodness' sake. As if he had any right to judge her.

She sighed. The needle buzzed away on her arm, hurting when it came close to her wrist but not hurting so much as, say, sprint cycling. She didn't know what to do for Kate. Just because Zoe was the one who had taken Kate's confidence away, it didn't mean that she knew how to give it back. It was easier to believe that Kate didn't suffer too much from it all; that she was unaware of how unfair it had all been on her. It was easier to hope that Kate didn't see how tired she was starting to look next to Zoe, or didn't notice how much the burden of Sophie was slowing her down.

It was all a bit shitty to contemplate. If Kate really understood what had happened to her – what was happening to her still – then the fact that she *wasn't* crying about it made Zoe want to cry.

There it was: a prickling in her eyes. Zoe charted it and connected it with the other points of reference; the pangs and lurches and catches of breath that she felt when she let herself think about Kate too hard. There did seem to be a constant pattern inside her – a constellation of disconnected emotions which, when viewed in its entirety, seemed to form the shape of someone who cared. But then again, you could connect the stars any way you liked. Some people saw a big dipper, while others only saw a plough.

Zoe was wary of the idea that on some level she might be a good person.

She eavesdropped as Kate's call with Jack turned sour.

'What's the matter?' Kate was saying. 'Oh, don't be like that. It's just a bit of fun.'

Zoe watched her face fall.

'It's just for an hour or something. You guys can wait that long, can't you? Okay, *Christ*. Tell Tom we're sorry. We shouldn't have sneaked out like that.'

Another silence.

'It's just a fucking tattoo, Jack. It's the Olympic rings. It's not like I'm getting Tony Blair's face.'

Zoe watched the confusion coming into Kate's expression, and wondered what Jack could be saying. It wasn't like him to be a dick about something like this. Zoe knew Jack, she really did.

In the autumn of 2002, they'd all been twenty-two. Jack had been winning some big races, and Zoe had been winning everything she entered. Pursuit events, sprints, time trials. All the other girls were racing for second place that season. Zoe was racing so often, she hardly needed to train. It went on like that all through the summer, and Zoe got used to the sight of Kate on the second step of the podium, viewed from slightly above. Now that they were friends, it was easy to make a joke of it. *Your turn next*, Zoe said each time, and they laughed about it while the medal ceremonies went on around them. It wasn't until Zoe lost that she realised it wasn't funny at all. In the autumn, one week before the National Championships in Cardiff, Kate beat her in a nocturnal sprint race in the Manchester Velodrome which was broadcast on national TV during primetime. Zoe couldn't bear the feeling. Tom had to force her to go out for the podium group and collect her silver medal. She had to stand on the second step and look up at Kate's radiant grin and her dainty little elfin cheekbones. It left an ache in her neck that lasted for the whole of the next week.

The Nationals were huge that year. Cycling was starting to get big, and the crowds were a thrill. All the finals were broadcast live on ITV. Jack won the sprint. Zoe and Kate had come through their heats and were scheduled to race each other next. While Kate watched Jack climb the podium, Zoe looked for his phone in his kitbag and sent herself a text. Later, while they were stripping off their warm-up suits by the side of the track and preparing to race, she pretended to receive it.

She gasped, then tried to look flustered. 'Oh . . .'

Kate put a hand on her shoulder. 'What is it?'

Zoe shook her head. 'Nothing. Sorry.'

She grabbed her helmet and shoes and headed for the start, forgetting to take her phone. That was all it took. On the line, Kate was in pieces. The sprint final was best of three, and Zoe didn't need the third race. On the podium, on the silver step, Kate couldn't stop crying.

It felt worse than Zoe had thought it would. In her room in the hotel they were all using, Zoe sat on her bed the whole afternoon, staring at her National Champion's sprint gold medal, wishing she could give it back.

At the end of the afternoon, Jack knocked on her door. He was shaking. He couldn't speak.

Zoe's eyes were red from crying. 'Is she still here?'

Jack shook his head. 'She's gone home.'

'You didn't go with her?'

'She wouldn't let me. I need you to phone her and tell her the text was from you.'

'She didn't believe you?'

Jack shook his head.

Zoe gestured helplessly. 'So why's she going to believe me?'

Jack stared at her for a long time, and she watched the despair come into his face as he realised she was right.

'Why are you like this?' he said, finally.

She started crying again then, and she couldn't stop. She didn't ask him to comfort her, and he didn't offer.

They went for a walk, by the harbour. She told him she was sorry; that it wouldn't happen again. It was a cold, grey day with the rollers ghosting in. Her hair was growing out by then, and it whipped and tangled in the wind. The seagulls sounded like angels who'd lost their jobs. The air tasted of salt. She threw her National Champion's medal into the harbour. It didn't splash into clear water. It snagged on a floating coil of blue polypropylene rope and hung from its ribbon, the gold glinting dully just below the grey surface. They watched it for a long time, but it wouldn't sink.

Zoe was back in Manchester twelve hours later, and she started training for Athens fifteen minutes after that. With less than two years to go, the work had a fresh intensity. Every yard she forced a bike around a track was one yard closer to glory. The sense of destiny made her skin tingle, but her mind was unsettled and it took her a fortnight to understand why. She realised she couldn't entirely focus on training until she'd apologised and made things right with Kate. It was a new feeling for her, this knowledge that her own wellbeing had in some way become linked with that of another. It was an unexpected snare. As the feeling intensified, a weakness grew in her body in direct proportion to it until she could hardly lift a barbell off the mat. Her unease mounted and she resented Kate more and more – almost began to hate her, in truth, for the fact that she liked her too much.

She invited her out to lunch, never intending to say anything about herself. She'd been planning just to do something nice for Kate and say sorry, but then it had happened and she'd told her about Adam dying and found herself crying in the middle of The Lincoln – actually weeping, with tears running down her face – while Kate hugged her and the pianist played *The Dukes of Hazzard* theme tune *affrettando*, getting faster and faster as he realised it wasn't cheering her up.

She worked out with Kate every day after that. Her strength returned straight away. She was amazed that Kate was able to forgive her for Cardiff. As the winter wore on, Kate asked a few times if she would consider seeing a psychologist. She heard herself agreeing, more to prove she was sorry for what she'd done than because she thought it could help. She committed to going once a week. Kate walked with her to the sessions and left her at the door with a smile and a supportive squeeze on the arm. Zoe sat in a chair that was self-consciously not a couch while the psychologist asked short, leading questions and then settled back in his own chair, which was carefully selected to set his eye level lower than hers.

He made the room into a silent vacuum that she was supposed to populate with memories. As though such things could safely be surrendered. As if they'd served their purpose, like the spent phases of a rocket, and could tumble soundlessly back to earth. There was no allowance made for her growing suspicion that her memories weren't done with her yet; that they still held unspent fuel; that to relinquish them now was to reduce her chances of escape. The more she talked about Adam, the more she felt the pull of gravity.

Talking made her empty and weak, even as the psychologist insisted that it was doing her good. At the end of each session he would steeple his hands, touching the fingertips to his lower lip as he offered a summing-up and humbly solicited her opinion as to whether his précis had merit. She found herself agreeing that she had a problem with anger, and that she suffered from an inability to accept the occasional defeats that were an inevitable and healthy part of being alive.

But it only made her more angry, hearing herself admit that she had a problem with anger. It made her feel defeated, admitting that she couldn't handle defeat. After every session Kate would meet her outside the clinic and they would go for coffee and Zoe would make sure to laugh and order an extra shot of hazelnut and admit that she really did feel much better.

Her results in training suffered. When she lined up for the practice sprints with Kate, she found she could no longer summon the old fury from deep inside her and focus it in her muscles. In place of the rage was a quiet ache, as chill and grey as the sea in November, and she was beaten even before the starting whistle blew. On the days when she watched Kate getting further ahead with each lap, her worst fear was that the psychologist might cure her.

Tom raced her against Kate every week and when she stopped winning altogether, she stopped going to the psychologist. She told Kate she'd turned the corner, and Kate was happy for her.

The next session, in training, she beat Kate for the first time in a month. For a couple of weeks she listened to the psychologist's patient voicemail messages suggesting that she return to therapy. After a while he stopped phoning.

Things intensified between Kate and Jack. Zoe tried to be happy while Kate told her about their plans – how they were going to buy a house together, maybe think about getting married and having children. Kate started inviting her back to their place after training, and she got used to chatting with the pair of them over tea. At first it was awkward, with Jack, but as she got used to it she found herself loosening up around him, to the point where she and Kate could take turns berating him for his music. Finally there came a morning when the three of them were laughing around the kitchen table, while Jack leaned back and Kate stirred the tea and Zoe did Tom's accent, when Zoe thought to herself: this is it. My life has finally started, and these are my friends.

Then, at the end of March, Kate and Jack argued. Zoe didn't hear about it from Kate. She only noticed a cooling-off in their banter at the training sessions, and an unexplained halt to the post-training invitations to Kate and Jack's house. Kate made excuses, saying she was tired or claiming other appointments, until it got to the point where they hardly spoke outside the track. Zoe was worried at first, then confused, then heartbroken. Her voicemails all went unanswered. Kate was her first friend – her only friend – and losing her was disorientating. For the first time in her life, Zoe found it hard to get up in the morning. She sat on the edge of the bed, holding her head, feeling vacant.

Finally she bumped into Jack at the velodrome and asked him about it. He told her he'd split up with Kate. They'd been talking, and the subject of Zoe had arisen, and Jack had made the mistake – mistake was his word – of admitting how he'd felt about Zoe at the beginning. There'd been an argument – a stupid argument, since it was all in the past. Wasn't it stupid? Wasn't it a sad row over water that had long since flowed under a very distant bridge?

Zoe had found herself agreeing that yes, it was a very sad row, over nothing at all, and then she'd gone back to her flat and lain awake half the night thinking about both of them.

A week later Jack travelled alone to the British Cycling spring training camp in Gran Canaria, a day ahead of Kate. Zoe was already out there. She knocked on his door, late at night. They told each other it was okay, but it wasn't okay. Kate was a thousand miles away but the more they tried to lose themselves in each other, the more her presence grew in the room. Zoe felt it – the first sense of unease growing into an undeniable tearing at her heart. Naked in bed with him, coming down off the euphoria of their first hours together, she saw in his eyes that he was feeling it too.

'I'm sorry,' he said.

She shook her head. 'It's fine. I'll go.'

He held her. 'You don't have to. Stay and just sleep, okay?'

They both pretended to, lying with their backs to each other and their eyes staring at the walls until a pale grey light began to seep beneath the blinds.

Zoe left him lying there, gathering her things quietly and tiptoeing across the floor to allow them both the dignity of the notion that, were it not for the fact that he was sleeping, one of them would have spoken words of farewell that would have been weightless, and wise, and made the whole terrible thing all right. It was important to leave space for the idea that such words were available to be spoken, requiring only to be plucked from the low-hanging branches of the dawn.

She walked down from the hotel to the beach, left her clothes in the dunes and stepped into the Atlantic as the nude sun rose through the waves. Three pelicans in tight formation flew low over the water, silhouetted against the light, gliding without sound. The horizon was youthful and smooth. With her toes just touching bottom, she faced out to sea and washed herself clean of the night. The water was soft and the breeze subtle. She surrendered her footing and struck out to sea in an easy freestyle.

Beyond the shorebreak, where the sea floor dropped off into sudden indigo, the bottomless cold engulfed her. Her chest tightened, and she gasped. The fresh breeze out here blew the tops from the waves in clear salt sheets which slapped at her. She had to turn her face from the wind, and float on her back to get her breath. It was the first time she had looked back. She sank and rose on the swell, and in the troughs she was entirely alone in the brightening folds of water, and on the peaks she saw that the beach was much further than she had thought. The hotel, and Jack, and training, and racing, were a low concrete block cresting the distant dunes. Out here, it was just her.

Her leg brushed against something big and heavy. She kicked out in terror, ready to fight, but the thing floated to the surface. It was a section of a wooden boat. It hung beside her, black with age and water-logged, sheathed in hard white barnacles on the underside. When she took a stroke away from it, it followed her, languidly, sucked along by the eddies her body made. She forced herself to be calm. She floated on her back, her limbs extended in a star, staring up at the blue-grey dome of the dawn. There, with her chill white body suspended in the ocean and tingling with the memory of Jack's, she felt the terror of having no one. The feeling was wide and cold and savage as the sea.

In the tattoo parlour, Kate dropped her phone on the floor and it disintegrated, the battery shooting one way and the shattered plastic casing the other. The sound broke through into Zoe's thoughts, and she looked up. Kate was staring at her.

'What is it?' she said.

Kate's hands were shaking. 'Tom's on his way here. He's got news.'

Silver-grey Renault Scénic

Mum had a white surgical dressing taped over her right shoulder blade. Sophie could see the corner of it above the neckline of her yellow T-shirt. She sat watching it from her seat in the back, while Dad drove them home. She tried to work out what it meant.

'Mum,' she said, 'what's that on your back?'

'It's nothing, Sophie.'

'Did you crash?'

Dad said: 'It's *nothing*, okay?'

He used the voice that made you fold back into yourself, like an anemone in a rock pool when you touched it with your finger. Sophie shut her mouth.

Mum and Dad were talking in the low voice grown-ups used when they didn't want you to hear. Grown-ups thought your ears were worse than theirs, but your ears were actually better. This is the order it went downwards in, for hearing: Jedi, bats, owls, foxes, dogs, mice, grown-ups.

'What were you *thinking*, anyway?' Dad was saying.

'Don't be a shit. You think this isn't bad enough?'

'I'm just saying, I mean . . . what was in your head?'

'I don't *know*, okay? Do I always have to know?'

'What? Is that your question? If it involves skin that's permanently attached to you, might it not be sensible to be *sure*?'

Mum said in a sad voice: 'It's my skin.'

Sophie's stomach sank. It was cancer. This is what it was. It was skin cancer on her back. That was why the surgical dressing was there. Sophie knew all about cancer, and Mum had it of the skin, and she'd gone for an operation. That's why she'd disappeared after training, because grown-ups always tried to be secret about cancer and things. But this is the order it went downwards in, for keeping secrets: Jedi, foxes, grown-ups. Mum had gone for an operation, and it had gone wrong, and now everything was bad.

Dad was saying: 'But the *Olympics* . . . I mean, shouldn't you have *got there* first?'

'We thought we were there, didn't we? We're number one and number two. No one else is even close. And now *this* happens. And if that isn't bad enough now I've got this fucking . . . *thing* on my shoulder.'

Sophie watched in the rearview mirror and saw how her mum's hands twisted around her seatbelt. Dad looked across at Mum, then reached out to touch her knee. She looked back across at him, and the sadness in her face softened slightly. Straight away Sophie felt better too. It was like Mum's knee was the okay button and Dad had just pressed it.

'I know,' Dad said. 'I'm sorry.'

'Mum?' said Sophie.

Her voice was so small that Mum didn't hear it. She tried again, filling her lungs with a hissing wheeze and forcing the sound out through the tightness in her throat.

'Mum?'

Mum turned to look at her and she reached out her hand, between the two front seats, to touch her.

'It's okay,' she said. 'It's actually not as bad as you think.'

'I'm sure you're right, darling.'

'Sometimes you'll feel really sick but if you do all your chemo you actually will get better. You will.'

She looked at her firmly, nodding so Mum would see how sure she was. Confusion came into Mum's face.

'Sorry?' she said.

'The thing on your back,' Sophie said. 'The cancer.'

Mum looked at her for a long time, and there was a strange expression in her eyes that Sophie didn't understand. She swallowed. She shouldn't have said cancer. She was used to it, but the new people took a long time. At the hospital a lot of them couldn't say the word, especially the grown-ups. The women said *I've got a tumour*, which made it sound small enough to catch hold of but not so small that it would slip through your fingers. The men said *I'm fighting the big C*, which was better for them because they could think of this massive C-shape from the alphabet posters attacking them, like a crab, and it was easier for them to imagine how they would fight something like that than some smaller, softer C, like a cell.

'It's okay, Mum,' she said. 'Dr Hewitt says it actually makes you stronger if you use its real name.'

There were tears in Mum's eyes. 'Oh, darling, I'm so sorry. It isn't cancer. It's only a silly tattoo.'

Dad pulled the car over to the side of the road and they both got out and climbed into the back seat. They unstrapped her and hugged her tight, and the three of them sat there while the dusk gathered and the early evening traffic rolled by with the rain flaring in its headlights.

'Whatever happens,' said Dad, 'it's nothing next to how proud we are of you.'

'What?' said Sophie. 'I didn't do *anything*.'

This made Mum and Dad laugh for some reason. Why were they proud of her, when all she'd done was to get it completely wrong? A tattoo was really different from skin cancer. Really.

Sophie sighed, exasperated. As soon as she'd survived leukaemia, she was going to have to survive these parents.

Beetham Tower, 301 Deansgate, Manchester

Zoe let herself into her apartment, dropped the key into the dish, and put a blue plastic carrier bag down on the enamelled lava work surface in the kitchen area. She took a screw-top bottle of white wine out of the bag and stood looking at it. She hadn't drunk alcohol since that rainy training ride with Kate, in the depths of the off-season, more than a decade ago. She didn't have anything specifically made for putting wine in. She didn't even know how much you were supposed to drink.

She chose one of the small, heavy white ceramic espresso cups and filled it. She brought the bottle and the cup over to the tall windows and looked down over the lights of the city. She sniffed the wine, screwed up her face and drank it. She stood for ten minutes, gauging the effect. In a body that was tuned to know its heart rate to the nearest beat and to process the afferent messages running through every highly strung nerve bundle with arctic clarity, there was no warm glow, just an immediate feeling of concussion and a sense of terror at the power of the chemistry. She poured again, and drank another cup.

When half the bottle was gone, she felt brave enough to think about what the rule change meant. If she wanted the Olympic place, she would have to fight Kate for it. She held the thought and turned it around. It was true that she was desperate for the place. Without it, she'd lose her sponsors, and she'd lose this apartment, and she'd lose a reason to keep her heart and lungs functioning. But to be sure of getting the place, she'd need to push her body harder than she'd ever pushed it before. There'd been nothing to choose between her and Kate at training today.

She drank another slug of wine and used the cold coffee cup to cool the raw Olympic tattoo on her forearm. Looking at those rings, she could hear the roar of the crowds in Athens and Beijing. She searched her heart and questioned whether she was capable of destroying Kate, just to hear that sound again. She closed her eyes, leaned her forehead against the cool plate glass, and wondered.

In the months after Gran Canaria – the spring and early summer of 2003 – she did almost no competition at all. She saved herself for the Track World Championships in Stuttgart, at the end of July. She was clocking world record times in training. She left Jack and Kate alone to rebuild their relationship, and she forced all her pain and confusion into energy on the bike.

She flew out early to Stuttgart. British Cycling set her up in the hotel that all the British Cycling squad would use when they came out. It was close to the velodrome and for the whole month before the event, she trained on the track she would race on. She battled a virus that sucked her energy and spaced her out, but the game had never been bigger, and every atom of her body was focused. She hardly even noticed she was in Germany. The language was different but the track was the same.

Jack and Kate came out together, with one week to go. They were happy together again, but not so solid yet that they could comfortably be around Zoe. She smiled politely at them when they met in team meetings or passed each other at the breakfast buffet.

The 2003 Worlds were the biggest they'd ever been. There were teams from as far away as Brazil and China. All the races were broadcast live on Eurosport. Zoe was sick with nerves and excitement. More than once, she threw up in her hotel room. She was calm, though. Her preparation had been impeccable. It was all over the press: she was going to clean up. The media was in love with her. In the *Guardian*, a popular philosopher wrote a piece about her work ethic. In the *News of the World*, there were photos of her breasts in Lycra, and speculation about whether she wore anything underneath. There was something for everyone.

The World Championships began in a blaze of camera flashes. In Stuttgart, on the last day of July and the first two days of August 2003, Jack got the most gold medals ever won by a British cyclist at the Worlds. Kate won two golds and a bronze. Zoe failed to even qualify for the finals in three of her events. She came second to Kate in the run-off race for the sprint bronze medal. She felt terrible in all her heats. Once, she even threw up on the start line. They had to delay the starter's whistle. A man mopped the track, then they drove off the water with industrial driers. Zoe lined up again to start. The whistle went and a hot weakness flooded her body. The other girls rode away from her as if she wasn't even pedalling. A clip of her, trackside, in tears of incomprehension, stamping repeatedly on her nine thousand pound state-of-the-art carbon fibre machine was soon all over the internet.

Tom arranged a taxi and took her straight from the track to a clinic. They were there for two hours. The doctors ran tests. Zoe waited. They ran more tests. She waited again, in a tiny white room with fashion magazines in German, and air conditioning that rattled. A doctor came in, all smiles, and told her she was pregnant.

'It looks like you are right at the end of the first trimester,' he said. 'Congratulations!'

Then, seeing her face, he said: 'Sorry, is that not the good word? My English is not so good.'

Zoe made him repeat the test. She didn't believe it was possible, not when she'd been training as hard as she had. He wasn't a specialised sports doctor, so she told him about the physiological changes. The way your body saw how low your fat stores were. How it registered the unbelievable pain you went through every day. How it naturally assumed you were dying, and made the necessary adjustments to your reproductive system. The doctor listened politely while she told him how her hormone levels had changed, how her oestrogen had fallen and her testosterone had built. She told him that she hadn't had a period for three years; that she hadn't used contraception since 1999. The doctor said that maybe she should have. The doctors were direct like that, in Germany.

When she walked out of the consulting room and into the lobby of the clinic, Tom was waiting for her. She smiled weakly and told him it was just a stomach bug.

Back in her room in the team hotel, she vomited again. She drank iced water. Kate was still at the velodrome, doing press. Zoe watched her on Eurosport. She was radiant.

She switched off and stared at the wall for an hour. Then she went online, made an appointment at an abortion clinic in Manchester, and started to rough out a revised training schedule for Athens.

Kate knocked on her door. She'd had the decency to leave her medals in her kitbag, but there was no hiding her victory. Gold blazed out of her: through her skin, from her eyes. It glowed in the air around her.

Zoe said: 'Happy now?'

'Don't be like that. I thought you might need someone to talk to.'

'I've got Tom.'

Kate paused. 'Great. Good. Well, look, I'll leave you to it, okay?'

Zoe sighed. 'Don't go. It's nice of you to come.'

Kate sat down on the bed with her. 'So what's wrong? Did the doctors say?'

Zoe gave a small, defeated laugh. 'Just gastro. Look, when we get back to England, let's . . . you know. Let's do something. Like go and watch a film, or whatever.'

'Not on our first date. I don't know what you've heard, but I'm not that kind of girl.'

Zoe laughed, but halfway through the laugh she started crying.

'Zoe? What is it?'

She sniffed. She bit her knuckles and whispered: 'I'm fucking *pregnant*, Kate.' Her face was crumpling so hard, the word came out in a squeak.

'What?'

'I'm pregnant. No one knows.'

'No one?'

Zoe shook her head.

'Oh. Wow. I mean . . . right.'

'It's okay. I mean, it's nothing. I have to get rid of it, right?'

Kate blinked. 'Oh *God*, I mean . . .'

Zoe swallowed. Her voice was broken. 'I know. But I have to. Don't I? I mean, I'm doing Athens. I'm not doing . . . you know . . . *baby*.'

Kate was silent.

'Kate?'

Zoe watched her face distorting, and it made no sense. It took her the longest time to work out that Kate was trying not to cry. She felt a surge of anger. What was Kate doing crying, when Zoe was the one whose life was in bits?

'What's your problem?' she said. 'I've got no *choice*, okay?'

'Zoe, please . . .'

'No choice at all. So don't guilt trip me.'

She watched Kate's red eyes rise up to meet hers.

'Is it Jack's?' Kate said quietly.

Zoe didn't feel the impact until a few seconds afterwards. She hadn't thought about whose child she might be carrying, only about how quickly she could stop carrying it. When the question came, the shock was so total that she couldn't make her face deny that it was possible.

Kate watched her, her face heavy with sadness.

'I knew something had happened,' she said finally. 'He was so quiet in the training camp . . .'

Zoe got up, left the room and went for a long walk alone around the streets of Stuttgart. She realised as she walked that there wasn't any different way to do the maths. She hadn't slept with anyone since she'd slept with Jack, and not in the month before him either. That meant two things: that the baby was his, and that sleeping with him had meant something to her, at least enough to break the pattern of her behaviour. Something had been growing in her emotions as well as in her womb, and she would somehow have to find the strength to get rid of both.

On the plane back to London, she was a wreck. She hadn't slept. She covered her head with a fleece and hugged her knees in a window seat, three rows behind Kate and Jack. Half an hour into the flight she stood and walked up the aisle to them. She wanted to say sorry. More than that, she was desperate to talk. Tom was furious with her and with Kate and Jack closed against her too, there was no one to speak with about the agonising choice she was trying to make. She reached their row. Sensing her looming, expecting her to be a member of the cabin crew, they looked up with the half smiles of people about to politely turn down the offer of coffee or tea. When she saw the shock come into their faces, followed by Jack's embarrassment and Kate's miserable confusion, she mumbled 'I'm sorry,' and hurried back to her seat.

There were photographers waiting at Heathrow. She walked through customs into a galaxy of flashes. Money had changed hands. Someone at the clinic had leaked the news. A reporter shouted at her. He was from Britain's biggest Sunday newspaper. From somewhere behind the crowd barrier he yelled: 'Zoe! Zoe! Are you going to keep the baby, or are you going to the Olympics?'

Once it was put like that, in public, it wasn't her choice to make any more. A hundred bright flashes caught the bone-white realisation on her face.

Kitchen, 203 Barrington Street, Clayton, East Manchester

After they'd eaten and Sophie was in bed, Kate put the dishes in to soak. On the windowsill above the sink was the drilled metal container holding the washing-up brushes, and next to it was the silver trophy cup into which Jack had counted Sophie's sixteen pills that morning. It was empty now.

'It's only the Olympics,' Kate said. 'I could just ditch it, you know. Spend more time with Sophie.'

She saw a pale and cautious fear flare in Jack's eyes.

'Stop that talk,' he said. 'You'll fight Zoe for the place, and you'll win it, and you'll go and race in London. You were neck and neck on the track today.'

Kate stared out of the window. 'I worry about fighting her. I think she's getting more unstable. I think she's losing it.'

'Don't make it about her. Think about how Sophie would feel if you quit. Think about how you'd feel.'

'What about you? How would you feel?'

'If you quit?'

'Yes.'

She watched the strain of it tightening his face.

'I'd quit too,' he said.

She nodded, believing he meant it but not believing he would.

She ran the cold tap and rinsed the suds off the baking dish. Maybe this was how it ended, after all, at thirty-two years of age. Not in defeat or glory on the track, but here, with a new load of their training kit in the laundry basket upstairs, and these three plain white plates with their pasta bake encrustations soaking in the sink, detergent breaking down the stubborn grease.

'Maybe I need some time to think,' she said.

'Oh Christ,' said Jack, holding his head. 'Since when was this about thinking?'

And he was right – it was terrible to hear herself saying such things. On the cork wall behind them were Sophie's drawings, from baby to eight years old. The smiling suns and the spaceships. Their daughter's footprints in yellow poster paint, making the petals of a sunflower. Kate remembered how she had held Sophie's skinny ankle to stamp each foot in its hour. With her other arm she had held Sophie up – this was before she could stand on her own. The strong stem and the broad leaves Kate had drawn herself, with a green wax crayon, while Jack was on the plane to Athens.

'Just think about it,' Jack was saying. 'What would you do, if you gave up?'

She waved a dismissive hand, then winced as the movement stretched her tattoo.

'There are other ways to make a living, right? I mean, unless all those commuters are faking it, there are other jobs.'

Jack stroked her cheek. 'Not once you've heard the crowd.'

She pushed his hand away, gently. In truth, the baying of the crowd had often frightened her. It set your adrenaline pumping, yes, but there was a particular silence at the heart of it. The crowd got thirty minutes for its lunch break. The crowd smoked outside its office building in the rain, stubbing out its cigarettes and disposing of the smouldering ends by inserting them through the metal grille of a wall-mounted disposal unit according to a directive contained in an email that had been circulated. The crowd was Jack, if his dad hadn't pushed him out of his comfort zone. The crowd was her, if her own father hadn't taken her to a bike race when she was six. It was the thinnest of separations, and the crowd noise carried easily across the space and haunted her.

She shivered. It was dark outside, and here were these dishes in the sink, and the laundry in the basket, and the orange blush of street-lamps revealing the rooflines. From their neighbours' windows, that warm and self-assured glow. That underlying flicker of TV. And in the sink, this scud of soap bubbles, thinner each time she looked.

Tom had always warned them about this: *One day, sooner than you think, your sporting life will be over.*

This soft sound of soap bubbles popping in the bowl.

This despair in her husband's voice as he said to her: 'Think about what's good for you, for once. You don't owe anyone else one more thing.'

She turned and watched him. 'Even so, I think I'd rather look after Sophie than fight against Zoe.'

'It's not an either/or. Oh Kate, is this about your confidence? I *know* you can beat Zoe. The only thing stopping you is the fear you might lose.'

She heard the sharpness come into her voice. 'I'm scared I might win. Winning is all she has. I'm nervous what she might do to herself if we leave her with nothing. I'm terrified of what she might do to *us*.'

She saw from his eyes that he felt it too; that he'd been struggling to formulate it until now. He didn't think past the immediate, this was the thing with Jack. The sheer simplicity of him was the reason they'd ended up with a life of such complexity. It wasn't his fault that she could deal with the complications and he couldn't. People had their natural habitats, after all, demarcated not in ecologies but in ages. He'd been perfectly adapted to being nineteen, and she was better at being thirty-two.

She kissed him, carefully, on the cheek, and both of them circled this thing that she had finally said out loud. They reached for ways to ring it around with more words; to make it safe.

Jack said: 'She can't hurt us any more, Kate. That was nearly ten years ago. We're older and wiser now.'

'So's she.'

'But what can she actually do to us, if we trust each other and we don't let her get between us?'

The question hung there between them.

Kate looked out of the window at the dark back yards and the dark terraced houses darkening further under the sudden hammer of rain. She could have had so many other lives.

When she was six, Dad had taken her to her first bike race. It was something they could do together, out of the house. Dad had seen the race advertised in the local paper – it could just as easily have been tiddlywinks, or judo.

Mum and Dad had argued at breakfast, that day. Kate was eating fried eggs. She didn't think about the argument too much. Mum had been grumpy for weeks – her new job made her miserable. She sold door to door, working for a company selling fabrics by the yard. Sometimes she went on road trips, and once or twice a month she had to stay the night away from home.

At breakfast on the day of the race, Mum snatched her plate before Kate had finished. She crashed it down by the sink. There were rings under her eyes. Dad said: 'We'll be back late, okay? I'll take Kate out for a pub lunch after the race.' He smiled and squeezed Kate's hand. She was thinking of a ploughman's, with the thick brown bread and the butter in a little gold wrapper. With cheese and chutney and pickled onions, strange and translucent, that you could prise the layers off one by one. Dad would have a pint of mild and she'd get a Diet Coke.

Mum said to Dad: 'Why do you always get to be the fun one?' And Dad said: 'That's rich.' That was when they argued. Kate put her fingers in her ears.

Sometimes, at night, she dreamed about finding money. Hundreds of pounds that she would dig up in the garden and rush inside and give to Mum, so she wouldn't have to work all the time.

Dad drove them to the race in the Rover 3500. The old car was beautiful. It was the dark, rich yellow of egg yolk. It was creaky and it rattled. But it was lovely and big and solid. It was your own world inside there, completely safe and unbreakable. Dad said she could sit in the front, for a treat. Mum was saying something. Dad closed the car door on the end of her sentence: 'What time are you planning on being—' Clunk. And then silence, because the doors were so big and heavy. And the smell of the vinyl seats. Also the smell of Dad. He did up her seatbelt. He wore an aftershave called Joop! with an exclamation mark, as if you were meant to shout it. Sometimes, when she was all alone, she did. Without really knowing why.

Joop!

Dad pulled out onto the road and she watched through the side window as Mum's lips moved.

'What's Mum saying?'

'I don't know.'

'Shouldn't we go back and find out?'

Dad sighed and squeezed her hand. He switched on the radio. The *Challenger* space shuttle had exploded, the day before. It had broken apart after launch. They were still talking about it – it was such a shock. One moment it was white and intact, like a milk tooth, a bright white shape in the clean blue atmosphere. And then the blue sky was full of the tiny pieces of white. Each colour was full of the other. Kate was sad because one of the astronauts was someone's mum. They'd said *Challenger go at throttle up* and then everything had disintegrated, the radio said. But Kate didn't want to hear. She hummed a tune with her fingers in her ears.

In the middle of the Rover's steering wheel there was a big, silver hexagonal bolt that held the steering wheel on. It was an instrument just like the others; always telling you that you were exactly eighteen inches away from death. People got killed by those bolts. The police arrived at accidents and they found dads with perfect hexagonal wounds right between the eyes, but no expression of surprise on their faces. They'd been aware of the risk. It had stared them in the face for years.

When they arrived at the race, Dad got her bike out of the boot. He held her hand and carried her bike to the start. There were forty or fifty kids there, and she was scared. Lots of the other girls were bigger than she was. Some of them had fast bikes, with drop handlebars and thin tyres. Hers just had Scooby Doo stickers. She hid behind Dad's legs till it was time for the race to start.

It was a grass track, with the course marked out by wooden stakes with thin orange rope strung between them. Kate was much faster than nearly all the others. She was so far ahead, she thought she'd done something wrong. She waited for someone to shout at her. Only one other girl was as quick as she was. They rode side by side for a while. Kate looked across and smiled, but the other girl didn't. Kate could have gone faster, but it felt mean to leave the other girl alone so she stayed with her. When they got back round to the start line at the end of the first lap, Dad was smiling. He gave two thumbs up. The other girl's dad was there too. He was shouting: 'Come on, come ON! You can beat her!' The other girl tried to go faster. Her face was getting red. Kate slowed down a bit, so that the other girl could too. They got around to the start line again. Dad cheered. The other girl's dad shouted: 'Come ON! You're quicker than this!' He was angry. Kate was scared for the other girl. On the last lap she slowed down even more, but the girl was getting tired. She clipped a stake with her handlebars and rolled across the grass.

Kate stopped her own bike and dropped it. With cold fingers, breathing in the muddy smell of wet grass, she picked up the other girl's bike. She said: 'Quick!' She was nervous because of the girl's dad. The girl looked at her. She was very small. She had mud on her face and the front of her tracksuit. She was starting to cry. Kate whispered: 'Don't.' She held the bike up and the other girl got on. The girl rode away, and the others all rode past while Kate was still getting back on her bike. She crossed the finish line last, in tears.

Dad said: 'That was so bloody unfair.' Kate was sobbing. She said yes, yes, yes, and she meant it was unfair that the other girl was scared of her dad. She couldn't explain it – why it made her sad that her life was easy; why she was scared of how happy she was.

Dad drove them away. The gears crunched. Dad drove faster than normal. His knuckles were white on the wheel. He said: 'You've got a kind nature, Kate. People will try to take advantage of that.' On the radio, they were talking about the objects they'd recovered from *Challenger*. A thousand tiny things had fallen to the sea, all at their own particular speed. There were mission patches floating on the waves. The heavy things had sunk beneath. Some of them would never be recovered.

Dad said: 'That girl shouldn't just have ridden off.'

Kate said: 'She was frightened. I wanted her to win.'

Dad was quiet for a long time, then he said: 'Kate, I'm more proud of you than if you'd won.'

He drove too fast around a roundabout. The tyres screeched. Kate closed her eyes and breathed in the smell of Joop!

Dad said: 'I'm sorry you had to hear all that, at breakfast.'

He said it quietly. He drove loudly. The bolt on the steering wheel glinted.

Kate said: 'It's just because Mum's tired.'

Dad said nothing. He drove faster.

He said: 'We're all tired, Kate.'

She held on to her seatbelt with both hands.

Dad drove straight past the pub.

Kate said: 'What about our pub lunch?'

Dad said: 'Let's see if Mum wants to come with us.' His voice was tight.

They got back home and Dad braked hard. Kate had to brace her arms against the glove box. There was another car outside their house, black and shiny and new.

She said: 'Who's that?'

Dad said: 'That's your mother's boss.' His voice was too quiet. 'Stay here while I go in.'

He made her wait in the Rover. That was okay. Nothing bad could happen while she was in there. Dad left the radio on. There was a lot of shouting from inside the house. She turned up the radio. They'd found hundreds of pieces of paper. They were sheets from flight manuals. They'd fluttered down to the sea. Some of them were just ashes. The heavy parts had sunk – the binders from the flight manuals, the metal binder rings. The instructions were floating loose on the sea. For how to fly to space. For how to reach escape velocity. Dad came out onto the driveway with Mum's boss. They were pushing each other. Kate was scared. She ducked down in her seat. She peeked over the dashboard. Mum was watching them from the front door, in her dressing gown. She saw Kate looking at her, and she looked away.

226

After the shouting, Mum left with her boss and Dad took Kate to the pub. She had a ploughman's lunch and he had pie and chips. He had a pint of mild. She had a Diet Coke, with ice cubes and a quarter slice of lemon floating in it. They didn't talk. The ice cubes in her drink were shaped like thimbles. If you held them upside down against the side of the glass with your straw, they filled up with bubbles. Dad sighed when he saw her doing it. She leaned against his chest. She whispered: 'Joop!' Dad said: 'What?' She said: 'Nothing.' She smiled at him. The ice cubes floated and clicked. Some of the words never sank and some of the heavier things were never recovered.

Dad smiled. He said: 'Before she left, Mum told me to tell you she loves you.'

She knew he was lying.

'Dad?' she said.

'Yes?'

'I'm more proud of you than if you'd won.'

Twenty-six years later, as she passed the plates to Jack to dry, she gave him the same quiet smile she'd given Dad that day.

'What?' Jack said.

'Maybe we're being paranoid. Maybe Zoe doesn't want to beat me any more than I want to beat her. Not if it means the other one can't go to the Olympics. I really think she's changed.'

He touched her arm. 'Well, one of you has to win.'

She tilted her head. 'Do you ever regret choosing me over her?'

He didn't hesitate. 'You know I don't.'

She scuffed a foot across the stained pine floorboards of their kitchen. 'Because this is the only track I really want to beat her on.'

Jack looked at her for a moment, then grinned.

'What are you smiling at?'

'We should sell tickets, then. If this is where the action is, we should get some seats in here, charge fifty quid a head, make a fortune.'

Wednesday 4 April 2012

Turkish Café, Ashton New Road, Manchester

Tom went to a place where they had all the papers. He tucked himself away at a corner table. He was the only customer, and it was too early in the morning. This was more of an evening place, with narghile pipes on the shelves and dark purple on the walls. From behind the brushed aluminium bar the waiter watched him with the polite curiosity reserved for old men who had become dislodged from their proper place in time.

Tom ignored him and spread out a paper. For a minute he couldn't bear to look. He waited, massaging his knees, watching the bright morning sun through the red, white and blue plastic strips hanging in the doorway. His coffee came, strong and muddy with sediment in a clear Pyrex cup. He eyed the newspaper sideways.

Everything about newspapers made him feel tired and defeated. The columnists were flies buzzing against a window, needing to be let out into life. The editorials chose their lines like intermediate skiers opting for the safety of the green and blue pistes, yet finishing with the rhetorical flourish and the triumphant fist pumps of a downhill champion skidding to a halt after a winning run. He wondered why people never grew weary of the bullshit. He hated that he'd allowed his athletes' lives to be so warped by it.

Every column inch had been an incursion into territory that he should have protected. If he'd been strong he would have said to Zoe: Have your termination or don't, and who cares what the papers say about you? If he'd had the integrity that the papers also lacked, he'd have made his riders choose, on day one, whether they wanted to be media faces with sponsorship deals or athletes with a single focus on results. Looking at the newspaper now was like looking at himself. He'd allowed his girls to race on the pages of the paper instead of the boards of the track – that was his failure.

He made himself look.

In the end the tattoo coverage could have been worse, but it still wasn't great. They'd gone big on Kate on the back page, and used Zoe for contrast. Kate was in the foreground, looking shy and excited about her tattoo. They'd linked the photo to the news about the Olympic entry change and treated it like a bet, as if Zoe and Kate had known before they had the tattoos done that only one of them could go to the Olympics. BRAVE KATE HAS SKIN IN THE GAME, was the headline. Under the picture the caption read, *Tats the spirit: Underdog Kate Argall gets inked alongside scandal-hit rival Zoe Castle, after shock ruling that only* ONE *of them can go for gold in London.* There was an inset photo of Sophie, bald under her *Star Wars* cap, smiling at the camera. The caption read, *Sophie: Mum's gold would mean so much to me.*

He sat in contemplation for a moment. His athletes were unravelling – this was undeniable. He'd always imagined that they could hang on, the three of them, for one last Olympics and then decide what to do. Now, though, he had to put his coaching head on and look the odds in the eye. The longer this went on, the more Zoe would get unbalanced and Kate would get demotivated. It didn't do to keep this tension between them, and as their coach it was his job to understand how to break it as quickly as possible.

If only he'd managed to straighten things out between them after Stuttgart, then maybe a lot of what had happened next might have been smoother. Instead, there'd been no reconciliation for months. Jack had become taciturn, taking his mood out on the track. However Kate had squared it with him, she hadn't been ready to forgive Zoe, and Zoe hadn't felt she'd been the only one to blame in any case. Zoe had felt resentful and trapped with her pregnancy, and Kate had suffered more with each day Zoe's bump grew. He'd done nothing – as a coach or as a friend – to get them talking. Finally the damage the silence did had brought them face to face on its own. He couldn't fail them like that again.

He drained his coffee and signalled for another. The radio was on in the café, playing Gold FM. Like the DJ said, they were number one with the solid gold hits of the 60s, 70s and 80s. Phil Collins came on, singing 'In the Air Tonight'.

The waiter arrived with the coffee.

Tom smiled at him. 'Brings back memories, eh?'

The waiter looked blank. 'What does?'

'Phil Collins.'

'Who is Phil Collins?'

Tom pointed at the speakers. 'Him.'

'Oh yes,' said the waiter. 'Very good music. Very nice.'

He nodded with pantomime enthusiasm and took Tom's empty cup away.

Tom wobbled his denture and a light sadness settled over him, like snow on a barbecue in winter. Away from the track, young people had begun to humour him. When they treated him like a

231

relic it made him think of future rooms where he would be encouraged to sit on wipe-clean vinyl recliners alongside others of his generation. He saw himself insisting that he'd once competed in an Olympic Games, while uniformed carers politely agreed with him. *I missed out by one tenth of a second*, he'd tell them. *One bloody tenth.*

That's lovely, Thomas, now eat up your soup or you won't be in top shape for the next Olympics, will you?

When he'd thought about old people's homes, he'd always imagined a soundtrack of Vera Lynn and the wartime greats. Now he realised that by the time it was his turn to be geriatric, the nostalgia music would be MC Hammer and Sade and Phil Collins. He imagined himself in a group of half a dozen tracksuited octogenarians doing seated light aerobics to Madonna's 'Vogue', and he understood immediately that he would need to kill himself in pretty much the same month that he retired from coaching. He would give himself maybe a week to get his papers in order, then find a sensible way of doing it. There was bound to be something involving pills – something relatively undramatic. He'd write a quick note, and then do it in a way that made the least possible mess for others to clear up.

He worried about who he should write the note to. An email to the police seemed overly self-pitying – it was surely an exaggeration to pretend there was no one else who needed to know. On the other hand, a suicide note would be a shitty way to get back in touch with his family. Matthew was best off not hearing from him again. This, too, was undeniable. He'd wanted his son to succeed where he'd failed and so he'd bullied him too hard in training. The kid had snapped one day and taken a bike lock to him, and that was the end of Tom's front teeth. A week later, his wife had left and Matthew had gone with her, and that had been that.

Sometimes Tom thought about it – had a flash of Matty's face for a moment, like now – but then his mind recoiled from the pain of it. It was okay, really. Each year the sharp edges of it grew softer.

In the empty café, Tom listened to Phil Collins and tried to analyse the lyrics the way he would if the artist was one of his athletes. Something was coming in the air tonight. Phil could feel it coming, so obviously it was something big. The guy had been waiting for this moment all his life, so whatever it was, it wasn't as if they came along every half hour.

These haunting chords; this echoing drum; this insistence that some cataclysm was imminent. Tom frowned as he thought about how he would advise Phil. He sat in the café and pushed his denture about with his tongue and stirred his coffee anticlockwise, languidly. His professional conclusion, finally, was that Phil Collins was just a fucker for never saying what the something was – this something that he alone had detected coming, like some balding airborne early-warning system with drumsticks and a reverb unit.

This was how Tom's mind rebounded from thinking about his son. Always, it skimmed the surface of the pain, then skipped off and attached itself to the nearest harmless distraction.

He looked at Zoe's photo in the newspaper. He knew there was grief in her past, as deep as his. He had no other explanation for the desperate way she behaved, or for the strong connection he felt with her. It wasn't love – he was too old for that – but it was a kind of unbearable affection. It wasn't even that she made him wish he was thirty years younger – life did that all on its own.

233

He growled at himself. It was frustrating. When all you knew was heart rates and lactic thresholds it was as if life gave you big emotions, but only these cheap little instruments to gauge them with. Phil Collins' lyrics held meaning the way a pocket mirror held the moon, and yet these insufficient things were all he had: these old pop songs in empty cafés, these gold medals his athletes had won, these small redemptions refunded by an idiosyncratic history that disqualified whole decades but counted every second in tenths.

Time had never behaved itself around him. It played like a scratched record, now repeating an endless phrase, now skipping whole verses so that things happened too late or too soon.

He could still feel the fierce pressure of Zoe's hands on his, in the delivery room. It was his fault that she hadn't carried the baby to term. It still haunted him that he hadn't been able to persuade her to stop training. All he'd managed was to slow her down slightly. She'd dealt with the pregnancy the way she would deal with an injury – keeping her training ticking over whilst accommodating the temporary restrictions on performance. Even when she was twenty-six weeks pregnant, he hadn't been able to get her to think of the baby as something that was actually going to happen. He'd talked to her about it at the velodrome one afternoon. He'd actually stepped out in front of her on the track so that she had to stop, and he'd held her handlebars while she struggled against him.

'Please,' he'd said.

'Please what?'

'Please stop. You'll hurt the baby.'

Her chest was heaving and the sweat was pouring off her. 'Don't be so melodramatic. I'm not pushing it. I just need to keep my basic fitness level up, and then as soon as it's out I can get back to race fitness for Athens.'

'Except that as soon as it's *out*, Zoe, it'll be a human being and you'll be its full-time bloody mother.'

She nodded and waited, as if further explanation was required.

'Well?' he said. 'Are you telling me the father's going to care for it? I got the impression he isn't involved.'

She threw her head back and laughed. 'You got that impression?'

He put up a hand. 'Look, it's none of my business who the father is, but you should consider asking him to help, at least. Babies are hard work. It's relentless. They need feeding and changing and carrying, day and night.'

'So I'll do those things. We'll work out how many hours it takes and I'll fit it in.'

'It's not like it's a list of tasks I can schedule round training for you.'

'Then what is it?'

'It's a life. You're supposed to give a shit.'

She looked past him, down the track. 'Of course I give a shit.'

'Then get off the bike, Zoe. You're twenty-three years old. All this will still be here for you when you're ready to come back to the sport. But right now, you need to get off the bike.'

She stared at him. 'It's Jack's baby, Tom. I'll get off the bike when Jack does.'

He was so surprised that he let go his grip on her handlebars, and she was so angry that she stamped down hard on the pedals and built up her speed way past any kind of safe limit. Each time she flashed

235

past him he begged her to slow down, but she only rode harder. Finally he just slumped in a seat and watched her ride.

After twenty laps Zoe slowed to a stop, racked her bike and warmed down slowly on the fixed machines in the centre of the velodrome. Tom took her a clean towel and an isotonic drink at ambient temperature.

'You okay?' he said.

She looked up at him. Her face was pale and there were black rings around her eyes.

'I'm sorry,' she said.

'Don't be. I'm just an old bastard who never got it right myself. I reckon you can do better than I did, is all.'

He arranged the towel across her back, and squeezed her shoulders, and used a corner of the towel to dab the sweat away from her face. She stopped pedalling then. She closed her eyes and leaned her head into his chest. He didn't know what to do with his hands, so he left them hanging helplessly by his sides. They stood there for a minute while the decelerating flywheel of the stationary bike made a mournful, descending note in the echoing space of the velodrome.

'I'm so tired, Tom,' she whispered.

'You'll feel better,' he said.

'Will I?' she said. 'Do you?'

He thought about it and then, because he was her coach, he said: 'Yeah.'

She smiled up at him. 'Liar.'

When it happened it was sudden. She got up from the exercise bike, took two steps towards the dressing room, and collapsed with a shout. He ran to her and she gripped his hands. When he realised what was happening, his legs almost buckled. He had just enough presence of mind to get her to change out of her British Cycling kit and into her civilian clothes. Whatever was going to happen now, he knew it would be easier for her without all the attention. When the ambulance came he got in it with her and she held on to his hands again, her eyes rolling. When the paramedic took his clipboard and asked him for the details of the patient, he gave them his mother's maiden name.

She was still gripping his hands, forty minutes later, when the paramedics wheeled her into the delivery room. They peeled off her clothes and laced a hospital gown around her, and Tom was careful not to look while they did it. The medics gave her injections to stop the contractions, but they didn't work. An hour after they'd arrived, the midwife told them that nothing was going to stop the baby coming.

'Are you the partner?' she asked him.

He shook his head. 'I'm just a friend. I'll wait outside, okay?'

Zoe gripped his hands. 'Don't leave me alone. Please.'

'I'll just be outside.'

She looked up at him, pleading. 'Please.'

Tom closed his eyes and opened them. 'Okay.'

The midwife looked levelly at Zoe. 'Just to confirm, are you happy for this gentleman to be present at the delivery?'

Zoe's face convulsed with the pain of a contraction. When it was gone, she looked up at the midwife. 'I don't have anyone else.'

'Is that a yes?'

'Yes.'

They gave her pethidine, and gas and air, and after that the contractions seemed to bother her less. He held her hand and dropped to his knees to whisper encouragement in her ear. Thirty-five years before, they hadn't let him in to the delivery room, but he told Zoe what he'd told his own wife just before they'd wheeled her away from him. He said what he'd said to all of his athletes, for decades: *Breathe*.

Zoe was disconnected with the shock and the opiates and the gas. She squeezed his hand and groaned.

'It's okay,' he said. 'It's okay.' He knew this was what you were supposed to say when it wasn't.

She rolled her head to look at him and her eyes were frantic.

'Tom,' she said. 'When they let me out of here, let's go straight back and finish the training session, okay?'

'Just breathe, all right? There'll be plenty of time for all that.'

She shook her head and writhed with pain. 'I have to get back.'

Sweat beaded on her face and her hand gripped his so hard that her nails drew blood. The midwife told her to push.

Tom was making sure to keep his eyes on her face, and Zoe had her eyes squeezed tight, and the doctors took something away but neither of them noticed, and no one explained anything to them.

Fifteen minutes later Zoe delivered the placenta, and both of them thought it was the baby.

'It's coming,' Zoe groaned. 'Oh God, it's coming.'

Tom felt an arc of tension rise in her body, and as it subsided he heard the heavy, flaccid weight of something coming out of her. He looked, expecting to see a newborn. Instead he saw a steak-sized parcel of gore in the midwife's hands. It was wrapped in a translucent and gelatinous jacket, like a clear dumpling. The umbilical cord trailed from it. He forced himself to look again, following the cord to the place that must be the belly button and trying to make sense of what he saw. He stared at the placenta for the longest time, thinking it to be the convexity of the belly, and searched at its extremities for the places where tiny arms and scrawny legs and an outraged little face should be. Not finding them, he felt a rising panic and a clawing shame that something had gone terribly and obscenely wrong. There was a hot metallic stink of blood, and the midwife was flustered and uncommunicative. Her attention was turned to what was happening now on the other side of the delivery room, where doctors and nurses were crowding around something on a table that was blocked from his sight by their bodies.

Zoe was flat on her back, exhausted.

'Is it okay?' she whispered.

Tom squeezed her hand and tried not to vomit.

'Yeah,' he said. 'Everything's fine.'

An orderly reached down with a latex-gloved hand and grasped the thing that had just come out of Zoe. Tom watched as the hand lifted the yielding mass into a large stainless steel dish, covered it with a plain green cloth, and placed it without ceremony on the middle shelf of the stainless steel trolley beside the bed. Of course, he thought – these people saw such things from time to time. It was natural that they were unsentimental.

So that's it, he thought. The thing wasn't viable.

He couldn't block out the image of its terrible malformation. He was only grateful that they weren't going to make Zoe look at it.

He knelt by her ear. 'Look, sweetheart,' he said. 'I have to be straight with you here. It was beautiful, but it was stillborn.'

She looked at him then, and he saw the relief in her eyes.

A few minutes later the doctors wheeled over the thing they'd been working on. It was a clear acrylic box, besieged by monitoring machines and perforated by cables. Inside was a tiny premature newborn, much

239

smaller than the hideous thing that the orderly had placed in the dish and taken away. This newborn was almost completely obscured by ventilating pipes, feeding tubes, protective headgear and plastic sheeting. Tom wondered why they were showing Zoe some other woman's baby. Maybe it was a psychological thing. Maybe if you'd just given birth to something monstrous, there was research that showed you needed to see a normal child immediately.

'What's this?' he asked them.

The midwife ignored him and smiled at Zoe. 'It's your daughter, Mum.'

Zoe waved her away as politely as she could while the orderly dabbed at her thighs with baby wipes. She explained to the doctors, clearly and calmly, that it was okay – that it was kind of them, but that she didn't need some other woman's baby. She told them it wasn't the end of the world for her that her child had been stillborn.

Tom watched their startled reactions.

'There's only nine months to go till Athens,' Zoe explained. 'I need to get back to training.'

The doctors had a whispered consultation, then hurried the baby away to the neonatal ICU.

Even when Tom grasped what had happened and talked Zoe through it, she didn't seem to feel any connection with the thing in the incubator. The doctors told her it was breathing mostly on its own. They were pleased – at twenty-six weeks, it was the best possible news. They set up a bed for Zoe next to the incubator, and they showed her how to scrub her hands and push them through the airlocked vents in the side of the box. She was supposed to touch the baby. Instead she fell asleep, washed out with fatigue.

Tom called Jack and Kate to the hospital. They came straight away and stood by the bedside, holding hands. They looked at the baby in its box. Kate sighed, and Jack held her tightly.

'She's beautiful,' said Kate.

'Yeah,' Jack said.

'She's got your little face.'

Jack said nothing; just looked at his daughter while tears ran down his cheeks.

Kate looked up at Tom. 'She told you the baby's Jack's?'

He nodded.

She looked down at Jack's hand in hers. 'What do you think?'

Tom shrugged. 'I don't think. I'm just here to help.'

They all looked at Zoe sleeping, on her side, with her knees drawn up. Her black hair was plastered to her face with perspiration. There was blood on the sheet that they all tried not to notice.

Kate stroked Zoe's face. Zoe didn't stir.

Kate knelt by her bed. 'Look what's happened, Jack,' she said quietly.

'I'm so sorry,' he said.

Kate didn't respond to him. 'She looks so weak. Zoe? Zoe? Oh God, is she going to be okay?'

'She'll be fine. Doctors say she'll be flat out for a while, but you know Zoe. She'll be breaking down the walls if they don't let her home in a couple of days.'

He tried to make it light, but Kate wasn't smiling.

'I should have just talked to her. It's been months since we spoke. I can't believe I just left her alone to deal with . . . all this.'

Tom touched her arm. 'Don't beat yourself up. It's not like any of us knew how to cope.'

Kate didn't take her eyes off Zoe. 'I'll make it up to her. She's my friend. And now look at her ... look at all this *blood* ... and she didn't have *anyone*.'

Tom nodded. 'But look at the baby, won't you? Don't tell me she isn't beautiful. None of this is something to be sorry about.'

They all looked in silence while the baby's pulse beeped softly from the monitoring unit attached to the incubator.

Kate stood and turned to Jack. 'What are you going to do?'

'I don't know.'

'Do you want to stay here with Zoe and ... your daughter? Do you want me to leave?'

He shook his head.

Kate hugged him around the neck and pressed her face against his. 'I should,' she whispered. 'I thought I could handle it, but I'm not a part of this. I should go.'

She looked at him with perfect desperation, got up and hurried out of the room. She paused in the doorway and Jack half rose from his crouch, but the despair came back into her eyes and she was gone.

Jack stood, looked Tom in the eye and nodded sadly.

'Oh, mate,' said Tom.

They hugged, briefly. Jack turned back to the incubator. He placed both hands on top of it and looked down at the face of his daughter.

'Coffee?' said Tom, after a while.

'Thanks.'

Tom went out for twenty minutes. He found a vending machine, bought a chocolate bar and ate it slowly to give Jack some time to get his head together. He bought two plastic coffees from another machine and held one in each hand as he reversed back through all the swing doors to the ICU. When he returned to the room, Zoe was still asleep and Jack had his hands inside the incubator, stroking the baby's cheek very carefully with the tip of one finger.

He said: 'Is she going to be okay, do you think?'

Tom put Jack's coffee down on Zoe's bedside table. 'I don't know. The doctors say she's twenty-six weeks. I don't even know how early that is.'

Jack nodded slowly, still looking down at the incubator. 'You think I'm an arsehole, right?'

'You talking to me, or the baby?'

'You.'

Tom sipped his coffee. 'I don't think you're an arsehole. You fucked things up, that's all. That's our primary role as fathers.'

Jack laughed sadly. 'I did it sooner than most.'

'Well, I always said you were spectacularly quick.'

Jack stared down into the incubator. 'Do you think she's all right in there?'

'She's probably looking up through the glass and asking the same thing about you. She looks snug as a bug.'

'Are you hungry?'

'Nah. I grabbed a Twix out in the corridor.'

Jack didn't answer, and Tom realised he'd been talking to the baby.

'Jack,' he said. 'Have you been seeing Zoe often?'

Jack shook his head. 'I slept with her once. After Kate chucked me out. It was a rough patch.'

'Think you could live with Zoe? Raise the kid?'

Jack turned to watch her sleeping. 'I'll help her raise the kid,' he said finally.

'No happy families, then?'

Jack looked at him. 'I don't love her. She doesn't love me either. I think it took us sleeping together before we could see that straight.'

Tom looked away.

'What?' said Jack.

'Mate, what is it with blokes your age? You've got psychological answers for everything. Look at Zoe. Look at her. She's fragile as hell, and just about the only thing that makes any sense to her is going to Athens. And now she's got a baby, and you've got away with it. Back in the day I'd have run you out into the bush and beaten the crap out of you till you took your bloody responsibilities.'

Jack looked him in the eye. 'You're not her dad,' he said quietly.

Tom stared back at him, blood pumping. He was so furious he could have punched him. Slowly, the pounding in his chest calmed down and he looked at the ground. His shoulders sagged.

'True,' he said.

Jack took a step back and ran his hands through his hair. 'I care about Zoe, but what am I meant to do? Emotionally speaking she comes up to here on me.' With the flat of his hand he indicated a planar surface two feet above his head. 'I think I could look after a baby, but I don't know how to look after her, and I don't want to. I don't love her, I love Kate.'

Tom looked down at Zoe. In sleep, the hardness was gone from her face. Her hands were tucked beneath her cheek and her nostrils flared softly with each breath. She looked very young.

Tom said: 'I think I can look after her, but I don't think she can look after the baby.'

Under the naked lights of the ICU room, Tom and Jack said nothing for a long time.

* * *

In the café, Tom finished his coffee. A measure of the thick sediment made it into his mouth and he ground it between his molars, tasting its bitter blackness. Phil Collins was still singing that he could feel it coming in the air tonight.

Tom was pretty sure that if Phil could be bothered to express the problem a little more honestly, he'd be able to coach him how to break it down into its constituent parts and solve it. This was how it worked, with coaching. If you were honest about the challenge, there was always a way to break it down.

Zoe hadn't wanted the baby; Jack hadn't wanted Zoe. Once Tom had expressed it like that, the solution had seemed straightforward. He'd sent Jack, Kate and Zoe off for a week to give everyone space to think about it, and he'd stayed in the hospital with the baby. Within a week Zoe was back in light training, and he was helping the nurses to change the baby's tiny nappies and switch the cylinders on her feeding tube. He slept in the bed they'd put there for Zoe, and he ate the food from the vending machines. The nurses called him Grandad, and he found it easier not to correct them. He called Zoe every day and asked her to come in, and some days she did. He would sit with her while they both looked at the baby's tiny hands swatting invisible flies in the incubator.

'Don't you want to hold her?' Tom asked.

Zoe twisted her hands together. 'I can't feel anything for her.'

'You can't, or you can't let yourself?'

Zoe hadn't taken her eyes away from the baby. 'If she isn't with me, it'll be better for her.'

'But are you sure you want Jack to take her? How do you know you won't feel different, a few months down the line?'

She pulled her knees up to her chin and stared at the baby.

'It's not about how I feel, is it? It's about how I am. I won't be good for her, Tom.'

A few days in, on one of Zoe's visits, Tom said: 'At least give her a name.'

'Sophie,' she said, without hesitation.

'Oh. You've been thinking about it.'

'I've been thinking about her all the time. I haven't been thinking about anything else.'

'Why didn't you say something?'

She closed her eyes. 'I didn't know if I could give her a name. I didn't know if I had the right.'

He hugged her. 'You just give her as much as you can. That's all any of us can do.'

The nurses wrote *Sophie* on the baby's wristband and wall chart. An unspoken optimism took hold in the ICU, now that the girl was attached to the world by more than her feeding and breathing tubes. The medical staff seemed to move more lightly, and a brightness came into their tone. Tom liked the name. There was something soft and hopeful about it that befitted a child whose claim to life was still provisional.

When Jack next came to the hospital, Kate came with him. They took over from Tom, taking it in turns to sit with Sophie while the other one trained. Tom watched Jack becoming the besotted father, and Kate falling in love with the baby too. He watched them for a month, with the same careful attention to positioning and body language that he gave to his riders on the track. Then, when he was sure it was going to work out, he helped them to arrange the legal papers. Jack had custody, Zoe had access rights, and the newspapers had a different story entirely. The papers would have destroyed Zoe for giving up her child, so Tom had her agent tell them that she'd had a stillbirth. It was the only cycling story the mainstream papers ran in the whole of the off-season. For a while they called her BRAVE ZOE, or TRAGIC ZOE, and they printed photos of her leaving training in dark glasses.

Three months later, Sophie was strong enough to leave the hospital with Jack and Kate. They waited another month, then announced through the British Cycling press office that Kate had given birth to a daughter and wouldn't be racing that season, but still planned to be fit for Athens. She didn't give any interviews, and Tom whispered into the ear of one or two reporters that this was out of respect for Zoe's loss. Jack did a three-minute segment on the BBC breakfast show and a light-hearted, self-mocking piece about new fatherhood in *The Times*, which appeared under his name with a photo of him in his racing kit holding Sophie gingerly, and was based on some vague notes he'd phoned in to the sub-editors at the paper. Because it had all happened in the winter, and Kate hadn't been seen in public since the Worlds, no one asked questions. She was just one more promising female athlete who'd put family first; Jack was just one more handsome guy rendered likeable by an anecdote about poo going everywhere at nappy change time.

Tom had run the whole deception. He'd broken every problem down into its parts and solved it. And in the years that followed, whenever Zoe broke down into parts, he'd done his best to solve her too.

Phil Collins faded out. Tom pushed his coffee cup away and looked at the newspaper photo of Zoe and Kate. Every day now the newspapers would raise the temperature. He knew they wouldn't all get through three months like this, before the Olympic qualifiers established which of the girls was going to race in London. Sooner or later, something would give. Zoe would do something stupid, or Kate would collapse under the pressure, or some hack would dig up the truth about Sophie. When you broke this problem down it had two parts: one, that the media was all over the rivalry between Zoe and Kate; and two, that they had a whole three months to make hay with it.

He put a fiver under his coffee cup, pulled himself upright and made his decision. He couldn't change the media, but there was a way of shortening time. He nodded at the waiter, hobbled out into the light, and phoned his girls one after the other.

Beetham Tower, 301 Deansgate, Manchester

It was still early when Zoe ended the call, put the phone down on the kitchen counter, and went to the window. It was a bright morning with cumulus clouds idling in the synapse between the skyline and the sky. She watched their shadows trailing at street level. The gaps between the shadows were surprisingly even. From up here you noticed patterns that seemed random when you lived on the ground. The clouds arranged themselves in the sky with the same instinct for separation as people in crowds. There were a lot of them up there, but you never saw them collide. There was no clumsiness in the way their ranked shadows marked a dappled time across the escapement of the city's roofs.

She put a hand against the plate glass to balance herself and lifted her ankles in turn to stretch her quads. Tom had phoned to ask if she would agree to race Kate the next morning, and to abide by the result. It would be better, he'd said, to get it over with than to tear themselves to pieces for three months while they waited for the formal qualifiers. She'd said yes without thinking, the way she always said yes to Tom.

Down in the city centre, on Princess Street and all along Portland Street, she picked out the adverts with her face on them. If she lost against Kate tomorrow, there wouldn't be another campaign. She'd be papered over with new ads. Here and there out in the suburbs, in this economy, a few orphaned posters might linger on the billboards. Green would be the last colour to fade. Her flesh tones would go first, then the silver edges of the ice cubes in the glass she held. Finally only her eyes would be left, with the slash of green lipstick and the fringe of green hair, tinted in post-production. She would look out across the grey streets from the white of washed-out adverts.

She shivered, and pushed the image away. She couldn't think of it happening like that. The only way she was going to wave goodbye to the sport was from the top of the podium in London. Tom must think she was going to beat Kate, or he wouldn't have asked her to race. He knew she wasn't built to survive a slow fade-out.

The only thing that kept her alive was winning, and without winning there was only blackness and despair. It had been like that since she could remember. She'd been born in a speeding ambulance after a very quick labour and the first sound she heard was sirens. What could you do, when you were born under a blue flashing light instead of a star sign? You could only keep ahead of your destiny. You could only count calories, and do 300 abdominal crunches every morning, and make your body your home.

At ten months she crawled faster than the other babies. When there were rusks and rattles to reach, she reached them first. At eleven months she toddled while the others only teetered. The old photos showed a blur of her in a tiny dress. At two she ran with her elbows sticking out, so no other kid could get past her.

Her mother found her second-hand machines to ride until she turned ten. Then, on the morning of her birthday, she raced downstairs and her first brand-new bike was waiting. It was wrapped in two kinds of paper, one a canary yellow, one red with stars. One roll hadn't been long enough. The bike was pink with white tyres, tinsel streamers on the handlebar ends, and a basket to put her doll in. She didn't love her doll, not so blindly that she was going to give her a free ride, so she unscrewed the basket to save weight. She loosened the screws with the point of a carrot peeler, then teased them out with her fingernails. She snipped off the handlebar tinsel with her mother's haircutting scissors. She knew boys rode their bikes quicker, and she reckoned maybe the difference was tinsel. She left it in plain sight on the kitchen floor, without sweeping it up, and she knew she'd get in trouble for it later. But if later really cared, it should try turning up at places sooner. She called upstairs to her brother Adam and told him it was time to race.

Adam was seven and a half, and much smaller than her. He rose up on his toes when their mother marked off their heights against the doorpost, but his mark still came a head below Zoe's. They had the same hair, a glossy blue-black. Their mother cut it for them while they sat on a three-legged stool in the kitchen, kicking their legs and listening to the Chart Show on BBC Radio 1. Debbie Gibson and the Fine Young Cannibals. It didn't matter if you were her son or her daughter: the haircut their mother gave was the one Luke Skywalker had in the first *Star Wars* film, the one where he journeyed throughout the galaxy but didn't meet anyone who took him aside and said:

Listen up, Luke, either grow it long and raffish or cut it properly and let's see those nice cheekbones. Zoe wanted to be a boy, and it upset her that Luke was so bad at it. Still, their mother wouldn't cut her hair short, and Skywalker's hair was what she had to settle for. Rather Luke than Leia.

They shared a bed in a small room under the eaves, and when their mother climbed the ladder to wake them each morning they'd be tangled around one another, puffy-eyed from dreaming, or wide awake and bickering about the details of a dream they'd shared. Their mother dressed them more or less the same, but she put butterfly-shaped hairclips in Zoe's hair, which Zoe could sometimes persuade Adam to wear if she took responsibility for him wetting the bed. As well as the hair, Adam had the same jade-green eyes and the same skill of not being in the room by the time you finished your sentence. They'd learned the trick of living fast and then accelerating away before they got in trouble for it. So of course she called for Adam when it was time to test her new bike from the top of Black Hill to the bottom. The handlebar tinsel was still on the kitchen floor, all mixed up with the jet-black clippings of the haircut their mother had given her for her birthday. She was supposed to sweep them up, but there was no time. Jobs like that, when you were ten, they took about two hundred years.

They lived in a small farmhouse with its own field at the end of a long lane. Their father had left when Zoe was four, so their mother did everything. As well as Zoe and Adam there were four dozen bantam hens and nine Jacob sheep. The Jacobs had four horns and devil eyes – they looked like Lucifer in a woolly jumper. There wasn't much to do apart from look at the sheep, and there weren't many cars in the lanes, so they rode their bikes wherever they liked. Black

Hill was their local mountain. It was 212 feet high, which was the highest altitude to which a human being could ascend without supplementary oxygen. From the top of the hill you could see the curvature of the Earth, if you held your head upside down at a particular angle.

The day of her birthday was hot. It was the alivest part of summer, the part where you could actually see the plants growing, out of the corner of your eye – although they froze the moment you looked at them. The wheat was on the turn but it was still fresh and green, with the poppies and the cornflowers spangling it. They rode out along the lanes, singing 'Back to Life' by Soul II Soul and taking their hands off the handlebars to clap out the rhythm. Swifts swung down to buzz them and flashed back up into the heights, screaming. When they reached the foot of Black Hill, they got off and pushed their bikes. The hill was so steep.

They shared a water bottle, one of the aluminium ones that the pro riders used in the old days. It was dented and scuffed, with just the vestiges of its original paint. Adam drank from it often and noisily, making sure Zoe noticed how pro it made him. It also made him have to stop and wee. She closed her eyes and listened and pretended that the sound of Adam's urine was hers, scattering insects and seeping into the soil and releasing the dark scents of clay and cool flint. She supposed boys took this consolation for granted. However bad things got, you could always make ants flee and beetles race for higher ground.

At the top of Black Hill they stopped to catch their breath. They tightened up their race helmets. It was 1989. It was before safety was invented. But Greg LeMond had just won the Tour de France in a futuristic streamlined hat – it had been on the television news – so she and Adam had made aerodynamic helmets out of chicken wire, paste and newspaper. The newspaper was the *Daily Telegraph*, which their mother took. Under the paste of Zoe's helmet you could see three quarters of the photo of the man in Tiananmen Square, standing in front of the tanks. The tank man was famous for being slow. Four tanks bearing down on him, every nerve of his body screaming at him to run, and somehow he stood his ground. It was the only kind of race you could win without moving.

Adam and Zoe drew up beside the oak tree they always used as a start line, and they turned their bikes so they pointed downhill. The lane was seven feet wide, lined with beech trees that roofed it in. The light was green and soft. She took the left-hand side of the road and gave Adam the right. She was older, so she could push him around like that. She chose the left side because the road curved to the left all the way down the hill, so her side of the road was shorter. She had a shorter line and she had a new bike with straight wheels. She was going to beat Adam hollow. He just grinned at her. He never worked out why he always lost their races. Or maybe he did, but he didn't mind. Adam just cared less than she did.

Their helmets were held on with string. You could see a fragment of a newspaper headline on the front of Adam's. It said JUBILATION AS. He grinned in the green light, with gaps where his grown-up teeth were growing, and the smell of blooming plants in the lane, and JUBI-LATION AS. She wondered: as what? They counted down from five and then they stood on the pedals. She began to inch ahead of Adam. Soon they were pedalling like crazy. She could hear Adam struggling for breath and giggling at the same time. The harder he chased, the quicker she rode.

They went so fast that her eyes began to stream. She couldn't see much, but there wasn't much you needed to see – just the high banks of the lane to steer between. The air roared over her ears, and she was shouting with the excitement of it, and so was Adam. You got up to this speed where the bike started humming beneath you, where the vibrations through the handlebars and the saddle drew you into a trance of concentration. You noticed everything. Every click of wing cases opening as ladybirds in the long grass verge took fright at your approach. Every concussion of tiny chips of stone, thrown up from the asphalt by your tyres and striking the tensioned steel of the bike frame. Time had the quality of indecisiveness. Everything was unusually quick and unusually slow.

She whooped. Adam echoed her, somewhere behind. Around the curve a car came quickly up the hill, black and soundless against the roar of the rushing air, and impossibly close. She saw the face of the woman who was driving it. She saw the O that her mouth made. Her lipstick was neon pink, unnatural. Zoe was hugging the bank to her left and the driver was hugging the bank to her own left, and Zoe shot through the gap between the car and her side of the lane. She was surprised. She thought: *You don't see many women wearing lipstick in these lanes*. Then she heard the bang, which was much louder than the end of the world, and she kept on pedalling.

She knew it wouldn't be true unless she looked back. She was certain that if she could ride faster than the news, the news would never reach her. This was the hour in which she began to emerge distinctly from the main fluid of time. She and time were oil and vinegar shaken up and left to stand: they began to separate back into magic and water. She rode flat out for twenty-five miles and when the police finally found her it was dusk, and she was on the dual carriageway, wobbling with exhaustion while juggernauts swerved and blared their horns. She was delirious. She asked the policemen if she was in trouble for cutting the tinsel off the ends of her handlebars and leaving it on the kitchen floor. They put her in the back of the police car, and they took off her papier-mâché helmet and laid it on the seat beside her. They took her to hospital and they gave her fluids, and later they gave her the news.

Her mother came to the hospital the next afternoon and drove her home, in silence. The tinsel and the hair were still on the kitchen floor. Her mother went to bed without a word getting said, and stayed in her room for ten days until her mind allowed her to answer the phone and consent to Adam being taken from the cold room and driven to the church to be cremated.

Cards and flowers arrived in the house. Zoe wasn't as sure it was over as everyone else seemed to insist. Several times a day she climbed to the top of Black Hill and raced down again, as hard as she could. The deal was, if she could ride faster than she had ever ridden before – if she could ride faster than time – then she would look around and Adam would be there again, racing along behind her. She was sure she could bring him back. There were so many deals she had made as a child, after all, and about half had worked and half hadn't. Once on Christmas Eve she'd slept in her sleeping bag on the floor, leaving her bed for Jesus to sleep in. In the morning she'd checked to see if the pillow had been slept on. It hadn't. But another time she'd ridden past a fox that had been killed on the road, without a mark on him, and he was still warm and his eyes glittered with black fire, and she made a deal that if she carried him to the foot of a silver birch tree and put acorns close to his head for when he woke up, then he would come alive again. And when she went back the next day to look, he was gone, and that was proof.

If she could cheat time of a fox, she could try to rob it of her brother. She rode down Black Hill again and again, faster and faster, and each time she looked back and Adam wasn't there, she thought: Next time I'll just go quicker. I'll never lose a race.

She didn't remember any one particular day when she stopped believing that winning would bring Adam back. She didn't know when she stopped looking behind her when she raced, to see if he was on her wheel. She just gradually grew up, and time with its self-regarding eye built a monument to itself out of her memories, raising it from the plains of her experience until it blocked her view of the past.

203 Barrington Street, Clayton, East Manchester

While Kate was still on the phone to Tom, Sophie came downstairs, hanging tight to the banisters and screwing up her eyes against the light.

'Tom,' Kate said, 'I've got to go.'

'Sure. Will you do it?'

'Yeah. I'll race her.'

'You can take a bit more time if you want. A week or two if you need to mentally prepare.'

She closed her eyes for a moment while she thought about it. 'No,' she said. 'I'm fine to race tomorrow.'

'Anything I can help you with? Anything you want to talk through with me?'

'No,' said Kate. 'Just have my bike ready.'

'That's my girl,' said Tom. 'Midday tomorrow then, okay? Come at eleven and get warmed up.'

'All right.'

Kate pocketed the phone and hugged Sophie. 'You okay?' she said.

Sophie was puffy from sleep. She broke out of the hug and looked at Kate as if trying to place her in the general taxonomy of species. 'Excuse me,' she said in a cracked voice, 'but what planet is this?'

'It's breakfast time on Earth,' Kate said. 'Rice Krispies or chopped banana?'

'Rice Krispies. Are you with the Empire or the Rebels?'

'Rebels. Juice or hot chocolate?'

'Juice. Where's Dad?'

'Training.'

Sophie groaned and sat down at the kitchen table with her head in her hands.

'You feeling okay, darling?'

'Yeah.'

'Really?'

Sophie pulled her knees up to her chin and looked out of the kitchen window without saying anything.

Kate felt a catch in her chest. She held Sophie close, noticing the slightness of her. It seemed that there was less and less of her each day. Kate closed her eyes and breathed in the smell of her daughter.

She'd loved Sophie from that first week in the hospital. She'd been totally absorbed – had adored her from the moment she saw her in the incubator. It just seemed obvious to her that no one so small should have to survive on their own. By the time she had sat with her at the hospital, for weeks, her heart quickening every time the unnaturally still little body moved an arm or opened an eye, Sophie had felt like hers. She'd taken naturally to the work of caring for her, of reaching inside the incubator to adjust her tubes, or to carefully wash her with a warm, damp cloth.

She'd been the one who mostly looked after Sophie. Jack had been happy to take his shifts, but Kate had found it hard to leave Sophie alone when it was her turn to train. There was always something more she felt she could do. The longer she spent with Sophie, the more in tune she became with the subtle rhythms of her sleeping and feeding, and the more she learned to work with those rhythms to nurse her into health.

When they took Sophie home they reaffirmed their commitment to equally divided childcare, but every time she saw Jack's clumsy attempts to look after Sophie, she found a new reason to stay and help. She could do every part of this new routine except pick up her kitbag and walk away from her daughter, even for the space of five hours.

In the end, Jack had ended up training far better than she had. A month before the Athens Olympics, he had won his place in the squad and Kate had missed out at the selection trials. She'd registered the fact with a dull shock that she buried under the routine of caring for Sophie. Then the double disappointment had come, when the paediatrician had told them that Sophie's immune system was still too underdeveloped to permit travel. It was perfectly normal with premature babies – it was nothing that time might not reasonably be expected to fix, he told her – but in the meantime Kate was going to have to watch the Olympics on TV.

She'd made a deal with Jack, when his plane tickets arrived and the reality of her exclusion finally started to hurt. After Athens they would take equal turns to look after Sophie, and both of them would get to race in Beijing. That had been their agreement.

In the end, missing out hadn't been as hard as she'd imagined. She and Jack had always planned to have children one day, once their track careers were over. If she let herself think of this like an ordinary accident – like a missed pill – then it was easier to think about. She told herself that Sophie was no different from one in three kids: unplanned, but not unwanted. She was happy for Zoe's successes, and the next day she felt no emotion more complex than joy as she watched Jack win gold himself. And then, when he proposed to her from the top step of the podium, she shouted 'YES!' out loud in their living room, two thousand miles away, alone with Sophie in front of their little TV. Twenty minutes later a dozen photographers were outside their house, and a camera crew let her talk to Jack live on air.

"Yes," she said again, more quietly this time. "Yes, I will."

On the doorstep Sophie smiled in her arms and that was the photo on the front page of all the papers the next day. Someone draped a Union flag around the pair of them to make the shot.

After Athens, a sponsorship deal came in for Jack. Nike were very generous. They could have moved to a bigger place somewhere quiet and nice, out in the southern suburbs, but they decided not to leave this ordinary street near the velodrome. They wanted to stay in real life. They filled their little yard with a plastic sit-on tractor, a sandpit, a tiny trampoline. They celebrated Sophie's first birthday in March 2005, not on the date of her birth but on the anniversary of the day they'd taken her home together from the hospital. Jack's dad got drunk, pulled off the oxygen mask he was dependent on by then, and gasped to Kate: 'Tae be honest, now that ye are family, it's better tae have all that bike nonsense behind ye in any case. The only reason women's cycling is even in the papers is because ae yer knockers in that Lycra, an' we don't want our granddaughter's mum getting that kindae treatment.'

She laughed, and she was pleased that Robert had called her Sophie's mum, but the next day she rode one hundred and forty miles. She left Sophie with Jack and headed out before dawn on her training bike. She turned right at the end of Barrington Street, rode seventy miles to Colwyn Bay, bought a bag of chips and ate them looking out over the Irish Sea. She was the only one on the seafront, in the drizzle. Then she rode home, flat out. She had a shower, made Sophie's tea, saw Jack's parents onto the coach back to Edinburgh, then phoned Tom to tell him she was ready to train again.

Tom and Dave helped them divide the waking day into four blocks of four hours. Six till ten, ten till two, two till six and six till ten. Each of them did two blocks of training and two blocks of parenting. Then they slept for eight hours, woke, and did it again, every day for three months without discussion.

When Jack's father died, it broke the routine for a week. At the graveside they stood hand in hand under an umbrella and watched the coffin being lowered. An arrangement of white carnations spelled 'DAD'. The undertakers had removed it from the coffin lid and laid it on the artificial grass, collecting rain. Kate wondered if they were supposed to take it home with them to Manchester. There was no useful anagram of the wreath; no obvious peacetime application. Were you meant to pixellate it, removing the carnations one by one and putting them in a vase? Or were you supposed to keep the arrangement intact, on the window ledge in the kitchen, until the earliest moment it could decently be slipped into the bin? When Kate's own father had died it hadn't occurred to her to spell anything out in flowers, and now she wondered if that meant she'd loved him too much, or not enough.

She squeezed Jack's hand and said: 'How are you feeling?'

'I don't know. Ask me after Beijing.'

'That's three years away.'

He sniffed. 'It's three years and two months. Let's talk about it when we've both got gold medals round our necks.'

They cranked up their training until the momentum was unstoppable. The fridge was racked with sports recovery drinks and Tupperware pots of kiddie food. The routine was endless. The floor of the shower was never dry. Childcare, training, shower, childcare, training, shower. Sleep. Repeat. Sunday was a recovery day. They laundered the Lycra. They froze pasta sauce in freezer bags labelled with the days of the week.

Her comeback event was the British Nationals in the autumn of 2005. The logistics were harder than the racing. She and Jack had to juggle heats, warm-downs, hydration, nutrition, finals, medal ceremonies and Sophie. The British Cycling staff were amazing. One of the girls took Sophie for the last day, when the intensity of the competition peaked. She walked around the technical area of the velodrome with Sophie on her hip, and Kate laughed and told the newspapers that her daughter was the only toddler in Britain who'd been assigned a personal trainer. She kissed Jack. She was perfectly happy.

She won the individual pursuit, the 500m time trial and the sprint. She beat Zoe in the finals of all of them. Jack won all his events too, but it was Kate on the front of the papers the next day. KATE'S GOLDEN COMEBACK, with a photo of her on the podium. Flowers in one arm, Sophie in the other. Sophie blinked at the camera flashes like a fruit bat woken from sleep. She wanted Kate's gold medals for herself. She put them around her own neck. She laughed, and the cameras loved her, and Kate became the face of Mothercare. They paid off the mortgage on the house, and they put Jack's mother in a nice new-build bungalow in the community she insisted on staying in.

As Sophie grew up, Tom fitted Kate's training blocks around Sophie's nursery hours. Sophie's first word was 'bye-bye!'

Her speech was slow to develop, but they didn't think much about it. She was happy and beautiful. Her second word was 'mutain', which meant: 'Mum is training'. She slept in between them on the bed. Kate loved it being the three of them, under the warm duvet, with Sophie's closed eyes twitching. She hadn't breast-fed her, but she felt she could feed her daughter with sleep. In the daytime she helped her line up her stuffed animals. Sophie told them off, mimicking Tom. She said: 'Iger or tain!' which meant: 'Tiger, you're over-training!'

In 2006, Kate and Jack cleaned up at the World Championships. In 2007, on her third birthday, Sophie was still smaller than she should have been. Kate marked her measurements on the height and weight chart. Sophie was slipping down the percentiles. Kate was worried, but Jack said: 'You know what the problem is? The girl's half English.' They were still making a joke of it at the end of that year. It was easy: they were still winning.

Manchester was great, and Jack and Kate agreed they were there to stay. Kids from the nursery came around for play dates, and Kate did her stretches while they tumbled together. Sophie liked playing with boys – she wrestled and fought and kicked, and she usually won. Kate and Jack could have done without the coughs and colds they brought, but it was nice to have that stream of tiny visitors. Sophie was the only one of the family with a social life.

Sophie blew out the candles on her fourth birthday cake weighing the same as she had a year before. She was taller, but you could see every one of her ribs. And yet you could see every one of Kate's ribs, too, and she was the face of healthy motherhood. Jack reassured her. They agreed that the average height and weight curves included a lot of kids who ate a lot of crisps. That made them dangerously fat but it didn't make Sophie dangerously thin.

They barely had time to discuss it in any case. They had a five-minute handover between training blocks, plus a quick chat at the end of each day if they could keep their eyes open. Every morning the alarm went at six and Sophie jumped on them, already dressed in her jeans and T-shirt and baseball cap. She tickled them till they couldn't pretend to be asleep any more. She yelled: 'Mum! Dad! Time to get QUICKER!'

Tom stepped up Kate's training again for the final push to Beijing. In head-to-head races, two times out of three, she was beating Zoe. Sometimes she won by a wheel-length, and sometimes there were only millimetres in it. She worked at a dangerous intensity. It could have made her ill. Tom paced every training session and monitored her blood counts to keep her just the right side of overtraining. Physios came to the house to work on her aches. A nutritionist planned her meals. British Cycling paid for someone to do the washing and cleaning. No British athletes had ever had the kind of monitoring and support that Kate and Jack had in the run-up to Beijing. Kate gave everything. She started beating Zoe three times out of four. She went to the edge of what was humanly possible and then, when all the hard work was done, they flew to China for the formality of picking up medals. Zoe flew out a month early, realistically looking at silver in the sprint and the individual pursuit but hoping that an extra week's training in the Beijing humidity might give her back the edge. Kate and Jack flew out as late as they could, since their family schedule was harder to translate to a new set-up. They topped off their training with one final superhuman blast in Manchester, then headed to Beijing to taper off and recover before the racing.

The flight was eleven hours. The cabin crew treated them like rock stars. Sophie had a cold, so Kate and Jack sat with their heads turned away from her, breathing shallowly, as if the germs couldn't find their lungs that way. Sophie sat between them, watching cartoons. Kate looked across her at Jack. This was the longest time awake that she'd spent with her husband in months, and she realised he was more beautiful now than when they had met. He was stronger; stripped down to the minimum musculature that would achieve his purpose. He was quiet and calm, in a sky-blue hoodie. His hair was just turning grey at the temples. He smiled. It made her shiver. She reached across and held his hand.

When the flight attendants brought a meal, Kate and Jack refused it. They were on their own eating schedule, and Sophie wasn't hungry either. When she fell asleep with her head on the fold-down table, Kate noticed she had a bruise on the back of her neck: a big bruise, purple-black and angry. She asked Jack how it had happened, but Jack didn't know. It was typical, really – it wasn't the kind of thing he noticed.

There were screens on the seatbacks, with a tiny picture of their plane tracking across the map. Here they were. She leaned across Sophie and kissed Jack, 35,000 feet above the central Asian steppe. Sophie had drawn a picture before she fell asleep – the stewardess had given her crayons. Kate eased it out from under her head because she was dribbling on it. She used the backs of her fingers so as not to get the germs. It was a nice picture. On the high branch of a tree, a baby owl was nestling between its owl parents. The daddy owl was blue, the mummy owl was pink, and the baby owl was carrying a lightsaber. Kate hardly saw the picture. She was visualising the Beijing velodrome. Tom had shown her videos of the inside. He'd given her this exercise to do on the plane: visualise victory. Picture every nuance. Own every inch of the venue.

Sophie slept all the way to Beijing. Kate hadn't expected that. She'd brought games, toys and books, and if those failed she was going to bribe the girl quiet with Jelly Tots. She had six packets in her bag. But Sophie just slept. When they landed, Kate had to wake her up. She awoke confused and angry, like a little animal at the vet coming round from anaesthetic. On her forehead there was a new bruise from where she'd fallen asleep on a crayon. But Kate wasn't seeing the bruise, she was visualising victory.

She couldn't believe they were finally in China. Beijing was like landing on Mars. Sophie's new bruise didn't fade, all through immigration and customs, but Kate thought: it's just a bruise. Sophie fell asleep again in her arms, and she held her so her breath went the other way. You didn't train for twenty years just to catch a cold right before your big event.

A car was waiting for them, and it drove them across the city. Sophie fell asleep on Kate's lap. They arrived at the hotel that the British Cycling squad was using, and Jack lifted Sophie out of the car. His fingers left bruises on her arms. Kate and Jack finally started to notice.

The two weeks in Beijing were a blur. Sophie was in and out of hospital. It was complicated. The doctors thought it was a lung infection. Then they thought she had a problem with her kidneys. She was running a temperature. The IOC gave them an interpreter. The interpreter had learned the vocab for twenty-eight sports, but she didn't know all the medical terms, so it was hard for Kate to judge how serious it was. Doctors talked at them and their sentences went on forever. Afterwards the interpreter would touch her arm. She would make a sad face, and her translations were short. *Doctor says your child quite sick.* The doctors watched the interpreter while she translated. Kate couldn't translate their expressions.

She and Jack took turns to train at the Olympic velodrome while the other went with Sophie to the hospital. When they weren't training, they sat with Sophie in their hotel room. Kate hardly slept. She woke up and went training. Or she woke up and cried. She woke up feeling too weak to ride, and went to the velodrome and watched Zoe getting stronger.

They did more tests. The interpreter came with them to the hospital again. They sat in a small room and waited for the doctor. There were no windows. There was a round table with a white plastic veneer and coffee rings. There was a clean white plastic vase with pale flowers. There were bright halogen spots. There was a painting in a plastic frame, of one white horse, running. The carpet was grey and there were grey stacking plastic chairs. They sat for half an hour, and the interpreter translated their silence perfectly. Sophie slept in Kate's arms, in her black *Star Wars* pyjamas. There were footsteps in the corridor outside. Each time footsteps approached, they all turned towards the door. Each time the footsteps passed by, they looked back at the floor. The air conditioning rattled. There was a fourth chair in the room. It was empty, for the doctor when he came.

The walls seemed to warp and shift. The hands of the clock

seemed to surge forward in a sudden gust, then stand for long periods becalmed. The room was adrift in time. The interpreter wrung her hands.

When the door opened, Kate jumped.

The doctor unbuttoned his white coat. He sat down. He put one hand on his knee. He checked his notes and looked up. He talked to them for a long time. Then he stopped talking and looked at the interpreter. She had brought a dictionary. She flicked through the pages. Then she looked up at Kate.

She said: 'Your daughter has leukaemia.'

'She has what?'

The interpreter checked the translation again, marking the word with her finger and showing it to Kate. 'Lew-kee-mee-ya,' she said. 'You are unhappy as one in ten thousand people. Now you must start angry medicine right away.'

Nearly four years later, at the kitchen table, Kate began counting the day's pills into the silver cup for her daughter. Already she could feel the adrenaline sharpening her gestures and scattering her thoughts in anticipation of racing Zoe the next day. She counted out the sixteen pills like old friends, knowing that by the time they were gone only one sleepless night would remain between her and the race that might be her last.

National Cycling Centre, Stuart Street, Manchester

In the afternoon, Tom wheeled his girls' race bikes up from the store and installed them on stands in the centre of the velodrome. Half a dozen riders from a youth squad were training on the track, and their coach's instructions rang through the otherwise empty building. Tom let the action revolve around him at a distance while he focused on his preparations.

He spun the wheels on both bikes, looking for trueness and alignment. He checked that the mechanic had installed the right gear for each rider. He made sure the tyres were new, and checked the air pressures. All of this was the mechanic's job tomorrow morning, but Tom didn't want to leave it that late to discover that some vital part was defective.

When his checks were done he stood between the two bikes, one hand loosely closed around a handlebar of each. In the way the machines were set up, you could feel something of the riders. Zoe's bike was bigger, with two more inches of height in the frame and three extra inches of reach. She rode with a bigger gear and used the long levers of her legs to power the pedal stroke around. Kate's ride was more compact, with a lighter gear that she spun till her legs were a blur, making up for her relative lack of power with a phenomenal work rate. Kate's machine was painted simple white, with a passport-sized image of Sophie's face smiling up from the top tube under the clear lacquer of the finish. The bars were wrapped with a light pink bar tape that was springy and warm to the touch. Zoe's bike was unpainted, so that the functional lay-up of the dark carbon fibre was visible under the matt varnish. Her bars had a black rubberised grip on the drops. On each side of the seat tube, visible from whichever side her opponent lined up beside her on the start line, was written UNDEFEATED in large gold letters in an Old English typeface. While Kate's bike was designed to make her feel at home in the cockpit, Zoe's was calculated to intimidate.

There was an intimacy just in touching these machines whose

frames fitted each rider as precisely as her own bones; these frames that had carried their riders, the two women he cared most about, to limits of pain equal to, and occasionally beyond, their emotional breaking point. Tom gripped the handlebars and grappled with the feeling it gave him to know that after tomorrow, one of these bikes would never be raced again. By 1 p.m. the next day he would be wheeling one of these machines back down to the British Cycling gear room, while the loser took their ride home with them as a souvenir, to sit in the hallway for a few months and then finally, when the pain and the shock had sufficiently receded, to be auctioned off to benefit a charity of her choice.

When he allowed himself to visualise the aftermath, the physical act of wheeling the winner's bike back down to the room where dreams were held in trust, he knew it would be better if Zoe won. It wasn't that he would prefer her to win – he'd never allowed himself to confuse the closeness he felt to her with a wish that she should prevail over his other athlete. It just seemed true, as the coach of both women, that if you extended your remit beyond simple results on the track and into the domain of their general welfare, then it would be better for Zoe to beat Kate tomorrow. Kate had reasons to carry on living if she lost.

It was shitty, though. If anyone deserved a go at the Olympics it was Kate. Back in Beijing, when Sophie was first diagnosed, there'd been six days to go before the cycling events. He'd caught up with them an hour after the doctor gave them the news, when they didn't know if Sophie was going to die or not. He'd been briefed by the doctors, and because it wasn't his own kid he'd had just enough detachment to ask some follow-up questions. He knew more than Jack and Kate did.

He'd had to fight his way in to the hotel through a press of reporters. Somehow, the media had worked out that there was a story. The opening ceremony was underway, and Jack and Kate weren't there, and the reporters had done their asking around. Britain's two best medal hopes, and some kind of medical emergency. That's all they knew, and Tom wasn't giving them anything else. He'd barged his way through the pack in the hotel lobby, stonewalled their questions, and got the general manager to take him upstairs in the service lift.

When the manager let him into the room, Kate and Jack were kneeling by Sophie's bed. Her eyes were motionless behind her eyelids. Kate's phone was going off and so was Jack's. The TV in the room was on quietly, showing the opening ceremony. There were fireworks, and showering silver stars from the roof of the stadium. All the teams were draped in their flags, smiling and waving as they lapped the track.

He made them both sit down on the end of the bed and he took away their phones. They sat there like children, looking up at him.

'Okay,' he said, 'I've been talking to the doctors, so let me break this down for you.'

He pointed at Sophie. 'Fact one. Ninety-one out of a hundred kids in her condition recover, so this is a very positive situation we're managing here. Fact two, you do not want to get her involved with the treatment protocols in this country, because none of us will understand what the hell is going on and you won't be able to make the right decisions for her. Therefore, fact three, one of you has to fly home with her in the morning. This is what I gather from talking with the doctors here, and I've also been advised by a consultant in Manchester who's ready to organise Sophie's admission.'

Kate couldn't look at him. She leaned over and buried her face in Sophie's neck.

Tom said: 'Unless you think there's another way to do this? We could assign someone to fly home with Sophie, but you're not going to let her go home without one of you, are you? Not to start chemo. If I thought there was any way we could still have both of you medalling at these Games, then that's what we'd be doing. But one of you competing is the best we're going to get out of this situation.'

Jack put an arm around Kate. He said: 'We'll both fly back.'

She squeezed his knee. 'Yeah. We'll both go.'

Tom knelt on the floor. He looked from one of them to the other. 'No.'

There was silence.

Tom said: 'I don't blame you for not seeing it straight, but this is all about winning outcomes. You can get Sophie better. And you can win gold. If one of you stays, you can achieve both of those things as a family. That's how you have to look at this.'

Jack said: 'No, Tommo. No.'

'Dave will tell you the same, Jack. Call him if you like.'

'You've talked to him?'

'Of course we've talked. We both reckon one of you needs to win now, for the three of you. You simply don't train as hard as you guys have trained to come away with nothing.'

Kate looked at Jack. Both of them were stroking Sophie's hair and face, as if they might make her better with their hands.

Kate said to Jack: 'Is he right?'

Jack held his head and grunted, as if containing an explosion in a limited space.

'And I'm sorry,' Tom said, 'but you need to think about the money side of this too. At least one of you has to keep your sponsor happy. The next couple of years are going to be hard, and the last thing you need is to drop both of your incomes.'

Kate turned to Tom, and he watched her forcing herself to breathe. 'Okay,' she said at last. 'Who stays, and who goes home?'

'That's the question, isn't it? I think you two have to choose.'

Jack groaned again, and the sound was so desperate that Tom found his own hands twisting. He wondered if Kate was getting her head around the situation more quickly because she was stronger than her husband, or whether it was easier for her because it wasn't her biological daughter who lay on the bed between them – dying, for all any of them knew. Maybe there was a deeper level of pain in the blood. Certainly when he'd told Zoe, she'd taken the news like a direct hit from a bus. She was only out there now, at the opening ceremony, because Tom had made her attend. They couldn't risk the media making a link between her and Sophie.

Kate looked at him. 'How would you decide, if it was just about the results?'

'On purely sports performance grounds?'

'Yes.'

Tom hung his head for a long time. He massaged the back of his neck.

'You know I hate this, right?'

'Yes.'

He looked straight at her. 'Jack's a sure-fire bet for gold, I reckon. And you're in the form of your life. If this was about results, I'd ask Zoe to take Sophie home.'

He watched her face carefully as the shock came into it. She drew closer to Sophie and held her, instinctively. 'No,' she whispered.

He pushed a little harder. 'Let's send Jack home with Sophie, then, and let you race. It's your turn.'

She shook her head and stroked Sophie's hair. 'I can't leave her,' she said.

She swallowed. She knew it was the end.

Jack put his hand on Kate's shoulder. 'But it's your turn,' he said.

She looked down at Sophie, and ran her fingers over her pale cheek, and neatened up the collar of her daughter's dress where it had become folded inwards.

'I just can't leave her,' she said simply.

Tom stood up and took a step away, to give them a little space. 'Then I'm sorry, Kate. You'd better pack your things.'

Kate said: 'Fine.'

He could tell she was concentrating on not crying. The next few days were going to be all about helping her to break the hours down into achievable goals: not crying, not screaming, not fainting. If she could perform these feats to Olympic level, there was a possibility that she would get through the week.

Jack put his head in his hands. Now that the decision was made, no one knew what to say.

The BBC sports anchor was on the television in the hotel room, looking serious. He was standing in the downstairs lobby, talking to camera. They cut to footage of Jack winning gold in Athens, and Kate on her doorstep accepting his marriage proposal on live TV, with Sophie in her arms and the flag draped around them. They cut back to the sportscaster, who had one hand on his earpiece and one hand holding the mic. *All we know at this time is that this looks like a grave, grave situation.*

Sophie woke up crying. She said: 'I feel *bad*.'

Jack cradled her head. He whispered in her ear: 'It's going to be okay, brave big girl. You're just tired. You're going home with Mummy for a nice rest.'

Puts the whole thing into stark perspective, the sportscaster was saying. *We can easily forget, underneath all the glitz and the glamour of an Olympics, that these are real people, real families like yours and mine.*

Tom watched Kate looking down at Sophie, and at that moment Sophie looked up at her and reached out her arms in that gesture small children make when they want to be held. The trust in her face was simple: she felt terrible, and it was something she knew Kate could deal with. She didn't know this was different from all the banged knees and the earaches and the bad dreams that Kate had spent years soothing.

Kate picked her up, and Sophie clung to her and laid her head on Kate's shoulder. Kate stood with her for a long time. Then Sophie reached out to Jack, and he took her and rocked her and whispered into her ear.

Kate walked to the window and looked down on the street where a crowd of cameras was already gathering.

Tom went over to her. He said quietly: 'More than anyone, I know what you've gone through to get to these Olympics and I know what it will cost you to walk away. In a few hours you will get on a plane with your daughter, and doing that will hurt more than childbirth. And do you know what? This is how you'll know you're her mother.'

Kate leaned gently against him. 'Thank you,' she whispered. Tears welled in her eyes.

'You can do this,' Tom told her. 'You can make your daughter better. The doctors tell me it'll be a hard and painful and slow road, but she is going to get well again.'

'I know I can do a hard road,' she said. 'I know I can do a painful one. But you'll have to help me deal with slow.'

203 Barrington Street, Clayton, East Manchester

As the sun sank below the bowed roofs of the terrace, Jack ran Sophie a bath and helped her get undressed. She was listless and vacant in the bath. She sat upright and twisted the flannel half-heartedly between her hands while Jack made up a story for her. He had Luke Skywalker and Han Solo pilot the *Millennium Falcon* through a difficult asteroid belt. Doing all the actions and sound effects himself, he had the two heroes beat overwhelming odds to defeat an attack fleet of TIE fighters. Then, since none of it provoked a response from Sophie, he had the exultant Han and Luke kiss passionately in the cargo bay of the *Falcon*. They were surprised in the act by Chewbacca, whose rage response showed that he had old-fashioned views on human love which were typical of his species and yet unbecoming in such a well-travelled Wookiee.

Jack watched Sophie's face but she only stared, glassy-eyed, at the taps.

'Are you even listening, missy?'

He snapped his fingers. 'Hey! Earth to Sophie Argall. Come in, Sophie!'

She turned her head slowly and squinted at him. Her expression was that of a naturalist who thought – but was not entirely sure – that she might have detected the outline of a well-camouflaged creature amidst the foliage.

275

'What?' she said.

'Are you okay, darling?'

She closed her eyes. 'I just want to go to bed, please.'

Her voice was a whisper that barely carried over the buzz of the extractor fan in the bathroom.

Jack lifted her out of the bath, towelled her, pyjama'd her and sat her on his knee to clean her teeth.

'It's going to be all right, honey,' he told her. 'You're going to be okay.'

'Yeah,' she said.

He kissed her on the forehead. Her skin was hot, but maybe it was just from the bath.

'Think you've got a temperature?'

She shrugged.

Jack found the digital thermometer in the bathroom cabinet and took a reading in her ear. The little screen said 101.5.

'I'm going to give you some Calpol,' he said. 'I don't want you to tell Mum, okay?'

'Why?'

'Because she's got a big race tomorrow. We don't want her to worry about a little thing like this, do we?'

Sophie shrugged again. 'I'm fine,' she said, but she let Jack feed her two spoonfuls of the liquid paracetamol.

He put her to bed and she went down without a murmur. She felt hotter than she had before. He knew he should say something to Kate and at the same time, he knew he shouldn't. He sat on the top stair for a long time, thinking it over before he went down.

Kate was sitting at the kitchen table with her eyes closed and her hands gripping the table edge, leaning to the left in her chair.

'Tea?' he said softly.

She frowned, still with her eyes closed. 'Shh. I'm visualising.'

He touched her on the shoulder. 'Visualise a cup of tea?'

She leaned her head against his arm. 'Yeah, go on then.'

He busied himself with the kettle and the teapot.

When he came back to the table, Kate said: 'How was Sophie?'

He put the teapot down. 'Great. We were doing a story and she loved it.'

Kate poured a cup and blew on it. 'I have trained you to use a teapot, Jack Argall. Of all that I have achieved, this will be my legacy.'

He studied her face. 'You okay?'

'Excited. I think I can beat her.'

'I think you can too. Just don't do what I did in Beijing.'

She smiled and held his hand. 'It's different now. Sophie's getting better.'

'Yeah,' he said, brightly.

He looked down at their hands, entwined on the tabletop.

In his first heat in Beijing, he'd lined up against one of the French riders – he hadn't even learned his name. He'd shaken his hand on the start line and tried out his French on the guy, in the name of international relations. He'd said: *Bonjour, feller.* The Frenchman had smiled but he'd looked scared shitless. Jack had felt sorry for him, coming up against Jack Argall in the first round.

That velodrome in Beijing was astonishing. It was packed. There were twenty thousand men, women and children in the stands, and half of them were taking photos. As the clock counted down to the start, the camera flashes increased like the souls of the saved until they weren't individual points any more but one great urgent web of light, shimmering and pulsating across the surface of the crowd like the signals flowing over the skin of a creature from the deep. And the roar the crowd made – it was colossal. It gave Jack the fear. He had earphones on inside his helmet, and an iPod tucked into the sleeve of his skinsuit. He was listening to the Drambuie Kirkliston Pipe Band blasting out 'Battle of Killiecrankie'. That was a tune to make the devil afraid, but it wasn't enough to drown out the din of the crowd. The whole surface of the track was trembling. He could feel the buzz of the crowd transmitted right up the seat tube of the bike, and through the rigid carbon saddle to his arse. The insides of his lungs vibrated with it. His teeth hummed as if they were picking up radio. The atmosphere sliced through his nerves, pulled them free from his carcass and discarded them like the string from a Sunday roast.

Trackside, there were TV cameras everywhere. They had a camera on a zip wire that hovered in to a foot in front of his face, like a huge black wasp. It showed his face, twenty metres high on the gigantic screen they had there, suspended above the centre of the velodrome. He had his helmet on with the blue silvered visor that came all the way down past his nose, so naturally he gave the crowd his Judge Dredd face. And they loved it, and they gave him a cheer and stamped their feet till the whole venue shook.

He looked across to the Team GB support crew in the technical area. His coach was giving him the hand signals to calm down, to focus on the countdown and stop playing with the crowd. So naturally Jack raised his hands high above his head and began to clap out a rhythm in time with the music in his ears. The crowd roared even louder. They clapped when he clapped. The noise was incredible. Twenty thousand souls from every nation on Earth clapping out the rhythm to 'Battle of Killiecrankie'. It was possible to forget, just momentarily, that Sophie was five thousand miles away, in a small room, starting chemo.

Playing with the crowd, he grinned. He watched himself clapping on the massive screen. It showed him in slow-mo. The muscles punched out so hard each time his arms engaged, there looked to be an alien under his skin, fighting to get out. *Christ*, he thought, *I really am stupendously strong.* The camera zipped in close to his face again and without thinking about it he yelled: *This is for you! Get well soon, Sophie!*

He looked across at the GB crew. Next to his coach was the mechanic. Two hours before Jack had even showed up, this guy had been here to disassemble his bike, clean it, lubricate it and reassemble it, using a chart recording his set-up preferences to the half-millimetre. The man had cranked every Allen bolt to within 0.5 per cent of its optimal tightness using a digital torque wrench. Then he'd examined Jack's tyres, inch by inch, with a magnifying glass, looking for the tiniest sign of damage. If he found anything, he replaced the tyre and started again. One hour before Jack had left the hotel, his coach had showed up at the velodrome, checked the mechanic's work, and made sure there were clean towels trackside and a static warm-down bike ready and cleaned for after the heat. Next to his coach and the mechanic was the assistant coach. Half an hour before Jack had arrived, the assistant had turned up with an insulated bag containing isotonic energy drinks for use during his warm-up, and high-protein recovery drinks for after the heat. All these drinks were brought to body temperature, in order to place the minimum physiological stress on his system. Next to the assistant coach was the team physio. He'd been monitoring Jack's pre-warm-up stretches and preparing the massage room for after his post-heat shower. Next to the physio was the GB medic, and he was on station in order to respond within fifteen seconds in the event that Jack should crash, or collapse, or go into some kind of seizure induced by the combination of adrenaline, twenty thousand cheering human beings clapping to his rhythm, and a bagpipe tune commemorating a victory by the forces of James VII of Scotland over William of Orange of England. Jack wasn't sure what the medical term for that would be.

He looked at all of these people – all of this apparatus that was supposed to make him win – and a hollow feeling grew in his stomach. He couldn't keep his focus away from the fact that Kate and Sophie were riding a harder race. The bagpipes careened around his head. The crowd drowned out the drone notes. He tried to keep his head in the game, but a chill was quickening inside him.

Two things happened then. One, the French guy rode away from the start line. Two, Jack's coach started making frantic hand signals, pointing at the disappearing Frenchman as he rode off down the track. Jack was thinking: *That's inexperience for you. The poor bastard's so nervy, he's gone before the whistle.* But his coach was still waving his hands and shouting, and the French rider was twenty metres down the track and looking back over his shoulder. Jack was thinking: *The guy's going to see what's happened, and he'll have to turn around and come back to the start line, which will be mighty embarrassing even for a man accustomed to the popular music of Johnny Hallyday and Jean-Michel Jarre.* But the guy didn't turn round. He put his head down instead, and sped up. So Jack turned off his iPod to get a better idea of what was happening. That's when he heard the entire crowd falling into a sickening silence. In the sudden quiet his coach was shrieking at him to go! go! go!

Shit, he thought, *I've only gone and missed the start.* But he knew that with the kind of effort he was easily capable of putting in, he could still catch the French rider. He was calm. He popped up from the saddle and powered down onto the cranks. The Frenchman had fifty metres on him, and he'd abandoned any tactics: he'd seen his chance and he was just going flat out for the line. Jack dug deep. He put everything into the chase, and by the end of the first lap the gap was down to thirty metres. He could feel his face contorted with pain, but it was working. As he crossed the lap line, his coach gave him a double thumbs up from trackside.

He wound it up even harder, forcing that last fraction of one per cent out of his body. He was getting there. The frame of the bike was flexing with each pedal stroke. It was the stiffest bike ever built, and it couldn't cope with the power he was laying down. By the end of the second lap, the Frenchman was only ten metres ahead. Jack's heart rate was at 195, power at over one thousand watts. The journalists covering the race from the press pit could have run a two-bar electric heater off him and still had enough power left over to drive their laptops. Jack was thinking, this is what they will write about me: *Awesome, awesome, awesome.*

And then he thought: *Sophie.*

A picture formed in his mind. He was alone in a room, holding Sophie's hand as she lay absolutely still. It was hard to tell, from the picture, if she was alive or dead. The image snatched his breath and broke his rhythm. He lurched, and for a moment he stopped gaining on the French rider.

He tried to get back on the pace. *Pedal pedal pedal. Breathe breathe breathe.*

But the image came back to him, more distinct now. Sophie's hand in his, her face a mask of stillness.

His coach was making more frantic gestures from trackside. He was shouting: *Step it up! Step it up!* At the end of the third lap, Jack was twenty metres behind. He wound it up as hard as he could, and his coach was shouting, *Let's go, Jack, that's it!*

The picture came back.

He couldn't block it out any more. All the force poured out of him, as if someone had pulled plugs from drain holes in the soles of his feet. The Frenchman beat him by forty-five metres. Jack was only just coming out of the curve onto the home straight when he saw him cross the line with his hands in the air.

The crowd was very quiet. There was a stillness in the velodrome. The humidity was overwhelming. Sweat poured off Jack in hot sheets. He slowed to a halt over two laps and grabbed the trackside rail to lean on. His chest was heaving. He was too exhausted to even get off the bike. The medic raced over with his bag. His coach ran up and put an arm around his shoulders.

'The fuck just happened there, Jack? Are you okay? The fuck was that all about?'

The pain was burning all through him. It was agony – he realised he was actually groaning. The medic was asking him: could he tell him the name of the Prime Minister? He had a stethoscope on Jack's chest. Dave was in his face asking was he all right? He sat there with his body shaking and he let the physio cool him down with a sponge, like you'd do with a racehorse.

His mind kept lurching between the moment and that terrible room where he'd sat holding Sophie's motionless hand. He was so frightened and confused he could have screamed. This was how a bull in a bullfight felt, bleeding from all the lances. He wanted to destroy things. He wanted to die right there, by the side of the track.

He wanted the world to be burned to ashes and all of the people to be gone and nature to start again without him.

The camera on the zip wire zoomed right up to his face, and he stood up and started yelling at it and trying to punch it away with his fists. He stared it right in the lens, to show that he wasn't broken. He was trying to stare two billion people down. Dave grabbed him round the shoulders and turned him away.

'Leave it, Cassius Clay. Let's get you out of here.'

'But the next race . . .'

His coach shook his head. 'We're going to concede, old friend. You're cooked.'

And that was the end of his Beijing Olympics. As they walked towards the dressing room, his legs buckled and he started to cry.

There was a man with a steadycam, walking backwards, capturing every moment. Jack looked up and saw him and said the only thing he could think of to say, right into the camera.

He said: 'I'm sorry, Sophie. I'm so sorry.'

In the calm of the kitchen now, he hugged Kate tightly.

'Just keep your head in the race tomorrow,' he said. 'There's nothing to worry about. Sophie's getting better, and you're in the best form you've ever been. All you need to do now is ride.'

Kate kissed him on the tip of his nose. 'Sport's so much simpler than life, isn't it?' she said.

'That's why it's so much more popular.'

Thursday 5 April 2012

Beetham Tower, 301 Deansgate, Manchester
6.35 a.m.

The morning of the race was cloudless and chilly. For the first time since moving to the tower Zoe did her warm-up on the roof deck, five hundred feet above the traffic, in the direct lightspeed blast of the sunrise, with the *Blade Runner* theme in her earphones. Sometimes life was okay. It was impossible not to be lifted by the elevation.

She had a spinning bike up on the roof, pushed up against the railings on the east side, and she took the cover off it now and clipped into the pedals, warming up as the sun climbed higher. As her heart rate rose steadily and smoothly up into the 130s, a simple happiness trembled in her: at the atomising brightness of the light, at the barely contained potential in her muscles, at the undertones of approaching summer in the cold clean breeze blowing in off the Pennines. As her heart rate hit 150 she felt as if she could unclip from the pedals, climb over these rails quite unfussily, and just fly. It didn't feel as if she weighed nearly enough to get hurt.

The feeling freaked her out. She dialled the resistance down, spun the lactate out of her legs, and came to a halt. Then she burst into tears, quite unexpectedly.

She calmed herself, unclipped from the spinning bike and went down off the roof into the cool marble staircase of the tower. She let herself back into the apartment.

In the living area, she watched herself on TV. She was all over the morning news. A psychologist in a lime-green skirt suit and gold book chain necklace was agreeing with the presenter that it would be better if Kate went to the Olympics.

The presenter said: 'A lot of our viewers will be asking whether it's acceptable for someone to represent Great Britain when she's being written about for all the wrong reasons.'

The psychologist said: 'That's exactly the point. Girls are inspired by these Games – *my* daughters are inspired by these Games – and they look to someone like Zoe for an example of how to be a success-ful female.'

Zoe flicked the TV to mute and felt herself balancing on the edge of control.

After coffee and 300g of steamed long-grain rice with dried fruits she stood under the shower and let herself imagine that she'd chosen another life. She imagined being Sophie's mother – feeding her care-fully, carrying her around like eggshells, giving her all those pills in the right order – doing everything she saw Kate do.

Her tattoo stung on one arm, the graze from her crash stung on the other, and she tried to hold them both outside the jet of the shower. She couldn't wash herself, only revolve futilely. She tried to get her head back into the uncluttered space where she needed to be to beat Kate.

It was frustrating that her mind was doing this to her, today of all days. There were days when she didn't think about Sophie at all. Then suddenly, like this morning on the spinning bike, out of nowhere, she would cry for a few minutes. Most nights she had dreams where she had lost something nameless and was frantically searching for it. At first she'd imagined it was gold she was looking for, but after she won gold in Athens, and again in Beijing, the dreams carried on. And sometimes, too, she had dreams where she was racing, and something horrible was chasing her, and would catch her if she ever slowed down. But then again, everyone had those dreams.

She got out of the shower, wrapped herself in a towel and went back to look at the TV while she dried her hair. They were showing yesterday's back page now, with the photograph of her and Kate in the tattoo parlour. Zoe stared at the inset photo of Sophie. She still found it impossible to link the child Sophie was now with the tiny thing in the incubator that everyone had insisted was hers. When she saw Sophie – at the track yesterday, for example, grinning in the basket of the butcher's bike – she found her appealingly mad in the manner of all children, and sobering in the manner of all the undifferentiated sick, but still, nothing really moved inside her. She felt more for Kate – she knew Kate had suffered, and was suffering, and it touched her.

Now, though, as she looked at the inset picture, it was undeniable that Sophie resembled her. There was much more of Jack in there, but by forcing herself to look, she could see a very slight ghost of her face in Sophie's. It disturbed her, watching this evidence of herself surfacing through the features of a man she had put behind her. And she *had* put him behind her. This was the one thing she had done that she was proud of.

In the sink in the kitchen area she ran cooling water across the hot rawness of her new tattoo.

What would her life be, if she hadn't given Sophie up? Would

Jack have left Kate for her? Would the three of them be together now?

She allowed herself to imagine what it would be like to have Jack in her bed, softly breathing, in place of the howling emptiness of the wind blowing in from the hills and swaying the tower in the gusts. An old anguish surged through her and she ground her nails into the raw tattoo, forcing a cry of pain.

On the TV, the psychologist was explaining that someone called Zoe Castle had all the classic markers of someone in denial. She counted off the telltale behaviours on fingers ringed with diamonds and tipped with cherry-red lacquer: the promiscuity, the insatiable need to win, the lack of contrition.

They cut to the back page of the newspaper again. The picture caption said, *Sophie: Mum's gold would mean so much to me.*

Zoe tried to remember the state she'd been in when she left Sophie behind at the hospital. Those days were clouded in her memory. When she thought back to them there was just the obfuscating haze of the analgesic drugs, and the certainty of tears if she tried any harder to access what had happened.

For the first time, she wondered whether Kate might not be some-one who had shouldered a burden that she couldn't carry, but someone who had arrived when Zoe was at her most vulnerable, and taken something from her.

She bit her lip and tried to think clearly. What if Tom was in on it too? What if Tom had liked Kate best all along? What if everything he had done was to manipulate Zoe and get Kate what she wanted? What if it wasn't in Zoe's interests at all to race against Kate today, and this was just one more of Tom's confections?

She pushed the thought away. It was wrong-headed, she knew it was. Tom was a good man and she knew how he felt about her. She liked him back.

On the TV, the psychologist was counting off paranoia, delusional thinking and pathological self-obsession on her fingers. There was so much wrong with this woman called Zoe Castle that the psychologist had to start counting on the fingers of her other hand.

Zoe closed her eyes, trying to block out everything but the calm visualisation of the race she would ride against Kate in less than four hours' time. The image of Sophie's face came to her instead. Something she had been fighting for years stirred inside her. It was a small ache at first, something barely differentiable from the rising crackle of emotion that wouldn't let her think straight this morning. She shifted her weight from foot to foot and clenched her fists so tight her nails bit into her palms, and slowly the ache grew into a hurt, and then a wound, and then a furious agony that she could no longer hold inside.

Sophie was her daughter, and she had let her be taken away. Whenever the thought had started to surface she had pushed it back under, into the cold depths where light rarely reached, but she had always known that this had to be part of why she felt the way she did, why she had spent all these years racing from one championship to another, bedding this man and that. Was this why nothing came close to touching the raw and inconsolable place inside her?

Her life was one endless loop that she raced around, with steep banked curves so she could never change or slow down. It just delivered her back to herself, over and over and over.

She'd thought she'd done the right thing. She'd believed it was best, given that she had no feeling for the child, to give her to someone who did. Now, though, all she could think was that in

288

giving up Sophie, she had given up life. She let the grief surface, and howled.

Later, when her tears had stopped, she felt cold and calm and clear. She went back up onto the roof. The sun was still bright but the breeze was freshening, and darker rain clouds were rolling in off the hills. By leaning on the rail and screwing up her eyes, Zoe could make out the street where the Argalls lived – the terrace of roofs that they must be eating breakfast beneath even now.

She felt the ache again, somewhere in between love and despair. The need inside her was frantic. She needed to see Sophie. She tried to get her head clear to race, but for the first time in her life she didn't know if she wanted to win.

Mum's gold would mean so much to me.

She shook her head violently, trying to get the thought to leave. She spat over the railings, and watched the white fleck spiralling down through the rising vortices to lose itself in the bright white tones of masonry.

She could barely remember how she had reached this height, but she could see now that it was a very, very long way down.

Forest moon of Endor, Outer Rim Territories, Moddell Sector, 43,300 light years from the Galactic Core, grid coordinates H-16 7.45 a.m.

Sophie saw Vader's real face for the first time as Vader lay dying. When the spirit was gone she held him in her arms for a long time. Though he had led a bad life, at the end he had been a good father. She took his body to a clearing on the forest moon of Endor, and built a pyre to cremate him. As the flames rose, the dream began to disintegrate.

Somewhere outside it, Mum and Dad were talking.

Dad said: 'Are you ready to race?'

Mum said: 'I think so.'

Sophie tried to open her eyes but she was still too sleepy. Through her eyelids there was light the colour of smoke. The sound of Mum and Dad talking was twisted around itself. Her chest hurt.

Mum's voice said: 'I love you.'

Dad's voice said: 'You too.'

Sophie smiled.

Mum's voice said: 'Is she waking up?'

Colours came into the light. Red first, then green, then yellow. It glowed through her eyelids. It was like the day finding its felt tips one by one, down the back of the sofa and in the cutlery drawer and wherever it last left them. Her head really hurt. She wanted water or juice or something, with a straw. Just to drink cold water or juice. She was so thirsty she could drink for a million years.

Mum said: 'Zoe's all over the TV again this morning. They were comparing me and her.'

'Aye, I saw.'

'Tom was right to get this over with. What if they dig around and something comes out?'

Dad said: 'Sssh, she's moving.'

She felt Dad's hand on her forehead, and she struggled to open her eyes and sit up. Her body felt as if it was getting reattached, like C-3PO when they put him back together after he got disassembled. But the wires were getting connected all wrong. She tried to move her legs but they wouldn't go. The last few mornings had been like this. It was getting harder each day to wake up.

The light grew stronger through her eyelids.

Sometimes, before you came awake, it was hard to stop being a Jedi. It was beautiful, the forest moon of Endor. They were radiant, the star fields of the Moddell Sector. Every day, more and more of you wanted to stay out there. It would be so easy.

She had to concentrate, that's what she had to do. She had to remember who needed her on Earth. So she said in her head over and over again: I am Sophie Argall, I am eight years old, my mum and dad are champions. I am Sophie Argall, I am the human wearing the pink pyjama bottoms and the *Star Wars* T-shirt, and Mum and Dad need me.

She felt a hand stroking her cheek.

Mum said quietly: 'What are we going to do? Do you think I should forget the Olympics?'

'No. Why?'

'To look after Sophie. To spend more time with her.'

'We've been through this. Focus on the race. You can beat Zoe.'

'I know.'

'Then do it, and then get ready for the Olympics. We'll worry about everything else afterwards.

'But what if there isn't an afterwards?'

'Don't say that.'

'But what if there isn't?'

'Please, stop it.'

'What if I make it to London and Sophie . . . you know . . . doesn't. And I'm sitting there for the rest of my life with a gold medal and the feeling that I could have done more for her. You know? Can you imagine putting that medal around your neck?'

'This is exactly how you mustn't think. Sophie's going to be fine.'

Sophie felt Dad's hand on her forehead again.

'Look,' he said, 'there's no point in both of us waiting for her to wake up. Why don't you go out for a ride, get your head together, go to the venue early like Zoe does?'

Mum was quiet for a moment, then Sophie heard her kiss Dad.

'Thanks,' she said.

'My pleasure. Now piss off and win. Call me when you've annihilated her, okay?'

'Jack . . .'

'Shh. No drama. You're the best. Get out of here.'

'I love you, Jack.'

'While I am only an actor paid to impersonate a man who loves you.'

'I hate you.'

'While I am merely indifferent.'

Sophie heard Mum leaving the room, then she heard Dad's voice again, soft and close by her ear.

'You okay, little one? Christ, you're really hot – you're burning up.'

She half opened her eyes and then she had to screw them tight shut again, because the light was the brightest light in the entire universe.

Sometimes Mum and Dad told her not to look straight at the sun. Well, this light was stronger than the sun. If you actually lived on the sun, this would be the kind of light that your mum and dad would go on at you not to stare at. It was that strong.

Dad said: 'Sophie? Can you hear me?'

Sophie knew she had to wake up properly now, before he could start worrying. Dad took a breath to talk again, and Sophie forced all of the Force into her muscles and sat up straight in bed, even though it hurt really badly. Her head thumped and she opened her eyes and the light was too much, and sick came out of her mouth. She sat there in this light that was brighter than the sun, and Dad was suddenly quiet and the room was quiet and everything was silent except for the fast, hard thudding of her heart against her ribs.

203 Barrington Street, Clayton, East Manchester
7.55 a.m.

'I'm fine,' Sophie said. 'I feel great.'

Jack cleaned up the sick and showered her. He dried her with a towel that he'd warmed up specially on the radiator.

'Are you going to be sick again?' he asked.

She shook her head.

'Sure?'

'Yes.'

He helped Sophie dress.

'Breakfast?'

'Not yet.'

'DVD?'

She shrugged.

'Games?'

'Okay.'

He found her iPad for her and watched as she swiped at it lethargically. He spooned more paracetamol into her, and she accepted it without taking her eyes off the screen. He pulled the *Star Wars* baseball cap over her small, bald head while she ignored him completely, her tongue wedged between her teeth in concentration.

Jack was relieved that her attention had settled on something. He went downstairs to get breakfast for them both and to count out the day's pills into the silver cup. He made a bowl of Rice Krispies for her and a bowl of granola for him, listening to The Exploited on the kitchen stereo. He went upstairs humming along to the tune, and when he reached Sophie's room she was slumped on the floor with her cheek pressed into the screen of her iPad and an endless line of letter Gs spooling across a text input window.

He grabbed her, sat her up and looked into her face. Sophie was unresponsive at first, then her eyes opened and she looked at him.

'*What?*' she said.

'Sophie, are you okay?'

'*Yes!*'

She pawed him away. Her cheeks were flushed and a string of dribble hung from the corner of her mouth. She didn't seem to notice.

'Did you faint, Sophie?'

Sophie shook her head furiously. 'I was just *resting*.'

'You fell down on the screen.'

Sophie shook him off. 'I. Was. RESTING!'

Jack hesitated. Maybe he was overreacting. Looking at Sophie now – at the force of her indignation – it was true that she didn't look too awful. It was hard to know what should be taken in your stride and what should stop you in your tracks. When he'd left, Sophie had been concentrating and engaged. When he'd returned, less than ten minutes later, she'd been fully unconscious. Did that need a visit to the GP, or a trip to the hospital, or a call for the air ambulance? Somehow you were meant to take responsibility, minute to minute, for deciding which events you would call manageable, now that none of them were.

He swallowed. 'I'm sure it isn't anything, but I do think, you know, that we should maybe pop by the hospital, and maybe get you checked out.'

Silver-grey Renault Scénic
8.45 a.m.

Jack strapped Sophie into her car seat and drove towards the hospital, faster than he should have.

'Dad!' said Sophie.

'What?'

'Slow down!'

'Sorry,' said Jack.

He braked momentarily, then gently brought the speed back up. He heard Sophie jiggling around in the back seat, and sighed.

'What is it? Do you need a wee?'

The poor kid was stressed because he was. His nerves were shot. He'd probably overreacted to Sophie's high temperature. These things happened all the time, but he'd panicked. He'd hurried Kate off to her race without making enough of a fuss of her, which was going to do God knew what to her morale, and here he was on his way to the hospital, where the paediatrician would smile reassuringly, call him 'Dad' and send the two of them home with instructions to give Sophie paracetamol every four hours until her fever abated.

He slowed down, wondering whether he should skip the hospital and go back home.

'Sophie,' he said patiently. 'If you don't need a wee, please can you stop kicking the back of my seat?'

She kept on doing it. Jack decided to ignore it for now. He eased the car into the nearside carriageway, which would let him duck into a side road, do a three-pointer and head home.

'Want some music?' he said.

She answered by increasing the frequency of her feet drumming on the back of his seat. He felt a flash of irritation.

'I'm not playing this game today, Soph. I'll take that as a yes, then.'

He stuck on De Rosa doing 'New Lanark' and sank back into the headrest while the guitars washed over him. He forced his hands to loosen their chokehold on the wheel. He needed to calm down.

He took a deep breath. 'I'm sorry I dragged you away from your game. Are you still feeling poorly?'

No answer from the back seat. The petulant drumming against the back of his seat continued, a little less forcefully but still enough to be annoying.

'No need to sulk, eh?'

Jack sighed, and deployed the windscreen wipers against the shower that was starting to fall. The cold April rain had the smell of change about it. It bothered him in a way he couldn't pin down.

The shower intensified. Jack dialled up the wipers to their top speed and cranked up the hot air to demist the windscreen. A side road was coming up on the left. He put on the indicator to signal into it, then hesitated and flicked it off again. The hospital was only a couple of minutes away. It might not be the end of the world to take Sophie for a quick check-up, then maybe grab both of them a hot chocolate from the vending machine in the hospital lobby. Sixty pence, option A3 – he knew the selections by heart.

'Sophie?' he said. 'If you stop kicking my seat, after the hospital we'll get a nice drink, okay? And then we'll go to the toyshop and I'll buy you a new *Star Wars* figurine. Any one you like. Okay?'

There was no answer.

'Sophie?'

Still nothing.

He angled the rearview mirror back to see her.

Sophie's head lolled in her seat. Her eyes rolled, her arms twitched.

He pulled in to the side road, whipped off his seatbelt and dived into the back. Sophie's legs were kicking spasmodically. He unstrapped her and laid her down. She kept on twitching. He held on to her arms and tried to make them still, but there was a terrible force inside her.

Jack felt the blood draining from his head. He couldn't think at all. He let go of her with one hand, took his phone out of his pocket and made the emergency call. The voice asked him which service he required, and he didn't know. The voice was cool and professional. It asked him: *Police, fire or ambulance?* Inside the car, De Rosa were unravelling the sad silvery fabric of a dream. Inside himself, all Jack could hear was a high, thin screaming. The voice on the phone asked him what was the nature of the emergency. Jack got it together enough to shout that he needed an ambulance, but in truth the nature of the emergency was that he and Kate had lied to themselves about what had been going on. The nature of the emergency was that they had drawn a curtain between their daughter's degeneration and their dreams of gold, and there was no obvious type of vehicle with any kind of specialist crew inside or any sort of siren on top that could possibly be vectored to his position to fix that.

National Cycling Centre, Stuart Street, Manchester
9.00 a.m.

Tom had the velodrome booked for four hours from ten o'clock. At nine he checked the girls' bikes over again with the mechanic, while the juniors trained on the track. In the kitchen along from his office in the warren of rooms underneath the track he made up a batch of isotonic drink, put it into bottles, and stacked them in a cooler. He took out more clean bottles and mixed the girls' recovery drinks. Zoe favoured a powdered protein shake made entirely out of freeze-dried excellence, which came in a gold and black tub printed with extravagant nutritional promises. The smell of it made Tom retch, but it was true that it was perfectly optimised for minerals and essential amino acids. Kate preferred skimmed milk whizzed up in the blender with berries and honey. Tom bought milk and soft fruit for her once a week and kept them in the fridge in his office, on the shelf above the blood and urine samples.

He poured the girls' drinks into their bottles and added them to the cooler. It was twenty to ten, and his hands were shaking with nerves. He lugged the cooler up to trackside and watched the juniors warming down. Their faces were aglow and they were larking about. They were the under-16s, and they still believed they were pretty lucky to be there.

When ten o'clock came he got the crew up from the maintenance room to sweep the track and run the machine around it to clean off every trace of sweat, lube and grease. He phoned the control room and got them to put on the full floodlights, the way they would for an evening competition. He had them initialise the Lynx photo-finish camera on the start/finish line. At ten thirty the physio came in and set up two stationary bikes to Kate and Zoe's dimensions, at opposite ends of the warm-up area.

With everything ready, Tom lowered himself into a trackside seat where he could see the main entrance. He waited for Zoe to arrive first.

Kate arrived at ten to eleven, skipped down the stairs and dropped her kitbag at the side of the track with a boom that rolled around the space. She kissed Tom on both cheeks.

He said: 'I don't need to ask you if you're ready.'

'I feel great. This was a good idea.'

'You sleep okay?'

She smiled. 'I can sleep when this is over. Is Zoe getting changed?'

'She's not here yet.'

Kate blinked. 'Okay.'

'Yeah, I know. Think she's found a whole new way to mess with your head?'

Kate laughed. 'Oh, come on. We're over that.'

Tom held out his hand. 'Still, you'd better give me your phone.'

Kate sighed as she handed it over. 'There's no need, really.'

Tom pocketed the phone. 'Race day rules. We'll keep the two of you apart till start time. We'll run this just like a big event. No contact. No psychology. I'll have you use the changing room one after the other, then I'm going to isolate you and have you warm up at opposite ends of the space.'

'Okay.'

Tom put his hand on her elbow. 'Just for once, let's make it all about what happens on the track, shall we?'

He sent her off to change, then sat down to wait again. Kate was out of the changing room at eleven and he sent her off with the physio to warm up on her stationary bike. At ten past eleven he phoned Zoe, but her voicemail picked up.

'Come on,' he said. 'You're meant to be here.'

At twenty past, three blazered officials from British Cycling arrived to witness the race. A shower was intensifying outside, and they came through the doors shaking out umbrellas and bitching about being called out. Tom briefed them on the race rules: best of three sprints, the winner to remain subject to the new Olympic selection procedure, the loser to formally announce that she was not available for selection. No journalists, friends or family supporters to be present, no press conference, no recording equipment besides the photo-finish camera. He gave each of the officials a copy of the governing documentation, and all four of them signed. Tom explained how the sprints would be organised, with one official to act as the approved starter while the other two would hold the girls' bikes steady at the start. The three officials would then umpire the sprints, with Tom recusing himself from the process.

Tom settled the officials in their seats and organised coffee and biscuits for them. At half past eleven, Zoe was still nowhere. To calm himself, he checked the girls' bikes over again. He brushed invisible spots of grit off the track. He tested the photo-finish equipment, walking across the line and calling the control room to check that the image was being triggered and displayed on their screens.

He called Zoe and got her voicemail again. He left a message that he struggled to keep unemotional. He went up to the reception area and looked out. The sky was graphite grey, the rain wasn't letting up and there was still no Zoe.

Kate was fully warmed up now, and Tom went over to the mat where the physio was taking her through some light stretches.

'All good?' he said breezily. 'Legs still attached?'

She looked up at him. 'Any news?'

He shook his head.

'What if she doesn't show up?'

He looked at his watch. 'She's still got twenty minutes. You know her. She's just playing with you. She'll be hiding around the corner, doing her own warm-up.'

Even as he said it, he was aware of the heavy rain hammering on the skylights high above their heads. Kate peered up into the glare of the floodlights, shielding her eyes with a hand.

'Yeah, but what if she doesn't come?'

Tom sighed. 'The officials are here. The papers are signed. If she's not through these doors by noon then you'll go to the Olympics and she won't. She knows the rules for today. You both agreed to be bound by them.'

Kate shook her head quickly. 'If something's come up, I wouldn't hold her to the rules.'

Tom nodded his head at the officials. 'These guys would. Unfortunately, nine tenths of the race is about making it to the bloody start line. You should understand that better than anyone else on earth.'

He watched her face as she took in the information.

She said: 'Let me call her, okay?'

'No. See? This is how she's getting into your head. She'll be here. You just need to keep your mind on your own race.'

Kate closed her eyes and took a breath. 'Okay.'

At ten minutes to twelve Tom heaved himself up the stairs to the reception area and stood looking out through the doors at the street. His chest was tight and he felt nauseous and angry. Why did Zoe have to be like this? Why couldn't she just use the talent she had to win on the track, without wrenching everyone to bits beforehand?

Outside, the rain was ending and the April sun glittered on the wet tarmac. Cars sent sheets of water arcing over the pavement.

Zoe came splashing through the puddles on her training bike, threw it down at the kerb and burst through the doors of the velodrome at eight minutes to twelve. She was soaked from the rain, her hair hanging wet and her kitbag dripping water onto the hard-wearing industrial flooring of the reception area.

She stopped six feet from Tom and stood looking at him, breathing hard. Steam rose from her wet jeans and her sodden black hoodie.

Tom's anger dissolved and he rushed to close the gap between them. 'What the bloody hell happened?'

She looked down and sniffed. 'I nearly fell.'

'Off your bike?'

She shrugged. 'Off my tower.'

He didn't know how to react. After a long pause, he said: 'At least you're warmed up.'

'Tell me what to do.'

He looked at his watch. 'Can you change in four minutes?'

'Yeah.'

'Do it. Your bike's ready for you. I'll see you at the start. We'll talk about this afterwards, okay? You and me. We'll go for a coffee. But right now, I just want you to go to that place in your head where you go when you race. Nothing else exists, okay? Don't look at Kate on

302

your way down. Don't look at the officials. Just get changed and walk to the start line and keep your eyes on me. I'll look after you, Zoe, okay?'

'Okay.' Her voice betrayed the faintest of tremors.

He held out his hand. 'Phone.'

She dug it out of the pocket of her jeans and handed it to him compliantly.

He put it in his own pocket. 'Why are you still standing here?'

She jogged away down the stairs and Tom followed her. Even in distress, there was a grace to the physics of her. While Tom hobbled, his ruined knees creaking, Zoe flowed easily, like oiled light. There was an unselfconscious sense of entitlement in her movement, as if space and time sucked in their guts to let her through, like starstruck bouncers on a nightclub door.

'Shit,' Tom whispered to himself. It wasn't till now that he'd realised how badly he wanted her to win.

A phone buzzed in his pocket. It was Kate's, and Jack's name was on the screen.

He picked up. 'Mate,' he said. 'It's me. I'm fielding Kate's calls till after the race.'

There was no answer from Jack.

'Jack,' he said, more loudly. 'It's me, Tom.'

When Jack's voice came it was choked and unnatural. 'There's a situation here. There's a fucking situation. I'm here at A&E and they've rushed Sophie away and I need to tell Kate to—'

'Right. Okay. Slow down.'

He'd reached trackside now. He turned his back toward Kate and the warm-up area and the officials, and cupped his hand over the phone.

'What are you doing in A&E? Kate didn't say anything.'

'She doesn't know. Sophie had a fever and I was taking her in for a check-up and it suddenly got worse. I mean it's really bad. I don't know what's going on, so can you please tell Kate that she needs to get here? Or, no, can I talk to her, please?'

Tom hesitated. 'You know what we're deciding here today, right?'

'Yeah, I know, Tom, but this is . . . shit, I mean it's . . .'

'Yeah, yeah, okay, I get you.'

Tom looked back towards the warm-up area. Kate was hopping from foot to foot, keyed up with adrenaline, watching for Zoe to come out of the dressing rooms. Her helmet was on, her eyes were hidden.

He exhaled deeply, to calm himself. 'Listen, it's your call. We're five minutes away from racing here. I'm going to be honest and tell you that Kate's looking pretty good for the win at this point. Do you need her there, or do you need her to do her thing here? It's your family. You need to decide what's best for it.'

There was a short silence on the end of the line. Then Jack said: 'Not tell her, you mean?'

'I'm saying tell her after the race. If she takes it in two and skips the shower, she'll be out of here in forty minutes. During which time you're there with Sophie and you can handle it. Kate's here and it's the biggest race she'll ever ride, that's all I'm saying.'

'Yeah, but if something . . . you know . . . *happens*, and I didn't tell her?'

'Yeah, and what if everything turns out fine, and you told her this now? That'd be the third Olympics she'd miss. I'm her coach, Jack. I'm keeping count even if you're not.'

'That's not fair, Tom.'

Tom sighed. 'I know. I'm stressed, you're stressed. Look, like I said, it's your call.'

Jack said: 'Can I talk to her?'

Tom looked over to the warm-up area. Zoe was there now, up from the dressing rooms, suited up and pulling on her gloves. He caught her eye. She looked at him desperately.

'Okay,' he said quietly into the phone. 'I'll put you on.'

He pointed for Zoe to go to the far end of the warm-up area, while he carried the phone over to Kate. As he handed it to her, it felt like a betrayal.

'Is something wrong?' she asked.

He kept his face neutral. 'It's Jack.'

'What is it?'

He shrugged. 'It's Jack.'

She took the phone in her gloved hand. 'Jack?' she said. 'Is everything okay?'

Tom watched his own face in the mirror of her visor. He watched the uncertain line of her mouth. Then, as she kept the phone pressed to her ear, he watched her begin to smile.

'Oh Jack . . .' she said.

She listened some more, and he saw how her face blushed beneath the visor and her smile became a full grin.

'I will,' she said softly. 'Thank you. Yes. I know I can.'

He saw how she leaned in to the sound of his voice, pressing it to her cheek.

'I love you too,' she said, and he watched two small tears appear from beneath the lower limit of her visor and course down to her jawbone.

When the call was finished, she turned to Tom.

'Thanks,' she said.

'What for?'

'For letting him wish me good luck.'

Paediatric Intensive Care Unit, North Manchester General Hospital 11.58 a.m.

Jack put his phone back in his pocket and collapsed into a chair. Static popped and hissed through his neurons. He didn't know if Sophie was asleep or unconscious, and the ICU nurses were too busy to tell him. His daughter was silent but her body still talked through the monitoring machines. They bleeped and took dictation. Jack watched as they traced out vital signs on screen. According to Siemens Instruments, Sophie's heart rate was 88. She was breathing, unassisted, 22 times per minute. He found his feet tapping along to the rhythms of the monitors. His body swayed to strange syncopations as it willed her to live.

On the phone to Kate just now, he'd been close to telling her everything. It was unbearable to have all this responsibility.

Watching Sophie with her breath misting the inside of the translucent green breathing mask, there was a terrible acceleration. The idea that Sophie could die had always been there, ever since the first diagnosis, and yet it had seemed like a bad place on a map, an Ivory Coast, somewhere not urgently frightening because fear itself kept you away from the place. You thought of it as somewhere braver people went, or at least as somewhere you'd have plenty of time to pack your bags for. And yet here he was, suddenly, in his tracksuit, with the house keys, the car key, his phone and five pounds seventy-three in the pockets, watching

Sophie do something that might actually be dying. This was the nature of time: it was a wide, elegant and gently descending spiral staircase whose last dozen steps were unexpectedly rotten.

He needed Kate. He needed to hold her hand. If this was the final fall, and they didn't fall together, they'd fall apart.

He tried to keep busy. He plugged in his earphones and stuck on The Proclaimers. He put on '500 Miles' because it was Sophie's favourite. When it got to the chorus he took out one of the earbuds and placed it in her ear. The rhythm of the song drifted in and out of phase with the beeping of Sophie's heartbeat. Her expression didn't change.

He leaned down to whisper that Kate was on her way; that Sophie should fight and hang on.

They were letting him hold Sophie's hand now, and for a while it had seemed like a good sign – an indication that she was out of danger. Now Jack began to think that the nurses were passing him a message that he was reluctant to understand.

At first they'd made him wait outside, gesturing to Sophie through the wired safety glass panel in the door. Sophie didn't know what was happening to her and Jack had done his best, but these were difficult hand signals to make: *You're fine, you're absolutely fine, all these doctors and nurses rushing around you are basically overreacting, but it would be rude to contradict them now that they've made such an effort.* It was a tricky message to pitch, through thick glass. You had to allow for refraction.

Sophie had smiled before she fell asleep. That smile, framed in wired glass, was framed inside Jack's head now. Doctors and nurses had ebbed and flowed, and he had found it impossible to isolate one individual from the green-gowned tide and ask them: is my daughter dying, or just sleeping? At this extremity, finally, there was shame. He was ashamed that his daughter had become so ill without him realising it.

Now, whatever was happening to Sophie seemed not to be improving or worsening. The monitoring machines were constant. Jack was fearful of breaking the spell or of calling any more of time's attention to Sophie's particular case. He sat very still. Inside this room now, with the monitors on, time was a diamond cut by Sophie's breathing and polished by her pulse. As long as these sounds persisted, it was crystalline.

National Cycling Centre, Stuart Street, Manchester
11.59 a.m.

Kate was careful not to look at Zoe as they lined up side by side at the start. Zoe had drawn the inside line for the first race, so Kate had her to her left. She didn't let herself think about the drama of Zoe's arrival, or of what might be wrong. She held on to the sound of Jack's voice on the phone, telling her that he loved her. She let the words ring in her head until they were the only sound she heard, until all her disappointments were silenced. She looked straight ahead down the track, adjusted her grip on the bars, and made her mind go quiet.

'One minute to go,' said the starter.

Her senses were keyed up. She swung her steering left and right, testing the adhesion of her tyre rubber as the torsional force squeaked it against the varnish of the track. As she turned the bars, the friction of her skinsuit irritated the fresh tattoo on her shoulder blade, sending a flash of anger through her. She tensed and relaxed her muscle groups in turn, transmuting the anger into potential. She noticed the

308

tiniest details: the ultrafine mesh on the backs of her gloves; the sandalwood notes in the perfume of the woman in the blazer who was holding her bike up by the back edge of its saddle.

As the starter counted down the seconds from ten, she let herself look across at Zoe for the first time. Zoe was staring straight ahead. Kate felt the expansion of Zoe's lungs and the tensing of her muscles as if they were her own. In the last few seconds before the start, she let her body fall in with the rhythms of her rival's.

When the starter's whistle blew, Zoe eased away from the line and Kate followed her at a distance of six feet, ready to close the gap quickly if Zoe pulled away. Zoe kept the speed to a crawl, craning her head back, watching for any twitch Kate might make to indicate that she was about to accelerate. Around the first curve they both hung low in the trough, and when the straight opened up again Zoe steered right and made for the high side of the track. Kate followed her up and they held their line there, accelerating to keep adhesion around the second curve, then maintaining the speed into the home straight. When they crossed the line at the end of the first of the three laps they were gradually picking up the pace, and Kate was still tucked into Zoe's slipstream.

Halfway round the second lap they were still cruising on the high side of the track, with Kate following and watching for any sign that Zoe was going to break. As they reached the apex of the curve that would take them back into the home straight, Zoe angled her head and set herself to dive down the banking to the well of the track. Kate reacted instantly to follow her, and she was fully committed before she realised that it had been a trick. Zoe kept her height and as Kate dropped down to the black line with her muscles screaming as she snapped them instantly to full power, Zoe dropped in behind her and tucked in to her slipstream just as the bell went for the final lap.

Kate understood the consequences immediately. Now that she'd lost the advantage, the only thing to do was to ride hard for the finish. There were no tactics left – they were both down in the well of the track, winding up to top speed around the shortest line, and Zoe was tucked in to her wind shadow. If she couldn't put down some extraordinary power now, Zoe would simply hang there until the last hundred metres and then accelerate out of her slipstream to slingshot past her for the win.

Now that there was nothing to think about, Kate was very calm. She wound herself up to the absolute limit of her power and used the image of Sophie to turn off the messages of agony exploding from her legs and her lungs. As they came into the last curve, sparks were detonating in her retinas from the effort. She flashed out of the curve into the last straight, sensing the disruption in the airflow and hearing the roar of the wheels as Zoe came out of her shadow and pulled alongside her. For fifty feet they were side by side. Kate pulled every atom of herself inside out and slowly, inchwise, Zoe's attack began to falter. From being alongside she dropped to an inch back, a wheel-length back, and with a cold, silent flicker of wonder in her heart, Kate realised she was going to win. She crossed the line a bike-length ahead of Zoe and began to wind the pace down, easing her pressure on the cranks and letting the bike pedal her around two laps as the speed slowly came off. As she slowed, she looked across and saw how Zoe rode in defeat, with her shoulders slumped and her head down.

Zoe looked across at her, gasping. 'I'll get the next one,' she said.

Kate shook her head, too breathless to speak, but inside her a small, careful hope was forming.

**Paediatric Intensive Care Unit, North Manchester General Hospital
12.05 p.m.**

Sophie came awake with a groan, and Jack's heart leapt. Her voice was muffled by the mask, and he had to lean in to hear what she was saying.

'Dad?'

'Yes?'

'Can I tell you something?'

'Yes.'

'When you die it's just the same, except you get a glowing line around you.'

'I know, darling. I've seen the films.'

'They're not just films, though. The Force is real.'

Jack looked into her eyes and saw the fear in them. He swallowed. 'Yes, darling. It's real.'

Slowly, Sophie smiled. 'Truly?' Her voice was a clockwork doll winding down.

Jack said: 'Truly.'

She closed her eyes. 'I've never felt like this.'

'Yes you have. You've been through much worse.'

'How do you know?'

'My job is to remember for you.'

'How do you know you're remembering right?'

'I know. When you're a grown-up, you'll understand. Everything is much clearer to us.'

'Am I going to die, Dad?'

'No, you're not.'

'Would you tell me if I was?'

'Yes.'

'But would you?'

Jack found the power not to hesitate. 'Yes,' he said. 'I'd tell you.'

They fell back into silence. The air smelled of urine and bleach. They searched each other's faces for doubt.

It was a relief when Sophie closed her eyes again, a respite from the gruelling work of projecting confidence. Only later came the shock as Jack realised what the closing of eyes might mean now. His mind was slow to adjust to the situation. It was still reacting to ordinary things according to their ordinary context. It saw his child's eyes closing and it thought: *rest*. It didn't think: *rest of your life*.

A few minutes later Sophie's eyes came open again. She looked around her in confusion.

'Why isn't Mum here?'

Jack squeezed her hand. 'She is here, darling. She's been with us all the time you've been asleep. She's just gone out of the room for a few minutes.'

Sophie looked relieved. Her head sank back into the pillows.

'Dad, it's so quiet in here.'

'Yes.'

A long pause. 'Why aren't there more doctors?'

'Why do you want more doctors?'

'So they can do more stuff. Make me better.'

'They are making you better. They found you had an infection. They've put you on antibiotics.'

'What if they're not here because there's nothing else they can do?'

'They're doing exactly what they should. Right now the best thing to do is to wait, and rest.'

'Then why are we here and not at home?'

'We're just in here as a precaution.'

'How do you know?'

'Because the doctors told me.'

'Would the doctors tell you if I was dying?'

'Yes they would.'

'How do you know they would?'

'I just told you! Grown-ups know things. It's like we have the special glasses and we can see the whole thing in 3D.'

Sophie opened her mouth to deny this, but then Jack saw the quickest flash of cunning in her eyes. The look vanished and Sophie's face became childish again, and simple.

'When do I get the special glasses, Dad?'

'When you're twenty-one, Soph.'

'That's ages.'

'Yeah.'

She waited for exactly six beeps of heartbeat and then her smile blinked off.

'I think the doctors don't tell you everything.'

'Why would they not tell me everything?'

'Because you might cry.'

She was watching Jack's face for a reaction and Jack was careful not to show her one. He hugged her instead. 'There's nothing to cry about. You're going to be fine.'

Later, when she drifted away from consciousness again, Kate called and Jack jumped up. The ringtone clashed with the rhythm of Sophie's heart rate and breathing. It shattered the crystal of time that had formed in the room. The fragments scattered, displaced by this new kind of time that arrived in old-fashioned rings, sampled from the bell of a vintage Bakelite receiver and encoded into the software of Jack's phone.

About to answer, he closed his eyes and listened to the dissonance. Heart, lungs, phone. The ringing went on and on, seeming to increase in volume and discord until there was nothing he could do but step outside the room to take the call out of earshot of the monitoring machines.

'Jack?' said Kate.

Her voice was beautiful in the sudden silence.

'Hey,' he said. 'How's it going?'

He could hear her elation even through the bad connection here in the heart of the hospital, with her voice modulated by the rhythmic ticking of some urgent pulse in the phone mast.

'I won the first race,' she said. 'I'm stronger than her today. I think I can beat her.'

'I knew you could do it.'

'I knew it too. We're on again in five minutes. If I win this next one, that's it. I've got to go now, okay? I'm not meant to have the phone, but Tom forgot to take it back off me. Don't call it, okay, 'cause it'll ring in my kitbag.'

He smiled. There was a lightness in his chest as his body responded to her voice, dumbly, as if nothing else was going on. The crystalline time of Sophie's room was gone now, but here was a new kind of time that shone on them both, that radiated from the warm glow of their voices on the axis of the connection. They could live here, just for a moment, and be happy. These were the moments you lived in, after all, these rococo twists of time. You could make them last forever, or until you told the truth.

He glanced back through the wired safety glass. Sophie seemed completely peaceful. The heart rate monitor still said 88. The breathing monitor was still on 22. Who was to say that she wouldn't simply open her eyes again, and smile, and everything would be okay?

He forced back the urge to blurt out the truth, to tell his wife to come quickly.

'Good luck,' he said. 'Go ahead and win it.'

After she clicked off the call, he went back into the room and sat by Sophie's bed. He closed his eyes and imagined Kate, untroubled by anything except the race ahead. He smiled because he had given her something rarer than gold: an hour outside time.

National Cycling Centre, Stuart Street, Manchester
12.29 p.m.

Zoe lined up on the high side of the track and watched Kate settling in to her left for the start of the second race. She knew Kate's start line ritual by heart: the redundant checking and rechecking of the zip on the back of the neck of her skinsuit; the regular bilateral twitch of her heels to confirm that her shoes were solidly mated with the pedals; the soundless movements of her lips as she recited whatever calming mantra she used to empty her mind. Zoe watched her as she bowed her head and stared at the likeness of Sophie that stared back at her from the top tube of her bike. She watched Kate's involuntary smile. She looked for weaknesses – for any telltale asymmetries in the way she sat on the bike that might indicate inflammation in a particular muscle group, or any deviation from her habitual start line behaviour that could indicate a concern. There was nothing. If anything there was unusual confidence in the way she sat; a fluidity in the line of her back and shoulders that spoke of straightforward strength.

Zoe sniffed, and settled her gloved hands on the bars. Kate's confidence didn't bother her. If anything it gave her a pang of regret that Kate's disappointment would be the sharper when she lost. Zoe had to win – she was going to win – but it didn't mean she had to enjoy ending Kate's career. It was just that winning was the overwhelmingly likely scenario. Zoe ran through her advantages. She was clearer-headed now than when she'd arrived. In the first race she hadn't been properly warmed up and her tactics had been all over the place. Now she was back in race mode. As well as being psyched up, she knew she had to be less tired than Kate. In the first race Kate had led at full power for an entire lap while Zoe had hung in her slipstream and only shown her face to the wind in the last few yards. Even though she'd lost the first race, she knew she was fresher for this second round.

The official starter checked that his whistle was in position on the lanyard around his neck. He shifted his weight to the balls of his feet. Zoe knew he would soon begin counting down from ten. As always, she knew that Kate would choose that moment to look across at her for the first time. On impulse, she unclipped her chinstrap and raked her helmet back on her head so that her eyes were visible beneath her reflective visor.

Ten, said the starter.

When Kate turned to look at her, Zoe was staring straight back. She watched the visible recoil as Kate saw her exposed eyes, then the rapid flick of her head as Kate looked straight ahead once more. Zoe tipped her helmet forward again, secured the strap, and noted the tension that had come into the line of Kate's shoulders.

Three, said the starter.

Zoe flexed her thighs, then her calves, jiggled her legs to loosen them up, then stood up in the pedals.

Two, said the starter. *One*. Time built up against a dam as he lifted the whistle to his lips, then flowed again as the sound released it.

Zoe let Kate take the lead and tucked in behind her. For the first lap she focused on unsettling Kate by ducking out of her line of sight whenever Kate turned around to look at her. By using Kate's own body to block her view, Zoe kept her wondering whether she was about to accelerate through her blindside. The result was that by the time they started the second lap, Kate was hanging deep in the well of the track, hugging the inner limit so that Zoe couldn't sneak up the inside channel. She was watching Zoe over her right shoulder, and Zoe began imperceptibly climbing up the gradient of the track and slowly increasing her speed so that she began to draw level with Kate.

Zoe found herself smiling. She loved this. She'd given Kate only two tactical options, and both of them were shitty. Kate could ignore the inexorable way that Zoe was gaining altitude on her, in which case it would eventually be too late and Zoe could simply use gravity to accelerate down the slope and cut in front of her. Or, if Kate began inching up the slope to cover against just that move, then she would be leaving the inside channel open and Zoe could dive down behind her and sneak through it.

Kate craned her head back nervously, and Zoe watched as her rival's indecision mounted. Sooner or later Kate would have to break out of the trap Zoe had set for her in the only possible direction: forwards, by putting down the power and starting the sprint proper. The problem for Kate was that she'd burned out her legs in the first race, so the earlier she launched the sprint, the more advantage she'd be conceding to Zoe.

Three quarters of the way around the second lap, Zoe forced the issue by suddenly powering up and climbing right up to the lip at the apex of the curve. Kate was half a pedal stroke too slow to cover the move. Instead, seeing that Zoe's height advantage was too great, she dived down into the well of the track and powered up her pedal stroke to maximum. With gravity on her side Zoe swooped down into Kate's slipstream and tucked in effortlessly. Kate pushed forward frantically in an attempt to create a gap between them. By the time they took the bell for the start of the final lap, moving at top speed, Kate was still leading out but Zoe knew she would catch her. She could see from the gradual wilting of Kate's posture on the bike that Kate knew it too. Zoe relaxed into her pedal stroke, conserved her energy around the last two bends as Kate began to slow, then popped out of her wind shadow on the last straight to take the race by a wheel-length.

She dropped down in front of Kate as the pair of them gradually slowed, making sure that her rival only saw her back wheel. She kept her posture strong on the bike, not allowing her head to drop as she gasped for air. She projected effortless strength until they both came to a halt, then she hopped off the bike as if the pair of them had been for nothing more tiring than a ride to the shops.

Later, warming down on the stationary bike, she looked across at Kate on the opposite side of the isolation zone Tom had set up between them. Kate was watching her back. Kate dropped her eyes and Zoe looked away as the truth of their situation sparked back and forth across the vacuum between them. Zoe's tactics had controlled the first two races and now, even though they had one victory apiece, Kate would go into the deciding race depleted.

Zoe knew that she should feel exultant. Instead her legs felt suddenly heavy, as if an unseen hand had dialled up the resistance on the stationary bike.

Paediatric Intensive Care Unit, North Manchester General Hospital
12.35 p.m.

The antibiotics dripping into her arm should save Sophie, this was what Dr Hewitt said. Jack wanted to believe it. She was still pale and drifting in and out of sleep. Jack held her hand and squeezed it from time to time, a submarine sending a sonar pulse, checking for the return pressure.

'All right?' he whispered.

'All right,' said Sophie. Her voice was still tiny inside the capsule of her oxygen mask.

'Really?'

'Yeah. I sound like Vader with this mask'

She squeezed his hand and Jack felt better.

Dr Hewitt pulled up a stacking chair and sat down at the bedside, facing Sophie and Jack.

'I've got good news and more news for you, Sophie. Can you listen carefully for a minute?'

Sophie nodded, a small movement against the green pillow with the name of the hospital printed in purple ink on the selvage of its case.

'Well, the good news is that we've run your bloods and they're really, really good. I'm delighted, and you should be too. I know this might seem odd to you when you're feeling so poorly, but your counts of bad cells are way down and if I had to take a bet on it, I'd say it looks as if the chemo is working.'

Sophie whispered, 'So why am I like this?'

'The immediate issue is that the chemo has made your body very weak. There's an infection in your Hickman line, and that's what's been making you poorly. Ideally we'd have spotted it earlier.'

Jack groaned. 'I'm so sorry, Sophie.'

'Don't beat yourself up. Often the symptoms are indistinguishable from the general fatigue. This is the problem. The infection can sit around the axis of the line for ages, and then for whatever reason it accelerates. We're going to take the line out and clean up a bit. Because the line's been in for a while there's been quite a bit of tissue formation around the insertion point, so we'll need to put you under for a few minutes while we whip it out. Okay with you, Sophie?'

Sophie hesitated, her eyes wide and worried above the mask.

'It's not a big deal,' Dr Hewitt said. 'First we'll clean your skin with a special wipe to kill any nasty germs that may be lurking there. Then we'll just make some little incisions, with a very small knife. You'll be under anaesthetic, which means you'll just be dreaming.'

Sophie stared at Dr Hewitt. 'What will I be dreaming about?'

The doctor looked at Jack.

'*Star Wars*,' Jack said quickly. 'I promise.'

She swallowed. 'Okay.'

Dr Hewitt said: 'We'll draw the Hickman line out slowly, and once it's clear of the vein we'll flush an antibiotic through the line as we withdraw it, which will treat the site of the infection. Then you'll need a couple of little stitches, and we'll put a dressing over that.'

Sophie's hand was trembling. Jack wished Dr Hewitt would stop. He squeezed her hand again and she looked up at him, stared for a few seconds without any expression, and then, suddenly, she smiled the widest, most perfect smile. Jack beamed back. There was no choice in it: his body just responded. It was the strangest feeling to have your courage given back to you by your own child.

'After the Hickman line is out, we'll take you down to radiology and the nurse will take an X-ray picture of your chest, to make sure that we haven't left anything inside. Then we'll bring you back up here and give you the once-over.'

Sophie grinned at Jack again, and he made a face. She giggled. The moment had a certain persistence. The April light from the windows seemed to Jack like the clearest light ever to fall. The rhythms of the monitoring equipment were better than any of the music on his iPod. The tiny pulse that went whum-whum-whum in his ears. *Beep, beep, beep. Pulse, pulse, pulse. An' AH would walk five HUN dred miles.* Sophie laughing. Him laughing back at her.

Dr Hewitt had said that the chemo was working. It dawned on Jack, only now, that this really was what he had said.

'After the operation, Sophie, you're going to feel very poorly, I'm afraid. Your chest will feel a bit burny and you might have a headache and feel tired and sick. You might even *be* sick, but that's perfectly normal and you mustn't worry about it. It just means the antibiotics are doing their job.'

Sophie crossed her eyes at Jack. 'Bleurgh!' she whispered. 'Sick!'

That set them both off, faces hot with laughter. Dr Hewitt talked louder, struggling to assert himself.

'Sorry, Jack. Sorry, Sophie. Are you listening?'

They were gone. They had the giggles.

Dr Hewitt smiled and shook his head. 'You two are really something else, you know?'

'Sorry,' Jack said. 'It's just been a really hard time.'

He looked up at Sophie then, and he had never felt so tired nor so happy. The machines bleeped. The afternoon light poured through the windows. The light was made in the core of the sun,

321

thousands of years before Sophie fell sick. It had reached this point at the same moment that she was getting better. It seemed to Jack like first light.

When a suitable time had gone by, Dr Hewitt said: 'Right then, Sophie. Shall we wheel you through to theatre?'

Sophie shrugged. 'Whatever, Trevor.' Her insouciance was a mist in the breathing mask.

Jack walked with Dr Hewitt behind Sophie's bed as two porters pushed it along the corridors.

Dr Hewitt leaned in to him and said in a low voice: 'There are certain risks involved in the procedure. Fingers crossed she'll be fine, but she's weaker than we'd like. I just want you to be aware.'

Jack's stomach twisted. 'What does that mean? How big are the risks?'

'Obviously we do everything we can to mitigate. We use the lightest anaesthesia, and we have a crash team standing by.'

Jack nodded. His hands twisted together as they walked the long corridors under the superstitious eyes of hospital visitors. Jack knew what they were feeling. A child like this – bald, frail and breathing through a mask – made the corridors quieten and onlookers draw back. Sophie cleared minds that had been filled with thoughts of mortgage payments, and unpleasant duties, and difficult conversations overdue. After she had passed they would reconvene, in groups of two or three, and confide to strangers that the moment had marked them. *It makes you think, doesn't it? It puts it all in perspective.* These are the things they would say.

In the operating theatre a smiling nurse handed Jack a surgical gown with a stylised dinosaur printed on it. She helped Jack to lift Sophie down from the bed and into a wheelchair, and she showed them to a little cubicle with a nylon curtain where Sophie was to change.

'I can do it myself,' Sophie said when Jack tried to help her.

Sitting in the wheelchair, she took off her *Star Wars* T-shirt. She put on the surgical gown and Jack did up the laces at the side. He tried not to think about them unlacing the gown and exposing her skinny chest with the Hickman line growing out of it.

On the cubicle wall there was a sticker from a sticker book. Someone had tried to remove it, but they'd only managed to tear the edges. It was blue and red Spiderman fighting black Spiderman. Sophie stared, transfixed.

'Am I going to be okay, Dad?'

Jack knelt down and turned his daughter to look into his eyes.

'Of course. Look at me? Of course you are.'

'Really?'

He smiled. 'You're going to be fine. I promise.'

This is what he said.

They let Jack hold her hand while she went under the anaesthetic. The anaesthetist pushed home the plunger on the syringe and told Sophie to count to ten.

Sophie stared up at Jack with defiance in her eyes. 'I'm going to count to a hundred,' she said.

Jack stroked her face. 'Start with one, Sophie.'

'One . . .' said Sophie, and fell soundlessly asleep.

Outer Rim Territories, Sluis Sector, 50,250 light years from the Galactic Core, grid coordinates M-19, region of space colloquially known as the Dagobah System
12.55 p.m.

An X-wing chased a TIE fighter through the infinite darkness of space.

National Cycling Centre, Stuart Street, Manchester
12.57 p.m.

With the match tied at one race each and his girls lining up on the start for the decider, Tom climbed the stairs and sat in the seat high up in the stands where he'd eaten grapes with Zoe thirteen years before. Up here it was easier to resist the temptation to coach her; to give her the nod of his head and the cyclonic motion of his hands that meant she should simply go hard straight off the start line. If she threw the playbook out of the window, went to 100 per cent power right off the whistle and opened up a gap on Kate, he knew Kate wouldn't have any answer. Kate's legs were shot, but Tom knew Zoe. She would still be thinking tactics. In the last race she'd used her head, conserved her power and resisted the temptation to blow Kate away completely. She'd kept her powder dry and won by the tiniest margin she dared. She'd won elegantly. The way Tom saw it, the danger was that she would try to win that way again. Putting down the power right from the whistle would be ugly and brutal, but it would get the job done. He wanted to tell her that, but this was the thing with coaching: you had to step back at exactly the moment you ached to step forward.

He watched Kate on the start line as she checked and rechecked her pedals. He put himself into her mind. She would be thinking of ways to slow the race down, and since Zoe had the inside line this time it wasn't going to be easy. If he could whisper in Kate's ear, he would tell her to go like a rocket off the whistle. That way if Zoe had decided to go to full power too, then Kate wouldn't have let a gap open up and she could tuck in to Zoe's slipstream, but if Zoe had decided to start slow then Kate could drop down in front of her, slow down, and use the lead position to dictate the speed of the race.

He swore at himself then, and he had to smile. This was what it had come to, after forty years of high-level coaching: his best tactical advice to his two best riders would be to ride their bicycles as fast as they were able.

It was unbearable, though, watching his girls lining up to hurt each other like this. In less than a minute the starter would step forward and then, three minutes after that, all of their lives would be changed. There was an intimate distance at which Kate and Zoe had held each other for more than a decade, now calling it friendship, now calling it rivalry, but always keeping each other less than a finished sentence, less than a ragged breath, less than a wheel-length away. This final race was the knife that would cut that link between them and send them falling into their separate lives.

If he was honest with himself, the reason he had come up here to sit on his own in the stands was not that he was afraid of giving in to the temptation to coach Zoe to win. It was because he was finding it harder and harder to resist the impulse to go down to the start line and beg the two of them not to race at all. You're thirty-two, he wanted to tell them, so why not give it up without killing each other first? Sooner or later you'll both need to climb down from the

Olympic heights and learn to walk quietly in the valleys with whatever remains of your strength.

He hated himself for the part he'd played in bringing this final confrontation forward. He'd done it to protect them from the media, but now he wished he'd played it differently. He raised his hands helplessly, wishing he knew how to make the signal that would make them look across at each other on the start line and understand all of this for themselves. A cyclonic motion, perhaps, but in the anticlockwise direction, meaning: please, when the whistle goes, forget everything I ever told you.

As the starter counted the seconds down from ten and the start line tension came into the bodies of his two athletes, his arms slowly dropped to his sides. He was the best coach he knew. He had nothing else in his life, and his focus was perfect and absolute. He knew everything there was to know about making human beings go quicker, but nothing at all about how to make them stop.

He fell back down into his seat as the whistle blew. It didn't surprise him at all that Zoe and Kate both did exactly what they should have done, going hard off the line. Because Kate had anticipated her quick start, Zoe failed to open up a gap on her and by the time they came out of the first bend Kate was tucked in to her wake. With the pace high, Zoe was doing all of the work and with each metre they raced she was conceding the energy she'd conserved in the first two races. She swerved across the track from the well up to the high side and back, trying to expose Kate to some air resistance. Kate responded well, matching every twist of direction that Zoe made.

As they entered the second lap, Tom watched with his heart hammering. His riders were at full speed now, swerving and ducking at thirty-five miles per hour with Kate's front wheel six inches from Zoe's back wheel as Zoe tried desperately to shake her off. Another lap of this and Zoe's legs would be blown, leaving Kate to pick her moment to pop out of her slipstream and ride past her. If Zoe couldn't drop Kate from her wind shadow very soon, then she would have to slow the race down to the speed at which the slipstream wasn't an advantage.

Even before it happened, Tom saw the risk. He rose to his feet again and his hands went up to his mouth. He watched Zoe signalling, by the relaxation of her shoulders and the slight lifting of her head, that she was slowing down. Either Kate didn't see it or she decided Zoe was faking, because Kate didn't slow or turn. At close to full speed, at the high side of the track, her front wheel made contact with Zoe's back wheel. Zoe's bike twitched and sent her into a high-speed judder, but she managed to control it. Kate was less fortunate. Her steering twisted and sent her over with her feet still locked in to the pedals. She skidded along the smooth boards on her side, her bike still attached to her. She came to a stop in the well of the track, screaming with shock and distress. In less than a second, everything was over.

Tom watched as Zoe slowed and looked back at her fallen rival. Kate had already picked herself up and was standing helplessly with her bike, gazing after Zoe. Zoe had slowed to a crawl now, craning her head back to look. Tom felt a wave of disgust. It was one thing to win by a stroke of luck – that was how it went in racing – but she didn't have to gloat. She should just quietly ride for the line now.

While he watched, Kate slowly raised her arm and gave the thumbs up. Tom's eyes filled with tears. All of her dreams ended by a crash – the worst way to lose a race – and here she was, five seconds later, accepting it and telling Zoe she was okay. As his heart rate began to wind down, Tom sighed. This was the reason Kate was going to be okay in whatever afterlife awaited her, while victory would only postpone Zoe's disintegration.

He began the painful walk down the stairs to console Kate and congratulate Zoe.

'Come on!'

Zoe's shout echoed through the velodrome. Tom looked up.

Zoe shouted again: 'Get back on!'

He saw Kate's confusion. 'What?'

'There's still a lap left, you lazy cow! You can stop when this is over!'

Kate hesitated. Her gloves were already off and discarded at the side of the track. She shouted: 'Are you serious?'

Zoe laughed. 'Yeah. Are you?'

Tom froze on the steps. Was Zoe actually waiting for Kate? He couldn't allow himself to believe it. He almost wished that Kate wasn't spinning the wheels of her bike to check that nothing was bent, and climbing back over the frame, and clicking a foot into the pedal. He couldn't bear to watch Zoe sprinting away from her before she drew level, or to witness the despair replacing the tentative hope in Kate's body language as she realised it had been a cruel trick.

It wasn't. As Kate brought her bike up to speed and clicked her second foot into its pedal, Zoe was still waiting for her, rolling at the slowest possible speed at which she could stay upright. By the time the two riders were abreast, they were coming into the straight that would lead them into the final lap. He watched as Kate and Zoe looked across at each other. They looked for a long time and then they looked forward again. Without anything being said they accelerated, side by side, and hit the line together. The bell sounded and both of them stood up on the pedals and launched the sprint.

There were no tactics now, just a flat-out blast for the finish. Kate squeezed into the inside and Zoe rode alongside her, both riders with their heads down, rocking their bikes from side to side as they wound up to an impossible speed. Beneath their visors their mouths gaped for air and the agony of the effort was written in the lines their jaws made. As they came around the first bend of the last lap Kate edged ahead by a few inches but Zoe pulled it back on the straight and went into the final bend half a bike length ahead. The inside line helped Kate to bring herself back, and as the two riders entered the finishing straight there was nothing between them. They flew down the last fifty metres in a blur of speed, matching each other pedal stroke for pedal stroke and breath for breath, and as they threw their bikes forward in the last desperate lunge for the line, they looked across at each other to see which one of them had taken it.

Post-operative recovery room, North Manchester General Hospital 1.15 p.m.

It had been a very quick operation – three strokes of the scalpel, then the deft withdrawal of the Hickman line. Almost before Jack had realised the surgeons had begun, the porters had arrived to wheel Sophie next door.

Here, the quiet and the stillness destabilised him. The nurses were gone for the moment – they'd left him alone with Sophie. The monitoring machines were set on mute. He asked the question with his eyes, but Sophie's breathing was so shallow that there was no answering movement of her chest. The rise and fall of it was his only pendulum, and without it this was a room outside time. He held her hand. Through the glass pane in the door he could see people moving in the corridor, arriving for their shifts, complying with visiting hours, oscillating according to their natural frequencies.

Jack whispered: 'Sophie?'

He stroked her face. There was a stillness in it beyond simple motionlessness. This is what frightened him more than anything. It looked like Sophie, and yet the anaesthesia had stilled even the echo of character that her face showed in sleep. These were Sophie's features, faithfully reproduced in their superficial aspects but unmoored from their animating spirit. *Very lifelike*, was the phrase that flashed into Jack's mind. He tried to unthink it, but you couldn't do that.

The air was neutralised for humidity, and temperature-controlled at 19.5 degrees Celsius. It was recycled air from wide-mouthed stainless steel ducts and it smelled of other people's tragedies. Jack closed his eyes and prayed.

Please don't take her, he said.

He waited. And then, when there was no answer either in the vocalisations of his mind or in the neutral pressure of Sophie's hand on his, and since Sophie's features were as still as a pool from which the wider sea had ebbed, he said: *If you let Sophie live, I will live for her from now on. I will hang up my bike. I will make her life my only gold.*

This was the deal that Jack tried to make with the universe. He was thirty-two. He realised that this moment, with Sophie's hand in his, in this little room, had been with him from the start. It had been with him, gnawing away at the underside of his small talk, when he stood in his boxer shorts while the tailor first fitted him for the

Athens Olympics. It had been with him, growing in definition in his mind's eye, while he held his head in his hands in the Beijing hotel.

He'd always been in this room.

He opened his eyes, hoping to see some movement, but Sophie was perfectly still.

National Cycling Centre, Stuart Street, Manchester
1.17 p.m.

Tom climbed up to the control room with the three race officials to look at the image from the photo-finish camera. The officials clustered around the monitor while the control room technician downloaded the picture. Tom wasn't ready to look. He sat on the far side of the little room, looking down on the track through the floor-to-ceiling safety glass windows. The floodlights were off and Zoe and Kate were arm in arm in the gloom, walking around the track with their shoes and socks off, warming down. As he watched, they looked up at the control room. He waved, but they couldn't see him. The control room glass was one-way.

He put a call through to Jack and got his voicemail. He was about to leave a message when the technician called over that the image was ready to view. Tom stood, walked the five steps to the screen, and made himself look.

Ten thousand times per second the camera had taken the narrowest cross section of the finish line, giving ten thousand microscopically thin vertical lines. The software had arranged the lines side by side, from left to right, in the order in which they had been taken. Tom squinted at the screen. You had to remind yourself that what you were seeing was the opposite of a normal photo, where space was frozen in time. This was an image created for use by professionals of the fractured second. It showed time frozen in space and it lent the strangest distortions to the bodies of the two athletes he knew so well. The quality of relative stillness translated well from space into time and so their arms and their faces were faithfully reproduced but their legs, which had been spinning so fast, were thinned at the top of the pedal stroke where they had been travelling faster than the bike, and thickened on the back stroke. The wheels of the bikes were neat circles, but the spokes described eerie parabolas from the hubs to the rims.

It spooked Tom to see his girls smeared across time like this. This was how he had lost out on a medal in '68. Back then they had used real film, continuously exposed as it was dragged across a thin vertical slit. The old machine had stamped lines on the image at intervals of one tenth of a second. That was what he had lost by: one tenth of a second, one eighth of an inch of time. That was the thinnest they could dice it, back in the day, and anything closer was called a tie. In those days they still left a fraction of a second for the idea that what God had joined together, no man should split apart.

He looked at Zoe's face, perfectly at peace as she crossed the line, and he was proud of her. It seemed to him that whatever happened on the line, she had won the race of her life. It was a symptom of this fallen age that the three race officials were asking the technician to superimpose a vertical red line that intersected the leading edge of Kate's front wheel, and making him zoom in, and pointing excitedly at the tiniest sliver of pale light between the fine red line and the foremost extremity of Zoe's front wheel.

'Shit,' Tom said quietly.

The senior race official turned to him. 'Is there a problem?'

Tom opened his mouth to speak, then shook his head. It was useless to explain that for most of his life there had been no technology in the world that could have separated his two girls today. It was impossible to express his outrage that they had atomised the second to the point where Zoe could lose by a thousandth of it.

'There's no problem,' he said finally.

'I'm sorry,' said the senior official. 'Do you want me to tell them?'

Tom shook his head. 'No, it's on me.'

The walk back down the steps to the track was long, with his knees protesting every movement. Zoe and Kate stood at the foot of the stairs, watching as he approached. He worked to keep his face neutral, and when he reached them he took Kate's hand in his right and Zoe's in his left.

'Kate won,' he said. 'By one thousandth of a second.'

He held their hands tightly for a moment, then released them. They turned to each other and stood in silence while the information began its slow metamorphosis into understanding.

He said: 'You can look at the photo if you like.'

Zoe didn't take her eyes from Kate's. 'No, it's okay. Well done.'

Tears welled in Kate's eyes. She shook her head and put her hands to her mouth. 'Let's race again.'

Zoe shrugged, helpless.

Kate turned to Tom. 'Can we do it again? Just the last race.'

'You know we can't.'

'I'm sorry, Zoe,' said Kate. 'I'm so sorry.'

Zoe didn't react. It worried Tom, the way she stood there with her hands loose at her sides and her eyes unfocused.

He put a hand on her arm. 'Come on,' he said gently. 'Let's talk.'

She shouldered him away. 'There's nothing to talk about, is there?

That's why they paint a finish line on the track, so you know when it's over.'

He sighed, and dropped his head. He had to find the strength to be her coach now; to provide the simple minute by minute instructions she would need to get through the next hour and the shitty days that would follow.

'Go and take a shower. Then get dressed and come and see me in my office. Okay?'

She sniffed and looked down at the raw Olympic tattoo on her forearm. 'Okay,' she said finally. Then she turned to Kate and tilted her head slightly. 'I'll miss you,' she said.

Kate took her hands. 'Zoe . . .'

They hugged hard, almost painfully, until Zoe broke it off and turned to walk to the dressing rooms. Tom watched her go, then he flipped down a seat for himself and indicated to Kate to take the one beside him.

'How are you feeling?' he said.

She looked at the ground. 'Like shit.'

'That's about right, I'd say. You're a good girl, Kate, but she didn't let you win. She only let you race.'

'I shouldn't have got up again. I shouldn't have let her bring me back in.'

'So why did you get up?'

Her face crumpled and her voice came out in a thin, strangled whisper. 'Because I've tried so hard, Tom. I wanted to win. I wanted to go to the Olympics.'

'And now you will. Unless you break three legs or someone pops up from nowhere in the next three months who's anything like as quick as you, then you'll be going to London. Think about that for a moment, will you?'

334

Kate held her head. 'I'm trying. But when I get there I'm just going to be thinking: *Zoe should be here, not me.*

He put an arm around her. 'Zoe is where Zoe is. If she hadn't let you back in after that crash she'd have lost more than the race, and I think she knows it.'

'I still feel like crap.'

He squeezed her shoulder. 'You'll handle it, Kate. It's about time you caught a break.'

They sat in silence for a moment, watching the maintenance crew buffing the track.

Tom took a deep lungful of air and exhaled it slowly. 'Kate?' he said carefully.

She looked at him warily, sensing the change of register. 'Yes?'

'You should call Jack.' He watched her eyes widening and he raised his hands. 'I'm sure it's nothing to worry about, but he's had to take Sophie along to the hospital.'

She jumped to her feet and the seat flipped up with a crash. Her nostrils flared. 'What? When was this?'

The truth was that it had been in another life, ninety minutes ago, when what happened on the track had still seemed vital. He tried to meet her gaze, but his eyes only made it to her feet.

'I'm sorry,' he said. 'I think you should go to the hospital.'

She was silent for a second, taking it in, then he watched as she sprinted away from him across the warm-up area and up the stairs to the main entrance.

He stood, folding his seat up quietly, and began the long walk down to his office.

Access gantry over main reactor core shaft, Imperial Battle Station colloquially known as the Death Star
1.55 p.m.

Vader said: 'I am your father.'

Sophie screamed: 'No!'

She woke up sobbing and confused. Dad was holding one hand and Mum was holding the other. There were tears in her eyes. She was wearing her race kit with a raincoat pulled over the top.

'It's okay, darling,' Mum said. 'Everything's okay.'

There was a burning place near her heart, and she put her hand to the familiar place where the Hickman line exited her chest. It was gone. In its place was a raw wound that hurt very badly when she touched it.

'I'm hit!' she said. Her voice was muffled and there was a mask obstructing her mouth. She struggled and tried to sit up, but Dad pushed her back down to the pillows.

'You're not hit, baby. It's the anaesthetic. You're going to feel a bit confused for a little while.'

Sophie blinked up at him. She looked around. There was a bank of instruments with wires trailing towards her body. She followed the wires to the points where they ducked under the edge of a sheet. The sheet covered her. She looked underneath and saw her own familiar body there, dressed in a hospital gown with a happy blue dinosaur on it.

Something was wrong. Dad's big strong hand was painfully tight on her small one. Mum's was too hot – there was sweat running down her arm. And the Hickman line was gone. This wasn't normal. She didn't belong here. This was the dream, she realised. She closed her eyes and tried urgently to wake up. There was a battle raging on the forest moon of Endor, and they needed her. This was no time to sleep.

'Sophie,' said Dad. 'Stay with us, okay?'

She opened her eyes again, irritably. 'You're not even real,' she said.

Dad grinned. 'That's my girl.'

She struggled weakly and tried to rip off the thing that was covering her mouth. Mum's hand closed around her wrist and stopped her.

'It's suffocating me!'

'Darling, that's your oxygen mask. It's helping you breathe.'

Sophie struggled for a moment, then collapsed back into her pillows. She lay for a while, catching her breath, then she opened her eyes wide.

'Am I late for school?' she said.

Dad looked at Mum, and Mum looked at Dad, and they both smirked.

'*What?*' she said crossly.

Mum leaned down and kissed her on the forehead. 'You are a bit late for school, Sophie. You're about two months late, but I'm sure you'll catch up very quickly. Fingers crossed, the doctors think you might actually be getting better.'

Sophie scowled. 'I'm not going in thicky maths with Barney,' she said.

Mum and Dad laughed, which was really annoying because everything she said now they seemed to think was hilarious.

She was so angry that she used the Force on them, which you were only meant to do in a battle and never with people in your family, but she was so enraged she couldn't stop herself. She raised her right hand, which was plumbed in all its veins with catheters that were taped down to the wrist, and she pointed her thumb and first finger at Mum and Dad. She narrowed the gap between her digits, and made the special frown with her eyes that caused the Force to flow from her fingers.

Her parents looked across at each other again and widened their eyes in fright. Sophie nodded with satisfaction – they weren't so cocky, now that the tables were turned. First Dad and then Mum put their hands to their throats and made small choking sounds, struggling for air.

When she decided she'd made her point, Sophie released them. Mum and Dad collapsed down into their seats, gasping, and when they'd got their breath back they held her hands while the monitoring machines showed her pulse slowly returning to normal.

'Do you want some good news?' said Mum. 'I think I'm going to the Olympics.'

Mum was watching her, waiting for a response. Sophie had been half listening, and because it seemed important to Mum, she made an effort. She ran the words over in her mind, trying to get the sense of them, but she was exhausted. The words made no sense. There were just these ten pink toes poking out of the end of her sheets. This shiny blue linoleum floor that made you want to roller skate. The bright, clean smell of the hospital, like electric washing-up liquid. It was beautiful and it made her happy but all of it was suddenly too much, and the darkness lurched again and swallowed her up and dragged her back down into sleep.

National Cycling Centre, Stuart Street, Manchester
2.05 p.m.

Tom waited for Zoe in his office underneath the track. She was taking forever in the shower, and he didn't blame her. There were two decades of racing to be washed away.

He got through to Jack, who told him that Sophie was very weak in post-op. He tried to put it outside his mind for now; to break it out of the problem space and concentrate on the needs of his athlete.

'My athlete,' he said aloud, feeling the sound of it in the dead air of his little room.

Unless she wanted to carry on in the sport at some more terrestrial level – and he couldn't really see her showing up to race at the Nationals any more, or the Northwest Seniors – then maybe she was no one's athlete now. What should you say to a woman like Zoe, now that no one was paying you to say it? As her coach he'd always known what to tell her. It had been easy to help when it had mattered how high she should keep her pedalling cadence, or how many grams of protein she should be eating a week before race day. Now that real life was the game, it would be easy for her to lose it. She would be helpless in a world where victory was rarely complete and defeat was often negotiable.

He didn't know what to tell her. He couldn't protect her the way he'd done when she was nineteen. He'd put her up in his flat in the week she spent at the hospital, after Jack's crash. He'd cooked for her, he'd talked cycling with her, and then when she'd decided she couldn't be with Jack, he'd hosted her for another week and tried to keep her head together. He'd looked after her the best he could, and there'd been a bond between them since then.

It was hard to see how he could help her now. He wanted to suggest that she come to stay with him again, but he was scared to ask. She might imagine he was in love with her; that he was a lonely old man appalled at the prospect of the remaining days of his life continuing to report for duty, one after the other, without her in them. She'd be right, of course – women always were – but maybe love wasn't the word. You surrendered the right to be in love with a thirty-two-year-old woman the minute you did something as careless as to be born in 1946. No, love wasn't it. It was just that without her, the incessant days would be sea lions at the zoo, mounting the podium and slapping their pliant fins to solicit some answering applause that he supposed he would have to train himself to produce. It was a trick that people managed. Maybe, with practice and an occasional glass of red, he could manage it too.

She came into his office, bleached by sadness, smaller than he'd ever seen her.

Since he didn't know what to say to her, he said: 'Tea?'

She nodded, and sat down on his desk while he made two cups.

He said: 'I'm proud of you. What you did on that track today was the best thing I've seen an athlete do.'

'Now I wish I hadn't.'

'Well, you're only human. I mean, I'm fairly sure.'

She managed a weak smile and they drank their teas.

She looked at him over the rim of her mug. 'What am I going to do, Tom?'

He pulled a pad and a pen off his desk. 'Let's make a list, eh? First we need to talk to British Cycling and work out a career path for you in the sport, find you a first coaching position, get you started. Then we ought to put together a press release. Before that you'll probably want to talk with your agent and your sponsors. Then we need to—'

'Stop,' said Zoe quietly. She held the heels of her hands to her forehead. 'I don't mean what am I going to do today. I mean, what am I going to do with the rest of my life?'

Tom blinked. '*Life* is a big word, isn't it? Let's break it down into smaller segments. Let's find a level of granularity we can plan around – we could say we'll take it a month at a time, or a week at a time, and treat each of those modules almost as a training unit . . .'

He was getting into it, using his hands to sculpt compliant units of time into the stuffy air of his office. He tailed off when he saw how she was looking at him.

'I just lost by a thousandth of a second,' she said. 'Don't tell me about weeks and months.'

He put the pad and pen back down on his desk, unmarked.

She looked at him, her knees jiggling nervily, her expression intent. 'You had a kid, right?'

He nodded. 'I still do, somewhere. Matthew. I haven't seen him for, I don't know, twenty years.'

'In all this time, you never talked about it.'

'Well it was never *about* me, was it?'

He smiled, but she didn't.

She said: 'Do you ever have those dreams where you're in the street and you've lost a child, and the dream goes on and on, and you search more and more frantically, and all you find is the kid's little shoes?'

The smile slowly faded from Tom's face. He looked at her wordlessly.

'The kid's fucking *shoes*, Tom. Sometimes they're full of blood, right up to the rim. They're so full that if you go up to them and press the side of the shoe, even very gently, then the blood wells up over the side and drips down onto your fingers. No?'

'Oh Zoe,' he said. 'When are you ever going to tell me what happened to you?'

She ignored him. 'I have that dream most nights. Other nights it's the one where something's chasing me. That's why I'm frightened of being alone. Do you never get frightened?'

He looked down at his hands. 'I reckon you get used to it.'

She exhaled unevenly. 'I don't get used to it. The only thing that ever helped me was racing. That's the only time I can't think about anything else.'

'Okay,' said Tom, 'so let's work on it. Let's look at some of the triggers that give you the bad dreams, and work out some coping strategies.'

She gave a short laugh, high and unsettling. 'The trigger is being alive. Think I should knock that on the head?'

'Don't even joke about it.'

She looked away. 'I suppose I've been making less of an effort to stay alive. I take risks I shouldn't. I ride out in front of traffic. I look down off the roof of my building and I kind of lean out and . . .'

'And what?'

Her eyes glittered as she stared at him, her face tight with tension. 'Can you help me get my daughter back? Can you help me get Sophie?'

Tom took a sip of his tea and put the mug carefully down on his desk. 'That's not the kind of question you can really ask your coach.'

She moved her hand to his, sweeping the tips of her fingers across his wrist. 'I'm not asking you as my coach, Tom.'

He fought against the shiver of pleasure that ran up the afferent nerves of his arm, found his spinal cord and evolved as it propagated through the more sophisticated matrix of his central nervous system into a sharp ache that was indistinguishable from longing.

He hesitated, then gently moved his arm away.

'As your friend, I'm telling you that you won't be thinking straight till you've come down off the back of this. It's natural that you feel like hammered shit right now. For a few days it'll feel like the world has ended.'

She reached across and took his hand again and held it in both of hers, studying it as if it was a map that might offer a way to navigate the conversation. 'I've trusted you since I was nineteen,' she said finally. 'I've never questioned what you said. When you suggested Sophie should go home with Jack and Kate . . .'

He freed himself again and put her hand back down on the desk. 'I never told you what to do. You didn't feel you were in a position to look after Sophie, and we all respected you for putting her into the care of someone who was.'

She glared. 'Well, now I am in a position to look after her, aren't I?'

He tried a smile. 'Give it a couple of days, will you? Get some rest, get your head straight, and then let's talk about Sophie. She's ill, Zoe. It's not the right time for her or for you to be getting into this.'

'So when is the right time?'

'I don't know. Maybe when you're not riding out in front of traffic.'

Zoe gripped the edge of the table. 'You could tell them you gave me bad advice, couldn't you? You could tell them I was lost and I didn't know what I was doing and you should never have let me give up my daughter.'

'Tell who?'

'Tell the courts.'

He sighed. 'You don't want to get the courts involved, Zoe. If you go to the courts then the media comes with it. You know what the media will say, if it all comes out?'

She looked at him and shrugged.

He forced himself to hold her eyes. 'They'll say Kate Argall gave up the Olympics for her child, while Zoe Castle gave up her child for the Olympics.'

She flinched. 'That's not fair.'

He shrugged sadly. 'Yeah, but is it completely untrue?'

'I thought it was true that I had to keep the pregnancy, because *you* said they'd never leave me alone if I got rid of it so I could race. Then I thought it was true that I had to keep quiet about being Sophie's mum, because *you* said the press would tear me apart if they found out.' Her voice rose, ringing with accusation.

'Don't tell me that wasn't true.'

'Yeah, but I'm tearing *myself* apart. This is worse than anything the papers could do to me.'

He tried to keep his breathing even. 'You were okay with it when you were winning. You took the golds and you stood on that podium and you raised your arms in the bloody air.'

She glowered at him. 'My arms, Tom? Let's look at my arms.'

She yanked up the left sleeve of her jacket and showed him the graze from her crash, still weeping through the gauze.

'This one is a true story,' she said. 'You'll go too fast, you'll crash and it will really fucking hurt.'

She jerked up her other sleeve and showed him the Olympic rings on her skin, lurid and inflamed. 'This one is a lie. *Swifter, higher, stronger*. It just makes you more and more lonely. People see me standing on the podium and they think they're seeing glory, and all they're seeing is the one shining minute when I rose up out of the mess I made to get there. Look at every single champion you've ever met. Look at me and Jack. We're wrong in the head. We spent our whole lives putting ourselves first. Now look at Kate, always coming second. The saints were all losers, Tom. But they don't give out medals for this' – she waved her grazed arm at him – 'they give them out for this.' She pushed her tattooed arm towards his face, hard, and he recoiled from it.

'You're not seeing it straight.'

'I can see it with my eyes closed, Tom, because it hurts. It fucking hurts.'

He sighed and sank back in his chair. 'You wanted to win. My job was to help you do it.'

She shook her head furiously, angry red blotches rising in the skin of her face and neck. 'I feel like my heart's been ripped out. I feel like I could start screaming and never stop. If you ever really wanted to help me, you'd have warned me eight years ago how I was going to feel today.'

He stared at her, incredulous. 'Please. I couldn't change you. No one could.'

She smiled savagely at him, almost a snarl. 'Then your job was just to sell tickets to the freak show, the same as everyone else.'

'That's not fair. I care about you. I always did.' He realised he was blushing.

She said: 'If you care about me, then let me stop all the lies. It's my turn now.'

He looked at her sharply. 'How do you mean?'

'I want to tell Sophie the truth. I want to do it today.'

He spread his hands in a pleading gesture. 'She's in the hospital, Zoe.'

Straight away, he wished he hadn't said it. He watched her muscles tense and her body spin on the swivel chair, configuring itself to get up and leave.

He grabbed her wrist. 'Please, don't go there now. Just give it some time. I've seen this before with athletes at the end of a long run. Today is the worst you're ever going to feel in your life, but believe me, you do have a future.'

She pulled away from him. 'Not without my daughter. I mean it, Tom.'

He looked into her eyes then, and he believed her.

'I'm going to tell Sophie the truth,' she said. 'I'm going to the hospital and telling her now.'

She got up from his desk and he stood to block her, but his knees flared with pain and his spirit sank. He fell back down in his chair.

'I can't stop you,' he said.

And then, when Zoe had left his small, airless office, he said: 'I never could.'

He looked down at his hands for a minute, then picked up his phone to warn Jack and Kate.

North Manchester General Hospital
3.30 p.m.

Zoe arrived at the main desk of the hospital and signed in as a relative. They told her where Sophie was, and she followed the signs to paediatric intensive care. She walked the long linoleum

346

lines of the corridors, feeling the weakness in her legs from the after-effects of racing. In defeat there was no endorphin high to offset the aches. At the junction of two thoroughfares she had to rest, taking her weight against the wall for a minute until the sharp pains in her ankles subsided. Hospital staff flowed by, moving with the undramatic efficiency of bodies rarely pushed close to their operational limits. The pain in her ankles made her think about Tom. Was this how it had started for him – the arthritis and the joint problems? Did it hit him the very minute he sank out of the sport? The body was like that – it had a capacity to hold itself together until it was allowed to fall apart. People walked out of burning buildings on two broken legs, only collapsing when they were safely away from the flames. Spouses died within days of each other, and they called it a broken heart.

Sparks of gold light floated across her vision, and the floor seemed distant and uneven. She hadn't eaten since before the race – she'd been too upset to remember her recovery drink – and now her blood sugar was crashing. She ignored the pain from her ankles and forced herself to move again according to the directions the receptionist had given her.

Kate was sitting in the corridor outside the entrance to the recovery unit, on one of a pair of vinyl-covered chairs that bracketed the double swing doors. Opposite the chairs there was an aquarium with slow fulvous fish gnawing at the thin green lamina of algae on the inside of the glass. There was a noticeboard with government posters recommending the daily ingestion of vegetables, and outlining how best to sneeze.

Kate looked up at the sound of Zoe's trainers on the lino. She didn't seem surprised to see her. Her face was blank, drawn with

347

fatigue. She was still wearing her racing skinsuit, with her raincoat over the top of it.

'Hi,' she said quietly.

Zoe scowled. 'Tom told you I was coming, right? I'm going in, okay?'

She put her hand on the push-plate of the door.

Kate didn't look at her. 'Just sit down, Zoe.'

There was something in her voice that made Zoe hesitate.

'You can't stop me,' she said.

'I know,' said Kate. 'So sit down.'

Zoe sniffed. 'Okay,' she said. 'One minute, and then I'm going through.'

She sat in the other chair and twisted it sideways to face Kate.

'Sophie's very weak,' Kate said.

Zoe felt the last of her own strength leaking away. The gold lights drifting through her vision multiplied until she could barely see. The chair seemed to lurch beneath her and the floor listed away so that she had to grip the armrests, or fall.

'Is she going to be okay?'

She watched Kate pressing her lips together, trying to control her emotions.

'We think so.'

Zoe sagged with relief. 'Thank God.'

Kate's mouth contorted for a moment, then settled back into a pale, tired line. She said: 'Are you okay?'

'I feel like I got the shit kicked out of me.'

Kate nodded. 'Tom said you were upset. He said you were talking about telling Sophie the truth.'

Zoe looked across at her. It was hard to see Kate as the winner, even now. Since they were nineteen Zoe had developed a habit of looking for the weaknesses in Kate's stance; the signs of hesitation in her face; the insecurities in her speech. She had leapt on every advantage Kate conceded, even though afterwards she had always been sorry. Now there was no more afterwards. It was hard to adjust to the reality that Kate had finally won – had won everything. There she was, sitting in the exact same kind of chair Zoe was sitting in, and yet the knowledge that Kate was going to the Olympics made her chair a throne. Zoe had spent so many years in awe of the Games that it was impossible to stop feeling the force of it now. All the power that she had invested in London was suddenly Kate's.

What made it worse was that Zoe hadn't even been beaten, not really – she'd given Kate a second chance at the race today because it seemed the right thing to do for Sophie, who wanted her mum to win so badly. Her *mum*. As she looked at her rival sitting palely across from her, it struck her with full force that Kate had never once truly beaten her at anything. Zoe had given up Jack, and surrendered Sophie, and gifted the Olympics. Kate had merely been there, pathetically hanging on in second place, in order to be the closest to Zoe when she loosed all these precious things from her grasp. While Zoe had battled with ghosts, Kate had hoovered up after her like a good little housewife.

Zoe's eyes narrowed as she felt some of her strength return. 'Yeah,' she said. 'I do want to tell Sophie the truth.'

She watched the tears welling as Kate took it in. In the tank on the opposite side of the corridor the imprisoned fish worried away at their thin layer of green slime, flicking their tails and sending up grains of gravel that fell in silence back to the aquarium floor.

'All right,' Kate said finally. 'You do have a right to tell Sophie, if that's what you need to do. But . . .'

She stood, came over to Zoe's chair and knelt to take her hand.

'You're my best friend, Zoe. I know how hard this is for you. I do trust you to do the right thing for Sophie. Will you wait, though? Will you wait till Sophie's stronger before we tell her together?'

Zoe looked down at her and felt a tearing force in her chest. This was how they always got you – Kate, Tom and Jack. They talked so sweetly that you felt an answering surge in the buried part of yourself that you so desperately wanted to believe could be you. You surrendered to it, just for a moment, and the next thing you knew they'd taken something else from you.

Hot rage rose through her. 'I'm not just talking about telling Sophie. I want us to do something about it.'

'What?'

'I want to be Sophie's mother, Kate. I want nights without nightmares. I want everything you took from me.'

Slowly, Kate shook her head. 'Oh God, Zo. I didn't *take* Sophie from you. I took her in, because you . . . couldn't.'

Zoe shook her head furiously. 'You took *me* in. All of you.'

She watched Kate's mouth twist in a soundless howl as she realised Zoe meant it. 'Please,' Kate said. 'Please.'

'Please, what?'

'You can't.'

'I can. If you won't do what's right, then I'll fight you in the courts. I was in pieces, Kate. I didn't know what I was doing.'

'Please. You're not thinking about what this will do to Sophie.' Kate collapsed against the arm of the chair. 'I can't stand this, I can't stand it.'

Zoe looked down at her coldly. 'Then you should have left me with something. You should have stayed down when you crashed today.'

Kate looked up at her through tears. 'Is that what this is about? Because you can have it. You can have my place in London. I'll phone British Cycling right now. I'll tell them I cheated. I'll tell them I sabotaged your bike. I'll tell them anything you need me to, Zoe, just please leave Sophie out of it.'

Zoe stood and stepped around her. 'No. I'm not going to let you trick me again. I'm going in there right now and I'm going to tell Sophie the truth.'

Kate grabbed hold of her arm. '*Please*. I'll give you anything.'

Zoe tried to pull her arm back but Kate clung to it fiercely, increasing the weight on Zoe's ankles so that she had to stifle a yelp.

'Get off me!'

'Please, Zoe. If you have to do this then at least don't do it now. Okay? I'll give you my place in London if you just leave Sophie alone for a month. Just let her get stronger, okay? If you love her at all, then take my place in the Olympics – take whatever you need – but just give her a few weeks to get better. Then you can do whatever you have to do. Just please – please – don't do this to Sophie now.'

Zoe snapped her arm away and broke Kate's grip. She put her hands over her ears to block Kate's pleading. 'I'm not listening to you any more. There's always a reason why you end up happy, and just for once I don't want to fucking hear it!'

Zoe stepped out of range of Kate's reaching hands and projected herself backwards through the swing doors, into the recovery unit. She walked quickly past the nurses' station, ignoring the pain in her ankles, blanking the uniformed woman who asked how she could help. She heard the swing doors open again as Kate followed her in. She hurried down the unit's central corridor, looking left and right through the narrow strengthened-glass windows of each room. The fourth room she looked into was Sophie's – she saw Jack sitting at the bedside and pushed her way in through the doors.

Jack looked up at her but she didn't acknowledge him. Her eyes fell on Sophie, pale and still, her mouth and nose covered with a translucent green oxygen mask. She stopped.

She hadn't been expecting this – for Sophie to be unconscious. She'd been holding on to the image of Sophie as she had been two days earlier, laughing in the basket of the butcher's bike while Kate pedalled her around the track of the velodrome. Zoe had pictured her under the weather – ill, perhaps, but sitting up in bed and smiling bravely. She'd even run through a few of the preliminary things she might say. *Sophie, remember how much fun we had at the track the other day? How would you like to have fun like that all the time?*

This perfect silence, this absolute stillness pulled her up short.

Sophie's face, motionless and waxy, was a perfect echo of a face that lay deep in the silence of Zoe's memory. Zoe raised her hands to her mouth and gasped. A rising dread flushed all the heat from her blood and she froze, staring at Sophie's face, fighting against the surfacing of another bone-white face that she hadn't seen since she was ten years old.

'Oh God . . .' she whispered.

She staggered, and gripped the steel guardrail of Sophie's bed to stop herself from falling.

Jack's hand was on hers and Kate's arms were hugging her around her shoulders but she didn't feel any of it. They were asking if she was all right but all she could hear was the cold, close silence of the room. The sharp disinfectant smell of the hospital quickened the memory that was rising unstoppably now. The hospital bed on its rubberised castors supported it and the green hospital sheets shrouded it, and as she sank to her knees the height of her eyes descended until she was ten years old again, and walking with a female social worker through the echoing, empty corridors of a hospital basement.

They'd given her pills to make her calm, but the only effect had been to lodge a high whining note in her ears and a dizzy, lurching confusion in her mind. Adam had come off his bike – that was all she remembered. Adam had come off his bike, and she needed to find him and take him home. She had to do it herself because their mother couldn't. Something had happened in their mother's heart or head that meant she couldn't get out of bed and she couldn't stop crying and shouting.

It was forty-eight hours after the police had picked Zoe up, delirious and riding erratically along the dual carriageway after the accident. Her legs still ached badly, and it hurt to walk.

'Is it much further?' she said. 'Which room is Adam in?'

The social worker stroked her hair. 'Adam's body, darling. It's that door at the end.'

The words were all mashed up in Zoe's head. The social worker was pointing at a battered, unpainted metal door at the end of the corridor. Zoe hurried towards it. She pushed against it but it was locked.

When the social worker reached her she knelt down and said: 'All right, darling. Now I do just want to check that you're still okay to do this. It's going to be very difficult for you to see Adam the way he is. I'm afraid it will make you very sad, but we've found that in the long run you'll probably be more sad, and more upset, if you don't actually see the body.'

Zoe wasn't listening. Now that they'd reached Adam, she couldn't bear that the social worker was making her wait. She pushed insistently on the door until the woman unlocked it for her.

Inside, it was very cold. There were no windows, just a set of overhead strip lights. The floor was tiled, and there was what looked like a sink and ordinary kitchen units along one side. In the centre of the room, Adam was sleeping on clean green sheets in a high steel bed. His head was towards her and she saw his shock of glossy black hair on the pillow.

She smiled with relief. 'Adam!'

The bang of the accident had been so loud, it was good that he was so peaceful. She'd worried that he might be injured and shouting with the pain, or just shouting for no reason the way their mother was. On the top of the kitchen units along the side of the room there was a pair of red rubber gloves, and nothing else. She didn't understand why there was no food in the kitchen, or why her brother was sleeping in it. Maybe he was as confused as she was.

He'd drawn the green sheet up over his face to make it dark enough to sleep. She padded up to the bedside and drew back the sheet and he didn't move at all; just lay there perfectly asleep. He was pale but he was himself, and so calm. She smiled and kissed him on the cheek and then her smile twitched, because his skin was chilly. She drew back and looked at him and noticed again how pale he was. She touched him.

He was so cold.

'Adam, wake up!'

He didn't open his eyes straight away, so she shook his shoulder. It didn't move the way it should have. Instead, his whole body rocked from side to side. She shook his shoulder and watched his feet following the motion, under the sheets, at the far end of the bed.

'Adam?' she whispered.

A terrible fear flashed over her and she let go of Adam's shoulder to make the fear be not true, and she ran out of the room and along the corridor. She was quick, even with the pain in her legs, and it took a long time for the social worker to catch her. She felt herself being picked up off the ground and held as she struggled to escape.

After a while she was too tired to fight any more, and she let herself be carried to a little room with a low table and carpet tiles and scratchily upholstered chairs. She listened carefully to what the social worker told her. The words came through more clearly this time, but since it was impossible that they could be true, she went into a kind of long and terrible dream for more than twenty years and she tried again and again to wake up from it. Athens didn't wake her and Beijing didn't wake her and then, finally, she did wake up, at thirty-two years of age, kneeling beside this hospital bed and watching Sophie's face on another green hospital pillow, pale and absolutely still.

Zoe's shoulders shook, and Jack and Kate knelt on either side of her and told her that everything was going to be okay.

They brought a chair for her, and the three of them sat by Sophie's bedside all afternoon. Slowly, as she watched the slight rise and fall of Sophie's chest, Zoe felt the ache of the day's defeat subsiding. She watched the natural, unconscious way that Kate tended to Sophie – now turning her sheet down when she seemed to be hot; now adjusting the strap of her oxygen mask when it slipped. Slowly, she remembered something she had forgotten in the bitter aftermath of Kate's victory: that this job Kate had been doing wasn't something that she herself could do. It wasn't just hard, it was always a wheel-length ahead of impossible. Looking after a very sick child was the Olympics of parenting. If Sophie had been hers to look after, through the long years of her illness, Zoe knew she wouldn't have made it.

The pain didn't disappear with the acceptance, but it slowly became easier to hold within herself. Each moment layered small consolations around it, working to smooth its sharp edges. Sophie was alive – this was the main thing. And Zoe had Tom, and Kate, and so she wasn't completely alone.

All afternoon the three of them sat in silence around Sophie's bed, never taking their eyes from her face, willing her to get well.

Finally, with the red sun setting beneath the ragged grey clouds outside the hospital window, Sophie opened her eyes.

She was quiet for a few minutes, looking around her and taking in the presence of Zoe, Kate and Jack. Kate fetched her a glass of water and took off her mask to help her drink it, and Zoe watched Sophie's calm eyes as she looked up into Kate's face and smiled.

'Mum?' she said in a cracked whisper. 'Why's Zoe here?'

Zoe felt Jack and Kate watching her.

She leaned in and took Sophie's small, warm hand in both of hers. 'I just wanted to tell you . . .' she said. Then she faltered, feeling the sting of tears.

'Tell me what?' said Sophie.

'Something I've never told you before. Something I should have told you years ago.'

Sophie blinked. 'What?'

Jack and Kate shifted on their chairs. Jack was about to say something, but Kate stopped him with a hand on his arm.

Zoe squeezed Sophie's hand and smiled at her. 'I just want to tell you who you've got as parents. You're a very lucky girl, Sophie. You have a dad who cares about you so much that he could hardly ride his bike straight for thinking about you, even in the biggest race of his life. There aren't very many men like that in the whole world, I hope you know. And you have a mum, Sophie . . .'

She swallowed and tried again. 'You have a mum who loves you so much that she was ready to give up the most important thing in the world for her, just because it was the right thing to do for you.'

She blinked rapidly, forcing back her tears.

Sophie looked at her quizzically. 'Yeah,' she said. 'I know.'

As the tears began, Zoe felt an arm around her and let her head fall onto Kate's shoulder.

'I'm so sorry,' she said. 'I'm just so tired.'

Kate's hands stroked her hair. 'Shh,' she whispered. 'It's okay. We're just tired because we've been racing so long.'

Two weeks later, The Townley pub, Albert Street, Bradford, Manchester

Tom came back from the bar with a double Scotch for him and a sparkling water for Zoe. She was sitting at a corner table, on a bench seat set into a wall alcove, with her chin on her knees, watching him.

'What?' he said. 'An old man can't have a drink after a day like that?'

She managed a small smile that lit up his mood a little. He was pleased with how she was doing. It wasn't the sun yet, but it was a candle in a basement. He'd take any kind of progression from the absolute darkness of those hours after her last race.

She pointed at the drink in his hand. 'But whisky?'

'If they made anything stronger, trust me, I'd be drinking it.'

She tried another smile.

He hadn't left her alone for a fortnight. In the daytime he'd kept her engaged with the simple tasks of winding up her sponsorship deal and moving out of her apartment. In the night, in his small flat, he'd looked into her room every half hour. He'd slept only in twenty-minute bursts shattered by the piping of his wristwatch alarm. Still, at his age, you needed life to forgive you more than you needed sleep.

This morning he'd organised a small white hire car with the rental company's sticker on the doors, powered by something that was nominally an engine. He'd driven her down south to the decaying Hampshire church with the overgrown graveyard that she'd never visited. It had taken them half an hour to find her brother's headstone. It was polished and lacquered black marble, in the shape of a teddy bear. The canonical features had been carved into the stone with inhuman precision using a computer-controlled router programmed by a manufacturer that presumably specialised in these stelae and produced them in short runs of ten or a dozen units at a rate determined by statistical algorithms to be proportional to the rate at which children passed away within the geographical purview of the distributor. At a later time, possibly further down the supply chain, the routed lines of the teddy bear's eyes and smile had been picked out in a patent-protected brand of weather-resistant gold paint that had the property of adhering to metamorphic stone when properly keyed in, and staying there pretty much forever.

Tom had hated the stone. The sense of disappointment at a world that had produced such an artefact and compelled this young woman that he cared about to look at it was almost more than he could bear. He'd taken it out on the grave's overgrowth of long sedge and bramble, ripping it away so violently that his hands were left torn and bleeding. The headstone, when they had finally exposed it, was stark and upright and unweathered in that flat field of lolling, rusticated crosses.

Zoe hadn't said a word, just silently stared at that terrible child's monument travelling in eternal locked formation with the softer stones of the elderly dead. Then, kneeling, she took out her first Olympic gold – the sprint medal from Athens on its faded blue ribbon. She hung it around the teddy bear's neck. From her jacket pocket she took the dented aluminium water bottle she and Adam had shared. She stood it up carefully on the grave, heaping the white marble chips to keep it upright on its uneven base. *You won*, she whispered. *You must be so thirsty.*

Walking back to the car, they had clung to each other for support. His knees were shot, her ankles were questionable, and both their hearts were in the kind of state where, if they had been any other muscle, he'd have recommended that they should be rested for the remainder of the season.

They'd sat in the car in silence for a few minutes before he started the engine.

'I should have come here twenty years ago,' she said finally. 'I should have dealt with it all in my head. That's what normal people would have done, right?'

He thought about it for a moment, then sighed. 'Let's both not get started on what we should have done.'

Zoe looked out at the churchyard. 'Is it always like this, when someone falls out of the sport?'

'Like what?'

'I don't know. It feels like dying. Or being born.'

Tom weighed it up, tapping his fingers on the wheel. 'No,' he said finally. 'I mean by the time they retired, the other riders I worked with had more or less figured out what they wanted to do next. Maybe that's why they won so much less than you. You never really thought about next, did you? Gave you a hell of an advantage on the track.'

'Was that not fair on the others, or was that not fair on me?'

He grinned. 'Sweetheart, fair is a hair colour.'

She'd laughed and they'd driven back north in a mellow kind of silence. They'd arrived back in Manchester and dropped off the hire car in the evening. They'd gone up to her apartment on the forty-sixth floor and packed the last of her things into a single Team GB holdall while the moon rose over the city through the tall plate-glass windows. Then they'd put her single Yale key into a plain white envelope and posted it through the letterbox of the solicitors who were handling the sale.

They'd stood out on the pavement, not knowing what to say to each other.

'I could go for a drink,' Tom had said.

Zoe had shrugged. 'I suppose I could go and watch you drink it.'

Now Tom was sitting opposite her and he positioned their glasses on the coasters. The pub was nearly empty. The blood-red carpets were patterned to camouflage whatever might be spilled on them in the future, and musty with the smell of whatever had been in the past. No one had put money in the jukebox and so it was choosing its own tunes. At this moment it was playing 'God Only Knows' by the Beach Boys.

'How are you feeling?' said Tom.

'Okay.'

'How are you finding the weather, down here where us mortals live?'

She flipped him the middle finger.

The baby-faced barman rang a brass bell suspended from the canopy of the bar, to indicate that time had reached a point of division. 'Last orders,' he called.

Tom frowned at his watch. 'Sure you don't want something stronger, Zo?'

She shook her head, and he reached over to touch her arm.

'You want us to go and see Kate and Sophie tomorrow?'

'Soon. Not just yet. I need some time to let it all settle.'

He watched her carefully. 'Do you regret not telling Sophie?'

Zoe sniffed and shook her head. 'No, I'm glad. Kate *is* her mother. Kate went through hell for her and I just . . . went.'

Tom squeezed her arm. 'You did the best you could. That's all you ever do. I wouldn't like you so much if that wasn't true.'

'But Tom, I love her. It's possible to love a child even though you can't be their parent. Isn't it?'

He smiled. 'I reckon so.'

Her eyes were still, the green of them muted and dull. There was a long way to go with her. Soon, maybe in another week or so, she'd start hearing the hints he was dropping. She still wasn't receptive to the idea that there might be something great she could do with her days. She talked about modelling deals, or becoming a commentator, or any of a dozen lives he knew would make her unhappy. Still, he wasn't going to give up. It was a patient business, talking comets down to the speed of life.

'Never mind,' he said. 'Everything's going to be all right.'

The barman was putting chairs on tables and spraying the kind of aerosol furniture polish that had the quality of simultaneously being citrus fresh and unsurvivable. The TV in the corner was showing the war in Afghanistan. The jukebox had moved on to Ella Fitzgerald singing 'Dream a Little Dream of Me'.

'You're a pretty nice person,' Zoe said finally.

'If your ankles get any worse, honey, then you'd better start being nice too.'

She smiled at him then, a full smile that lifted him to a place he hadn't been in weeks.

Slowly her mouth sank back into a soft and serious line. 'You're good to me,' she said quietly.

'You're the story of my bloody life,' he said. 'Why wouldn't I be good to you?'

The barman gave two strikes on the big brass bell and said: 'Time, ladies and gentlemen, please.'

Three years later, Sunday 5 April 2015

National Cycling Centre, Stuart Street, Manchester

Jack sat next to Kate, high up in the stands, watching Sophie train alone on the track. They didn't talk, only listened to the rumble of her wheels on the boards and the beeps from the lap timer. They liked to wait up here, out of Sophie's line of sight, letting her get on with it. They liked to listen to Zoe's excitable shouts as she coached their daughter.

Sometimes, as Sophie carved around the high banking and dropped snugly back down to the racing line, they felt their own hands twitching on phantom handlebars, and the muscles in their legs aching to fire. Their heart rates climbed and they were there on the track with her, roaring round those polished maple curves, pushing the biomechanics to that perfect edge where everything clicked and their minds became still.

When it carried them away like that, they had to close their eyes and slow their breathing and remember that their time was gone. It persisted only in the immutable stillness of Jack's gold from Athens, buried in the ground with his father, and in the daily motion of Kate's gold from London, swinging in its rightful place on the end of the light cord in the understairs toilet of their home.

After all the years of speed, the greatest challenge of all was to make themselves sit still, up here in the dark of the stands. This was what you learned, after all the racing was over: that the hardest laps were the ones you did after the crowd had gone home.

'Kid looks good, doesn't she?' Jack said after a while.

Kate watched Sophie grinning as she swooped into another curve. 'Yeah, she looks really quick.'

'Think she'll go gold one day?'

Kate was about to warn him against hoping for too much, but she closed her mouth. Who was she to say what the probabilities were? Sophie had come back from leukaemia. She had fired the Death Star's destructor beam into the limitless constellations of space, and hit exactly the right target. She had beaten those kinds of odds.

They watched their daughter. Dark locks protruded from under her crash hat. When she took the helmet off she liked to wear her hair in side buns, and she had a tendency to accessorise with a belt and a blaster. Strangers who saw the Argalls now were more likely to diagnose a fashion disaster than a medical one.

Sophie had bulked up as quickly as they had. With remission from leukaemia had come respite from some of the allergies and intolerances. With her off the chemo and them off their training diets, the family had become partners in second breakfasts and midnight feasts. Sophie's cheeks were filling out. Jack's jeans were three inches bigger at the waist. They had eaten themselves back to normal, or as normal as any family could be whose daughter was currently circling the national velodrome in a custom-made Princess Leia Lycra outfit under the supervision of an Olympic quadruple gold medallist at seven o'clock on a Sunday morning while her school friends were all at a sleepover.

Jack squeezed Kate's knee. 'Youth Nationals this summer. Think we should let her compete?'

Kate thought about it. 'What does Zoe say?'

'She told me Sophie was going to beat the other girls so badly they'd need counselling.'

Kate laughed. 'She doesn't change.'

He felt the anxiety catch in his chest. 'But I don't know. Is it safe for Sophie to push herself so hard, physically?'

'She says she feels great.'

'But that's what she told us when she was practically dying. I mean, how do we know what to believe?'

Kate hugged Jack around the waist and nestled her head into his shoulder.

'We'll see the truth on the track,' she said quietly.

They both looked down at the action. Far below them, with fits of echoing giggles and rivers of foul language, Zoe was psyching their daughter up to race pace. In the fading years behind them, the vast crowds shouted their names. Far above them all, and falling through the skylights high in the vaulted roof of the velodrome, the brave April light was golden.

author's note

Cycling is hard. The training is brutal and relentless, the racing desperate and dangerous. Researching this novel I spent some time on a bike, seeing how far I could push myself and trying to record how it felt. I am a willing but poor cyclist, and with every turn of the pedals I am more in awe of the champions. There are barriers of physical and emotional pain which they can push through and I cannot. They are extremely brave people, and I feel it is important to record some of their real achievements here.

At the Athens Olympics in this novel, Zoe Castle won gold in the women's sprint and individual pursuit, while Jack Argall won gold in the men's sprint. In reality, gold in the women's sprint was won by Lori-Ann Muenzer of Canada, gold in the women's individual pursuit by Sarah Ulmer of New Zealand, and gold in the men's sprint by Ryan Bayley of Australia.

At the Beijing Olympics in this novel, Zoe Castle won gold in the women's sprint and individual pursuit. In reality, Rebecca Romero of Great Britain won gold in the women's individual pursuit while Victoria Pendleton of Great Britain won gold in the women's sprint.

May their victories be remembered, and their characters celebrated, forever.

At the time of writing, the London Olympics of 2012 are still a year away. Good luck to all the athletes.

Caring for sick children is the Olympics of parenting. While researching this story I was allowed to shadow Dr Philip Ancliff, a consultant haematologist at Great Ormond Street Hospital, where seriously ill children are brought from all over the world. I was present in the room while Dr Ancliff, a brilliant and compassionate man, broke the news of some very serious diagnoses to the parents of some very sick children.

Nothing prepared me for the emotional impact of witnessing parents' reactions at times like these. And nothing has ever filled me with more hope and anticipation than to see how those parents, together with the amazing team at Great Ormond Street, subsequently cared for their unwell children. Parents and staff alike seemed to step up into a state of focused grace in which all worldly concerns were cast off until all that remained was love. As a researcher, it was like being embedded with angels.

I am sometimes depressed or discouraged by the behaviour of institutions and individuals in this world, including myself, and I have frequently struggled to find something I can look up to without fear of being let down or disillusioned. For me, Great Ormond Street Hospital is that thing. It embodies not only a pure spirit of mission and selflessness on the part of the staff, but also the astonishing progress made by doctors and scientists. Only four decades ago, a diagnosis of childhood leukaemia was a death sentence in nine cases out of ten. Today, through advances in medical research, the odds have been reversed and nine out of ten children will enter remission.

There is, of course, far more work to be done. If you have a spare moment then I would urge you please to visit the website of the Great Ormond Street Hospital charity, where you can find out about children with conditions like Sophie's, and learn about the extraordinary things that can now be done for them. If you are moved to donate, then I believe you will be effecting one of the most efficient conversions of money into love available anywhere on our planet.

www.gosh.org

Thank you.

Chris Cleave
London
2011

thanks

This novel evolved through six drafts and Jennifer Joel read all of them. Her insightful critiques and unfaltering support meant everything to me. Thank you, Jenn.

Peter Straus is a brilliant man who always has my back, and I'd be nowhere without his wisdom and strength.

Suzie Dooré is a unique and courageous editor who rescued me from oblivion and who continues to rescue me on nearly every page.

Thanks and admiration to everyone at Sceptre and Hodder & Stoughton, especially Carolyn Mays, Carole Welch, Jamie Hodder-Williams and James Spackman.

Alasdair Oliver is the art director for my books. I think he does a beautiful job. If you first chose this book because it looked good, I owe him one.

My very grateful thanks also to Simon Appleby, Tina Arnold, Leena Balme, Nikki Barrow, Auriol Bishop, Amber Burlinson, Maite Cuadros, Stephen Edwards, Harriet Ferguson, Ben Gutcher, Katie Haines, Lucy Hale, Kerry Hood, Jonathan Karp, Jessica Killingley, Sarah Knight, Laurence Laluyaux, Eleni Lawrence, Job Lisman, Bea Long, Zoë Nelson, Gunn Reinertsen Næss, Jorge Oakim, Marina Penalva, Jane Rose, David Rosenthal, Louise Sherwin-Stark,

Eleanor Simpson, Mathilde Sommeregger, Henrikki Timgren, Francine Toon and Synnøve Helene Tresselt.

Thank you to my cycling friends for getting me up to speed: Matt Rowley, Matt Hinds, Jake Morris, Neil McFarland, Ian Laurie, Jonny Moore and Alex Cleave.

A very special thank you to Danielle Ryan for the incredible support she has given to my family.

And thank you, as ever, to my family and friends.

find out more

Go to Facebook.com/ChrisCleaveBooks
for extra material, including:

Book tour updates and photos

•

Interviews

•

Articles about Chris Cleave's
inspiration for *Gold*

tell the world

If you want to talk about *Gold*,
join in the conversation:

via Chris' website: www.chriscleave.com
on Facebook.com/ChrisCleaveBooks
on Twitter: @chriscleave or #goldnovel

If you have something you want to ask
Chris about *Gold*, your question and
his answer could appear online,
and in the back pages of the
paperback edition.

read more

Chris Cleave says:

'My first novel, *Incendiary*, asked the question: how much of our freedom should we sacrifice in the name of some sense of security? It was about terrorism.

My second novel, *The Other Hand*, was about the politics of refugees and immigration, and the question I was asking there was how much of our comfortable lives should we give up in order to help those who are less fortunate than ourselves? It's this age-old question of charity, and where you draw that line. When do you get to the point where you can look at yourself in the mirror in the morning and say: yes, I think I've done a fair deal in distributing the luck that I've had as a person between myself and my own family, and between other people who have less.

I try to make these things personal, I try to make them small rather than geopolitical.

With *Gold*, I've taken that argument further, I hope. I try to write these stories that take universal human themes – what Faulkner called 'love, pity, pride, compassion and sacrifice', the things that we care about, the things that define our lives – and I try to make them small enough to see because those are all big words that mean very little unless you can enshrine them in a story.'

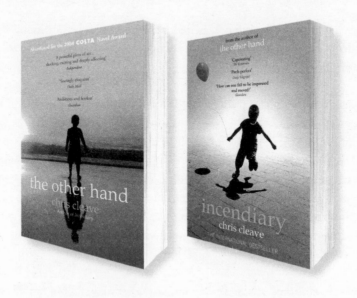

The Other Hand and *Incendiary* are both available
from Sceptre in paperback, and as eBooks.